The Art of Murder

Carol McKee Jones

Copyright © 2016 Carol McKee Jones

All rights reserved.

For Rob

Paris was great, wasn't it!

Acknowledgments:

With thanks to my son, Joe, for his support while I worked on The Art of Murder, and to all the 'test' readers, whose comments and suggestions were invaluable (Valerie, Trisha, Carolyn, Louise, Rob).

Special thanks to James Ferron Anderson for his excellent editing skills, his eagle eye in spotting errors, and assistance with improving the text.

Thanks to mum and dad and my Irish family for their encouragement.

Finally, a nod of acknowledgment to the beautiful city of Paris, its restaurants, cafes and galleries – we had a wonderful time following in Liam's footsteps!

Chapter 1

Sunlight, darting through horse chestnut leaves, painting pictures on paving stones: shapes flickering in the warm wind, shades of black and grey.

Liam paused as his eyes were drawn to the dancing images. He was suddenly aware that the coat he wore was too warm for the day, and weighed as heavy as a sack of slack on his shoulders. He took a cloth from his pocket and wiped his forehead. 'Art washes away the dust from the soul', he whispered the quote he'd seen on a plaque in Montmartre. Yet not even art, he knew, could wash away his sins. A woman in a silver-grey suit tutted when he dropped the cloth to the ground. She wagged a finger and pointed to a bin at the side of the road. He picked it up and dropped it into the bin. The woman gave a nod, a slight approving smile, and continued on her way. He watched her red heels rise and fall as they clicked on the hot pavement. She vanished amid the throng winding down the boulevard. A heat haze shimmered just above the ground and he wondered if she'd been a mirage.

"If only..." he found himself saying. Perhaps desire would cast a spell and transport him back twenty-four hours. Back to raindrops, beating against the pavement, sucking colour from the cityscape. Then, the ever present crowds had scurried by, faces hidden by umbrellas, hats and headscarves. The absence of the street peddler who sold small pots of peonies at the corner of Rue de Berri was notable. The lucky sod had stayed tucked up in bed, Liam imagined, wishing he'd done the same.

If only the sun had glowed as bright as it did today, he might have lazed on a bench watching animated tourists take photos of the gardens, the River Seine, the *bateaux-mouches*, and each other. Click, click, that simple sound would've been music to the ears. He could have inhaled the sights and smells

1

of the city: chocolatiers with quirky window displays, smart Parisians with scarves looped round their necks, rose petal perfume so sweet it almost masked the city's petrol fumes. Then there was the scent of lavender. Yes. Lavender was the scent he most associated with Paris. If he'd lingered and enjoyed the buzz and cut and thrust of the moment, then it wouldn't have happened.

Liam stopped at a newspaper stand. His eyes fixed on a clutch of postcards suspended on a metal rack: Sacre Coeur, the Louvre, the River Seine, a dark blue band mirroring the intensity of the sky. Alouette's eyes. His finger trembled as he raised it and traced the tip across one glossy postcard: the Pont Neuf, Paris's oldest bridge, stone glowing gold at sunset, arches curving. Alouette's lips. So lovely, yet he wished he could close his eyes and transport himself far away from this city of light.

"*Bas les pattes!*" The long-nosed man behind the counter growled. Startled at how vulnerable and subservient he felt at the reproach, his hand dropped to his side. He hunched his shoulders, threw a narrow-eyed glance at the newspaper seller, and moved on.

He passed a music shop. The doors were thrown wide open, one on each side. Glass and steel, shiny arms luring in, embracing browsers. *Thump, thump, thump.* His face twisted into a scowl as the hip-hop beat pummeled his eardrums.

His legs weakened and he collapsed onto a bench, next to a pair of older women who spoke in high-pitched voices. He couldn't grasp what they were saying, but from their creased foreheads and pursed lips, he guessed they were complaining about something. Silence fell over the bench. The woman next to him shifted the corner of her cherry-red coat away from him. He stole a glance. The woman's nose was wrinkled, her chin lengthened in apparent distaste. He tried to remember if he'd washed that morning. Then he recalled, he'd been so pumped up from the events of yesterday, he had lurched from his bed of leaves in the park onto the streets, without washing in the toilet of a nearby café. The clothes he wore were those he'd slept in: an oversized brown raincoat which skimmed the ground, beating the dust and dirt on the pavement as he walked, a green tee shirt, and a pair of trousers, several sizes too big, hoisted up by a leather belt. He liked the noise of the coat as it swished against the concrete, almost, but not quite, mimicking the scratching of his granny's broom as she swept the front doorstep. A thought crossed his mind that made him smile: how ironic it would be if the mayor of Paris recognised his contributions to the city's street cleaning efforts and awarded him a 'good citizen' medal. He shook his head - under the radar, that's where he wanted, no, needed, to be.

The woman in the red coat might have viewed him with kinder eyes if she'd met him when he'd first stepped off the Eurostar onto the marble sheen of the Gare du Nord. His hair, thick and fair, with only a whisper of grey. The type of hair, he fancied, women liked to tease and ruffle with manicured fingernails. His features then, still passably pleasant, his eyes bright, sky-blue, full of hope. Hopeful the mistakes he had made could be put right. If she'd seen him before his locks had turned greasy, streaked with white and tangled, she might have pouted in his direction with her lined lips and raised her pencilled brows in a come-hither gesture. She might have seen him as a potential young lover, or at the very least, a fellow human being.

The women got up and strode off without a backwards glance; the sound of their footsteps faded as they hurried away. He realised he'd taken on the mantle of a pariah, no more highly regarded than a flea riding on a rat's back. Like the flea, he'd transformed into a parasite, an opportunist who preys on others. His mother, Mary, with her soft, white waves and creamy Belfast accent, would turn in her grave if she could see what he'd become.

"My darling boy, all possibilities exist. You can be what you want, who you want. No need to take on the sins of the parents." He'd been impressed by her eloquent words, although he would have appreciated a more direct response to the simple query as to who his father was.

A young woman pushing a pram swerved and made for the part of the pavement furthest away from him. Her beige coat, which matched her hair, hung like a golden waterfall on her shoulders, the material soft, naturally bending with the contours of her body. Her skirt, bag and shoes were black. Elegant and balanced, Liam observed. His own life had never been like that. He wondered if the child in the pram had ever puked or pissed on this perfect creature. Probably not, he concluded. Some people were destined to follow a smooth path through life, gliding across an ice rink rather than chipping away at a cliff, one step up, another back down.

He squinted to get a closer look at the pram. Royal-blue body with silver and white trim. Silver Cross, he imagined. He'd once dated a woman who had a pram just like that, but that one was old, fished from a skip. The blue enamel was scraped, ignoble rather than royal, and the white on the body had faded to cream. She'd used it to ferry her booty to and from the local market: old books, china, glassware, anything and everything. Liam recalled one day, more precious than he had then realised. Billie, that was her name, had bought a load of secondhand books at the Sunday market. He'd offered to help her manoeuvre the pram, stuffed to the brim with the dank smelling objects. At the top of a steep hill, he'd let go of the pram handle. He'd clutched his stomach and bent over, laughing and wheezing at the same time as Billie's legs propelled her down the hill in pursuit of her mouldy treasures.

Liam had tried to make amends for the prank by helping her gather up the books and organising them in neat piles in the pram, but the only thing that would calm Billie down was the promise of half a dozen cans of Tennent's.

"If only I'd known," he whispered. If he'd known what lay ahead for him, he would have pursued Billie, maybe settled down with her, played the antiques game as part of a couple. A tin of beer in front of a real coal fire, Matisse prints hanging on the walls, cut from a book and set in secondhand frames, rather than needing to see the real thing in a gallery.

These were things he could have had, if only he'd been gifted with foresight. He could have learnt to love her hair, the colour of trodden wheat, her laugh, thick and dirty as molasses, her figure, short and sturdy. Liam shook his head picturing Billie's stash of books. Not fit to light a fire. Not one worth more than fifty pence. Bundle of rubbish, it just about summed up his life.

The woman and the Silver Cross pram shimmered down the boulevard. The pram, he acknowledged, contained a much more precious cargo than Billie's old books.

A patch of cloud shading the boulevard edged away. The midday sun beat down, bright and fierce. Coats and jackets were tossed over shoulders and arms in a synchronised wave that reminded him of a chorus in a ballet performance. Nostalgia washed over him. Had he really once been to see the Bolshoi Ballet at the Royal Opera House? He'd been a little in love with the principal dancer, Anna something-or-other unpronounceable. Her black hair, pulled back in a gloss bun, framed her heart shaped face. Her body, pliant as a piece of warm plasticine, was encased in beaded gossamer which glittered under the spotlights. Her feet were silky perfection at the end of shapely legs. He had been so hypnotised by her beauty he'd almost failed to notice two women in the audience, shoulders draped in fur stoles, and wearing a uniform of glitter and black underneath. Afterwards, he'd eyed them as they clambered into a black cab, clutching champagne flutes, hooting with laughter, their skirts hoisted up. One of the women had pressed her face up to the window and had given a cheeky wink as the cab pulled away. Divorcees rather than widows, he'd concluded with regret. One of those women, he later realised, might have taken him under her diamond-encrusted wing, shown him a good time, might even have come to his rescue.

"Swan Lake," Liam said in a loud voice. "It was Swan Lake."

Heads turned to look at him and then turned quickly away. A thought crossed his mind - could it be that his face was etched with witness marks, visible evidence of his misdeeds? People were so afraid of him, they pretended he didn't exist.

A passerby, a man with a puffy hairdo, wearing an orange jumper, sidestepped to the right, passing the bench at a distance of several feet.

"*Oui monsieur*. You're right to be scared," he muttered. "If you'd even glimpsed what I witnessed yesterday, you'd hail a taxi and order it to whisk you away to the other side of Paris. Another country, even."

He looked down at his shoes. He'd never been a natty dresser, but how could he have sunk this low? The leather on one shoe was split, allowing the lining to poke through. He could feel the warmth of the pavement through holes in the soles. If it rained, his feet were in for a soaking. He bent down and took a closer look at his shoes. Spots, like drops of paint, sprinkled across the leather. Rust coloured spots, a shade or two darker than the tan shoe dye. Drops of blood.

Images of the contours of two bodies flashed into his mind. One on top of the other, features and limbs obscured by a brown blanket. The salt in his tears stung his parched lips. He tried and failed to catch the eye of a man in a white kaftan. Maybe a glass of water, the light touch of a hand on his, confirmation he still had human form?

He shook his head. He was a London dealer, wasn't he? Did even a fragment of the hopeful man who bought, sold and traded antiques for a living, still exist?

A tapping noise distracted Liam from his distress. An old man with a cane passed by. He walked with a limp, back hunched, leaning heavily on the cane. The steel tip connected with the pavement with force as it rose and fell. He was reminded of a time, several months ago, when he'd heard a similar noise. That was the moment the nightmare had begun. *Tap, tap, tap.*

Chapter 2

Several months earlier

Rain brushed across the East London streets and gusts of wind rattled window panes. Figures, gender hidden in the half light, hurried past. The weather reflected the country's mood: grey and bogged down in recession. Liam sat at his desk, flicking through invoices, wondering which one he should pay with his last few hundred pounds. Just enough money to pay a bill, not enough to take that trip to Paris he'd been promising himself, he thought regretfully.

The intercom buzzed three times. This was followed by the tap-tapping of the knocker on the door downstairs. He got up from his desk, went over to the door and switched on the light. He only did this when it was absolutely necessary: when the sun had slipped behind the roof opposite or the sky was black with storm clouds.

It was late in the afternoon so he concluded the caller was unlikely to be a debt collector. As far as he was aware, or could remember from his childhood, those after your money usually operated first thing in the morning, trapping their prey when the victim was still groggy. The morning was a slow time when the rituals of washing, dressing and breakfast had to be followed. Lulled into a false sense of security from a night's rest, a door might thoughtlessly be opened or a knock answered in anticipation of the postman delivering good news. At least that's how it'd been in his home.

Another tap. This time louder and more urgent. Bone against wood. He opened the office door and made his way down the narrow staircase. He was curious. Members of the public or fellow antique dealers usually weren't so persistent. He opened the front door of the building.

"Me old son." Liam caught a faint whiff of brandy as an older man brushed past him.

"Victor", he murmured. He closed the door and studied Victor, who stood at the bottom of the stairs, clutching the handle of brown leather suitcase. Victor, who was normally in reasonable shape, looked as though he'd shrunk. Liam reached over and squeezed his arm, even under the wool cloth of Victor's coat it felt sharp, jagged and bony rather than muscular.

"Come on up. Tell me what I can do for you," Liam said in a soft voice. He followed Victor up the narrow staircase, noting the older man's right shoulder was tilting downwards. The bag he struggled with was clearly heavy and Liam experienced a pang of guilt that he hadn't offered to carry it upstairs.

Victor sat down opposite him. Liam opened a drawer in his desk and took out a bottle of Glenfiddich.

"I was just about to indulge. Join me?"

Victor nodded, his eyes fixed on the bottle label, as though he imagined the contents might provide an antidote to his troubles. Liam poured two glasses. Only an inch or two of liquid remained in the bottle, so he took care to ensure Victor had the larger measure. Victor held his glass up to the light and twirled it round. Slivers of amber flashed on the walls. He lifted the glass up to his nose, sniffed, then gave a smile of approval.

"Vanilla...and some sort of smoke. Oak, I think. Nectar of the gods. Fucking gorgeous," he said with the enthusiasm of a sommelier sampling a newly discovered wine. "Won't be seeing much of this where I'm heading."

"Verdict tomorrow?"

"Old Bailey, no less. I'm honoured."

"Any idea?"

"Not expecting a party with cake and candles."

"How long do you think?"

"Life, at least twenty, if the judge has her way," Victor shrugged. "On the other hand I could get off. Who knows?"

"Worst case scenario, you can always appeal."

"Blondie - my brief - is drawing up the papers as we speak. Just in case. No flies on that girl."

Victor got up, walked over to the window and peered out.

It was almost dark as night but the street lamps weren't lit. A notice had been stuck on a lamp-post the week before announcing a partial blackout, part of a money-saving scheme by the council. Street lights would be switched on according to time of day, rather than responding to degrees of darkness.

"Looking for someone?" Liam asked.

"Just admiring the light...or lack of it. Makes me feel like that bloke that used to be on the telly. The one with the glasses and hat and no face."

"The invisible man," Liam laughed.

Victor went over to Liam's desk and picked up a silver framed photo. A woman with fair ringlets hanging just past her shoulders had one arm around a chubby, angel-faced boy. The boy held an ice cream cone in one hand. A 99: a swirl of white with a chocolate flake inserted near the top. The boy held it up for the photo. He had a triumphant expression on his face, like a runner carrying the Olympic torch. In the background a fairground carousel sat motionless and devoid of customers. The faces of the horses were frantic and menacing rather than jolly. This gave an eerie edge to the pleasant seaside scene. Perhaps things hadn't been as rosy as the photo, at first glance, suggested?

"Brighton beach?"

"Margate. Day trip."

"Can't see no likeness in you now to this." Victor's eyes softened as he studied the photo.

"A lot of water under the bridge, Vic. Life knocks you around and it shows in the face," Liam said, although he considered he'd grown into his own awkward looks easily. He'd inherited his mother's thin Irish skin and rarely sunbathed, so in his early forties only a few wrinkles had appeared on his forehead and round his eyes. 'Chuckle lines' he liked to call them. Enough to give an air of maturity, not enough to age him. His crowning glory was a full head of fair hair, just a few shades darker than his hair in the photograph.

Victor nodded.

"I'm glad your mum had a good send off."

Liam was silent for a moment, remembering his mother as he sipped his whiskey. It was strange, he reflected, when he thought of her he didn't recall the cocoon of lily of the valley cologne that followed her as she moved. Neither did he hear her Belfast lilt. When she came to mind, he pictured the bright jumpers and cardigans she liked to knit. Never more relaxed than when wielding a pair of knitting needles and balancing a ball of wool on her knee. 'Warmer than shop-bought rubbish,' she'd claimed each time a new one was produced.

Across the table, Victor's face gave nothing away. Was he here just for old time's sake, to reminisce before he disappeared from circulation for a while, or did he want something? Liam noticed how frequently he glanced at his suitcase which seemed to be glued to the lower part of his leg. Why was he carrying a case around when he was about to go down for murder?

"I still don't know how to thank you. What you did for Mum those last few months."

Victor nodded and gave a sly smile. He already knows how I can thank him, Liam thought, that's why he's here. But he would do whatever Victor asked. If it hadn't been for Victor's generosity, his mother would have lived out her last few months in a substandard care home. Victor had visited the old woman and insisted on moving her to a state-of-the-art facility, one with specialist dementia care as well as a cinema, hairdresser and a memory wing, an area constructed to mimic an old fashioned shopping street. The windows of the false shop fronts displayed goods available in the past: tins of Spam, Pretty Polly silk stockings, Cussons Imperial Leather soap. Wrought-iron benches, the type found in parks, were provided so patients could sit and contemplate.

'They tell me it's the short term memory that goes first, so Mary will love this,' Victor had said when he'd encouraged Liam to look at the home. Liam was in full agreement with him; the eyes of the men and women resting on the benches were calm and reflective, rather than filled with fear of the modern world with its jarring noises and flickering devices.

He was humbled that this godfather of the antiques world, who'd taken him under his wing and taught him the business, had stepped in to help him. He'd been struggling to keep his head above water financially so Victor had set up a direct debit covering the fees. 'For as long as Mary needs it,' Victor had said. They both knew that wouldn't be long. It would be a short-term loan, paid back with interest, Liam insisted. Victor had been firm: Liam would pay him back, when the time was right for Victor. He looked across the table. The older man's gaze was, unusually for him, steady. One hand was still attached to the handle of the case, the other drummed an upbeat rhythm on the desk. Victor knew what he wanted.

He finished his whiskey and set the glass down. He picked up the glass again, and, without thinking, licked the remaining droplets which clung to the inside. Victor laughed.

"Times must be bad."

"The recession and bloody online auctions. Killed my business stone dead. Every Tom, Dick and Harry's an antique dealer now. You can see there's not much stock lying about. Can't buy cheap enough to turn a profit." He swept his hand around the office, noticing for the first time the brownness of the room. The Persian rugs with their intricate and colourful patterns had been rolled up and taken to auction the day before, whisking away any vibrancy from the space. Now, all that remained underfoot was lightly stained tan wall to wall carpeting, which the rugs had hidden from view. The walls were dark cream, the desk and chairs a mid-brown wood. Several Victorian landscapes hung on the walls, subtle and serious, dominated by brown, olive and cream tones.

"You were always too law abiding. Gets you nowhere but the poor house."

Liam shrugged. *He* wasn't about to spend twenty or more years in prison. Times were tough now, but then most of his life they'd been tough, aside from a few good years before the internet, like mould in a loaf of bread, permeated and corrupted the antiques business. There was also the divorce.

That had cleaned him out and he'd had to start all over again.

His childhood had been equally rocky. He barely remembered the first two years of his life in the attic room of his grandparent's South Belfast terraced house, but he remembered in fine detail the series of damp London flats he and his mother had moved to, along with the evictions and the tears and pleadings of his mother as stocky bailiffs regularly turned up and carted away their belongings.

Mary was a single mother. When Liam had quizzed her about the whereabouts of his own father, she'd insisted he'd never had one. 'Just me and you, my wee mawn.' Her blue eyes had danced with mischief as she spoke. Liam, who'd had sex education classes in school, had argued that such a thing wasn't possible, but Mary had been firm. 'Not the first time such a thing's happened. You believe the story about the Virgin Mary, don't you?' Later, social workers, who became involved in their case, quizzed her about his dad. The father would have to pay maintenance and a boy needed a man's influence in his life, they insisted. His mother had given them the same story: she'd never been with a man, had woken up one day, pregnant. They'd left the flat with red, frustrated faces and he knew she was having a laugh at their expense. And when he asked who the seedy looking trickle of men - some with Belfast accents - who visited were, she gave an exaggerated flutter of her eyelashes and beamed a carefree smile. One day, it dawned on Liam that one of these 'visitors' might be his father. After that he didn't ask again, although sometimes he'd lain in bed, eyes closed, hoping that when they opened again, he would see a photo of his dad hanging on the wall opposite. George Best, Dennis Law, Bobby Charlton, any of these footballing legends would fit the bill.

"Mary loved you. She had a good end. Just as important as a good beginning," Liam said.

"She was like a mum to me. Even knit me one of those woolly jumpers. I suppose that makes you my younger brother." Victor's eyes misted over.

"Anything, Victor. If you need anything, just ask."

Victor nodded and groaned as he lifted the suitcase and edged it onto the desk.

"Heavy bugger!" He tapped a code into the locking mechanism and the lock clicked open. He reached in and withdrew a bound wad of notes. He slapped it on the desk in front of Liam, then grinned and flipped the lid of the case wide open, revealing stacks of similarly bound notes.

"Mainly fifties, a few twenties. Must be around three quarters of a million here."

Liam nodded. Victor had a reputation for being a hard man. Those who didn't know his gentler side weren't surprised when he was accused of murdering an associate who'd dobbed him in for receiving stolen antiques. If he'd committed the murder, he had been careful: there was no sign of a body. Still, they both knew the verdict could swing either way.

The older man's aura of shiftiness wouldn't have helped his case. He was constantly tapping his fingers on a table, a chair, his knees, any solid surface. Liam suspected he suffered from undiagnosed ADHD. Victor's eyes flitted back and forth, always observing, rarely resting. His tics were annoying and Liam imagined they wouldn't impress a jury.

Liam's face reddened as he gaped at the money.

"Do you want me to pay someone? To arrange…comforts inside?"

Victor shook his head.

"No. Fags and protection all taken care of. This is my life insurance, my pension, if you like. The taxman got a whiff of unpaid taxes and is on the case. The authorities'll try to get their hands on all my stuff. The lot. When I get out, which I will hopefully soon, they'll leave me with nothing, take every last brass farthing, at least that's what the clever dicks think. This is my under-the-mattress stash. It'll get me a new start. Panama or somewhere like that, where the weather's warm, the women fragrant, and the booze cheap as chips. I tell you, boy, I've had enough of this dump."

"You want me to hold onto this for you?"

"That's it. You were always a smart one. Shame about the

honesty."

"Not all the time!" Liam laughed.

"No, but not dirty enough."

Liam got up and went over to the safe. He opened it and Victor began loading the money, taking care to ensure each stack was exactly on top of the one below. Liam smiled, imagining Victor, in another life, folding towels for a living in Harrods. "We are what life makes us," he muttered to himself.

Victor held back one of the smaller bundles of notes.

"Four thousand here. You look like you could do with a helping hand."

Liam hesitated, then took the money.

"I'll pay you back."

Victor got up. He held out his hand and Liam gripped it tightly. It'd be a while before they clapped eyes on each other again, he suspected.

"I'll look after your belongings with my life."

Victor narrowed his eyes and sucked in his breath. Even though the office heating had clicked on an hour earlier, Liam was chilled by Victor's look.

"My future-and yours-is dependent on that, me old son."

Liam flicked the light switch off. He sat down at his desk and listened to Victor's footsteps gradually fading, then the lock of the front door clicked. In the darkened room he stared at the outline of the safe.

Even though the safe was constructed of cast iron, he imagined he had X-ray vision. He could see the money stacked up inside, the legacy of Victor's dodgy dealings taunting him. He decided to take one more look, to verify the notes were genuine. After all, if Victor had given him counterfeit notes and later claimed they'd been genuine when handed over, he was fucked. He crouched down, opened the safe door and pulled out a few stacks of notes. He nodded when he saw they were all Bank of England, thus harder to fake. He removed several fifty pound notes from the middle of a bundle and followed all the rules of checking if the notes were genuine: running his finger across the surface, checking the words 'Bank of England' and the number '50' were in raised print. Held up to the light, the metallic thread running through appeared as a continuous dark line. The watermark, a not-so-good likeness of the queen, was also where it should be.

Satisfied he wasn't risking his own freedom by handling forged notes, he picked up Victor's glass, threw his head back and drained the last few drops.

Chapter 3

The following day, Victor phoned. In a voice empty of emotion, he told Liam he'd been convicted of murder.

"Blondie was matter of fact. She expected me to be found guilty this time round. Has a few tricks up her sleeve for the appeal."

He did a mental calculation. If the appeal wasn't successful, Victor would probably serve at least twenty years. That would make him well over eighty when he got out. Liam commiserated with his old mentor but Victor was upbeat, assuring Liam that he would soon be a free man.

"Larry could be in Venezuela for all they know, boy." Larry was the man Victor was convicted of murdering. "Verdict won't stick," he added. Liam wasn't so sure.

He opened his desk drawer and rummaged through, finally locating what he was looking for: an invitation to an Scottish Colourist art exhibition that evening. Liam dealt mainly in old paintings, but he also bought and sold anything he could get his hands on: first edition Dickens, Chinese porcelain, glassware. He'd even dabbled in Irish property just before the market took a downward turn. In Liam's world the deal and gamesmanship took precedence over everything else. Spit, shake, subsequent profit. This was his mantra.

As usual for that winter, it was a cold and rainy evening. Runny noses, fingers white with chill, and clothes wet through, had been the norm for too long, he grumbled to himself. He shed his overcoat and umbrella at the gallery door and made his way into the exhibition room. The heating was on full and the warm, moist air gave off a faint whiff of damp dog fur. He turned up his nose in distaste at the smell which reminded him of a cardigan he'd worn one winter in place of a coat. The wool fibres of the cardigan were permanently swollen with moisture and he swore that the second a raindrop fell from the sky, the cardigan stitches opened up to trap it.

A glass of champagne was thrust in his hand and he took a moment to admire the bouncing golden bubbles. There was something about this particular shade that spoke of sun, holidays on the Cote D'Azur, afternoons on the beach in Juan Les Pins, stretched out on yellow and blue striped loungers. The promise of balmy weather on a cold winter's day.

He took a sip of champagne and found himself distracted by a painting by Samuel Peploe, a Victorian artist born in Edinburgh. He set the glass down.

"The Coffee Pot," he murmured. Paintings of this quality rarely appeared in small exhibitions, and now here it was, at his fingertips, the holy grail of Peploe's work. He'd been astonished to read in an antiques gazette that this very painting had recently sold for almost a million. He gazed in awe at the painting: sparkling silverware and glass on a white tablecloth, set against a dark background. Subtle colours creating a lush atmosphere on the canvas. The subject was simple but Liam was entranced, noting that Peploe had taken the use of colour and shade to a different level. His eyes fixed on a slick of light grey on the white tablecloth, which magically created folds in the material. Then they shifted to streaks of white applied in deft strokes to the coffee pot, giving the effect of glinting silver. If he'd had the money he'd have bought it.

"Fat chance," he muttered. Earlier, an envelope from the bank had dropped on the doormat. He'd made some poor business decisions recently so the news wasn't good. He'd thought about it on a scale from bad to terrible before slitting open the envelope and scanning the statement. His eyes had clamped on the red font and the minus sign ahead of the numbers - two hundred and twenty thousand pounds in the red. Victor's generous donation would barely make a dent in this.

He found himself shaking his head as he mentally listed his assets: rented office, rented flat and a few pictures worth around a thousand pounds in total, some miscellaneous antiques and books he hadn't yet sold, none worth a significant amount. Then there was also the Asprey brooch his mother had left him, a 1970s diamond piece set in platinum, gifted to her by a lover. Although Liam hadn't been fond of the mean-faced man who, with great fanfare, had produced the brooch from his pocket during a family dinner out, his mother had cherished it. 'Generous with money, but not in spirit', she'd told Liam when, after a near violent argument, she had shown her lover the door. Afraid he might return when they were out to retrieve the brooch, she'd wrapped it in a hankie and had hidden it under a loose floorboard in the bedroom. Unless he was in a life or death situation, Liam decided, he too would hang onto the brooch.

Deciding to concentrate on enjoying the moment, he moved closer to the painting. He was an admirer of Manet, and favourably compared Peploe's work to that of the great Impressionist, whose technique often involved painting light areas first, followed by tones and darker colours. The effect was one of richness, creating a thick and oily surface, layer upon layer of texture. The process, he imagined, was similar to weaving intricate patterns through a fine oriental carpet.

He moved on to a street scene by another of the Colourists, John Duncan Ferguson. A wave of envy engulfed him when he read the artist's background information. Ferguson had moved to Paris in the early nineteen hundreds and had hung out with Matisse and other artists. He nodded. One day, preferably soon and money permitting, he would take a long holiday in Paris. He'd visit galleries, eat food in brasseries with chandeliers and brass lanterns hanging from the ceilings, and walls decorated with swirly art nouveau tiles. He would drink in glamorous bars: champagne in the afternoon, then gin and tonic as an aperitif before dinner, and a Chablis, crisp and chilled, with his meal. Afterwards, a good cigar would round off the experience. If he was very, very lucky, he might lure fit women to his bed. He couldn't claim any talent in the arts, but there was no reason, aside from a negative bank balance, that he couldn't aspire to follow in the more earthly practices of the great painters.

He was still studying the street scene when a hand gripped his shoulder.

"Bloody hell - must be at least twenty years. Where the hell have you been hiding out?"

Liam turned. A grin spread across his face.

"Will! Still a cheeky bastard."

His eyes were drawn to the sheen of Will's slick suit. Bespoke Saville Row, he told himself as he eyed the navy pinstripe jacket. The front edge flicked back revealing purple silk lining. He wished he had made more effort to dress for the exhibition, but he'd judged the dark grey tweed, the lucky jacket he wore to auctions, to be just fine.

"I see you're doing well." Liam tried to mask the envy in his voice. The last time he'd seen Will was after their final 'O' Level exam. Will, who had a reputation for being work shy, had stayed on at college, telling Liam he was aiming for a few years dossing at university. Liam had fewer choices. He was old enough to turn his hand to some sort of work and his mother needed the extra income. He'd embarked on a series of low paying jobs: shelf stacking in a supermarket, cleaning on Brighton's Palace Pier one summer, lackey at an auction house, which had the upside of teaching him the antiques business. The one thing Will hadn't done so well was in maintaining a head of hair. The only hair that remained on Will's head was a slick of grey above each ear. He ran a hand through his own hair and smiled inwardly. They were like two primates, preening, circling, sniffing out each other's level of success.

"Heady world of finance. Stocks and shares and all that." Will pointed to two similarly dressed men. "We came in to shelter from the rain. What about you?"

"I'm into art. I like Peploe."

"I mean what do you do now?"

Liam shrugged. "This and that. I buy and sell. Anything from paintings to antiques."

Will's eyes darted up and down as he scrutinised Liam.
"Doing well?"

"Swings and roundabouts in my business, but on the whole pretty good."

"Family?" Will asked.

Liam shook his head. "You?"

"Wife and two kiddies - and a dog. Private schools and healthcare. Can't afford not to do well." He fumbled in the inside pocket of his jacket. Liam noticed the name of Will's tailor: Carter & Son, a well-known Saville row company. Will pulled out his wallet and extracted a small colour photo. Liam was taken aback when he saw the image of a handsome red setter.

"This is Rex. Isn't he a beaut?"

Liam nodded, not sure what to say next. In the space of a few sentences they'd established that their lives were worlds apart, yet the embers of the friendship and understanding they used to share still gave off a faint glow.

"Hmm. Well, it's been good running into you." Liam surprised himself when he realised he meant this. How long had it been since he'd spoken to a friend? For some reason he didn't include Victor in that category. He held out his hand. Will ignored the gesture.

"Look, we're having a meeting with someone. A deal we can't pass on. Why not come with us. Have a drink at the bar, on me, and we can catch up later. I'll chuck in dinner."

Liam hesitated then nodded. Why the hell not, he told himself. The unpleasant bedfellows of poverty and bankruptcy lurked just around the corner, why not live it up one night?

He hugged the bar while Will and his companions sat at a table in deep discussion. Will had set up a tab and Liam had consumed two large whiskeys by the time Will joined him.

"That was tough!" Will exclaimed, wiping his forehead with a bar napkin.

"Office politics? Nice place to conduct business."

Will looked sheepish. "Em... not really office. To tell the truth, this is nothing to do with my job. The chap who joined us is from a tech company. He's giving us a few leads on a new development."

"Leads? You mean information."

"Bits and pieces. A nudge in the right direction, if you get my drift."

"Nudge in the right direction? You're not talking about insider information, are you?"

"We don't call it that," Will smirked. He rubbed his fingers together. "This could set me up for life, and no one gets hurt."

"Lucky bastard," Liam said. He had to get up at the crack of dawn for the antique markets at Kempton Park and Ardingly to set up his stall or coax a bargain from another dealer, and even then he had to haggle his head off. He gave Will an admiring look. With his smooth patter and devious ways, his friend appeared to have stumbled upon the proverbial pot of gold.

Will cocked his head sideways and narrowed his eyes.

"What?" Liam asked, ploughing into his third whiskey with gusto.

"You said you're doing OK...as you're an old friend, no reason why I shouldn't count you in. Double your money in a few months."

"Sounds too good to be true, mate."

"Too good, yes. I suppose it sounds like that, but it's certainly true. Insider trading goes on all the time; this is the tip of the iceberg. I trust you'll be discrete?"

Liam nodded. His mind was fuzzy from the whiskey, but he was a dealer and this was a potential deal. He was still wary.

"I don't know. I may have access to money - a lot of money - but I need to be sure."

"Opportunity of a lifetime, not to be missed," Will said after a moment's silence. His voice had risen an octave higher, words quickening, buzzing with eagerness. "I'm putting my house up as collateral, that's how sure *I* am."

"What about the dog?" Liam laughed.

"Rex is for keeps. Not so sure about the wife and kids. Might put them up too."

"Tell me more."

"I'm talking education. A company called Zarek. They've built an online education system. State of the art. This is going to be big; a revolution in teaching. Imagine, Liam, lectures delivered by experts instead of teachers. Stephen Hawking lecturing on physics, Hillary Mantel teaching creative writing, Brian Cox on astronomy - a pretty face for the girls. It'll change the way our schools operate, the way our kids are educated."

"Put a lot of people out of work as well."

"Swings and roundabouts." Will narrowed his eyes. "Revolutions bring about new opportunities."

"So, this is a new system. It's still in development. What if it's a dud? What if it doesn't work?"

Will tapped the side of his nose. "Information is king, Liam, and I have it from the monarch's mouth that the company already has a fistful of airtight contracts. It's all under wraps at the moment, but soon, when the news is out, the price will soar through the roof."

Liam and Will continued the discussion in a city bistro. They stayed there all evening, dining on fillet steak and drinking red wine so strong it was tinged with purple. Their faces were animated, their souls filled with greed as each discussed the merits of investing in a company that was relatively unknown, but was also a potential goldmine. Finally, Liam was persuaded by Will's argument. Contracts had been signed so where was the risk? Will was a city trader, Liam reassured himself. Surely he knew what he was doing?

He weaved his way back to his office, opened the safe and took out several bundles of notes. He sat on the floor and flicked through them, without breaking the seal. Doubts still niggled at the back of his mind: could he afford to risk Victor's money? But would he ever get this chance again?

He thought back to a day at Goodwood, when he'd been given information on a race that had been fixed, from someone who worked at the stable. The horse in question, Champagne Charlie, came in at 40 to 1. Unfortunately, he hadn't trusted the source and had ignored the tip while all his mates had cashed in.

He slipped a fifty pound note out from one bundle and fingered it. How much of Victor's pension fund should he risk? A voice in his head whispered that he should put the money back in the safe, lock it up and forget he'd ever clapped eyes on it. But another, even stronger voice, told him that even if his old mentor was successful with his appeal, which he doubted, it would be months before he got out. He would have time to replace the cash and make himself a tidy profit into the bargain. Double or triple your money, Will had assured. Judging by the earnest expressions on the faces of his co-conspirators, Will knew his business inside out. He smiled. That was good enough.

He slid the note back in place and put the bundle in his briefcase. Around ten thousand, he estimated, enough to test the waters. He hesitated, then clicked the briefcase shut. The opportunity of a lifetime had just dropped into his lap, he'd be a fool not to snap it up.

Chapter 4

Several weeks later, Will called at Liam's office. In one hand he carried a backpack. There was a slight smile on his face, an air of triumph radiating from him, like an actor attending the Academy Award ceremony when they knew the golden statuette was a sure thing. He set the backpack on Liam's desk.

"All in there. The lot you gave me...and more. Told you it'd be worth it." The words tumbled out, as though they'd been kept prisoner for too long.

"We've made a profit?"

"Four thousand in three weeks, that's *your* cut. Am I a genius, or what?"

Liam unzipped the backpack and looked inside. He raised his eyebrows. "Magician more likely." He looked back up at Will. "What now?"

"Are you happy with that? Four thousand enough to see you through old age and beyond?"

Liam got up from his seat and looked out the window. Did he want to keep struggling, like the poor sods he frequently watched heading to and from their places of work. Modern slavery, he called it. And if his business didn't buck up soon, he'd be a slave, without a home, with only job-seekers allowance and the state as his master.

"No," Liam said.

"No what?"

"No, not enough, and no, I'm not happy with my future prospects. I'm not meant to be poor. There's so much I want to do. Maybe buy some decent art, a few antiques, travel. A stint in Paris maybe."

Will shrugged.

"You mentioned more where that came from." Liam pointed to the bag.

"It's not really a risk, Liam. The proof's in the pudding, and what a fine pudding it is." Will sighed. "Liam, governments are awash with your and my money, which they seem hell bent on throwing at IT. All we're doing is diverting some of the spoils into our own pockets."

"I don't know…" Liam said.

"Mate, a couple of years ago I was just like you. Jittery, afraid of my own shadow when it came to taking chances. Then I watched the experts, 'who dares wins', that was their motto. Still I hesitated. Then came the chance of a lifetime: a new patient IT system that would change the way hospitals operate. None of this going to your local establishment for treatment. Patients were to be treated in areas of expertise according to their symptoms. Pain in the bum for the families at visiting time, but great for patients."

"I've never heard of that scheme."

"They dropped the idea halfway through. Spent a couple of billion though before it went belly up. I was too chicken to invest but a few million dropped into the lap of my good friend and colleague, Tristram. Living it large in the South of France now. Champagne Charlie, we call him. Needless to say, I vowed never to let a golden opportunity slip by again."

Liam blanched. In his mind he saw the image of Champagne Charlie: sleek, refined head, intelligent eyes, longer than average neck. His shoulders were well sloped and hindquarters muscular. As fine a horse as he'd ever seen, yet he had been too afraid to place a bet on him. Liam went over to the safe and hesitated for only a split second before opening it.

"Look in there," he said. "How many puddings will that lot buy?"

Over the next few months Zarek's shares slowly climbed. Not once did they dip so Liam concluded Will was the genius he'd claimed to be. Then it happened. The share price began to fall, at first edging down so slowly the chart barely registered the change. Then there was a sharp dip. Liam checked online and bought the Financial Times. Both sources registered concerns with Zarek's ability to complete the complex system before their competitor, Extus

Education, who were in the process of designing a similar system. He called Will and suggested pulling out.

"Sell! We're about to get out hands on a fortune and you want to bail out. Holding your nerve, Liam, that's what investing's about. You sell at the top, not the bottom. Only the bold profit."

"They've signed contracts already?"

"Sure thing. In the bag."

The shares dipped below the purchase price, then plunged further on a daily basis. A newspaper article declared that serious bugs were discovered during Zarek's initial testing, so system redesign was required. Via another newspaper article, he learned that contracts had been anticipated but not actually signed.

He had difficulty separating rumour from fact, and Will's platitudes were rarely available to quell his nerves. Sleep eluded him and his insides constantly churned from fear. A burning in his belly told him an ulcer was on its way. The only bright spot on the horizon was Victor's prison sentence. Victor would be tucked away in his cell for a long time and many years would drift by before he'd be let loose on the outside world.

More than once, when the press regarding the deal was negative, he phoned Will and asked if they should sell. On one call, he'd been extra jittery, his voice trembling, words jumbled up. Will had calmed his nerves and persuaded him to hold tight.

'Hold tight!' He'd forgotten how much he hated business clichés. They were words that filled empty space but had no real meaning: moving forwards, pushing the envelope, thinking outside the box, win-win. Will was a master of these phrases.

One morning, in the office toilet, he studied his face in the mirror, barely recognising the man who gaped back at him. Bulging pouches under haunted eyes added ten years to his real age, he took a step forward so his face was only inches from the glass. The whites of his eyes had turned pink with fine veins threaded through. Worst of all, a few strands of grey had slipped into his hair. He banged his fist hard on the sink, causing it to shudder and a pipe to dislodge from the wall. After making temporary repairs with masking tape, Liam strode into his office and picked up the receiver of his phone, a GPO bakelite model from the 1930's. There was no hesitation in his finger when he dialled Will's number. Before Will had the opportunity to speak Liam uttered the words 'Sell. I want you to sell now, Will'. There was a decisive click on the line. This was no telecoms incident or accidental break in the connection. Even across the line, he could smell Will's fear. It seeped through the wires like the sweet, spicy odour of toxic mustard gas. Minutes later, Will called back. His voice was steady and officious, as though he was reading from a script. Liam imagined this was the same tone he used when he delivered bad news to a distant client, someone with whom he'd no personal connection.

"Bad news I'm afraid. Things have gone pear shaped. Further difficulties with system development. I'm quite sure you'll understand. Pick up a copy of today's *Financial Times,* that'll explain things better than I can. I'm gutted, I really am." Liam drew a deep breath. Will didn't sound gutted and what was he trying, in his oblique way, to say? Was the money gone, had it vanished into some sort of digital thin air? There was a click on the line again. When he tried to return the call, Will's phone rang continuously.

Liam hurried to the newsagents on the corner and bought the *Financial Times.* His eyes widened as he read the headline at the top right-hand corner of the front page: *Zarek Pipped to the Post in Contracts Race by Extus Education.* No, no, not this. He imagined he'd screamed these words aloud and was surprised to hear no cries echoing off the office walls.

Liam's eyes were drawn to the newspaper again. A drop of perspiration slid down his chin onto the paper. He imagined it crimson. A droplet of blood. His blood. He reread the first few lines of the article on the business page: *Zarek computes the cost of software failure as promising start-up fails to deliver innovative online education system.*

Zarek. He wished he'd never heard that name or, more importantly, invested Victor's money in the company. To Liam, the world of technology was a mystery, shrouded in strange terms and processes. He couldn't distinguish a bit from a byte, and had absolutely no idea what a 'cookie' was or what it did. He might just as well have bought rolls of scratch cards or gone into a bookie's and placed the money on any old nag. A man wearing a blindfold, sticking a pin into a horse-racing schedule, would have made better choices than he had. What state had his mind been in to gamble all the money on Will's venture? Fool, madman, vulnerable, or just plain greedy - perhaps all of these labels should be pinned to the lapel of his jacket.

It was funny, Liam thought, how bloody obvious things were in retrospect: Will's snazzy suit, the slickness of his patter, the aura of desperation behind the grin. All of these should have warned him that Will wasn't the financial wizard he proclaimed himself to be. How many other people had been taken in by hotshots in smart suits, he asked himself. The global banking crisis had produced misery for businesses, governments, entire nations. He supposed Will had known the game was up for him and his pin-striped brethren.

Will had been subdued when he'd phoned earlier and told him to buy the newspaper, but there was also a formality in his voice, telling him that his old friend had made this type of call many times before. When he finally reached him again, Will was curt and to-the-point. The news was bad, terrible even, but Liam had been fully aware of the risks, Will was quick to point out.

"Time, I need time to sort things out. Keep your hair on," Will had said. He'd a meeting organised with his Zarek contacts in a few days and some of the investment, if not all, might be retrievable. He'd do all he could to claw back Liam's money, he said without mentioning specifics. Before Liam had time to ask exactly how he intended to change Zarek's fortunes, Will had hung up.

The following day, Liam sat at his desk willing the phone to ring, yet he still flinched when it did. He reached across the desk. His quick hand brushed a patch of ash from the edge of a Meissen plate he occasionally used as an ashtray, exposing a posy of delicate pink, blue and yellow flowers. At the other end of the line he heard wheezing, followed by incoherent words, yet the voice was immediately recognisable. It sent a chill down his spine.

"Victor."

"Unsafe conviction. Told you she was good," Victor finally said.

"Your barrister?"

"Who else? I'm hardly shacked up with a woman," Victor said. "Been a while. Couple of months."

"I... I've been busy... taking care of business. Good news then?"

"Might make bail soon."

"I'm happy for you. Delighted. When'll you know?"

"In a day or two."

"That's great. I'll buy a bottle of Moët. We can celebrate."

"Buy a couple of bottles. The first thing I want to do is get pissed. You can imagine the second."

Victor's laugh culminated in a fit of coughing. Too many fags, Liam thought. But then, what else did Victor have to do with his day, other than smoke and plot a bloody end for anyone that crossed him?

"I've been to hell and back. Put me through the ordeal of a criminal trial, the bastards did. Imagine, Liam, twenty years, a murder sentence, just because of a speck of blood in the boot of my car. And me an innocent man!"

"Can't imagine what it was like," he said, injecting false sympathy into his voice. Could Victor read him, tell he was scared? "If - when - you get off, what next?"

"Can't say. But these bastards'll try to stitch me up any which way they can. They're already after the house, the car, anything they can get their mitts on."

Liam gave a low mumble of sympathy.

"Those books I left with you? Still all right?" Victor said.

"Books?"

"Yes. The case full of books. Belonged to me old granny, they did."

He made a conscious effort to steady his voice. "Yeah man, they're fine. All good."

"I'll collect them as soon as I'm out."

"Can't wait to see you."

Liam's hand shook as he poured himself a whiskey. If only he hadn't succumbed to Will's flattery and the lure of money for nothing. He'd spoken to Will three times that morning and his former friend was still fobbing him off with the promise of yet more meetings with Zarek contacts. He suspected Will was playing for time. He knew he should go round, take Will by his Saville Row lapels and threaten to slit his throat if he didn't come up with some form of refund, but that was Victor's style, not his. Victor would not be as understanding with him as he'd been with Will.

He drained his glass, rolled up the *Financial Times,* the bearer of the catastrophic news, and pressed it into the rubbish bin. He played out his next meeting with Victor. It could only end one way - badly. Until this situation was resolved, he would need to put distance between Victor and himself. Basic survival instincts kicked in, telling him he had to go, leave London, get as far away as possible. He picked up the Meissen plate from his desk. It was a Marcoloni, circa eighteen hundred, gilding around scalloped edges, pretty sprigs of flowers on a bluish white porcelain base. It was worth about two hundred pounds in a good market. He removed the newspaper from the waste bin, wrapped a few pages round the plate and put it in his briefcase.

He took a final scan around the office. There was nothing tangible of any value and most of the memories he would be leaving behind were bad or sad. When he'd sat at the oak desk, which was mock-antique rather than the real thing, he'd received the call from the nursing home telling him his mother had died. Six months ago, an associate from Dublin had called to tell him that work on the development in Rathgar he had invested fifty thousand pounds in had gone belly-up. It had joined a host of other ghost developments in Ireland and in a split second, dreams of a cushy future fishing on the River Shannon and rooting round antiques shops in small riverside villages, had fizzled out. If he'd had arsonist tendencies, he would have struck a match, dropped it on the carpet, and watched orange flames lick the floors and walls until they turned black and crumbled away.

A grim smile was fixed on his face as he shut the door quietly behind him. He had screwed everything up. To Victor, betrayal would cancel out any trappings of friendship. As far as money was concerned, Victor wasn't a sentimental man. Victor would likely deal with him in the same way he'd handled Larry. There was no option, only one thing he could do.

He exited the building; his shoulders slumped forward as he faced the wind and rain outside.

Chapter 5

It took Liam less than half an hour to pack a small suitcase with personal belongings. The option of going cap-in-hand to his bank manager to arrange a loan for a trip was out of the question, so he rooted around his flat, looking for objects to sell. He boxed up three Victorian watercolours. All were landscapes: trees, rivers, cows, one featured a boat. They were pretty enough, but worth only a hundred or so apiece. He scanned his bookshelves. Most of the books were worth little more than a pittance so he decided to leave them. He owed two month's rent so perhaps his landlord could make a quid or two when he disposed of them. He picked up a small book with a green cover which lay on the coffee table. He leafed through the first edition children's book, *The Tale of Peter Rabbit*. The images were fresh and just as colourful, he imagined, as when Beatrix Potter had the book printed in 1902. As an art lover and collector, this was one he'd wanted to hang onto, but it was worth at least seven hundred pounds to a member of the public, maybe four hundred to a dealer. He put it in one of the boxes. He placed another book, a signed, authenticated, first edition of Mark Twain's *Huckleberry Finn*, which interested him less as it contained no illustrations, in the same box.

"A thousand pounds in a good market," he said aloud, then shrugged. Unfortunately a good market didn't consist of selling in haste to fellow antique dealers. He often referred to his colleagues as tightwads, but he was pragmatic and realised this also applied to him.

"Buy cheap. Hold. Sell dear." Unfortunately he didn't have the luxury of holding.

He was encouraged when the first dealer he visited, a woman called Lesley, who had a crush on him, bought the lot, paying cash.

"Holiday, you say, Liam?" she crouched down and edged the heavy steel door of the safe open after they'd concluded negotiations."

"Mixed with business. You know what it's like."

"Never a dull moment in the trade. Right?"

She stood up and placed three bundles of notes on the counter. She counted fifty and twenty-pound notes, one by one, into his palm, occasionally lingering over a note, throwing a teasing glance. He blushed, shamed at Lesley's obvious favour, humiliated that he would owe her one.

When the counting was complete and all the notes safely folded into the inside pocket of his tweed jacket, Lesley brushed off her skirt and ran a hand through her hair.

"You look tired, knackered even, like you could do with a rest." Her voice was heavy with sympathy. "When you get back, look me up. A friend of mine has a cottage in the Scottish Highlands. No antiques shops nearby. I could take some time off…"

He forced a smile. No point in telling Lesley he wouldn't be back in the near future. Anyway, she wasn't his type. She was brunette, which he liked, but she was too plain for his tastes – and her eyes were set slightly too wide apart. That scared him and he wasn't sure why. He liked his women classically good looking: Audrey Hepburn and Ava Gardner sprang to mind. He wouldn't kick lookalikes of either of these women out of his bed. He knew this was a paradox as he was in the habit of pulling on the first thing he found on the floor when he tumbled out of bed in the morning: wrinkled trousers dropped on the floor the night before, a crumpled shirt, he wasn't even beyond giving his boxers a second go. Women he'd dated at home didn't seem to mind but he suspected he'd need to up his game in his destination city - Paris.

When he boarded the Eurostar, thanks to Lesley, he was just over two thousand pounds richer. This would do, he told himself, until Will came up with at least a partial refund. He crossed his fingers and tried to view his flight from England in a positive light. Maybe the gods would look down on him with benevolent eyes and this would turn out to be an adventure. He pictured himself as a modern day Sydney Carton, the young barrister in Dickens' *Tale of Two Cities*. 'It's a far, far, better thing…' he began to quote mentally. No, strike that, he told himself, he was fleeing England in disgrace rather than doing something noble. And, in any case, hadn't Sydney Carton lost his head?

Look the part, dress the part and live the life. He buoyed up his spirits from the second class carriage of the train. He thought about his visit to the Colourist art exhibition, carefully airbrushing Will from the memory. Ferguson. Hadn't he envied Ferguson? Hadn't he longed follow in his footsteps?

The first time he'd visited Paris he had also taken the Eurostar. It was 1993, a few months after the opening of the tunnel. He was in his late twenties, felt like a lifetime ago. The whole thing was still a novelty and the fact that the train sped its way towards France under the weight of the Channel waters was exciting yet baffling at the same time. Wouldn't the weight of the sea be too much for a few steel girders to hold back? What if the tunnel caved in? He didn't try to understand, he wasn't an engineer. What was incredible to Liam was the ability to travel from central London to Paris, have lunch, and then return home, all in the same day.

He had taken his future wife, Lily, paying for the trip with the proceeds from the sale of two Dresden Monkey Band figurines: the cellist and the trumpet player. The twenty minutes in the tunnel had seemed like hours but he still remembered the exhilaration pumping into his veins when daylight flooded back into their carriage. They'd made it.

He and Lily had lunched at the Brasserie Escargot near the Boulevard du Montparnasse. He couldn't recall what the main course was, but they both had starters of escargot topped with parsley and the most pungent garlic he'd ever tasted. The trip had been expensive and should have left pleasant memories, but Lily had spoilt it with her constant complaining: the funny food, the length of the wait for a taxi at the Gare du Nord, the inability or reluctance of the driver to converse in English.

As he watched the rolling hills of Kent give way to the flatter landscape of Normandy, fear overwhelmed hope. The frequent clutches of windmills, sails rotating round and round, mirrored the nerves that swirled round his stomach, pinching his internal organs, making it difficult to draw a breath. He was leaving his old life behind, the things he knew, the skills and acquaintances that made his day to day life bearable. He'd never been rich and had made some disastrous business decisions, but before Will there had been hope and the option of picking himself up, brushing off his losses and starting anew was still there to cling onto.

There had also been the ever present hope of the 'big find', the undiscovered Rubens, the Turner sketch lying dusty in an attic for centuries, only surfacing at a boot sale when the attic was emptied. Liam hadn't been that fortunate, but there were enough minor wins to hold his interest in the antique business. *The Tale of Peter Rabbit* he'd picked up at a car boot sale in Brighton several years ago. It was a first edition, identifiable from the leaf design on the endpapers. His face was straight as a poker as he'd skimmed the front pages, hoping for a signature. Even though there was none, it was still worth a bob or two. The young woman behind the stall had been happy enough to part with the book for two pounds. He'd given her three. This was the same book he'd just offloaded to Lesley for four hundred pounds. A tidy profit, even if he said so himself.

"Run rabbit, run," he whispered, likening himself to Peter Rabbit and Victor to Mr McGregor, the gun-wielding farmer.

Liam left his suitcase in his hotel room and went for a walk. Meandering through the warren of Left Bank streets, he imagined that in the past he might have hung out in this district with the likes of Sartre. The ghost of a bohemian ambience lingered in the fabric of the buildings, the shabby-chic hotels, the ornate bistro facades. In the late nineteenth century, the café, Les Deux Magots, once the site of a novelty shop, was the place to be seen. A guide book he'd found on the Eurostar, told him that Rimbaud and Sartre had regular seats there. Stopping in front of the café, Liam took a guess at which seat Sartre would have occupied. The right side, behind the window, gave the best view of the boulevard in all weathers. If he had to place a bet, that would be it. He closed his eyes and pictured Sartre: hair swept back, owlish glasses, chewing on the end of a pipe. Despite Sartre once proclaiming 'hell is other people', he suspected he would have been a people watcher.

He passed the nearby Café de Flore. He was tempted to sit at one of the small round tables and idle the late afternoon away, but decided to leave that for another day, when everything was sorted and he had Victor's money back.

He stopped to admire the window display of a high-end second-hand clothes shop in a cobblestone street off the Boulevard du Montparnasse. The sleeve of a calfskin jacket hanging in the window, fluttered when the door opened. It appeared to be beckoning customers inside, so he went in. *Look the part*, he reminded himself as he brushed the sleeve with his hand on the way past.

Inside, the shop was gloomy aside from one corner where a sliver of a sunbeam shot through a gap in the window display. Dust particles floated on the beam of light, tiny stars in a mini universe. He sniffed. The scent of mothballs and violet permeated the air. A middle-aged woman with plump cheeks and a scarlet beret pulled low over her forehead, sat behind the counter. A large brooch in the shape of a spider was fastened to the front of the beret. He wondered if the brooch had a hidden meaning. Was he a luckless fly, about to become trapped in a spider's web? He gave her a quick once-over. *Know your adversary*. Her eyes, a startling coffee shade, were also studying him. Suddenly too bashful to try out his only slightly better than schoolboy French, he pointed to the jacket in the window. She got up and, accompanied by a wash of violet scent, made her way round the counter. She reached into a cut glass dish, took a handful of small lilac coloured sweets and tipped them into her mouth. She pointed at the dish. 'Monsieur.' He smiled but didn't take a sweet.

The woman bundled her black satin dress up above her knees. Her surprisingly shapely legs were encased in knee length black stockings. She muttered under her breath as she climbed into the window to fetch the jacket.

"One careful owner," the woman said as he helped her down. She held up the buttery-soft suede coat with one hand and unbuttoned it with the other. She swept a hand over the navy lining. Liam recalled how impressed he had been when he had glimpsed the purple silk lining of Will's suit jacket. If that thief, Will, could have a fancy jacket, then so could he. He pointed to the five hundred euro price tag.

"Expensive."

"Quality. Armani. Five hundred."

"Too much."

"Bargain."

"Two hundred."

"Monsieur is making a joke."

"Two hundred and fifty."

"… takes the food from my mouth."

"Two hundred and fifty. Final offer." Liam began to move towards the door.

"Three hundred. Final offer."

Liam hesitated, then nodded. He counted out the notes and the woman dropped the jacket onto the counter. Liam shrugged. He removed his beige jacket and slipped his arms into the sleeves of the suede coat.

"Monsieur has done this before," the woman said sternly, dipping her hand into the glass jar. "Bargaining, I mean."

"Many times," Liam said with a smile. He didn't mind her sour manner. He had won the deal, and that was all that mattered. It would have been more unusual if his adversary had taken her loss with good grace and congratulated him. He left the shop lighter in pocket but also lighter in spirit. The deal had lifted his mood.

Chapter 6

Liam's stomach growled as he sat down at a table in the hotel brasserie. He shook his head as he scanned the menu. Too expensive, all of it. Despite the inflated prices the lure of living in the moment was strong, so he gave into temptation and his ravenous belly and ordered smoked salmon and a glass of champagne. As he waited for the food and drink to arrive, he willed himself to switch off the mental movie of Victor rapping on his office door:
Victor frowns, he taps his fingers on the wood between knocks and shuffles from one foot to the other. His forehead creases, eyes narrow and cheeks redden. He rattles the door, then puts his shoulder against it.

The waiter set the food and drink on the table. Liam took a long gulp of champagne and the movie of Victor faded away. He jabbed his fork into a piece of salmon, turning it over, admiring the orange hue of the flesh and the oily yet silky texture, before tucking in. Afterwards he was still hungry so he ordered cheesecake and strawberries. The wedge of cake was thick and not too sweet, the strawberries, large, red and luscious.

The hotel was the first one the woman at the tourist bureau at the Gare du Nord had recommended. Its rates were twice as high as the daily budget he'd allocated himself on the journey to Paris. He had been grateful, overwhelmed with relief, when the clerk, a blonde who reminded him of an ageing Bardot, leaned across her desk and cosily conversed in English. He'd thrown caution to the wind and had booked four nights.

His mind buzzed and crackled with delight as he drank in the sights and smells of Paris - the glamorous women, wine, fashion, and menus offering soupe de poisson, cassoulet, gratin dauphinois. All these were in plentiful supply, there to test him, to challenge the senses. He put his troubles to one side and imagined he was on holiday. In a few days perhaps, with all troubles ironed out, he might climb back on the

Eurostar. Why not make hay while the weak winter sun shone? The image of Victor, his wiry frame, snake-like eyes, his inability to forgive, once again slipped into his mind. He covered it with an imaginary blanket.

He went up to his room and texted his contact details to Will. Afterwards, he climbed into the king-size bed and drifted off. The following morning, he was woken up by a knock on the door. Paris, he was in Paris, he realised. The spacious and light room, the white bedspread, the large picture on the wall of a ballet dancer in front of Notre Dame, confirmed this. His stomach churned as he got out of bed. Will knew where he was so it might be news from him. Good news, Liam hoped. As he put his hand on the door handle, he pictured Will, on the other side of the door, a bottle of champagne clutched in one hand by way of apology. Perhaps things had been sorted out or maybe the newspaper article about Zarek's collapse was premature. People got things wrong, he'd be the first to admit that. When he opened the door, a uniformed bellboy held out a long yellow envelope. Liam shook his head and snatched it from the boy. The young man frowned but stood his ground, hand outstretched. Liam squinted and scanned the front of the envelope: a telegram from London.

"Who the hell sends telegrams these days?" Liam dropped a two-euro coin into the bellboy's hand. He ripped the envelope open and scanned the contents. The short sentences marked a line between his past life, with its ups and downs, and his current ill fortune. He read them again, just to make sure he had fully understood their meaning:

Sorry old boy, no kind way to put this. Zarek definitely tits-up. They've scrapped the lot. Tried to salvage some of our investment, but no luck. We've lost everything. Don't hurry back.

He was incensed. Didn't Will understand he *couldn't* go back? Not if he didn't want to vanish like Larry. He had gambled with Victor's money. Only an idiot would do that.

He sat on a bench in the Tuileries gardens. His hand shook as he crumpled Will's telegram into a ball and chucked it across the pathway. *Don't hurry back.* There was finality in these words. A line drawn under hope. A marker struck through the promise that things would right themselves.

"Imbecile," a man's voice yelled.

His eyes were drawn to one of the stalls which edged the pathway. A giant of a man stood next to the stall, his body taut, apparently ready for action.

"Sorry?" Liam said.

The man bent down and picked up the ball of paper. He drew his arm back and aimed the ball at Liam. His forehead barely stung as the object connected with it. He got up and strode across the path.

"Now look here…"

His gaze dropped from the trader's icy glare to a painting propped up on the stall. He picked it up and studied it. A landscape: a rocky coast, chalk cliffs which swept down to the water's edge, whitecaps frothing on a blue-grey sea. It was painted in oils, using similar techniques to Peploe, layering depth and texture. To his eye, it also had the realism of a Hopper painting and he felt an achingly beautiful loneliness. Puffs of purple flowers sprouted from the cliff face, lending the powerful subject a hint of delicacy. Despite the constant hum of traffic on the boulevard, he imagined himself perched on top of the cliff, an olden-days king surveying his kingdom. In a place like this he would be able to rest and recover his senses with no interference from the rest of the world.

"Perfect. Like entering a dream world," he said aloud. Perhaps it was the pall of melancholy that hung over him, but a painting had never touched him quite like this before.

The trader grinned and the prospect of confrontation dissolved. His teeth and fingers, Liam noted, were heavily stained with nicotine, the dirty yellow contrasting with the purity of the painting.

"Want to buy?"

"I love it. How much?"

"Three hundred." The trader clicked his fingers and Liam

suddenly remembered the telegram, the source of today's disappointment.

"Perhaps…no, I shouldn't." The enthusiasm he had shown had probably doubled the price of the painting. Normally, he was proud of his poker face. Under usual circumstances he would never have blinked an eye or shown a flicker of interest, even if the item was desirable and a bargain. But, he acknowledged, nothing about this day was normal.

"I give you two for one, a real bargain," the trader said in surprisingly good English. Liam perked up.

"You don't mean you've more than one of these?"

The man pointed to one side of the stall.

"A few more there by the same artist."

"I'd love to meet him."

The trader bowed. "Pleased to make your acquaintance."

"You – you did these?"

Liam raised his eyebrows. This man, with his ebony hair, probably dyed, leathery skin, and muscular frame didn't fit the romantic profile of an artist. In his mind, an artist was sensitive, precious about their work, an individual who would shun worldly pleasures, even food and drink, to buy their next canvas or acquire specific shades of paint: Burnt Sienna, Vandyke Brown or Naples Yellow. Yet, when he gave it a moment's thought, didn't Picasso disprove this stereotype? Hadn't he been fond of a dish of hearty eel stew, and weren't his last words *'Drink to me, drink to my health. You know I can't drink anymore.'*

"Painted in my attic." He reached out his hand. "Gerome Dubois, born in Arles, resident of Paris and, as I said previously, pleased to make your acquaintance."

"From the south. Van Gogh territory. That explains it." Liam shook his hand.

He picked up another painting and held it up. Light fell on a forest of trees. Layers of green and brown. Textured. Honest. He felt as though he could lie in the shade of these trees and forget his troubles.

"They're not signed."

Gerome picked up a marker and scribbled his name at the bottom left hand corner of each canvas. "This okay?"

He nodded and shrugged. Gerome had won this deal. "That'll do fine."

He took out his wallet and counted out three hundred euro. Gerome wrapped sheets of newspaper round the paintings.

"Pleasure to do business," he said.

Liam tucked the newspaper parcel under his arm and made his way back to the hotel. Back in his hotel room, he removed the wrapping and studied his purchases. Earlier, he'd told himself that Gerome had won the deal, but now it dawned on him that it was he who was the winner. Gerome was a true master. Steered in the right direction, he could become famous, his work worth a small fortune. He propped the paintings against the dressing table mirror, then went over to the bed and stacked the pillows on top of each other. Now he could lie back and admire his purchases in comfort. Two hours later he awoke feeling more refreshed than he'd been in a long time. The room was filled with a sensation of peace that not even his troubles with Will and Victor could shift. He was distracted by the beauty of the paintings again and it was a quarter of an hour before he remembered the telegram.

Liam called Will's mobile, but it was switched off. He tried Will's work number and was connected to his extension. As the phone rang and rang, he pictured the empty desk at the other end, the drawers cleaned out, not a trace of the prior occupant. He left a message with the receptionist who said she hadn't seen him for several days. Every so often his eyes were drawn to the paintings. Finally he got up from the bed and turned them round, so the painted side faced the wall. They were a distraction and he needed his wits about him to contemplate his next move. He was stuck here for the foreseeable future with limited funds. There was no way he could face being poor in a city like Paris.

He left his room and wandered down to the brasserie. He

needed to devise a plan, a route out of the situation he'd found himself in, with Will's assistance. Instead he sat on a stool at the leather-clad bar and drank two glasses of champagne.

When he returned to the room, he called the main number of the brokerage.

"Mr Grey? No longer with us," the receptionist said in a clipped voice.

"No longer with you... You don't mean deceased?" Despite the balmy temperature in the room, he shivered. Had Victor already been released? Had he discovered the link between Will, himself, and his missing fortune?

"He came in just after you called earlier. Said he wouldn't be back."

"Can I have a forwarding number?"

"Unfortunately he didn't leave one," she said. "His departure was untimely, a surprise to all of us. We'd like to speak to him. Urgently. So if you can supply a number, we'd be grateful."

"If I had his number, why would I be asking you for one?"

"True," the woman said. "Still, if you hear from him, you'll let us know, Mr..?"

Liam ended the call. Just as he thought, Will had deserted the sinking ship. And, from the conversation with the receptionist, it appeared he'd caused havoc at work. How much of his clients' money had Will invested in Zarek? How much chaos had he caused his company? But to Liam that was nothing compared to the mayhem Will had caused in *his* life. He'd just turned forty-three and was virtually penniless. His mind launched into a series of 'if only's', a habit formed in his younger days. If only he'd had a father, he might have learnt boyish things: how to kick a ball half decently, how to handle women without being a doormat, how to be a man. If only they hadn't moved so much, he might have done better at school. If only he'd held onto Victor's money then Victor might have thrown some cash his way to reward his loyalty. He could have declared bankruptcy and started all over again.

But Will's tired clichés had sealed his fate: buy the rumour, sell the news, and, you'll never go broke taking profits. Despite these run-of-the-mill clichés, he'd been hooked and had behaved like a fool, kneeling before the altar of greed.

"Money," he said, "is truly the root of all evil."

He lit a cigarette, lay back on his pillow and drifted into a trance. Through the haze of smoke his eyes lit on the paintings. He reached for a glass of wine poured earlier and alternated between sipping wine and taking long drags on his cigarette. When he'd stubbed out the cigarette, his last Marlboro, he got up and rummaged through the pockets of his jacket. He took out a packet of Gitanes, bought that morning, and opened it. The first drag of the dark tobacco had such a bite the room began to spin. He put a hand on the bedside table to steady himself.

"Needs must," he muttered. From now on he would smoke cheaper cigarettes and drink table wine. He wouldn't give up dreams of a good life, it would just be a cheaper one.

"Art, cigarettes and wine. What more could a civilised man want?" he said aloud. Then he remembered he'd also dreamed of nestling his face in the bosom of a Chanel clad brunette. Without money, that dream was on hold.

Chapter 7

Liam tossed and turned. He gave up trying to sleep and got out of bed. He went to the window and looked out.

The dying embers of night had still to cast off their grey veil, but a hint of light threatened over rooftops opposite. There was no noise outside, aside from the brushes of a street cleaning vehicle scraping against concrete. Without looking at the clock it was evident it was very early. He sat down at the desk and switched on the computer provided by the hotel. He waited for Google Mail to load, although fear rather than anticipation lurked in the pit of his stomach. He was disappointed but not surprised to see there was nothing from Will. The evening before he had dashed off several emails to a private account Will had set up, where details of the deal with Zarek could be freely discussed.

"It was all supposed to be OK," he muttered as he reread the emails. The first one said simply 'where the hell are you?' The second, sent an hour later, said 'Look, I don't want to know where you are – but what the fuck happened to my money?' There was no reply from Will. It appeared he had vanished into thin air.

Liam scanned the websites of the main financial press. One had an article on the failure of Zarek's system. The final test phase, it said, had thrown up errors which would take months to correct and delivery of the system was fatally delayed. In the meantime, Extus had snatched the educational provider contracts from under Zarek's nose. Time-to-market was king in technology development. You took chances, even launched a product with minimal testing, to prevent a competitor's product from gaining the market share, that's what Liam now understood. The story Will had sold him wasn't the same story he was reading now. He logged onto another newspaper's site and found an article on a breaking scandal involving Zarek, who were accused of encouraging investment by providing false insider information. He gave a low whistle.

"Insider trading *and* fraud. Double-dealing bastards," he said in a very loud voice, not caring if his next-door neighbour could hear him.

He logged off and shut the computer down. If they found Will, his own part in the scandal might be uncovered. His part was minor, a slap on the wrist, a few months community service at the worst, maybe a fine. But despite these attempts at reassurance, there would be no going home. Victor had a different sense of justice. His was more final.

After breakfast, he decided to go for a walk to silence the voice which repeated the words poor, destitute and up-shit-creek on a loop in his head. He pushed through the revolving doors and turned left. It was a fair morning, a chill in the air but the blue in the sky was already deepening. Smartly dressed people trickled down the boulevard, towards offices, coffee shops and other sanctuaries, he imagined. He examined the effortless chic of his fellow pedestrians. A silk scarf, casually tied at the neck, elevated a plain shirt and black jacket to high fashion status. Unlike Englishmen, Parisian men appeared unafraid to be seen in bright colours. This morning, pink was a particular favourite, worn in the form of cravat, shirt or sweater. One man even wore pink and black checked trousers.

He did a double take as two youngish women passed by. One was blonde, the other brunette. Contrasting beautiful bookends, he remarked to himself, although his tastes swung towards the brunette. Each woman wore the uniform of scarf knotted at the neck and expensive looking handbag slung over the shoulder. He wondered if their fashion sense had been passed down via their mothers, or if lessons in chic were timetabled in school. He sighed. This was a world in which he longed to be an active participant. If the deal with Will had been successful, he could have rented an apartment with large square rooms and high ceilings, in a good area, preferably the Left Bank. The attractive women he passed in the street might have queued up to date him. Now that he was down on his luck, women like that probably wouldn't give him a second glance.

Liam was aware that he lacked style. When he looked in the mirror he saw average, run of the mill. He doubted that women with expensive tastes would be queuing up to share a carafe of cheap table wine, drunk in a run-down bar. What he had always suspected was most likely true: money equalled happiness.

At the corner of the street, a man was seated on a low stool, a jug was on the pavement next to him. He was surprised to see someone begging so early, but perhaps that was good business strategy, the early bird and all that. There was a bench nearby and he had a sudden impulse to sit down and observe the man at work. If he didn't want to be similarly homeless and destitute, he reflected, the plight of this wretch might propel him into action.

He bought a newspaper from the newsstand, sat down on the bench, and pretended to read. Over the top of the paper, he watched as the occasional passerby dropped a coin into the jug. At the clink of the coin, the man, who Liam judged to be between thirty and forty, twitched, flipping the opaque sunglasses he wore further down his nose. He wrinkled his nose and the glasses sprang back into place. An older woman opened her mouth and roared with laughter. She rummaged in her bag, then dropped a coin into the jug. Clever, Liam thought, as the man mimicked the actions of an antique character money bank - flip, slide and clink

The man stood up and put on a navy jacket, almost, but not quite, blending in with the pavement catwalk. He walked over to the bench and sat down. Although the man's jacket was smart, Liam edged his coat closer to his body.

"No need to move. It's OK," the man said.

"Sorry?"

"I have enough." He patted the space beside him on the bench.

"I wasn't..." he began, then he realised it was pointless denying that sitting next to this man made his skin crawl. In Liam's mind, beggars were living ghosts, invisible to most of society. You might pay your dues by donating a euro or two, but you certainly didn't interact with them.

"You were watching me."

Sensing trouble ahead, he shifted to the corner of the bench. "I wasn't. I was reading the paper."

The man shook his head. "I saw your eyes, over top of newspaper. You were pretending to read. Not same as reading."

"I was amused by your trick."

"Ah, automaton, that is name of trick. My father taught me."

His father? Liam was immediately ashamed at his own preconceptions. Why did he find it difficult to visualise this man with a father, or any sort of family. He stole a sideways glance. In his blue jacket the man took on a middle-of-the-road appearance. He could be a local government clerk, a bank clerk or shop assistant. When he'd first spotted him, Liam had noted an ethereal air about him, like a vagabond sticking two fingers up at convention. Close up, he saw that he was well groomed, with dark oiled hair combed neatly in a side parting, and clipped beard. His eyes were clear and his face unlined. Old yet not old, Liam observed. In his current state of paranoia, he was wary of engaging with the stranger, but he was also curious.

"Your English is good. Excellent, even."

"School, tourists, television, girlfriend. Mainly television, but many ways to learn language. I maybe go to England as soon as I gather enough cash."

"Why?"

"Plenty of Czech in London. Lonely here and I cannot return home – yet."

The man reached out his hand.

"Borivoj from Besiny, beautiful small town in mountains." Liam nodded but didn't shake his hand. Borivoj moved his hand closer to Liam's so they were almost touching. "You can shake. Very clean."

Liam gave a limp handshake, barely connecting with the

other man's hand. "Er… Liam."

"Liam. Like actor, Liam Neeson, from *Schindler's List*? A fine film. Maybe you are cousin?" Liam smiled and shook his head. "See, we are friends," Borivoj said, nodding his head. "Liam. My first English friend."

"Irish, actually. Originally from Belfast. Northern Ireland, that is. Moved to London when I was young."

"Ireland. Nice country, I hear. Maybe I go there instead."

"I'm curious. How did you end up here?"

"Where?"

"Paris. Living on the streets."

"Streets? Ah, no. I rent room in hostel when I have good week. A few times I sleep in doorway, but not many. People are generous – but not too generous."

"Why Paris?"

"Very easy. Paris is beautiful city. I saw it on television, in books. You say goodbye to home, hoping for better life, but in reality it is not. You do one job and then another. Not much pay and treated... not so well. You don't want to work here any more but you also don't want to lose face and go home. I think expression is 'with hand between legs'."

"Tail," Liam corrected. "It's 'tail between your legs'."

"Strange expression, when we humans have no tails. English is not always logical. You have another expression, 'the other man's grass all the time greener'. I suppose that is why I am here. But what about you, friend, what is your story?"

"You could say I'm on holiday."

"Are you not enjoying holiday?"

"Why do you say that?"

"Your eyes. They tell story. Sadness, maybe worry. When you were watching me, I was watching you. You were curious, intrigued by me. Most people, even those who donate some cents or euro, don't really notice a person. They see sad situation and react as parents or religion has taught them. Automatic - I like that word, powerful, snappy. They don't really think when they throw coin in cup, but they feel good. Like going to confessional in church. Clean and righteous."

"I suppose you're right." He flinched as Borivoj's hand brushed the sleeve of his jacket.

"Nice. How can a man be troubled when he can afford such coat?"

"It's a long story."

"Designer?"

"Armani," Liam said, his voice deepening with pride.

"You must be rich. You stay in very nice hotel."

His eyes narrowed as he took a closer look at Borivoj. He patted his jacket pocket, verifying the comforting bulge of his wallet.

"How do you know where I'm staying?"

Borivoj slipped his sunglasses, which he had placed on top of his head, back on.

"Magic glasses, Liam."

"Really?" He wouldn't have been astonished if this was true. There was something otherworldly about Borivoj and it wasn't anything to do with his begging or busking or whatever he called it. Perhaps, he thought, it was simply a cultural difference. He hadn't travelled much in the past, and had certainly never come across someone from the mountains of the Czech Republic. But, he realised, they had something in common - they were both exiles.

"No," Borivoj laughed. "I saw you leave hotel. When you live like me you don't miss anything. Survival, you call it."

"Living on your wits, that's the English expression."

Borivoj nodded. "Why so serious. Something on your mind?"

"I have a few - one or two - issues," he admitted, suddenly glad to have someone to talk to. Over the past few years he'd been so busy dealing and making ends meet, he had neglected the human and social aspects of life. Not that he was the clingy sort who needed bosom buddies. The divorce had taken care of that and had knocked any vestiges of sentimentality from him. He had lost everything including the semi-detached house with the half paid off mortgage, and was so despondent he'd declined to take any of the contents, including his ten year old black and white cat, Mannie.

"Maybe I can help," Borivoj said.

"I need to work things out on my own. But, believe it or not, you have helped."

"I meet you later for drink." Borivoj shook the jug, rattling the coins inside. "Profitable morning."

"You're kind, but no, I need to be alone."

Borivoj shook his head.

"Alone not good. Come meet Alouette. She will make you feel better."

Liam raised his eyebrows. Borivoj raised a hand.

"Alouette is friend. Kind woman. We take glass together sometimes. Le Coq Bleu, Rue la Boetie. Come, join us later." Borivoj got up from the bench. "I must work." He returned to the corner and removed his jacket, revealing his worn shirt with its frayed cuffs. He sat down on his stool and winked. "Don't forget, Le Coq Bleu, be there or…"

"Be square." Liam laughed, despite his current state of despair. He was heartened that in the midst of turmoil, humour still existed. He had a strange feeling that life was, in a subtle way, laying out a set of lessons: don't judge too quickly; don't fall for flattery; don't expect a fortune to drop effortlessly into your lap. If he was clever enough to pick up on these lessons, to become a dutiful student, perhaps he could begin again.

"You English have crazy language."

As he continued down the boulevard towards the Louvre, this positive outlook evaporated. There were two certainties in his life. The first was the prospect of facing Victor's rage if he returned home, the second was an empty bank account. In his wildest dreams he could never have imagined being stupid enough to land himself in either of these situations.

For the moment he'd cling by his fingernails onto sanity, aiming to fill the day with pleasurable experiences - a morning in the Louvre, savouring the beauty of paintings by artists like Rubens, Da Vinci, Watteau, and others who saw the world with gifted and magical eyes. Afterwards, an espresso in an atmospheric café would round off the experience. But then again, a delicately prepared Sole Veronique and a fine Sancerre in a top brassiere, in the company of a charming woman, was an experience which could rival, if not surpass, art. He sighed, imagining he could smell the fictional woman's perfume: Chanel Number Five or something in the same price bracket?

At the Place de la Concorde, he wandered back to the market stall where he'd purchased the paintings. Grey smoke floated up from behind the stall. Behind a wall of canvasses, Gerome lounged on a deckchair. The gap between the stall and the railings behind was small, making his body appear larger. Around six foot two, Liam noted, thinking that he wouldn't want to tangle with him. Although the sun was out, an icy wind cut across the Place de la Concorde. Gerome shivered in a light cotton jacket more suited to late spring. Liam concluded he was having an unprofitable morning as his eyes were narrowed and his pursed lips moved occasionally as though he was silently arguing with someone. Gerome raised a fat cigar to his lips and took a puff. Liam savoured the cigar's earthy aroma. This was the smell of dealers in the market; the aftermath of business successfully conducted. A pint in one hand, a cigar in the other, he could practically hear the dealers' hoots of laughter when they'd got one over on Joe public. Gerome glanced up, his eyes brightened when he saw Liam.

"*Bonjour, mon ami*, my good friend." He set his cigar on the edge of the stall, stood up and clapped his hands. "Not so warm today."

"Bright...but chilly. Almost cold enough for snow."

"Snow? I hope not today." Gerome patted the sleeve of his jacket."

"May I?" Liam pointed at the paintings.

Gerome nodded and sat down again. He picked up his cigar and took a slow drag. His eyes followed Liam's movements.

None of the paintings caught Liam's eye, which pleased

him as he was, he reminded himself, almost broke. He stepped back and raised a hand in a gesture of farewell. Gerome sprang out of his chair.

"Wait. Gerome beckoned him round to the other side of the stall. He pointed to the deckchair. "Sit." Gerome reached into a crate and took out a painting.

"For my special customer." Liam drew a deep breath as Gerome held up a portrait of a beautiful woman.

"One of yours?" he asked, although he recognised Gerome's distinctive style. He was playing for time, allowing his mind to process the vision in front of him. Love at first sight. He would give every cent he had to burrow into the canvas and simply be a part of it.

"My very best effort," Gerome said proudly.

To his own astonishment, tears welled up in Liam's eyes. The painting told his story: a tale of his desires, a statement of what he didn't have. A nude, the most beautiful woman he'd ever seen, was reclining on top of a bed. But the word 'beautiful' didn't do her justice, he felt - she was a goddess. Her image and vulnerability were captured with such precision and feeling, he forgot he was looking at a painting. He fancied if he reached out and touched her skin it would feel warm, moist, velvety. Her black hair was layered in oils so cleverly it appeared to be swaying in a seductive manner. It tumbled in waves to just below her breasts and he was reminded of how he'd felt when he'd watched waves beat against chalk cliffs near Eastbourne on a stormy day. They had been so majestic and powerful, he had shrunk both in stature and presence before them. He had sensed their danger, yet a strange intoxicating dizziness had overcome him as he stood still, watching and anticipating the power of a giant wave washing over his body. Danger, that was the word he was looking for. This woman was dangerous in the most seductive of ways. He took a deep breath and forced himself to look away from the painting. Curious, he turned to Gerome. The man was a puzzle, a painter with few social graces or charms, yet he'd persuaded a woman like this to pose for him? Perhaps he'd judged the proverbial book by the cover too quickly, just as he'd given Will's patter too much credit. In times of stress, he realised, his powers of judgement fell short of basic standards.

"Two thousand," Gerome said.

He felt disappointment, as though it was a physical attribute, creep from his head, through his body, to his toes.

"I can't afford it - but it's really great. You're a fantastic artist. I don't know why you're not famous."

"He's still alive." A man who stood behind the adjacent stall chuckled.

"*Ta gueule!*" Gerome growled.

The man immediately ceased laughing and shifted to the far end of his stall.

"Mehdi likes to joke," Gerome threw a menacing look in the unfortunate Mehdi's direction. Gerome skirted round Liam, blocking his exit. "We can deal," he said.

Liam was sorely tempted. The woman was truly a goddess. If he couldn't possess her in real life then surely a painting was better than nothing? Then he pictured himself: money gone, ejected from his hotel, with only the pavement and paintings for company.

"No. I shouldn't. I can't right now." Sadness enveloped his whole being. In all his years of dealing he'd never allowed himself to become attached to an object. The closest he had come was with the Peter Rabbit book. There was something about the innocence of the young woman who'd sold it for a few quid that reminded him of the book's value. Even then, hadn't he only just parted with it?

Gerome, who was still barring the exit from the stall, stroked his chin. His eyes scanned Liam, up and down, several times. He reached out and fingered the end of one of the sleeves of the suede coat.

"Fine quality."

"Designer. Armani," Liam said indignantly. Earlier Borivoj, now Gerome. He wished his new friends would keep their grubby fingers off his expensive coat.

"Fake?"

"Certainly not."

Gerome gave a small, apologetic bow. "So sorry, a man of quality, a man like you who recognises quality, would *never* wear a fake." Liam nodded and attempted to navigate around Gerome's large frame. Gerome pointed to his chair. "Sit down there and we'll deal."

Having no choice, other than shoving Gerome to one side, he sat down and gave him a defiant look. He was a dealer, if Gerome thought he would get one over on him then he had another thing coming. All the same, he could sense his heart beat faster, his blood pressure rise.

"Your jacket and one thousand for the painting," Gerome said.

"It's wonderful but I've told you, I can't afford it. I don't have a thousand to spare."

"Jacket and five hundred."

Liam folded his arms and shook his head. If Gerome could play silly buggers, then so could he.

"Okay. Jacket for the painting. Straight exchange. A good offer."

Gerome waved the painting in front of his face. He imagined he could smell the woman's musky perfume.

"Who is she?"

"Just someone I know."

He took a deep breath. 'Fuck caution,' he told himself. Why not clutch at even a sliver of happiness? He had an idea and pointed at the painting.

"The jacket and a meeting with her. I want to take her to dinner."

"I don't know if that's possible…"

"Is she married?"

"No. I'm sure not."

"If I can't meet her, then no deal." Liam's right eye twitched, as it always did when he was aroused. There was a deal to be had and he was determined to seal it.

"Okay then. Deal," Gerome sighed. "But you have to wait.

She's gone down South for a week to visit her sick mother."

"Truth?"

"Yes, you can trust me. Why would I lie? Anyway, you can find me easily. I'm here most days selling my humble paintings."

Liam got up and once again attempted to negotiate round Gerome. Gerome pointed to the jacket. Liam set the painting down and slid his arms out. He gave his jacket to Gerome, who put it on.

"Nice, nice," he said. "A bit small, but still elegant."

Feeling the chill in the air, Liam headed back to the hotel. He shivered as he walked briskly. Was this an omen of dark times ahead? It dawned on him that for the second day in a row he hadn't made it to the Louvre, but that didn't matter as he had an eerie feeling that something more precious than the Mona Lisa was pressed under his arm.

On the way back, he made a decision. Tomorrow, instead of booking a few more days of luxury, he would move to a cheaper hotel. Earlier he'd checked the bill at reception and had been shocked to discover that, including meals, the total amounted to almost half of his funds.

He stopped by reception and asked the clerk to prepare the final bill for the following morning. Back in his room, he dialled room service and ordered a bottle of wine. He looked around his hotel room, taking in the understated luxury. It was a shame, he now realised, that he hadn't fully taken advantage of his surroundings. Sure, he had enjoyed the medium-soft mattress, the goose-down pillows, the starched white duvet cover which felt cool and silky against his skin. But he hadn't paid much attention to the large flat screen television or to the computer with free internet access, which he'd barely used aside from trying to contact Will. Nor had he opened the mini bar which contained a half bottle of Moët, pistachios, chocolates and other treats. In the bathroom, when he'd used the shower, he hadn't luxuriated in the thickness of the towels, nor rubbed the small bottles of creams and lotions into his body. 'You don't miss something till you don't have it', he remembered his mother saying as she and his eight year old self watched bailiffs whistling and joking as they removed scrappy old bits of furniture from their flat. He dismissed those thoughts. His younger self had vowed never again to be in that position, and anyway, this very instant he had a roof over his head. The only thing that was missing was a healthy bank account. If he could find that bastard, Will, he would put his hands around his neck and throttle him.

He turned on the tap and ran a bath. He tipped several bottles of scented oil into the steaming water and switched on the Jacuzzi. A few minutes later, he climbed into the bath clutching a glass of wine in one hand. He lay back as the hot water and oils soaked into his skin. The moment was all that counted, and right now he felt good. The bathroom door was ajar and through the opening he could see the painting of the beautiful woman, which he had propped up on his pillows. She appeared to beckoning to him.

Chapter 8

Liam sighed. Given the dimensions of the paintings, and the bulk of the bathroom towels and dressing gown he'd helped himself to, he had accumulated a considerable pile of luggage. There could be no hesitation, no piddling around, he needed to find cheaper lodgings right away. The same bellboy who had delivered Will's telegram helped him carry his luggage to the lobby and load it into a cubicle. The boy chattered in broken English on the way down. Tips were poor these days, he complained, and he was dependent on these acts of generosity to pay for his sick mother's medication. Liam barely noticed the monologue as he was too deep in thought. He was a whisker away from homelessness and all his wits were needed to keep a roof over his head.

He paid the bill, counting out the exact amount in notes and coins, ignoring the bellboy who shuffled from foot to foot nearby. 'I'll wager you're better off than me, mate,' he wanted to say, but held his tongue. Perhaps the lad's mother really was sick, and maybe his father, just like his own, had buggered off.

When he left the hotel, he paused and glanced along the street. He was relieved to see no sign of Borivoj. He wasn't in the mood for conversation with the talkative Czech, although he had to admit that yesterday, when he was at his lowest, he'd found their brief encounter uplifting.

Today, there was no desire to confide in another or to be commiserated on his run of ill fortune. From an early age, he'd discovered that he functioned best when he tucked his feelings away and got on with what he called the dirty business of life. In any case, his mind found it impossible to process what had just happened. Had he really gambled with a criminal's money, frittered the pension fund of a man who'd killed, and was capable of killing again? Surely he wasn't that much of a idiot.

He took his phone from his pocket and stared at the

screen. Perhaps he should phone Victor and try to explain what had happened? The urge was fleeting and vanished before he'd answered his own question.

He made his way down the street, intending to head away from the elegant district of his current hotel, towards the upper end of the Champs-Elysées. The guide book he'd found on the Eurostar indicated the hotels in that district were mainly two and three star and were more suited to his shrinking budget. His mind tuned into autopilot. Deal with the practicalities, it instructed. As he turned the corner, he heard Borivoj's distinct voice.

"Liam, nice to see you."

Borivoj's stool was partially hidden by a rack of newspapers. Liam briefly contemplated ignoring him and continuing on his way, but before he could turn the corner, Borivoj stood up, blocking his passage.

"Something...not right," he frowned. "The coat. Why such dull coat when you have Armani?"

Liam was wearing a beige parka he'd bought some time ago in England. It was warm and functional and certainly not cheap, but Borivoj had a point, it was dowdy. This was a coat designed for an older man, to keep out wind and rain, a functional garment with the sole purpose of protecting the wearer from the elements.

"I sold it. Exchanged, to be exact."

"Hmm." Borivoj stroked his beard. "Exchanged for what?"

"A painting."

"Armani for painting. How strange. Must be good one."

"Just something I found on a market stall."

"Market stall? Not so good quality. These paintings are two for penny, made for tourist. You've been had."

Liam shrugged. Borivoj had a point, many of the paintings he'd come across were pretty and evocative of Paris, but nothing special in the grand scheme of art. Gerome's work was different though, more than a cut or two above the rest. A comment from someone, he couldn't remember who, popped into his head, but before he could examine it Borivoj distracted him with a new trick. His glasses were hanging on a thick cord fastened around his neck. He puffed out his chest, like a courting pigeon, and the glasses sprang into the air. He ducked down, positioning himself under the glasses and they landed on his head.

"Nice trick," Liam laughed. "Your father?"

Borivoj shook his head.

"Alouette. She is very disappointed you didn't come to meet us, so we invent new trick. Maybe you will come this evening?"

"I'm moving today."

"Leaving Paris?"

Liam shook his head. "Moving to a cheaper hotel. Near the Arc du Triomphe, I hope."

"No shit! Alouette and I will meet in bar near there later. Do you know Le Chat Rouge?"

Liam was faintly amused at Borivoj's semi-fluent English punctuated by American slang. The Czech man was sharp, with a good ear for languages.

He shook his head. "I don't imagine I'll be in the mood for going out."

"Not very good tourist, Liam. Many tourists want to shop, eat, drink, have fun. They have list of art galleries to tick off and I win by getting euro each time I point them in right direction. But never mind. All different. If you change mind, ask hotel to give directions. Le Chat Rouge, guaranteed fun. That is why people go for holiday, isn't it?"

Liam continued on his way. When he arrived at the Place de la Concorde, Gerome's stall was not visible amongst the carnival of striped tents and amusements. He was relieved as he had no appetite to see Gerome wearing his suede coat. It was more than a garment to keep him warm, or help him compete in fashion stakes, it was the symbol of his new life in Paris, his freedom and survival.

Had buying the paintings been the right thing to do, he asked himself? But they'd already given him as much pleasure as the coat, so you could say both he and Gerome were the victors in this particular deal. Then there was the added bonus of the insanely beautiful woman and the possibility of a date with her. That tipped the scales in his favour. Sixty:forty to me, he muttered to himself.

It suddenly dawned on him that Gerome might never return. Could he have promised the date, knowing that the woman would never agree to it? Perhaps, he concluded, she had never set foot in Paris and Gerome had painted her somewhere else.

Instead of heading towards the Arc du Triomphe, he took a detour. He arrived at the glass and metal pyramid, the main entrance to the Louvre. It was years since he'd been inside, and then it had been easy to wander in, scan the signs on the walls, and find the paintings he was interested in. Now he found himself in a cavernous structure which reminded him of an airport check-in area. He passed a guide who was praising the beauty of the pyramid.

"You are standing inside an incredible work of art," the guide gushed.

Liam shook his head as he hurried past. If this was a work of art, he told himself, then god help the art world. Over the past decade the art scene had striven to outdo itself with flaky concepts, which in his mind weren't real art. Where was the skill in placing a bunch of painted dead caterpillars on a bush and then calling it art. And what about the crazy people who paid a fortune for these mad works? Were they so deranged they preferred these installations to a beautiful Manet, Peploe or Renoir? It could, of course, be argued that many such investments had paid off, and the pop stars and impresarios who had invested their money, had pocketed small fortunes when the price of modern art had rocketed.

"Emperor's new clothes," he muttered. But on the other hand he acknowledged that he was probably a dinosaur, with tastes in art firmly anchored in the past.

He wandered around looking for the entrance to the Old Masters wing. Finally he stumbled upon hall eighteen which was hung with twenty-four Rubens paintings. As he made his way around the magnificent, marble floored, high-ceilinged gallery, Ruben's large paintings with their dark subjects did nothing to uplift his spirits. A group huddled in front of one painting. Intrigued by the subject, a curvy woman pointing a dagger at her breast, he lingered at the edge of the group. The guide spoke in sing-song French. He picked up the words: suicide, mort, mari. "Suicide, death, husband," he whispered. Goosebumps rippled on his skin. Suicide was the act of a weakling, in his opinion, and he would never contemplate ending his life. Or would he? He left the building in worse spirits than when he'd entered.

He stopped at a coffee shop in a belle époque building nearby. Inside, he found a haven of cosy bookishness. Lighting was soft and calming, walls were lined with shelves of books, old and new. A layer of dust sat on top of the books. To Liam's eye, trained in the tricks of the antiques trade, the dust was sprinkled on top for effect. The glass of the mirrors on the walls was mottled, although the frames appeared newish and in very good nick. He observed they were hung at a height which would enable customers to view their reflections as they read or contemplated over a coffee or two. A waitress approached his table. He ordered a brandy. She raised her eyebrows and went back to the bar, muttering under her breath. She returned a minute later and slapped a large brandy on the table. He interpreted this as disapproval and noted that she had the air of someone who was fed up serving gormless tourists. He looked around, none of those he assumed to be locals were drinking alcohol. Instead, they sipped water or drank from tiny cups.

Several customers were seated on a long bench by a window. Some were hunched over laptops, one held a fountain pen over a blank sheet of paper. They wore the same expressions of concentration on their faces as they appeared to agonise over the right word. *Le mot juste.* He assumed they were writers as they possessed the seriousness of olden day clergy ministering to the flock. Their writing would one day reveal their genius to the world, at least that's what he imagined they thought. He smiled inwardly: at least *he* had a grip on reality.

Liam gulped the brandy down. It was adequate but nowhere near the standard of the fifty quid Armagnac he'd once consumed in a top restaurant back in London. This was during a brief, golden period in the antique business, when sets of Dickens books would sell at three times their real value. Still, right now the alcohol fulfilled its purpose, numbing his senses and clearing his head of jumbled up images of how he might kill Will or be disposed of by Victor. He likened the brandy to DDT sprayed by a crop sprayer, destroying a fog of insects. Short term victory, long term failure.

The centre of Paris was compact, easy to move around on foot. The metro, with its cold tiled walls and floors depressed him, even though it was cleaner than the London Underground. He remembered how Lily had hated the tube. When she'd worked in the centre of London she often moaned about her fellow commuters, describing them as 'a great unwashed tide of humanity'. He didn't care about race, creed, colour and washing habits, he simply hated the crush.

Paradoxically, it was in the midst of this tide of humanity that Lily met the man she embarked on an affair with, the man who ended their marriage. She'd never described in detail how she and James had met, and the only thing she would admit to was meeting him on the way home. They had apparently locked eyes in the tube for weeks before James had made a move. A series of drinks was followed by dinners, all with plausible excuses. Then Lily began to stay with friends overnight. One night the friend she was staying with called to speak to her. It was only later, when the drama, arguments and recriminations had been put to bed, that he asked himself why *he* had been the one to leave. Her solicitor was better than his so she had managed to hang onto the house. The day of his departure he'd looked at her properly as though he was seeing her for the first time. She was more beautiful than the image he carried in his mind. Her dark hair, dyed even blacker, hung past her shoulders. She wore loose track pants and a tight tee shirt, showing off her toned upper body. He'd wanted to hurt her back, but the only thing that sprang to mind as he stood in the front path was 'I always preferred the cat to you.' Yet he hadn't even taken the cat! A year after the break up, when the bitterness had softened, he joked with a mate that he should buy that bastard estate agent, James, a drink for taking Lily off his hands.

He continued up the Champs Elysées. The grand avenue, once the centre of Paris society, had been edged out of its fashion status by gentrified Saint Germain. At the upper end of the boulevard, chain stores competed for business. Record shops had the latest music, currently hip-hop, blaring out. He passed a shop where the music was playing at least forty decibels louder than he could tolerate. Liam had always associated Paris with mood music, the music of love, sung by crooners like Piaf and Aznavour, rather than rappers. This aggressive drum and bass resembled music of war. Perhaps an omen, he thought darkly. He pulled up his hood and turned into a side street.

A warren of narrow streets of mixed fortune criss-crossed this district. He stopped at the entrance to a two star hotel, admiring the swirling art nouveau ironwork fixed around the portal. Next door was a brasserie. The door was open and the scent of garlic mixed with grilling shellfish floated into the street. The aroma was so strong and enticing, he wondered if the restaurant had performed an age old trick and put scallop shells covered in garlic butter under the grill to lure in hungry diners. He had a quick glance at the menu outside. It was pricey, so much so he was dismayed to realise he wouldn't be in a position to dine here until his fortune took an upward turn. Hang onto every cent you can, an inner voice instructed.

He stood and listened. A scooter buzzed by, followed by another. A woman leaving the beauty salon opposite shouted her thanks and goodbyes in a high pitched voice he'd noticed was peculiar to many older French women. These noises he could tolerate.

He pushed open the hotel door and approached the front desk. Behind it stood two tiny elderly women. He imagined picking them up and putting them in his pockets, one on each side. Both women had similar features: blue-grey hair, aquiline noses, sucked-in cheeks adorned with puffs of pink. Their two sets of eyebrows were drawn in an upwards arc in reddish-brown pencil and each wore the same shade of rose lipstick. The skin on their faces had loosened, settling in mirror-image folds around their chins. One of the women looked up from the register. She set her fountain pen on the table.

"*Oui?*" The other woman echoed this a split second later. Liam shook his head. Had he entered another dimension?

"I'm looking for a room for a few weeks, maybe a month. Could I see one of your rooms?"

The woman he spoke to turned and gave her companion a knowing look.

"*Anglais.*"

They conferred for a moment in rapid, heavily accented French. One of the women reached up and lifted a set of heavy iron keys off a hook. She made her way round the desk.

"Follow me." She cupped her hand and beckoned towards a curtain. "If you please, monsieur. Fourth floor."

She pulled the curtain to one side and he followed her wiry figure up a winding staircase. He sighed, realising that if he liked the room he would have to cart all his belongings up the four flights of stairs. His breathing was shallow when he reached the top, yet the old woman walked in front of him with a spring in her step. She opened a door at the end of the corridor and Liam squinted as he entered the darkened room. She opened the shutters. Light flooded in revealing a spacious room with heavily scratched parquet flooring. A large bed with an iron bedstead was pressed against one wall. Opposite, was a walnut veneered wardrobe and matching set of drawers. A door led into a bathroom which was not in any way lavish.

There were no thick towels or small bottles of shampoo or shower gel. But that didn't matter, he reasoned, as his luggage contained these luxury items from his last hotel. The woman watched him with brown, beady eyes.

"Tele." She pointed to an old fashioned television sitting on a chest in a corner of the room. Liam mentally ticked off his list, which wasn't as much 'wish' as 'hope': clean, shower, bog, bed and television.

"How much?"

Her eyes moved up and down, scanning his whole body. He imagined she was taking in the quality of his clothes and the state of his shoes. Was she judging his wealth, deciding how much to ask? In that case, he was glad he wasn't wearing the Armani coat.

"Fifty a night."

"Forty-five and I'll take it for a month."

The woman hesitated as though she was about to haggle. She clicked her tongue and shrugged.

"Oui monsieur. One week in advance at reception, now."

He followed her downstairs. Just over three hundred a week. That would leave a pittance for food. Still, it was a place to lay his head while he planned his future. In the past, he'd allowed accidents to provide the roadmap for life. If James hadn't flirted with Lily, would he still be with her? And if Victor hadn't gone to prison, would he occupy the same office, the same flat, have the same bills stacked up? Rather than setting his own agenda, life was a runaway car on a hill, an accident rather than planned.

The woman who'd shown him the room disappeared behind another curtain in the reception area. He took out his wallet and approached the desk.

"What did we agree?" the woman's double, who stood behind the desk, asked.

"Forty-five a night. A week in advance. That's what I agreed with your sister."

The woman snorted. "Sister? I have none."

"Well, she looks like your twin," Liam said apologetically.

"Monsieur is mistaken. I have been alone here all day."

Liam shrugged. He wasn't in the mood for an argument and a tingling across his forehead told him another splitting headache was on the way. He paid the first week's rent and left to fetch his baggage. He shook his head as he walked along the street, he was tired and confused but hopefully he wasn't losing his mind. Hadn't there been two women at the desk? According to the woman he'd just handed a wad of notes to, there was only one. Perhaps the whole affair with Will had affected his mind more than he had realised?

When he returned to his room he hung the towels taken from the previous hotel in the bathroom. He arranged the small bottles of shampoo and oil on the shelf next to the toilet. With a bit of imagination, he told himself, this could be home from home for the next few weeks. He switched on the television, hoping the background noise would block thoughts of Victor from polluting his mind. It didn't. He switched it off and sat in a chair by the window, gazing onto a patio with a single skinny palm tree in the middle. There was a telephone on a side table and he contemplated ringing reception to see if it was possible to have food sent up, but then he imagined the elderly woman, struggling up four flights of stairs with a tray of god knows what. He recalled the scent of shellfish cooking in the brasserie next door. How he'd love to blow a fortune on a lavish dinner there.

"Bad idea, Liam," he muttered.

The sun dropped behind the building facing his room. The room which had at first appeared charming in an old fashioned way now took on a glacial and hostile air. A musty smell he hadn't noticed earlier lingered, despite the open window. Probably mice, he acknowledged. Still, as long as they left him alone, he was happy enough to share the room.

He went into the bathroom, combed his hair and splashed water on his face. He located his best jacket in the wardrobe, put it on and studied his reflection in the mirror. There was a large white stain across one lapel. He took the jacket off and rubbed the lapel with a damp facecloth. The colour faded slightly but the stain's outline expanded. He sighed and hung the jacket in the wardrobe again. A mess, both physically and mentally, that's what he was.

He put on his beige coat, made his way to the bedroom door and placed his hand on the handle. He retraced his steps and checked the bathroom sink, as he had a mild phobia of leaving the tap on. He repeated this four times, then he was ready to leave and make his way downstairs. He was lonely and needed someone to talk to.

The old woman was perched on a tall, swivel chair behind the reception desk. Her eyes took on a mischievous glint when she gave him directions to Le Chat Rouge. Despite having been on duty all day, she appeared alert. He wondered if she was indeed a twin. Perhaps she and her sister were bored and had decided to play a joke on a hapless tourist?

He strolled back onto the Champs Elysées and pulled up his hood again when he passed the record shop, still blaring hip-hop to all and sundry passing by.

Chapter 9

Le Chat Rouge was down a broad street, ten minutes' walk north of the Arc du Triomphe. Here, the grand old buildings of the city's core gave way to apartment blocks, launderettes and takeaways. He scanned posters fixed to the wall, which advertised jazz and country gigs. Bands had American names: Smoky Joe and the Catfish were playing the following weekend, supported by Daisy and the Desert Roses. In the vestibule, a doorman in a dark suit, crisp white shirt and bow tie, greeted the slow trickle of customers. For some reason, he couldn't say exactly what that was, he'd pictured the bar as seedier, a spit and polish job with clouded glasses and dirt ingrained into the tables and floor, a patina of Paris night life. From the outside at least, Le Chat Rouge resembled a cool Chicago jazz club.

Inside, he squinted as his eyes adjusted to the relative gloom. Ambient lighting, combined with the burgundy upholstery of seats arranged round dark wood tables, radiated intimacy. Brass lanterns inlaid with a mosaic of richly coloured glass hung in a line above the long bar, sprinkling a rainbow of colour onto the counter. An array of whiskey bottles, the liquid inside each varying in colour from amber to reddish brown, was lined up on glass shelves. Black Bush, a strong Irish liqueur whiskey and a particular favourite of his, sat amongst these. A hit of that and troubles would melt away, like ice in a warm drink. He looked around the room; not too many customers but it was still early. In a booth in a far corner, Borivoj's bearded silhouette was only just visible. Borivoj's jaw was moving up and down so Liam deduced he was talking to someone.

He ordered a drink and set a twenty euro note on the bar. The barman set a saucer with his change next to the drink. Liam flinched when he counted the coins: three euro and twenty cents. 'Fool and his money, easily parted', he muttered to himself as he pocketed the coins. He picked up his glass and made his way to Borivoj's table.

A wide smile flashed across Borivoj's face when he saw him.

"May I join you?" Liam asked.

"Of course, friend. A drink, perhaps?"

Liam held up his glass. "Already have one. Sorry, I didn't see you when I came in. Bit gloomy in here."

"Please. Sit down. Meet Alouette."

In a corner of the booth, he saw the darkened form of a female. The woman's hair skimmed the top of her shoulders, her features were barely visible. He blinked rapidly, his eyes still unaccustomed to the dimness. He sat down and Alouette leaned closer, out of the shadows. Soft pink from a wall light fell on her face, painting her skin rosy. Her hair was jet black, glinting. "This," Borivoj said with pride in his voice, "is friend, Alouette."

Liam reached out his hand.

"Pleased to meet you."

"See, Alouette, I told you he was real gentleman. English. No. Irish."

The woman smiled. He had a better view of her now. She was older than he'd first thought, with even, pleasant features. She leaned across the table, shook his hand and then slid round the booth. She raised her face up until it was just a foot away from his. He imagined she was going to kiss him on both cheeks, his heart fluttered in anticipation. Instead, she brought the palms of her hands up and lightly clapped his cheeks.

"*Comme un phantom* – a ghost. You didn't tell me he was so pale."

Borivoj shrugged and laughed as she slid back to the far end of the booth.

"You need some of my rouge." She fished a compact from her handbag and Liam recoiled, wondering if he should abandon his whiskey and scurry back to the hotel. Hadn't he learnt his lesson? Didn't he have any inkling of how to avoid trouble? He decided instead to take a large slug of his drink, which sent a hit of warmth rushing through his veins. Forget rose-tinted glasses, he told himself, amber glasses were just fine.

"Don't worry," Alouette waved her rouge brush at him. "I'm freshening up. The rouge isn't for you."

His eyes had become accustomed to the lack of light. He watched Alouette as she opened the compact and critically studied her reflection. The mirror of the compact reflected light onto her face as she painted her cheeks with a fine layer of brown powder. She was probably in her fifties, around ten years older than he was. Fine boned, a classical beauty once, he noted. Her face was symmetrical, eyes evenly spaced on either side of a straight nose. The flesh around her jaw had slackened, but the ghost of an elfin face remained. Her lips, sensuous and full, lovely if looked at in isolation, were the only disappointment: Alouette, it appeared, was or had recently been a smoker. Evidence of this came from tiny lines etched around her mouth. Still, he thought as the whiskey took effect, he wouldn't mind kissing her.

"She's great. Didn't I tell you?" Borivoj said.

Liam nodded. "Alouette…not a typical French name, is it?"

She shook her head. "It's a…." She looked up at the ceiling.

"Nickname?"

"I like to sing," Alouette said.

"Ah, hence the name. If I'm right, the translation of 'Alouette' is 'lark'?"

Borivoj's eyes misted. "She sings so beautifully I am reminded of home: mountains, lakes. Then I'm sad, but in sweet way. Show him, little songbird."

Alouette nodded. She took several deep breaths and began to sing.

Liam smiled. Here he was in Paris, listening to an attractive woman sing La Vie en Rose. A bit cliched and he wasn't exactly following in Ferguson's footsteps, but he felt as though he'd stepped into an old romantic movie. Magic. She stopped abruptly and he applauded.

"Terrific. I take it you're a singer. Professional, I mean."

Liam, who had expected a quick chat and one drink, an antidote to his loneliness, found himself warming to the strange pair.

"I wanted to be. I suppose I was born at the wrong time. When I was young, I liked the classic love songs of Piaf and Charles Trenet. Do you know the song *La Mer*? That was Trenet, but not many people are aware of that fact. They think it was some clever American writer. My friends laughed at my taste in music and called me old fashioned. They thought only British music was cool: The Beatles, Rolling Stones, Rod Stewart. But even now Rod Stewart has come round to my way of thinking. He likes the classics."

"Did you have some success?"

Alouette shrugged. "I performed in shows and had a few roles in revues for tourists. I was a Piaf impersonator at one time, but then the audience changed and suddenly they were too young. They weren't interested in listening to a middle-aged woman warbling songs they didn't know. So if I'm being honest, then no, I wasn't very successful."

"What do you do now? I mean, do you have a job?"

"You mean do I work in an office, typing, filing or something equally mundane? That would destroy me. I had the good fortune to have been given a small bequest from an aunt. It's securely invested, pays the rent and leaves me enough to get by."

Borivoj's hands were clasped, his head bent, as though he was deep in thought. He looked up. "Being a street performer is not easy. You see me doing tricks for euro or two. As with others in same situation, I have no control over audience. If they choose to watch and walk away without dropping as much as a cent, that is up to them. I have no choice. I have to perform. Trapped like elephant or tiger in zoo. Money is food, place to live."

"I assume you do well sometimes?" Liam eyed the elaborate cocktail Borivoj was drinking.

"Some weeks, yes, some weeks, no."

"What did you do back home?"

"I was fisherman."

"In the mountains?" Liam raised his eyebrows.

"Fish can live up mountains too. We have nearby lakes," Borivoj said defensively. "Trout, perch, pike. I took the tourists fishing in small motor boat. Old but trusty."

"Enterprising," Liam smiled. "I suppose you could dust off the fishing rods if you go home."

"No fishing. They took away license." Borivoj's eyes became guarded.

"I have had no work for over two years," Alouette said. "No wonder my agent dropped me, but then none of us are immune to the problems of life."

Liam raised his glass. "I'm in full agreement. In my case trouble and problems are like unwanted children. Once they're here there's nothing you can do about them."

"You have children?" Borivoj asked.

He shook his head. "Figure of speech. Just another way of saying I have problems too."

"Borivoj told me about you. He said he had encountered a tourist who looked like he was balancing the weight of the earth on his shoulders. But, how can you have problems if you have a comfortable warm bed and good food and wine. If there is enough money in the bank to enable you to travel?" Alouette challenged.

Liam was thoughtful for a moment. The whiskey Borivoj had just set in front of him was loosening his tongue. Slow down, he instructed himself.

"You hit the nail on the head. That's exactly my problem - I don't have a lot of money. I lost it. Almost everything I had." Borivoj and Alouette looked at each other.

"How did this happen?" Borivoj finally asked.

"A bad investment. I trusted the wrong friend. He…he let me down," he said weakly. In reality he wanted to bang his fist on the table, to shout that Will was the devil incarnate who had wrecked his life and who didn't give a toss about the mayhem he'd caused. He wanted to ask what sort of person sends a bad-news telegram and then buggers off.

"If it's not too impertinent, can I ask if your losses were... high?" Alouette asked.

"As I said, I lost almost everything."

"Yet you are here in Paris," Borivoj said.

"It's complicated. I had to leave quickly."

"Can you not do something?" Alouette insisted. "Go back to England and fight your friend. Get a lawyer." She waved her hands. *"Je ne comprends pas."*

He shook his head. "There are other things. Matters too delicate to discuss." Victor's features popped into his head: his nervous tic, his tapping fingers. He'd been his mentor and friend, had dipped into his pocket to help Liam out on a few occasions. Then there was the flip side of Victor. The unforgiving side if you crossed him. There was no doubt that Larry's disappearance was linked to his quarrel with Victor. 'An eye for an eye. Just be certain you never piss me off,' Victor had once whispered when Liam had bid against him at auction. He'd dropped out of the bidding immediately.

"So if you go back what will happen?"

Liam shrugged. "Who knows? Probably something bad." As he took another gulp of whiskey, it dawned on him that his guard was slipping and he might have said too much.

Borivoj reached out and touched his arm. "Your secret is safe with us, friend. We all have things we do not like to talk about."

"Like fishing," Liam winked, wondering how much of Borivoj's fishing was legal.

Another tray of drinks arrived and Liam opened his wallet and took out a fifty euro note. His brain was fogging up pleasantly, so he didn't blink an eye when the waiter gave him a five euro note as change. He threw his head back and poured half the whiskey down his throat. His insides were so warmed he felt as though as a wood burner had been lit in his belly. He suddenly felt invincible and thumped his fist on the table.

"I won't accept the hand fate has dealt me. I'll find a way to make money. You'll see."

After intermittent bouts of melancholy and indignation, Liam went to the toilet, then left the bar without saying his goodbyes. The Black Bush had left him horny and in the mood for intimacy. For a split second, he thought about inviting Alouette back to his hotel for a nightcap, however, she had given no indication that she was even slightly attracted to him. He was surprised that he was having these thoughts about a woman at least ten years older than he was, as that wasn't his style. But was the attraction born from desperation or did he simply want someone to mother him and soothe away his troubles?

He arrived at the hotel alone. On the walk back he had passed few people: two dark-skinned men taking a night stroll, several people hugging doorways, a group of youngsters hanging around the entrance to a twenty-four hour drug and record store, a man with a tattooed face, leading a pit bull.

The front door of the hotel was locked. He pressed the doorbell several times before hearing the sound of slippers slapping across the marble reception floor. The old woman he'd met earlier opened the door a crack. She tutted as she allowed the front door to swing open.

"Monsieur is late." She pointed at the clock on the wall above reception.

He shrugged. He wasn't in the mood to trade insults with her. He didn't care if it was five o'clock in the morning, which it wasn't, and he was oblivious to the pungent odour of Black Bush, oozing from his pores. He weaved over to the curtain leading to the stairs. The woman followed just behind him and he turned and made a swatting motion with his hand. She swore under her breath and hurried into the room behind reception. He pulled back the curtain and carefully picked his way up the four flights of stairs. He fumbled with the room key. Finally the lock turned and he stumbled into the room and threw himself onto the bed. He closed his eyes and opened them again as the room began to turn faster than a carousel he'd once ridden on Brighton beach. He was distracted by something on the walls of the bedroom and a part of his brain told him he might be very drunk. The paintings he had bought from Gerome had replaced the hotel's cheap prints. He didn't remember hanging them, yet despite the strangeness of the moment, he was comforted by the subjects: the soothing glade, where he could stroll and forget all his worries, the cool rock where he might sit and reflect. The woman in the third painting was reaching out, wiping his fevered brow.

"Thanks, Lily," he muttered.

Sleep came quickly, but it was disturbed and turbulent. Bailiffs in black uniforms heaved and hoisted possessions from a flat he and his mother had occupied in London. His mother threw herself on top of a small white wooden desk she'd retrieved from a skip. He saw himself, transformed into an eight-year old, with both he and one bailiff pulling at opposite ends of his mother's skirt as though it was a rope in a tug of war. When they let go, she gave up fighting for the desk and tumbled to the floor. He then observed himself hiding the paintings in the wardrobe and barring the wardrobe door with a chair. The beautiful woman from the painting was at his side and he promised to save her from Gerome, who had suddenly appeared, and was even bigger in his dreams than he was in real life.

With all the fury and ferocity he could muster, he set upon Gerome, pounding him with his fists. He was hot and anxious. A few times he opened his eyes and was relieved to find himself alone in the hotel room, with Gerome's paintings still hanging on the walls. He threw the bed covers off because he was feverish and they were wet. Minutes later, a chill invaded his flesh and bones and he pulled the covers up tightly round his body.

In the midst of nightmares, fever and chills, it dawned on him that he was ill. The image of the two women at the desk popped into his head, then there were three, then four. He managed a coherent thought. Perhaps he had been fevered for several days without realising, and that was why he'd imagined two identical women at the front desk. And had he really met Borivoj and Alouette at a bar? Borivoj, he decided, was real, but Alouette with her melancholy voice and fading looks, seemed like a cliché, a figment of his fever. 'Victims of time,' he muttered aloud as his own and Alouette's losses merged in his troubled dreams. Looks and money, and everything else people held dear, eventually wasted away.

At around eight o'clock in the morning, the phone rang. He stretched out his arm and picked it up, struggling to hold the receiver to his ear.

"Breakfast is served in reception," the old woman said.

"No... I'm not feeling well."

He put the phone down and pressed his head into the feather pillow. He had a throbbing headache that he was sure wasn't whiskey induced.

"Flu," he muttered. That was the last thing on earth he needed. How would he cope alone in a foreign city? But then he realised there were few friends he could call on at home in an hour of need. Maybe Lesley, but she wanted something in return.

He drifted off to sleep again. A knock on the bedroom door woke him. "Go away," he mumbled.

The knocking persisted. He climbed out of bed and stumbled to the door. When he opened it, there was no one in the hallway. His eyes were drawn to an object on the floor - a tray with a large bowl of milky coffee, a plate with several pieces of French bread, a pat of butter and a small jar of jam.

Momentarily lucid, he remembered he hadn't eaten dinner the previous evening. In fact, he realised, he hadn't eaten for at least twenty-four hours. He spread the jam on the bread and devoured it in several bites, then downed the pale, milky coffee in one go. Afterwards, his stomach ached and churned. The sweetness of the jam surged back into his throat. He fought off the urge to throw up and crawled back into bed, drawing the covers up round his body.

Waves of fever and chills continued. Perspiration slid off his body dampening the sheets, the duvet and starched pillowcases. He began to hallucinate, visualising the paintings leaping off the walls, then bouncing up and down on the mattress as though it was a trampoline. He was very fond of his market purchases and this wasn't such a terrible thing as they appeared to be enjoying themselves. However, when he hoisted himself up to join in the game, he tumbled out of bed.

He was vaguely aware of several pairs of hands lifting him, arranging the covers over his body. There was impatience rather than tenderness in their touches. The small group lingered at the foot of the bed, conferring in whispered, worried voices, interrupted by sighs. Occasionally they broke off the discussion to point at him. He forced his lips to curl into a strained smile, although he didn't feel like it. His head pounded, as though it had been chopped at with a meat cleaver, and on top of that, hadn't he just lost everything he'd worked for in his entire life? How could they expect him to be civil? The voices faded and he dropped off into a deep sleep.

Chapter 10

When he came round he was immediately aware of a weight pressing on his body, pinning it to the mattress. He was alarmed to discover the weight was simply a feather filled duvet. He raised a finger and tried to flex it. It barely moved. He realised he had been ill. Very ill. His body had survived a heat which he likened to being placed in a pizza oven and toasted, and a cold as intense as the waters under an ice fishing hole. Had he simply caught flu, or was this sickness a punishment, something he'd brought upon himself as he couldn't bear the notion of a life of poverty? Was there anything tangible or intangible to go back to? His heart sank as he pictured his empty office and flat, the empty space beside him in the bed he'd once owned.

He focussed on his immediate surroundings and was bewildered to discover that the charming, musty, sparsely furnished hotel room had transformed. The walls were now painted green, not the sickly pea shade typically found in soup cans and doctors' waiting rooms. This was a feminine shade with a hint of rose. A warm yet calm colour, soothing to the eye. He was baffled. How had he not noticed this pleasing colour yesterday? And what had happened to the original prints hung on the walls? When he'd returned from the bar, the paintings bought at the market were hanging in their place. Now, both the prints and paintings had mysteriously vanished and he found himself staring at a black and white photo of a beautiful woman with shoulder length hair and elfin features. He surveyed his surroundings. The heavy brown furniture was gone and in its place was a modern cream wardrobe and dressing table. In the distance, he detected a voice singing sweetly and wondered if he'd passed away and was lucky enough to have been transported to a charming room in the afterlife.

The singing stopped and a woman's head popped around the door.

"I thought I heard shuffling," Alouette said as she entered

the room.

Liam narrowed his eyes. "You're real."

"I hope so."

"Where am I?"

"My place. I'm Alouette, in case you don't remember. We brought you here."

"We?"

"Borivoj, the Czech guy, and I. We all took a drink together at Le Chat Rouge."

"I remember. Sort of. But how'd I get here?"

"When you left the bar, Borivoj followed you back to your hotel. You were angry and very drunk. He was worried. You might have fallen over or got into a fight. He was content when he saw you go safely into the hotel. The following evening, he went back to invite you for a drink. When he told the old woman on the desk he was your friend, she demanded he take you away. You hadn't paid your bill, she said, and you were ill, possibly contagious. Borivoj has a room in an unsavoury building. Temporary lodgings. He is embarrassed that he has fallen on hard times so he didn't want to bring you there. He called me and I went over. We packed your suitcase, helped you into a taxi, and transported you here."

"I don't understand," he said. "I'm sure I paid the bill."

Alouette shrugged and gave him an odd, yet sympathetic, look. He was mortified at his predicament and tears welled up in his eyes. He had no idea why he was crying and he didn't relish breaking down in front of this kind stranger. Perhaps the show of emotion was simply weakness resulting from his illness and the trauma that bastard, Will, had put him through. Victor, he didn't blame so much.

He realised with dismay that he was probably moved by the bone of pity Borivoj and Alouette had tossed at him. Lily hadn't shown a sliver of compassion as he'd trudged down the front path of their house, trailing his belongings behind in a wheelie suitcase. He'd turned and looked at her, a mixture of wounded pride and hate on his face. His beloved cat,

Mannie, had jumped into her arms. Both cat and woman had worn smug expressions on their faces.

"How long have I been here?"

"A few days. Four or five. A little less than a week."

Liam was suddenly aware that he was naked under the duvet. His face reddened as his fingers curled around the top of the cover.

"Ah that…" Alouette said. "You were soaked so we changed your clothes. The fever continued so we decided it was more hygienic to sleep without clothes."

"We?"

"Borivoj and I. Don't worry, you're not a matinee idol, but I've seen worse." Liam's teeth began to chatter. "I'll make you some soup." She disappeared and the singing started up again.

His eyes were closing, his brain humming 'Knockin' on heaven's door', the original Bob Dylan version, a favourite from his youth, when Alouette returned carrying a tray with a bowl of tomato soup and a chunk of bread.

"Don't sleep yet, you need to eat a little to build up your strength."

He edged into a half seated position. It suddenly dawned on him that the paintings he'd bought from the market were nowhere to be seen. Aside from his clothes and the brooch, they were all he had, all he possessed in the world. "My paintings. Did you bring them?"

Alouette nodded. "We packed everything into the taxi. You were shouting, causing a commotion in the hotel room. You wouldn't leave unless we brought the paintings. We were worried that we were stealing them but the old woman said she'd never seen them before. You are a strange one. You say you've lost all your money, are hunted by criminals, but you're worried about a few paintings. I have to admit the artist is very talented, but we're hardly talking about lost Van Goghs."

Liam took several spoonfuls of soup. He set the bowl on the bedside table and lay down again. For the first time in years, the cloak of cynicism he usually wore had been neatly folded and tidied away out of sight. He felt cosseted and comforted, although he knew the comfort part wouldn't last. It never did. Temporary lodgings came and went: B&B's, flats and houses, his office, hotel rooms. Even his marriage had been transient. The only thing that had remained steady in his life was the longing for a deal, money, and the good life it could buy. When the chips were down, this desire burned even brighter. He'd never thought of himself as materialistic, but this was a paradox as he knew true freedom required money. Without this you were a wage slave. He had vaguely dabbled in the writings of Marx when he was younger and even Marx agreed with him - money could set you free.

The following morning, after a dreamless sleep, his bones no longer ached and he had the vague impression that his legs might support him if he stood up. He edged out of bed and dressed. He made his way along the hallway until he found the bathroom. On the way, he saw Alouette curled up on the sofa in the lounge with a blanket over her.

Liam turned the shower on low so it wouldn't wake her. After drying, he looked in the mirror. Red, puffy eyes stared back at him. He patted his stomach. Flesh was loose across his belly. Although his complexion was normally fair, today it was grey, reminiscent of the shade of a mist over the Sussex Coast on a rainy winter's day.

He had a sudden longing to be somewhere he could call home. Where would he end up next, he wondered? He had left England in such a hurry, he hadn't given much thought as to what he would do, or plan how day to day life might pan out. He had vaguely hoped to turn his hand to some sort of dealing as that was where his real skills lay, but his command of French was poor to medium. While he could ask for things in shops and restaurants and could understand many of the words spoken on TV, stringing together a coherent sentence was another story. Without fluent French surely dealing would be impossible. But was that simply an excuse, he asked himself, when most of the people he'd met had a good grasp of English?

The smell of freshly brewed coffee drifted from the kitchen doorway. Liam stood awkwardly by the door and Alouette turned and looked at him.

"You look well." She threw back her head and laughed. A fierce heat rushed to his face. He knew he was a mess, a shambles of a human being. How long, he wondered, would she tolerate his pale features, dowdy clothes, the presence of a stranger in her flat?

Neediness was a trait he despised, yet this was not the first time he'd found himself in a vulnerable position, dependent on the kindness of others. When Lily had ejected him from their home, he'd persuaded a friend to put him up. Like Alouette, Michael had given Liam his bed, with Michael reduced to sleeping on cushions spread across the living room floor. Liam had outstayed his welcome. Too depressed to work, he'd claimed, and any antiques he could have sold were in his old house. He hadn't wanted to go over there as James, Lily's lover, had moved in and was apparently greatly taken with the cat. After several weeks of lying in bed until mid-afternoon, drinking too much red wine, and watching TV into the early hours of the morning, his friend had gently suggested that it was time to move on. When he'd protested he was still suffering from the blues, Michael's tone had hardened. A few days later, while he soaked in the bath, Michael had packed his suitcase and set it by the hall door. This prompted him to splurge his remaining cash on the deposit for a rented flat. Right now, he missed the flat's familiar white front door with a spy hole at eye level. The rotting-cabbage smell from the rubbish disposal chute next to his flat had always annoyed the building's residents, but he'd give all he had to be back there. Alouette appeared to have a good heart, but goodness had its limits. How long would she put up with him?

"You're kind. I look like something the cat dragged in."

"Cat? I don't have one. Come and join me for breakfast."

She pointed to the table and Liam sat down. Alouette

poured two cups of coffee and then set a plate of croissants, a warm French stick, and a pot of jam that gave off a strong scent of burnt raspberry, in the centre of the table. She sat down opposite him. The table was small and circular and the distance between them was no more than eighteen inches. Although she was not his usual type, he felt awkward, shy as a schoolboy on a first date. Alouette gave an encouraging nod and he picked up a croissant and spread it with jam. The outer shell of the croissant was burnt black on top, the inside, light as air. The jam delivered tiny explosions of sweet and sour. He devoured the croissant in seconds. Alouette pushed the plate across the table.

"Have some bread, spread it with the jam. The sweetness will perk you up, give you energy."

He nodded and took a piece of bread. He spread it thickly with the raspberry jam and it also quickly disappeared. He stared greedily at the remainder of the bread on the plate.

"Not too quickly. You'll make yourself sick."

Weariness washed over him. He leaned back in his chair and tried unsuccessfully to suppress a yawn. Alouette wagged a finger at him. Her fingernails were raspberry red, almost the same colour as the jam. He stopped himself from leaning over and licking them.

"You're still weak. I'll change the sheets and you can go back to bed."

Liam climbed in between the starched sheets. Cool and crisp, otherworldly, like a cloud. This was the most content and comfortable he'd been in his entire life, at least that's what flitted through his mind. However, the demon that existed in a dark part of his brain surfaced again, the same one that had tempted him to gamble away Victor's money, the one that had urged him to waste his precious funds on the expensive hotel. Soon, the demon whispered in his ear, Alouette would tire of playing nurse and she would ask him to leave. He made a swatting gesture, batting the demon and its useless chattering away. Peace, that was all he wanted, all anyone wanted. Right now he was peaceful, better off than in a bland hotel, which he couldn't afford anyway. He looked around the cheerful but sparse room. Perhaps Alouette was short of cash, maybe she'd welcome a paying lodger?

What was her relationship with Borivoj, he wondered? Were they lovers or simply friends? He realised he'd never had a proper female friend. Billie was the closest, but even they had slept together. Afterwards things hadn't been the same. Billie had become clingy, suggesting improvements to his clothes, his hair. She'd even hinted at moving into his flat. That was the last straw and he'd declined to answer any more of her calls. Strange, he reflected, he now thought of her with a fondness reserved for nostalgic glimpses into a rose-tinted past, and wished he'd taken up her offer. Perhaps someone like Billie would have stopped him from taking a risk and gambling with Victor's money. Over the years, there had been plenty of lovers, one night stands, even a wife, but none of these had been simply friends. Liam's thoughts and worries dissolved in the cloud of comfort in which he lay, and the coolness of the sheets triumphed. He drifted off not caring what experiences the rest of the day would bring.

That evening, after a dinner of chicken stew and green salad, Alouette and Liam settled on the sofa. She poured two glasses of wine and switched on the television.

"A nice red, don't you think? I don't normally have this with chicken, but it will give you iron. Good for the blood," Alouette said. "Good for the nerves too."

"Were you ever a nurse?" he asked, curious at her apparent in-depth medical knowledge.

"My grandmother was a *paysenne*. Countrywoman, I think you say. They have intuition, know more than many doctors."

"Is that photo you, or someone in your family?"

"Photo?"

"In the bedroom. Hanging on the wall."

"Oh, that old thing. It's been there so long I'd forgotten. Doesn't look like me now, but that was the photo my agent used to promote me. I was better then."

"Beautiful. You mean beautiful. Still are," Liam said gallantly.

"And you, Liam. Your face is not wrinkled and old, yet I can't imagine you young? You have a tired, how would you say – troubled – air. The type of aura you find in old people who are fed up with living."

"It's difficult to remember being young."

"What were you like?"

"Driven, focused, much the same as now, except longer hair and in better shape."

"Married?"

"Once. That was enough."

"Children?"

"Never wanted kids."

"Maybe that's why she left."

"Who?"

"Your wife. You said you were once married. I don't know why I am assuming she left you."

"Kicked me out. Found someone else. I've never given much thought as to why she fell out of love."

He curled his fingers round the stem of the wine glass. Was Alouette peering into his soul, and at that moment did she know him better than he knew himself? He and Lily had discussed children, but it had been Lily rather than he who had decided against a baby. She wasn't ready, she'd said. In reality, she hadn't been ready to have kids with *him*. But perhaps it was his fault. Perhaps the chaotic and financially unpredictable life in antiques, the ups and downs in fortune, didn't suit Lily's vision of a prosperous, stable life. The life that James, her cat stealing lover, was able to provide.

Not wanting to continue dwelling on the past, he took another swig of wine. Onwards and upwards, with a few unexpected twists in the middle, had always been his motto. At the moment, upwards seemed a very long way away.

"What about you?"

Alouette turned and stared at the TV screen. She bit her lip.

"Enough idle chit chat. I want to watch this programme."

Liam smiled, yet he could feel a tightness in his chest. Alouette's voice was sharp, dismissive, was she already fed up with him?

After almost half an hour attempting to watch a soap opera in French, he gave up and went to the bedroom. He opened his suitcase, took out his mobile phone and scrolled through contacts, stopping at Lesley's number. He hesitated, then dialled it. Fuck it, he told himself as he listened to the phone ring, why on earth had he come to Paris when a free cottage in Scotland was on offer? A few moments later, she answered. Her voice was slightly slurred and his mind flashed back to the antique fairs and events where they'd crossed paths in the past. Lesley had usually been propping up the bar, or if she had a stall, she would have a glass of white wine in her hand and a bottle under the table.

"Lesley, it's me." His voice was low. He kept an eye on the door.

"Liam." Her voice was flat, expressionless. Liam couldn't tell if she was happy or disappointed that he'd called.

"I'm in Paris," he said.

"Ah. The working holiday."

"Exactly. Just like I told you." This was going well, he congratulated himself.

"What can I do for you this fine evening, Liam?"

"I'm almost ready to come back. That cottage you mentioned, I thought we might go straight there. I've had flu, so I need peace and quiet - and your lovely company, of course."

He measured his words as he spoke: not too lovey dovey, not too offhand. There was silence on the other end of the line.

"Lesley? Are you still there?" He imagined he heard a noise, the popping of a cork.

After a moment she came back on the line. "So you want to go to the cottage?"

"Yes." A warm glow coursed through his body, Lesley would come to his rescue, it would all be okay.

"Well, you can fuck off."

"Lesley!"

"I went round to your flat to see if you were back. You know what I found? A pissy little thug, hanging around, waiting for you. He asked me if I knew you. Of course I said no. I could tell he was trouble right away: squat, big shoulders, flattened nose, tattoos up his neck and his face. There was a bulge in his jacket. Not sure if it was a truncheon or a gun."

"I don't know..." Liam began.

"Enough lies. I went inside the building and found your landlord removing the rubbish bits of furniture you left. He said you hadn't paid your rent. Had the cheek to ask me to fork out for you. After me paying over the odds for that tat you brought in."

"I take it the holiday in Scotland is off?" Liam said weakly, as the receiver at the other end of the line was banged down.

Without removing his clothes, he climbed into bed. With almost nothing in the world, he had to hang onto his current sanctuary.

Chapter 11

Liam had been at Alouette's for several weeks. The days had flowed like tributaries into a river, natural, unforced.

She lived in a different world, not the dog eat dog one he'd come to know, but one where calm appeared to be the ultimate goal. She was not forced to participate in the external world, as most of society were, not dependent on either a man or market economies for a living. Although she was not rich in a monetary sense, she was rich in freedom.

He stood by the front door. Light poured in through a south facing side window, warming his face. He rubbed his hands together and drew a deep breath: today he'd test the endurance power of his legs. See if, out in what he now called the unforgiving world, he could perform the actions of putting one foot in front of the other and continuing this process until a destination was arrived at. This morning there was no particular destination in mind, however he was aware that Alouette could, at any point, ask him to pack his bags and go. He reached out his hand. There was a time lag between the message from his brain instructing him to open the door and his fingers gripping the front door handle. During this brief moment, she emerged from the kitchen, waving a white dishcloth.

"No need for surrender," he said in a fake cheery voice. "I'm just off for a walk. Need to build up strength. You won't want me hanging around forever." He worked his face into a smile, which, if he had looked in the mirror, he would have described as brave. Bravery, Liam hoped, was the way to a woman's heart. The day Lily had announced her affair with her estate agent friend, courage had deserted him and he'd collapsed in a heap on the sofa. Perhaps if he'd shown courage and stood up to her, she'd have respected him more.

"You mustn't tell me what I want. Let me judge for myself." Alouette stuffed the dishcloth in her apron pocket. She untied the apron and hung it on the kitchen door handle.

"I could do with a stroll."

Alouette tucked her arm into Liam's as they made their way along the street. The gesture was friendly rather than romantic, yet even through the cloth of their coats he could feel the tingle of flesh against flesh. He edged closer to her and smiled. To the onlooker they might resemble old lovers who'd grown out of the physical side of their relationship, but still wanted to preserve their closeness. He glanced at her face. Almond-shaped eyes set at perfect angles above a long, Parisian nose. Her full lips were still surrounded by tiny creases, yet there was an additional sensuousness about them this morning. He pictured her in clichéd French clothes: a striped tee-shirt, black beret on the side of her head, a long, black, diamond encrusted cigarette holder suspended between fingers. Elegance and sense of style was a gift age couldn't spirit away, he realised, and he wouldn't mind fucking the version of Alouette his mind now painted.

"Euro for them?" Alouette said and laughed. "I, of course, mean 'penny for them'." He looked confused and she gave a playful sigh.

"What are you thinking, Liam?"

"Two things." He pointed to a fence with a thick box hedge behind it. "One: you're lucky to live near a park. And two…" His eyes scanned the street ahead, looking for a point of interest. They fixed on the red and white striped awnings of a café. "Coffee. I'd like a coffee there."

"My local, nicely chosen. Although the coffee I make at home is better."

Inside the cafe, he helped Alouette out of her coat. She performed the action with grace, as though the coat was a snowflake which had drifted onto her shoulders. He hung it on a coat hook by the door.

"May I?" he said, standing to attention next to the chair opposite Alouette.

"Paf!" she exclaimed. "You Englishmen are so uptight. You play at being gentlemen when all you think of is sex." Liam blushed.

"Sex? No, I wasn't thinking of us having sex. I mean, sex is the farthest thing from my mind. Although I don't mean I wouldn't want to have sex with you. You're very attractive so of course I would. But I wasn't thinking of that, I was just admiring the décor. The smell of coffee. Almond, dark chocolate. So deep and lush. And dammit…something in the kitchen smells good."

"Good. Neither of us is thinking of sex so we are on the same page." She passed the menu over. "Sounds like you're hungry. Eat what you like."

Alouette ordered an espresso and Liam a filter coffee and an omelette. The pale yellow and runny eggs which slid across the plate turned his stomach. He had lied to Alouette, he wasn't at all hungry. He ate a small piece of omelette and washed it down with coffee.

"I'm sure you could do better," he said, setting the fork down on the plate.

"Perhaps you have things other than food on your mind," she smiled. In an instant her smile turned to a frown. The trill of the doorbell. A clatter of heels on the wooden boards. A high pitched, female voice, calling a greeting.

"*Cherie!*" A fair haired woman, around Alouette's age, rushed over and kissed her on both cheeks. She pointed to a chair. "May I join you and your…"

Alouette hesitated, glanced at Liam, then nodded. "Vanessa, this is Liam."

"Liam…English. Another Englishman. You astonish me, Alouette." Alouette flushed and looked away.

This Vanessa, he thought, certainly wasn't a welcome visitor, but it appeared Alouette was too dignified to give her the brush off. He felt surprisingly protective towards her.

"It's been a while. A year or so? I thought you must have moved from Paris. Maybe retired to a quiet village," Alouette said.

"Surely you have heard? I have a part in a revue. One of the stars. Singing and dancing. We're very successful. We've been on a tour of South America." Vanessa flipped back her golden fringe. "We're off again soon: Germany and Austria this time." She reached over and placed a hand on Alouette's arm. "I was hoping to bump into you. If you're looking for work, perhaps I could help you. Get you a small part. Not much money I'm afraid, but it would be something not too taxing." She looked at Liam, her lips creased into a smug smile. The expression 'cat that got the cream' slipped into his mind. "But possibly your young man wouldn't approve?"

Liam studied Alouette's reaction to Vanessa's words. Did he detect a trace of wounded pride behind her otherwise impassive features? Vanessa had mentioned an Englishman. Could this man have broken Alouette's heart?

"Actually..." he said, running a hand through his hair. This was a gesture he'd used in the past when he needed to buy time. When he'd been undecided if he should bid for an item at auction and the auctioneer had threatened the final hammer strike, he'd drawn his attention with a cough and had played for time by running a hand through his hair. Thrown off guard, the auctioneer usually paused, giving precious additional seconds to assess if the item in question was worth bidding for. His biggest win using this tactic had been a seascape by William Edward Webb. He'd never heard of Webb and had missed checking out the painting in the auction viewing, but a quick search on his phone during bidding, one of the few technical functions he had mastered, told him the painting was worth more than double his three thousand pound bid. Fortunately, the hair scratching and ruffling actions with his right hand had distracted the auctioneer from observing his left hand flicking over his phone screen.

"I'm a theatre agent. From London,' he said. 'We're looking for a chanteuse. Someone to play a Piaf-type role in the West End. We're in negotiations with Alouette as we speak."

"This is a business meeting?" Vanessa's face flushed. He nodded.

"Alouette has quite a voice. One in a million, don't you think? West End first, then Fifth Avenue." Liam put his hand on top of Alouette's. "If she's willing to take the part, that is."

The waiter arrived at the table and stood by Vanessa's chair. She shook her head, handed him the menu, and stood up. "The time...I forgot I was supposed to be somewhere else."

"Nice to see you, Vanessa. I'll look out for you when your show is in London. What's the name?" he said.

Vanessa left without replying and Alouette turned to Liam.

"Always gallant. You stand at the table until I'm seated and now you save my reputation. You're a true gentleman."

Not like the other Englishman Vanessa mentioned, he thought. He considered asking who the man was, but Alouette's eyes were bright and mischievous. She was clearly still enjoying the prank he'd played on Vanessa, so why spoil the moment.

"Vanessa is not really a friend. She likes to humiliate me, to throw barbs in my direction. In reality, I know she has funded her own revue. Ah well, none of us likes to feel like a failure in life." She reached over and tipped her coffee cup against his. "*A l'amitie…* to friendship, Liam."

Warmth radiated through Liam's body. He had a friend in Paris. Perhaps he wasn't as alone as he'd thought.

"By the way, I'm impressed."

He hesitated for a moment, wondering if criticism would follow her random comment.

"What've I done?"

"It's what you haven't done. Cigarettes. You were smoking when we first met at Le Chat Rouge, yet I haven't see a cigarette near your mouth since you came to my place."

"Ah that…actually I did have a cigarette, one only. When I thought I'd recovered I had a shifty smoke out the bedroom window. I almost threw up. It felt like inhaling the contents of an old sock. I guess the illness knocked the enjoyment out of me."

"Not a bad thing. I, too, gave up suddenly. One morning, two years ago, I woke up a non-smoker. Just like that. It was so easy."

Liam smiled. He'd pleased her and that made him feel good. He wasn't a natural people pleaser and liked to think of himself as a free thinker, a man who knew his own mind. But Alouette made a difference. She was a good person. She deserved more than he could give.

Later that evening, in his room, he lay back on the bed and conjured up a memory of a place in Belfast: the Ormeau Park. An expanse of green near where his grandparents lived. This wasn't unlike the park he'd glimpsed on the walk with Alouette earlier. Clusters of trees interspersed with grassy lawns. Flower beds of different shapes, sizes and filled with vivid reds, pinks and violets. Contrived yet pretty. A playground with swings, a slide and climbing frames lay at one entrance to the park. There, on one visit, he'd found children who didn't know of his chaotic background and playfully mimicked his London accent. He was exotic and different to them. That stretch of green was the place he'd felt safest in his childhood.

His eyes intermittently flickered open and closed. One minute he wished he was back in the Ormeau Park, the scent of the bread baking in the nearby bakery drifting across the road. The smell, which embedded itself in the fibres of his clothes, had made him feel like his skin and bones had morphed into a warm bread roll. The next minute he remembered where he was and his fingers clutched at Alouette's lavender infused sheets. He inhaled deeply, not wanting to loosen his grip.

He was almost asleep when the bedroom door opened. A sliver of light from the hallway cut across the room and he was vaguely aware of a shadowy figure climbing into the bed. He wasn't alarmed. He could smell the scent of rose that normally wrapped itself around Alouette. She lay down, her body inches from his. He sensed her knees bend, yet the action was executed so carefully, they didn't creak or brush against his back. Even though their bodies had no contact, he felt her warmth occupy the empty space between them.

"Asleep yet?" she asked in a low voice.

"No – not yet." He didn't want to ask why she was here as this was the most intimate moment he'd had in ages. He wondered if he should reach out and wrap an arm round her, but that would suggest he was imagining she wanted physical contact. He wasn't sure that was the case.

"You're wondering why I'm here?"

"It's not important."

"I'm not looking for sex, just in case you're worried."

"I wasn't. You're an attractive woman, Alouette. And you have a good heart. I'm glad you're here."

"You remind me of someone who was once very important to me. When we were in the salon earlier, I had a great urge to confide in you. To tell you a story about me that few people know."

"Borivoj?"

Alouette laughed. Her laugh was low, almost inaudible, barely disturbing the quiet night air.

"Borivoj would die if I told him my story. He has become a good friend over the past year, but he has no idea who I really am… and what I am capable of. I'm sure he sees me as a mother figure, someone he can call up if he needs reassurance. He needs plenty of that. Life can be hard for immigrants. There is little support network, good jobs are hard to come by and accommodation is expensive. In any case, I can't confide, I don't want to shock or disappoint him."

"I'm not easily shocked or disappointed," he yawned. "I'm listening."

"I need to be sure I can do this. I have been hiding my past, my secrets, for so long I don't know if I can bear to speak the words."

He reached out, gripped Alouette's hand and squeezed it. He tried to make out her profile, but darkness consumed it. A wave of exhaustion overcame him. He made a brief effort to suppress another yawn, but the pleasant fog of sleep was too compelling. His eyes closed and almost immediately he began to snore.

Chapter 12

Alouette's story:

Alouette withdrew her hand from his. She listened to Liam's breathing become even, then turn to a light snore. She began to speak in a voice that was barely higher than a whisper.

"You asked me about the photo on the wall. That was taken when I was in my thirties, before the event that destroyed my career and my future. I was happy then. You can see it in my face and in my eyes. Spotlights, the stage, adoration, it all lay in front of me, like a beautiful, lush garden. It could have been wonderful, I could have been famous.

One day I was sitting in my agent's office waiting to see if I had been successful in my audition for a musical. I was a good singer so I was filled with confidence. A little bit – what's the word – cocky, even. There were a few other women seated in the room and we were all secretly studying each other. I think the phrase in English is 'checking out the competition'. The door opened and a man came into the room and sat down. It was strange and funny how the demeanour of the women changed from one of throwing dark glances at each other to pretending butter wouldn't melt in their mouths. They fluttered their eyelashes and crossed and uncrossed their legs. Some of the better endowed women pushed their breasts out and others pouted. I didn't do any of this as I was more confident with my sexuality. I looked up at him and gave a warm smile. He seemed grateful. I'm sure he was intimidated by a roomful of females. The other women were visibly upset when the man came and sat down next to me. He was handsome, very handsome, and when he spoke to me it was with a funny upper-class English accent. I had studied English at school and had visited London several times so my English was reasonable. We began to chat and it was as though all other people in the room disappeared and there was only us two. He told me I looked like Audrey Hepburn, who he greatly admired. I replied that I probably sang better than she did. We both laughed. His laugh was deep and manly, as though he was enjoying the joke. I can still hear it.

My agent came out of his office and called me in to see him. He told me I was successful in my audition and that I would start in one week's time. I was delighted with the news but slightly less enthusiastic when he told me the musical would be performed in Quebec first before returning to Paris in several months. He was astonished when I said I would think about accepting the part. You see, Liam, I had been without work for several months and this was my big break." Alouette turned, verified Liam was still asleep, then continued.

"I went out to the reception and sat down again beside Trevor. His face was pale, like yours. Somehow I've always gone for men with milky skin. They say opposites attract so maybe I was looking for my mirror opposite. He was called into his agent's office and all of a sudden I felt as though my heart had been torn apart. I was instantly in love with him and would have done anything to be with him. I was confused. We French understand amour… love. It happens and there's nothing you can do. My career had always come first yet at that moment I didn't care if I never sang again.

Trevor's next job, he told me over dinner that evening, was in London. He had a bit part as a French villain in an English movie. How strange that you had to come to Paris for a part in an English film, I told him. Fate, he said. 'If I hadn't come here I wouldn't have met you.'

My agent was very angry when I turned down the part in the musical. I was in my late thirties, beautiful and in my prime, but very close to being too old to play certain parts. This was my big break and maybe my last chance. The agent banged his fist on the table and spoke to me as though I was a naughty child. He said my career would be washed up if I was going to be choosy. I didn't care and gave him a big smile as I left the room: love's arrow had pierced my heart, surely and instantly. When I left that office I had changed, grown from a girl, star struck for the stage, to a woman. Every day, when I saw Trevor, my heart burst into song. I felt as though the streets of Paris were my stage and the passersby my audience.

When Trevor went back to England to work on the film, I went with him. We were a couple so it seemed the most natural thing to do. He was from a market town near Brighton. He brought me home to meet his parents, and to save money we decided to stay with them. His parents were well-off, his father some kind of doctor, the mother stayed at home. They were stuffy and traditional. They wanted their son to settle down with a nice English girl and not some floozy he'd picked up in Paris. I cooked and helped his mother with the washing up and other household tasks. I tried to be the kind of woman his parents would want their son to marry but when I became pregnant, things got worse. His parents were constantly chattering in Trevor's ear about how I had trapped him and how his career would be ruined because of me. Their words, like bacteria, infected him. He began to resent me. He criticized the way I ironed his shirts, said my baking was inferior to that of his mother – and it truly wasn't. I suppose it was inevitable that he would turn to his former girlfriend, who his parents greatly approved of, for consolation.

I needed space, to escape the reproachful remarks and looks of his parents. I persuaded him to rent a flat nearby. We moved but my new happiness didn't last. Before long, Trevor began to stay out late and sometimes didn't come back to the flat for days. I'm French and broad minded. I wouldn't have minded sharing Trevor's body but I couldn't support sharing his soul."

Alouette stopped speaking. She reached up and wiped away a tear with a corner of the sheet. She had imagined confiding in a relative stranger would be hard. She'd been wrong: it was like a novice climber trying to conquer Everest. Yet as she spoke, she felt a strange weightlessness. Her heart had been encased in stone, now truth was chipping at the stone, whittling it away. She listened for a few minutes to Liam's even breathing and occasional snore, then she continued.

"I was four months pregnant when my hormones began to fluctuate badly. Trevor had been away for several nights and when he came back we rowed. He told me it was over between us and he was going back to his former girlfriend. He stormed out of the flat. Driven by fury, I got into my car and followed him to her apartment. I saw them embrace on the doorstep and then sat in the car, watching their silhouettes shadow-dancing through the blinds. I waited for a while and then got out of the car. By this time I wasn't thinking, I was moving instinctively, self-preservation, you might say, or maybe it was vengeance.

I strode up the path, not sensing my feet on the gravel, nor hearing my shoes crunch and flick pebbles across the pathway, yet I could see them shoot this way and that. I moved, propelled along by an unseen being. I pressed the doorbell and listened to the theme music from *The Godfather* play. Loud and garish, suitable for a woman with no taste. When no one answered. I pressed again. *The Godfather* theme started up and when it ceased, I heard the sound of footsteps on the stairs. A fair haired woman opened the door. She didn't know who I was so she appeared curious rather than upset at seeing me. Before she could speak I hit her over the head with a wrench I'd found in the car boot. Somehow I'd carried it in my hand without sensing its steely menace or the damage it could inflict. The woman fell to the ground and blood oozed from a gash across her forehead, like the petals of a poppy unfolding on her pale skin. Strangely enough she looked beautiful then – before I'd judged her to be somewhat plain.

I stood there with the wrench in my hand, staring at her. A minute later, Trevor came down the stairs and found both of us. When he saw what I'd done he was both concerned and furious. After all, I was carrying his child. He phoned an ambulance, shoved me back in the car with the wrench and told me to go back to our rented flat. I waited all night, trembling in our living room, for either the police to arrive or Trevor to come home.

He spent all night at the police station and most of the next day also. Margaret, that was her name, was in a coma in hospital and they weren't sure if she would live or die. Finally the police believed Trevor's story that he was a family friend and he'd found Margaret in the doorway when he came to visit. A neighbour vouched for his story, telling the police they had seen a dark haired woman ringing the doorbell. I was surprised they didn't come looking for me.

Trevor packed me back off to Paris immediately. He was concerned for his child, he claimed, but I knew that he just wanted rid of me. He gave me some money and told me to disappear. If I ever set foot in England again, he said, he would tell the police what I had done.

I was so distraught I became ill, unable to eat or drink. I lost the baby and also my will to live. When I tried to commit suicide, I was taken to a convent to recover. The nuns gave me back my self esteem. I could carry on again, but I wasn't the woman I'd been before I met Trevor.

I later found out from someone who had befriended me in England that Margaret had recovered and she and Trevor had married."

Alouette stopped speaking. Liam was still snoring and she was glad he was asleep. She had wanted to unburden herself for so long, but she couldn't bear the look of shock, reproach and even horror, on the face of the chosen listener. It was good Liam was here. He reminded her of *him*. For years she hadn't dared even to speak his name, yet all of a sudden the feelings and remorse she had hidden over the past decades had surfaced. She was compelled to confide in someone, and she'd done that. It didn't seem to matter that he hadn't heard.

Liam's illness and his personal problems reminded her of the madness she'd suffered on her return to Paris. Her lunacy, she knew, was a means of cleansing her body after committing such an awful deed. Telling the sleeping Liam her story had been strangely cathartic. For years she had carried the demons of her actions with her. Perhaps now, if it wasn't too late, she would be free to love again. Maybe Liam, maybe someone else. Right now, she felt nothing but a gentle sadness.

Chapter 13

Liam pieced together fragmented memories of the night before. He reached out his arm, aware something strange had taken place: that he'd had close contact with another human being. The sheet next to him was cold. Could the warmth of Alouette's body next to his have been a dream? And if her sing-song voice had lulled him to sleep with a story, which he thought it had, he couldn't remember the exact content. He vaguely recalled her mentioning an English lover, giving up her career for him, then not much else. He'd fallen asleep quickly, so he knew they hadn't made love.

As drowsiness lessened, he recalled how she'd lain, near enough for him to sense her presence, but not close enough to imply intimacy. She hadn't crept in hoping for a quick tumble, she was there for another purpose. Liam had absolutely no idea what that was.

He lay back and analysed his immediate situation. Alouette was a new friend, a strange woman with a hypnotic charm. She'd been kind enough to take him in, but there was a protective covering, like the husk on a grain of rice, surrounding her. Enigma. Enigma was the word he was looking for. What was she thinking? Was she verifying how far she would go in helping him? Ascertaining if he was trustworthy? At any moment the rug could be pulled out from under his feet and he could be given his marching orders. He'd encountered fickle women before. He knew that the moment you felt you were secure was the most dangerous one. Rescue at the hands of Lesley was out of the equation and he wasn't sure if he was glad or sad about that. It wouldn't have been a long-term relationship on his part, but god, what he'd have given for six month's respite in a remote Scottish cottage.

He imagined himself in professional mode, standing shoulder to shoulder in an auction crowd, bidding against other dealers and members of the public for the same item.

He felt a warm glow as the hammer fell and his bid secured the imaginary item. He stretched his imagination even further. He was standing at the head of a classroom of homeless and destitute people, advising how they might buck up and get out of their dire situation. At the back of his mind, though, he was aware of the complexities that landed people in dire situations: a child might muddle through a troubled family life, then later go off the rails with drink or drugs or crime. Digging the way out of a pit of despair wasn't easy, he knew. Best not to fall in, he told himself.

In the past, some of his best ideas had been crafted between the sheets. Bed, in his mind, was for contemplation, decision making and sex, though not all at the same time. It had been one morning in bed, after a particularly heavy night out with his teenage friends, that he had decided to jack in his part-time job on the pier and concentrate on antiques. He'd had enough of boozed-up tourists tossing their crisp packets and uneaten chips on the ground, and he loathed the flocks of seagulls that appeared to take delight in aiming their droppings at the bit of the deck he'd just mopped. He had seen the possibilities in the antique world. The old boys who'd played the game for decades, who knew their hand-knotted Persian silk rug from the more *ordinaire* cotton version, and who, with a wave of a hand, might snap up a bargain. They could pick up a Chinese pot and tell if it was Ming or a twentieth century copy. Then they'd snap it up for a song if the seller didn't know what they had. In Liam's eyes these experts were modern day treasure hunters: Indiana Joneses in tweed jackets.

He was fascinated by the rings which operated at some auctions. These were groups of buyers who conspired to bid together, to close other buyers out, resulting in a low hammer price. The item bought might be later sold at an illegal private auction. Ring members possessed a combination of knowledge, craftiness and a willingness to sail close to the wind and incur the wrath of the police antiques squad. It was in such a ring he'd first met Victor. Victor was bolder, quite prepared to not only sail close to the wind, he was also willing to point the proverbial boat fully into it, allowing the sails to billow and propel him at great speed, leaving the antiques squad floundering in his wake.

Victor was successful and he, unfortunately, was not. His gains were offset by losses. An early eighteenth century blue and white Dresden writing set, a rare thing, had supplied the deposit on his first Irish property. Subsequent auction gains had been sunk into deposits on two more properties. When the builders downed tools and the property magnate who had sponsored the development disappeared, he'd lost everything.

The old Liam, a different person who shared only his name, had shrugged and carried on. Easy come, easy go, was the motto in the antiques world and losses were offset by gains, yet with the internet, all that changed. Amateurs, anonymous, gaping at computer screens in their bedrooms, bidding via a click of the mouse, muscled in on dealer's turf. Online auctions made creating a ring more difficult so profits were much harder to come by.

He wished he could time travel back to the days of his first auction. He'd left the building singing 'money for nothing and your kicks for free'. There had been fire in his veins that day, he still remembered the euphoria. But he had also experienced that same high when he'd first clapped eyes on Gerome's paintings. The big man was a freak. Rough. Probably poorly educated and completely unaware of his huge talent. There was a profit to be made from Gerome's gift. The profit would be his, he just needed to draw up a plan.

He became aware of a man's voice in the hallway. He got up and dressed. He hurried to the bathroom, splashed water on his face and dried off with one of Alouette's thick red towels. Raspberry – *framboise* – was how the label described this shade. Perhaps this was her favourite colour. He made a mental note to buy her a bunch of flowers in this shade, ran his fingers through his hair and checked his reflection in the mirror. Satisfied he was presentable, Liam entered the living room.

Borivoj sat on the sofa balancing a cup in one hand, and a muffin on a plate in the other. His features were pinched and serious. He sat upright, his back straight as a rod. His overall demeanour was delicate and refined, more suited to attending a genteel tea party than performing tricks with sunglasses on a street corner.

"Good morning," Liam said warmly. He held out his hand, then pulled it back when he saw Borivoj's hands were occupied.

"Good morning to you." Borivoj narrowed his eyes and fixed them on his cup.

"I have to thank you…" Liam began.

"No need," Borivoj interrupted. "I would do same for anyone. Any fellow human being."

"Still, you saved me from the clutches of those witches at the hotel. Stole my money, they did."

Borivoj frowned. "Witches…money? No idea what your meaning is."

"Never mind," Liam said as it dawned on him that Borivoj's mood was less than friendly.

Alouette came into the room. There was something about her demeanour, something missing, but he wasn't sure what it was. Her hair was the same, her clothes neatly pressed, her lips curved into a small smile. One hand brushed back a lock of hair which had fallen across her cheek, the other smoothed her apron. Intimacy, Liam thought, that's what it was. There was no hint she recalled the closeness of their bodies the night before or even a sliver of embarrassment that the episode had taken place. Was this the same woman who had lain beside him the night before or had it all been simply a dream? But when he took a closer look, he saw her eyes were pink rimmed.

"Everything OK?" Liam asked, sensing a gloomy atmosphere in the room.

"Fine," Alouette said.

Borivoj shrugged but didn't reply.

She turned to Liam "Coffee?" He nodded. She gave a small shake of her head and left the room.

"Have you two been arguing?" Liam asked.

Borivoj nodded. "We have argued."

"Can I help?" he asked eagerly. They had come to *his* assistance, perhaps he could repay the kindness by resolving the dispute.

"Arguing - yes. About you," Borivoj said in a clipped tone.

"I don't understand."

"I did not know what to do when old women ask me to remove you from hotel. I could not bring you to lodgings, they are not so nice and they might charge me more if another person arrives. I phoned Alouette and she came over. I told her not to bring stranger home. She insisted. But a woman alone must not do that!"

"I thought you both agreed I should come here. I was ill. I couldn't muster up the strength to swat a fly. What's the problem?"

"I don't know about fly, but I have never before seen Alouette like this. So upset. It must be something you have done, despite her claims that you haven't laid arm on her."

"Finger. It's finger, not arm. I haven't laid a finger on her." He held up his hands and wiggled his fingers. "I'm innocent. Don't know what you're on about, mate."

"So, you have not done anything to upset?"

"Not guilty," Liam said firmly. "Make that definitely not guilty."

Borivoj shrugged. "Maybe not – then I apologise. Women are strange, difficult to understand. I thought Alouette was impervious to ups and downs of normal women but I was incorrect."

"All women, in my experience, are hormonal. You should have seen my ex-wife!" Liam laughed.

"No jokes. My English is good but not that good," Borivoj said. "In any case I suppose you will depart soon?"

"When I'm better."

Alouette returned carrying a tray with a jug and a coffee

cup. She poured a cup and gave it to Liam. Borivoj raised his hand. "No more for me. I must to work."

He got up and Liam noted that he was wearing a jacket with thick padding in the shoulders. "Going for the retro look?" He laughed at his own joke.

"No need for comedy," Borivoj said darkly. "I look better than you any day, even in charity shop clothes."

Borivoj left without saying goodbye to him. Liam heard raised voices at the front door. Despite not understanding the exchange, he was aware that Borivoj and Alouette were discussing him. She came into the living room and picked up Borivoj's empty cup and saucer. Her hand trembled and the cup rattled against the saucer. She paused and looked at him. He could not read her gaze but right now she seemed as fragile as a Lalique vase.

"Is there a problem?" He got up and placed a hand on her shoulder.

"Nothing. It's nothing."

"Borivoj doesn't want me to stay here," he said. "This is your apartment. What do you want? I'll go if you think that's best." He put a hand behind his back and crossed his fingers. He needed to stay here, for there was nowhere else to go. Not in Paris, not in London, not in Belfast, particularly now his grandparents were gone.

"Do whatever you feel like," she said coldly.

"Do you mind if I stay until the end of the week? I'm still a bit shaky."

She nodded, muttered something softly in rapid French, and left the room.

Liam spent the next few days alternating between resting and taking short walks. He avoided the park, which reminded him too much of childhood, and the café with the red and white striped canopy. On the fourth day, when he swung his legs out of bed, renewed energy flowed through his limbs. He pulled the bedroom curtains across. Light flooded in. Two blackbirds on a tree next to the window hopped from branch to branch.

Although it was early, Alouette was already out. He sighed with relief. The last few evenings she'd been in a reflective mood, eyes fixed on the TV screen, yet he suspected she wasn't really watching the programmes. And even though he'd fended off sleep, anticipating the turn of the bedroom door handle, she hadn't come. Liam, who was hoping to stay here for a while, wasn't sure if he should be happy or worried. Lodger versus lover, which was best, he asked himself? The former was less complicated. Perhaps he could offer a small rent in exchange for a bed on the sofa? Given Alouette's current dour frame of mind, he would need to brush up on his powers of persuasion. Right now, she existed in another time, another place, and he wondered what that was.

He shook his head. Like Borivoj, he had difficulties understanding women. In his experience, they blew hot and cold. One minute they wanted you, the next they played hard to get. Lily was the queen-bee of that sort of behaviour. One anniversary, she had prepared a special meal: candles on the table, oysters and champagne for starters, Lily wearing a sexy, low cut red dress. Their relationship had been up and down for a while and he suspected she wanted to show him up. He was prepared: a bouquet of pink roses, box of chocolates, oversized padded card with hearts and a sentimental message, nicely boxed set of smelly bath stuff. Lily received the flowers with a wide smile, although she threw in the offhand comment 'red roses were her favourites, she liked the pink, though'. Her eyes had narrowed when she'd opened the card. Nothing inside except a large X. He could still picture her rifling through the leaves and petals of the roses, then slitting open the chocolate box seal with a fingernail. Her eyes had glittered. 'You rascal, where've you hidden it?' He knew then that he was in trouble. The oysters were tipped in the bin. 'They were off,' she'd declared in a chilled voice. Lily drank most of the champagne quickly, grumbling that none of the presents she had hoped for had materialised. Liam had been bewildered. How was he supposed to guess she'd wanted an airline ticket to Rome?

How, he wondered, could he persuade Alouette to let him stay? His powers of persuasion had never worked so well in the past, but was that because he'd been lazy, had made little effort to cajole? He dismissed the idea of flowers and shuddered as Lily's image came to mind: tight dress, heels, flowers tossed in the bin alongside the oysters, in the heat of their row. He stroked his chin. Perhaps wine or dinner in a nice bistro. Alouette was a woman who deserved the finer things in life. Luxury, surely that was the key to a woman's heart. There were few treats in Alouette's fridge. No champagne chilling, no filet mignon or lobster, no rare cheeses or Jamon Iberico, which he was partial to when he could afford it.

Alouette had mentioned a small legacy from an aunt. That was how she made ends meet. Yet it was evident money was in tight supply. Perhaps rent in exchange for kipping on the sofa would be welcomed? If she agreed, staying here would buy breathing space. Paris was as good a place as any to wheel and deal, and perhaps, with Gerome's paintings, he had discovered something worth wheeling and dealing in.

Chapter 14

The end of the week came and went. Mindful that Alouette could ask him to leave at any moment, he hid his inner turmoil, appearing calm as a swan above the water, but with feet paddling frantically below. On several occasions, while Alouette was cooking, he'd lingered in the kitchen, intending to broach the subject of staying on. Each time he'd bottled out. If she turned him down, then he might have to pack his bags immediately and head off to god knows where.

Her chilly mood gradually thawed. The day before she'd chatted after dinner. A soap she usually watched was given a miss and she had been extra appreciative when he had cleared the table and insisted on washing up. 'I could get used to this,' he imagined he heard her mutter, but then he realised it might be wishful thinking on his part.

It was a bright morning, the first cloudless day of the week. Liam put his coat on and made his way to the hallway. "Wait a second," Alouette called from the bedroom. She emerged wearing a tweed coat and black felt hat. As they made their way along the street she tucked her arm in his. Liam smiled to himself. The disagreement, whatever it was, had resolved itself. They went to the café with the red and white striped canopy. As he was helping her out of her coat, he noted the sadness had gone from her eyes.

"I'm nearly better, I could shift to the sofa. You'd have your bed back," He could hear his own voice quiver with nerves and wondered if Alouette could hear it too.

"As long as you don't lounge on my sofa all day.' Her smile was mischievous and he wasn't sure if she meant him to take her seriously. 'You know how much I like my soaps," she added.

"Anything," he said, surprised to discover he really meant this.

"I'm imagine you will become bored with nothing to do. You can use my laptop if you want. Ride…surf…the internet for antiques or art. You never know what you might find."

The following morning, when Alouette was out, he logged onto her laptop. He opened the mailbox Will had set up. A flash of rage welled up when he saw there were no new emails, no updated contact details, no information on Zarek, nothing on the police investigation. Nothing. It was no real surprise that Will had gone underground, maybe even left the country. Had he even bothered to take his family with him? A burning pain burrowed from his stomach to his back.

"Definitely an ulcer," he said aloud.

The suspicion of Will having the time of his life on Victor's money annoyed him so much he decided to get some fresh air. He put on his coat and picked up a ten euro note he'd left on the dressing table. He put it in his inside pocket. His fingers brushed against a piece of paper. He took it out, thinking it was an old receipt or bus ticket. A phone number was written on the paper. Fear washed over him as he remembered tearing this from his address book as he packed, and shoving it in his pocket, before disposing of the address book in the rubbish chute. This was Victor's landline number. Liam wasn't even sure if he had a mobile. He realised that if he dithered for even a minute he might end up ripping the paper into tiny pieces and flushing it down the toilet. He sucked in his breath and punched in the number. After a moment Victor answered.

"It's me," Liam said, instantly regretting what he'd just done. There was a moment's pause on the other end of the line.

"Liam." Victor said softly.

"I thought you'd change your number, that's why I haven't called."

"Understandable."

"I'm sorry."

"What happened?"

He was astonished by Victor's calm, measured voice which implied he might have forgiven him. Perhaps he had misjudged the whole situation badly. Was the money Victor had given him a mere drop in the ocean. Could he have offloaded similar sums with other friends?

"I invested your money. I was trying to help you out, to turn a profit. Thought you could use the extra cash."

"Aren't you the thoughtful lad!"

He examined Victor's voice for nuances, signs of anger or sarcasm, and found none.

"So…you're not pissed off with me?"

"Do I sound it?"

He gave an unsure laugh. "No. Not really. I wouldn't blame you if you were. Where are you now?"

"Still here, in London, on bail. A friend put up the cash."

Liam's eyes narrowed. Had Victor put a slight emphasis on the word 'friend'?

"I'll make it up to you," Liam said.

"Water under the bridge. You can come back now. No need to hide out…wherever you are."

"Christ, you're amazing," Liam said. "Not sure if I could be as cool as you."

"Cool is good, Liam. It's exactly how I need to be."

"You'll get off this time?"

"Probably. No need for you to worry, Liam, it's all in hand. You can come back now."

"Now?" Liam paused. "No grudges?" He remembered the look on Victor's face when Victor had opened the suitcase. Pure lust. Then he recalled the hooded eyes, the frown on Victor's face when he'd first talked of Larry's betrayal. 'No one crosses me and gets away with it', these were his exact words.

"You're forgiven. For Mary's sake."

Liam shook his head. Neither past friendship, nor memories of his mother would allow Victor to forgive him.

"Like hell! If you get your hands on me, I'll disappear like Larry."

"You fuckin' twat. Get back here now. Right now. We've things to discuss."

"A one sided discussion," Liam said shrilly, "while you torture me."

"Bastard. Where are you? I'd slit your throat right now if I could."

Liam switched off his phone and tossed it on the bed. A fresh emotion replaced the anger he'd felt towards Will. Fear. Victor now had this mobile number. He wasn't sure how these things worked but Victor was bound to have someone who owed him a favour. Maybe someone he'd been inside with, some tecchie genius who could track him down in a matter of minutes. Liam picked up his phone and stuffed it in his pocket. He would have to buy another one. This phone, he'd throw in the Seine. If Victor and his associates followed the electronic signal, then they'd find themselves mired in mud at the bottom of the river, along with all the other pond life.

"Best place for them," Liam said aloud.

Liam's stomach ache worsened. He was never going home, he realised, at least not until Victor was dead. Paris was his home for now and he would have to make the best of it. He'd made poor decisions in the past: the Irish properties, taking up with Lily, abandoning his cat, dinner with Will. He'd hoped that since his arrival in Paris his decision-making skills would have improved. The call he'd just made told him they hadn't.

He abandoned ideas of a walk when Alouette returned from the market with two bags of groceries. The browned top of a baguette jutted from one of the bags.

"I thought I would cook something special," she said. "Lasagne. Italian. All men like Italian food."

He breathed an inward sigh of relief. Alouette's good humour was surely back in place.

"I thought afterwards we might see a band."

"Out?"

"Yes, out, Liam. There isn't a band hidden in my small flat. A night out will perk you up."

"Le Chat Rouge?"

"My favourite. Good idea."

After dinner, they made their way through the streets of Paris, towards the jazz club. The meal had been heavy and satisfying: pasta with a rich meat, tomato and basil sauce. If he could have chosen, he would have made his excuses and gone to bed after eating. However, as they strolled past old and new buildings, the stars twinkling above, light flooding from windows, he had to admit that this was the closest to being happy he'd been in a long time. He slipped his arm through Alouette's, she didn't seem to mind, and glanced at her profile. Her lips were curved into a smile. He willed himself to fix this moment, rather than the call to Victor, in his mind. He was well fed and cared for. She seemed happy too. What more could anyone want?

A band was already playing when they took their seats.

"Swing, not my favourite," she said. He noted that even in the dimmed room, her eyes glittered.

"Do you want to leave?" he asked. In reality, now they were settled into their seats, he was looking forward to a night of music and the warming hit of a few glasses of Black Bush. He licked his lips as the waiter deposited their glasses on the table.

She shrugged. "It's fine. We should stay. I can't say why, but I want to suck the pleasure out of each day. I'm not being melancholy when I repeat the saying 'to live each day as though it's my last'".

Liam raised his glass and tipped it against Alouette's wine glass.

"Amen to that. To friendship, Alouette."

When they returned to the flat, she stood in the doorway, watching as he arranged the duvet and pillows on the sofa. A look of regret flashed across her face and then she was gone. He lay back on his pillow and reflected. Was moving onto the sofa the right thing to do? Surely Alouette had given up her bedroom for long enough? The look he'd just seen in her eyes told him otherwise. Unspoken words: loneliness, fear, sadness, desire, lingered in her wake. She was so controlled, reading her was almost impossible. In his current mellow mood, he would have relished the comfort of a warm body against his, but keeping Alouette onside was vital for future plans. Making love, he knew, would be a game changer.

Chapter 15

Over the next few weeks, Liam and Alouette grew closer, yet each night he slept alone on the sofa. One night, however, on his way to the bathroom, he noticed the bedroom door was ajar. As the bathroom door clicked shut he thought he heard her call out. He resisted the urge to go to her. In any case, he felt gratitude towards her, not love, so why rock the boat?

She was a woman who appreciated routine, he discovered. Between seven and seven thirty in the morning there was a flurry of activity: shower running, footsteps back and forth in the hallway, doors opening and closing. Half an hour later, the front door creaked open, then shut, quickly and without ceremony. The flat was silent until around nine, when a noisier Alouette returned. Bags crackled as they were unpacked, the kettle bubbled, footsteps clattered on the kitchen floor tiles. That was his alarm call, done without a word, scathing look or raised eyebrow. He understood it was time to fold up the sofa bed and tuck his pillows and blanket behind it.

This routine took place between Monday and Friday. Weekends were different. The sounds and actions associated with weekends were languid and carefree: jazz on the radio, Alouette singing, a visit to a gallery or a shopping trip. A stroll followed by a glass of wine in a café. Life was peaceful so he was happy to fall in with her suggestions.

As the weeks drifted by, he came to appreciate knowing exactly where he stood. When life was ordered there was no ambiguity. This was a novel concept for Liam. For the first time he knew what was expected of him: how to behave, what to pass comment on, where boundaries lay. Alouette liked to discuss her soaps, so he became familiar with their story lines. She enjoyed talking about food. After dinner she would discuss what they might have for dinner the following day. To his amusement, they frequently ended up with salad, cold meat and cheese. He discovered they both liked blues, jazz and old films. Both were fans of Hitchcock and Van Morrison.

Alouette's predictability provided him with an oasis of calm. He had no trouble fitting in with her needs. Easy. That was the word he used to describe this period in his life. Yet he was still aware that a sour look or an impatient sigh might turn everything on its head. If he was less than affable, she might suddenly realise what a pain in the ass he really was.

Borivoj visited several times. He was barely able to mask his suspicion and disapproval of Liam. Although he admired Borivoj's loyalty to Alouette, Liam didn't relish these visits. Once, when Liam walked him to the apartment front door, Borivoj leaned over and whispered into his ear, 'She'll see through you soon enough. Once she does you'll be gone.'

This comment once again brought his greatest fears to mind. Broke and homeless. That thought filled him with terror. If you were that far down in the gutter, how on earth could you pull yourself back up, he reflected? Offices, shops or factories wouldn't be queuing up to employ someone who didn't have the wherewithal to keep a roof over their heads. And women would hardly be flocking to rescue him. Sinking that low would be akin to finding himself trapped under a sheet of ice. The effort of chipping or scraping the way out might prove too much.

Borivoj's comment sent him into a state of flux. Life was smooth right now but what if Borivoj was right, what if Alouette tired of him? Money, he knew, was the missing link, the final number in security's combination lock. He took his mother's Asprey brooch from his suitcase and held it in the palm of his hand. Three larger diamonds set in platinum, and fifteen smaller stones clustered around these. He moved nearer to the window. The stones sparkled, throwing prisms of light onto the walls. He'd planned to hang onto the brooch until he was an old man, at least eighty, maybe even ninety. And if there were children, planned or unplanned, then the brooch would pass to them. That's what normal people did with their assets, wasn't it? Normal. That word was a mystery to him. He had observed other people go about their daily business, yet how often had he understood what made them tick? He shrugged and resolved to let the brooch go.

He sat at the desk in the living room and Googled lists of Paris jewellers. He found a jeweller, near the café by the park, which offered valuations. With a heavyish heart, he wrote down the address.

As he was getting ready to go out, he had a sudden thought. Why not kill two birds with one stone? Selling the brooch would give immediate security, but Gerome's paintings would, he hoped, provide for the future. He arranged the paintings side by side on the bed and studied them. They were still as stunning as when he'd first clapped eyes on them. He gave an appreciative whistle. Finding masterpieces like these on a market stall was every dealer's dream. As he traced his finger across the painted skin of the nude, he resolved to take control of his life. He would take one of these paintings to a dealer for valuation.

It dawned on him that he was itching for a deal. Deals were his lifeline in the past. When the rent was overdue, a book, a piece of china or one of the watercolours hanging in his flat might have been offloaded. Once he'd sold a jug he was using as a table ornament. It had gone for a 'monkey': five hundred pounds. He hadn't been particularly surprised, having done research prior to selling the jug. It was eighteenth century, used for serving beer or cider, made of soft paste porcelain, enamelled and gilded. The jug's remarkable feature was the moulded head of Admiral Rodney, who fought for the British in the American War of Independence, on the spout. The spout alone had pushed the value of the mediocre jug up a few hundred quid.

If he could make just one similar deal here, in this foreign city, then confidence might pump back into his veins. This was a win-win situation. Turning a profit would enable him to buy more of Gerome's work. He recalled an article he'd read in an art magazine on the value of paintings and how this could be manipulated by investors, who saw paintings as capital rather than art. There was no reason he couldn't do the same thing. This idea was still in its infancy, but if the paintings had the same impact on the art buying public as they'd had on him, he might be onto a winner. Sell one, buy publicity, sell the next for two or three times as much.

He examined the painting of the nude again. A bowl of apples sat on a table next to her. The fruit, which sat parallel to her right breast, was painted with red, green and white brushstrokes. The effect was so lush and lifelike, he found himself licking his lips. Next to the apples was an empty wine glass. What was the artist trying to say? Had the woman just finished the wine? Like Eve, was she about to bite into the forbidden fruit?

He tucked his mother's brooch into the inside pocket of his jacket, set the painting of the nude on top of the wardrobe, wrapped the painting of the cliffs and sea in newspaper, and left the apartment.

Outside, a different Paris had awakened. Shiny paving stones took on a yellow cast. Branches appeared to have sprouted buds overnight. Birdsong was louder and more joyous than before, and strangers occasionally smiled at each other. After all, spring was a season where things were reborn. As the sun warmed his bones, his optimism grew. Life would improve. He'd find a way to cut through his swathe of bad luck. His ill fortune couldn't be described as a blip, it was more a tsunami, a calamitous wave of misfortune. But today he allowed himself to feel hopeful. He found himself whistling *La Vie en Rose*, the tune Alouette had sung when he'd first met her. Surely he could allow himself the indulgence of seeing the world through Alouette's rose-tinted glasses?

He left the brooch at the jewellers. The owner was quick to assure him that he had several clients who would be interested in such a fine piece and who might pay cash. He was both cheered and sad that the valuation had been around fifteen thousand euro. This was enough to force a sale. If it had been less, he might have considered holding onto this last memory of his mother.

Eager to be far away from the jewellers, he walked for almost an hour, carrying the painting under his arm. He found himself in the warren of streets off the Boulevard Montparnasse, the home of Paris' glitzy antiques shops and galleries. He stopped and studied the paintings in the window of one gallery. Their elaborate frames made them appear more important. He nodded: the painting he carried stood on its own artistic merits and didn't need such fripperies. He took a deep breath and turned the door handle. He was unsure if this was the right place to begin his new career as a Parisian art dealer, but it was a start. 'Back in the saddle', he muttered as he went inside.

The shop interior was decorated in burgundy and gold, giving off a whiff of opulence. To his trained eye the decor smacked of pretentiousness. Dusty barns which served as auction rooms could hold more treasures than the fanciest antique shop. Shops like this were designed as magnets for the rich rather than aiming to attract the knowledgeable. The people he knew in the antiques business rarely crossed the threshold of this type of establishment.

Inside, spotlights providing the sole illumination, threw light and shadow across the gallery. Each spotlight was positioned to flatter a specific painting. Most of the paintings gave the impression of being old. In the art world, he knew, few things were exactly as they appeared. An old painting might turn out to be a copy, or even if it was genuinely antique, it might not be valuable. A rich impresario might fuss over a piece of modern art with little substance and begin to collect these dubious pieces. With high-profile ownership and provenance, their value was raised and, overnight, a quirky, worthless piece of art could become priceless. He appreciated the fun in these pieces, but where was the art?

Goosebumps crept up his arms as he realised he could be on the cusp of something big; approaching another set of life's crossroads where an action or event defined a future pathway. The artwork he carried was more competent than the works hanging on these walls. What if he'd found something of merit and was creating a 'eureka' moment in the art world? What must it have been like for painters like Manet, who crossed boundaries and broke with tradition, fathering a new and innovative style of painting? For years, they might have been laughed at and turned away from galleries. Perhaps they'd even starved for a while or earned a pittance painting portraits in Montmartre's Place Du Tertre. He recalled a brief encounter there with a silver-haired artist: 'How about a portrait, handsome boy?' The artist had smiled and shrugged when Liam with equal politeness had declined.

He made his way to the rear of the shop, giving the works on display a cursory glance. Pretty gilded ornaments but nothing more, in his opinion. An assistant dressed in a slick charcoal suit and white shirt sat behind a Chippendale writing desk. The assistant looked up from his laptop and frowned when he took a seat opposite. He realised he didn't look the part. The flu or whatever his illness was, had drained his skin of colour, and earlier he'd dressed so quickly, he had no idea what he was wearing. He glanced down at his feet and was relieved to see a pair of brown shoes rather than the beige slippers Alouette had bought him.

The salesman cleared his throat. Liam looked him in the eye. He had frequently dealt with auctioneers, art dealers and property magnates, some of whom he'd considered pricks. This salesman, despite his expensive, silky suit, was no more intimidating. Liam leaned back in the chair, relishing the challenge of a deal. The salesman looked down at the newspaper bundle on the desk.

"Speak English?" Liam said.

"Of course. Can I help you?" The salesman kept an eye trained on the bundle.

Astonishing, Liam thought, how the man opposite could convey so much meaning with just a few words. From the salesman's tone, he understood the questions: 'why are you here when this is clearly a high class establishment?' and 'why are you contaminating my desk with your badly wrapped parcel which probably contains junk?' Despite all his faults, his mistakes with money, women and property, *he* would never have treated a complete stranger as an inferior.

"I'd like you to look at this painting. Tell me what you think."

The man narrowed his eyes and cocked his head sideways as though he hadn't understood.

"You're an expert, aren't you?" Liam said sharply, using the voice he'd wheeled out in the past to get one over on fellow dealers at auctions. It was all about bluff, making your opponent think you had something important, something they wanted and needed. Even though Liam wasn't a brawny man he knew this voice could be intimidating. It told his opponent that he wasn't a man who liked to be crossed and suggested consequences which might or might not be dire, dependent on his mood. Not that he would ever follow a verbal threat through.

"I think you'll want to see this," Liam added.

Under Liam's steely gaze, the assistant caved in. He pointed at the newspaper and nodded. Liam carefully unwrapped the painting. The assistant lifted it up by a finger on each side. He held it up so light fell on the painting.

"Well painted," he exclaimed after a moment's pause. He took one of the shop's paintings off its hook and hung Gerome's painting in its place. He took a step back. A puzzled expression worked its way across his face and Liam gave himself an imaginary handshake. Bullseye. The painting was making its mark.

"I'm not sure what this is," the salesman said.

"Peploe's style, with a touch of Hopper thrown in. I've not seen anything like this before. Great, isn't it?"

The assistant shook his head, took the painting off the hook, and set it on the desk. "As you can see all of the paintings we sell are antiques. This isn't old but neither is it contemporary art."

"I know it's neither fish nor fowl but does a good painting need a label?" Liam drummed his fingers on the table. "In your opinion, is it good? Is it saleable? That's what I want to know." He was becoming impatient. This was not the outcome he'd expected.

The man shrugged and tapped his pen on the table.

"It doesn't fit any category I know, so it might be excellent or it might be terrible."

"I don't understand. You can't tell me if a painting is good or bad?"

"I know I couldn't sell it in this establishment, monsieur. It's not an important piece. I don't think something so freshly painted could have any sort of provenance. Our customers would *never* purchase something like this."

"I see," Liam said. "You can only judge if a painting is good by how much you can charge for it."

"A piece of art is only as good as its value."

"God help your customers, then." Liam picked up the painting and strode to the front door. Behind, he could hear the rustling of paper. When he glanced back, the assistant was pressing the crumpled newspaper into a waste basket.

He hurried down the street, eager to be far away from the shop. When Alouette threw him out, as Borivoj said she would, he would need money to pay rent, to eat, to buy the odd bottle of wine and newspaper. The money he'd make from the brooch sale would cover those needs for a few months, but then he'd be left with nothing. He imagined he saw the words 'Skid Row' repeated in flashing lights on the street walls. How on earth was he to strike a deal and earn a crust in a foreign city where he didn't understand the local dealing customs and had no idea which antiques were in fashion? Money begets money, he muttered to himself. He watched the passersby, their faces lit up on this beautiful spring day. In contrast Liam's mood had plunged and he likened his venture into the posh shop to taking a dip in the North Atlantic in winter.

He entered a café and carelessly set the painting on the floor by his table. It was still beautiful in his eyes but perhaps his mind had been affected by illness and only he could see its merits. To the salesman in the art gallery, Gerome's painting had come across as the dabblings of an amateur. He sighed. Did he have 'gullible' tattooed on his forehead? He mentally ticked off his recent financial disasters. First, and by orders of magnitude the greatest swindle of all, Will had relieved him of Victor's money. Then the old woman in the hotel, who probably *was* one of a twin and who liked to play tricks on idiot guests, claimed he hadn't paid his bill when he was one hundred percent sure he had. Finally that loudmouth Gerome had flogged him worthless paintings. In the eyes of the world he was a fool. He recalled Gerome's first word to him: *imbecile*. How right he'd been. He smouldered with rage as he drank his coffee.

He became aware of a group of people, across the café, focussing their attention on his table. He stared back. They broke off their gaze and entered into an animated discussion. One woman stood up. The others in the group nodded towards her, deferentially it appeared. He imagined she was the group leader. She made her way over to Liam's table. He flushed. It had been a while since an attractive woman had hit on him. He looked up.

"Excuse me," the woman said. She pointed to the chair opposite him. "May I?"

"By all means," he said in a charming voice. Despite his sour mood, the lure of an attractive woman was still strong. The woman in front of him glowed. Beige raincoat, blonde hair, tanned skin, golden suede shoes. Her snub nose was sprinkled with freckles, but that added to her charm. He likened her to a piece of bait on a hook, with he, the bewitched sea bass.

"I was just heading off."

"No, don't go. In fact, can I buy you a coffee?" she said.

He nodded and watched her stride up to the counter. He raised his eyebrows when she placed the order in excellent French. She returned to the table.

"You speak French well. Better than me," Liam said.

"Art tours and exchange trips. The kind kids don't want to

go on, but that benefit them in the future. But, pardon me. At first I thought you were French."

"Irish actually. From Belfast originally. I'm Liam, by the way." The woman's face broke into a smile.

"Elaine. American, as you might have guessed. Lots of creative types come from Ireland, I believe. I spent a tortuous six months on *Finnegan's Wake*, then I discovered the joys of *The Dubliners*."

He studied the woman for a moment. Her eyes glittered and danced. He had seen that look before on the faces of bidders just before the auction hammer went down. She wanted something and he was curious to discover what that was. He was accustomed to chasing women, now the boot was on the other foot and it appeared he was being pursued.

"What can I do for you?" he asked as the waiter set a coffee in front of him.

"I don't mean to be forward - are you an artist?"

Liam shook his head. "Not guilty. Although I've been accused of being an artist of a non-painting variety in the past."

Elaine looked confused. "I'm not sure what that means. I noticed the painting on the floor and thought you might be the artist."

"Oh that," he said flippantly. He hesitated for a moment. The woman had hunger in her eyes, they sparkled and danced as they flickered from his face to the side of the table. If it wasn't him she desired, then it might be the painting. "I buy and sell paintings. I'm a dealer. A finder of extraordinary pieces."

"I… we all… have been admiring your painting. May I take a closer look?"

"Be my guest." He picked up the painting and set it on the table.

"Oh my, it's even better close up! That's unusual for art, in my experience."

"The artist is unusual." He injected a knowledgeable note into his voice.

"Is he French?" Elaine's eyes were fixed on the painting as

she spoke.

"Very. The genuine article."

She took a deep breath. "I'd like to meet him. Would that be at all possible?"

Liam sighed inwardly. He'd experienced a brief adrenaline rush as he envisaged an imminent sale. Now it appeared, this woman simply wanted to meet a French artist. Part of the tourist experience, he thought ruefully. Liam shook his head firmly.

"He's very private. A bit nervous. Skittish as a prize racehorse, actually. Too talented for his own good."

"Is he very old? He paints skilfully, with an experienced hand."

"Oldish," Liam said.

"Can you humour me by sticking around for a few more minutes? I need to have a chat with my group." She pointed to her colleagues who were eagerly eyeing the proceedings.

She returned to her table and sat down, clicking her fingers several times.

He watched from the side of his eye as the group conferred and glanced over occasionally. There were smiles and nods. His heart pounded. The sweet aroma of an imminent deal was in the air.

She returned to his table and sat down and without saying a word. She gazed again at the painting.

He coughed. "Anything else?"

"Is this for sale?" she asked, with a slight tremor in her voice.

He studied her features. *Know your adversary.* He had seen burning desire etched on certain men's faces when a beautiful woman entered a room and they wanted to seduce her; he'd battled with rivals at auction for a painting or piece of china and had seen the fire in their eyes as they bid much higher than the item was worth. They'd lost all sense of reason and would have sold their grandmother into servitude to seal the deal. This woman was no different.

"It might be...for the right price. Although Gerome is old,

his health's not too good. He might not paint much longer."

"Gerome, Gerome. So French," Elaine said, verbally caressing the name.

Liam bit his lip and looked upwards, fixing his gaze on the ceiling. He could hear the woman's breath quicken. Putty in the hands. He suppressed a smile.

"How much?" she asked.

He tightened his grip on his coffee cup, preparing for the inevitable haggle. Still, the painting had cost him a mere three hundred. If he could move it on for at least three thousand then he would have made a thousand per cent profit. "Five thousand. Euro, that is."

Her body sagged and she wiped a bead of perspiration from her forehead. "It's hot, isn't it?"

He was too busy gauging her reaction to his offer to respond. Her body language told him she was relieved. He cursed himself for not asking more and he cursed the salesman in the gallery for making him doubt the quality of the painting.

"I'll take it." She smiled, showing off her even white teeth.

"I wasn't planning on selling, but I can see it's going to a good home." He shook her outstretched hand. "You've bagged yourself a bargain. It'll have to be cash, though."

"Can I meet the artist?" Her face glowed as she picked up the painting and studied it so closely the tip of her nose brushed against the canvas. He wouldn't have been surprised if she'd pursed her lips and kissed it.

"Unfortunately he's not in the best of health. He's quite ill at the moment."

"Oh!" She didn't appear disappointed. "Do you have any more of his work?"

"A few pieces," he said. "Interested in seeing them?"

"Hell yes!"

She left the coffee shop. Two of her colleagues drifted over to Liam's table and examined the painting. They appeared shy, bashful. One blushed and muttered he knew nothing about art and that Elaine was the expert. Liam smiled pleasantly and toasted them with his coffee cup.

"A good buy. Lucky for her we crossed paths," he said.

Elaine returned with a large brown envelope. She set the envelope on the table. "It's all there. I'm sure you'll want to check."

He quashed the urge to stack the notes on the table and count them, one by one. Elaine deserved his respect. "No need."

She reached into her bag, took out a notebook and set it on the table. "I'll need a receipt."

He smiled, then opened the envelope. Clearly *she* trusted him less than he trusted her.

"I suppose I should count it then."

"I'm going home in a few days. Bring what you're prepared to sell to the hotel and we might do business." She gave him a card with the name of her hotel and its phone number printed on it.

"Are the paintings for you or are you selling them on?" he asked.

She tapped the side of her stubby nose. "That would be telling!"

On the way back to Alouette's, Liam bought a bottle of Moet. An extravagant gesture, he knew, but hadn't he just sealed his first Parisian deal? The thrill of earning a few thousand euro in a matter of minutes had lifted his spirits and he wanted to share his good fortune. Alouette had nursed him while he was ill, so why not repay the kindness? He wouldn't divulge details, though, until his business with Elaine was done and dusted.

He passed a small bistro near the apartment. The exterior was painted in opulent red and gold shades. The flashy colours caught his eye and lured him over. He studied the menu chalked on a board by the door. Exorbitant prices, he noted, but his wallet was fat and the array of dishes made him salivate. A starter of Foie Gras would be just the ticket and perhaps afterwards, some rump steak or good, honest, steak tartare, accompanied by a fine Bordeaux, might boost his vitamin levels. A classic crème brulee or tarte tatin would round off the meal nicely. He went into the restaurant and booked a table for two. The enthusiastic waiter winked and pointed to a secluded corner of the room. Liam nodded, although he had peace and quiet rather than seduction on his mind.

Adrenalin coursed through his body when his mind, like a seamstress manually undoing a row of stitches from a delicate garment, unpicked the deal he'd just executed. Exhilarating, but he realised that he still missed the cut and thrust of auction day where victory was more about getting one over on an opponent rather than simply raking in money. The journey, he recalled once thinking, was where you got your kicks, not the arrival.

Chapter 16

Alouette's tongue tripped and danced as she climbed into the sofa bed. "Move away - over, I mean to say." She nudged Liam's arm with her elbow.

This was the end to an evening where both had indulged in an orgy of feasting on rich foods, champagne and wine. Fired by the success of the day, he'd ordered a second bottle of Bordeaux to accompany dinner, and despite a strong espresso afterwards he could barely remember the garlicky taste of the Foie Gras or the bite of the steak tartare. He couldn't remember how he'd ended up in bed, nor could he recall the walk back to the apartment or climbing the forty five steps up to the front door of the flat. The marble stairs must have echoed back the clatter of Alouette's stilettos, yet he didn't recall hearing such a sound.

She peeled off her nightdress and leaned in towards him. He was already naked and her fingers aroused him.

"Sure you want it?" He managed a coherent thought. She was his friend. He didn't want to take advantage of her.

"No streengs...strings, I mean," she laughed. "Don't be so uptight, *mon petit chou*."

If he had been completely sober he would have thought through the consequences of sleeping with his landlady: would he be staying here in the future as her lover or her lodger? And what if the affair didn't go the distance? Would she pitch him onto the streets? Then there was the remote possibility that he might meet Gerome's raven haired model and fall even more in love with her than he already was. Would he juggle both of them or would he let Alouette down? But, even though these thoughts flashed through his mind, none of them lingered. He was just as tipsy as Alouette and as much in need of physical contact.

She clambered on top of him. Her body, which appeared trim when clothed, was bony when naked. He wrapped his legs around her as their bodies moved rhythmically, then faster. Finally she groaned and slid off him. Liam, who hadn't climaxed, tumbled over until he lay on top of her. Suddenly his stomach lurched and he staggered to the bathroom, where he threw up.

The following morning he awoke nauseated and feeling as though his head had been pressed under the wheels of a lorry. In the distance, there was a sweet singing. He edged his body into a seated position. There was no indentation in the pillow beside him, nor rumpling of the sheets, yet he recalled Alouette's knees, unfleshy and bony, pressing into his thighs. They had made love, he remembered. He hoped he'd performed well. He stopped preening when he recalled that sex always resulted in consequences: ducking and diving, a steady relationship, in Lily's case, a ring on the finger. Rather than Alouette recalling his performance, he hope she'd blanked out the previous night's goings on.

"Coffee," Alouette called out from the general direction of the kitchen.

"Strong, please," he shouted. He lifted his hand and held it out flat in front of him, palm facing downwards. It trembled. He got out of bed and slowly rose to his feet. So far so good. He dressed, tidied away his bedding, and made his way to the kitchen.

He stood at the open door, watching Alouette glide about, quick and smooth as though she was on roller skates. Evidently in high spirits, she hummed a few lines from an upbeat song Liam didn't recognise. She wore her usual uniform of black trousers and black sweater; the silk scarf knotted round her neck was embossed with a jazzy, dolly-mixture type pattern. Her eyes were smudged in dark eyeliner, and red shiny lipstick made her lips appear fuller. The whole effect was sleek, elegant and sexy, reminding him of a cormorant, feathers oily and reflective, poised to strike. She turned and grinned.

"Up already? I thought you might need more sleep to revive you."

"Why, what did I do?" he bluffed. "Can't remember a

thing after the starter. Nice meal, was it?"

"Yes. I don't usually drink so much, but it was a special occasion, wasn't it?"

She stood on her tiptoes and planted a firm kiss on his lips. It wasn't a passionate kiss, which didn't surprise him as he had been sick during the night and hadn't yet brushed his teeth, but it *was* proprietorial.

"Drink up." She poured two cups of coffee and gave one to him.

He returned to the living room and sat on the sofa. Alouette followed and sat next to him, her thigh brushing against his, not appearing to notice his awkwardness. How very English I am, he thought. A Frenchman would take the morning after in his stride. He would be confident, making phone calls to his wife, kids or business associates in the presence of his mistress, without blinking an eyelid. But he wasn't French and he wished he hadn't arranged last night's dinner or at the very least hadn't invited Alouette. It was years since he'd mixed so many drinks. A cocktail of champagne, wine and brandy swirled round his stomach. Drinking too much equals poor decision making. This was an equation he knew like the back of his hand, yet yesterday he'd let his guard down and indulged in a moment of madness. Suddenly the apartment felt like a prison from which there was no escape. Everything he owned in the world was here. This was his home. It dawned on him that Lily's betrayal was still controlling his life and shaping the way he viewed women. On the other hand, maybe it was he who had pushed Lily away? Could he track his sometimes casual behaviour towards the opposite sex to his childhood? Did all men who grew up with only a woman as a reference point, spend the rest of their lives pushing against this mother figure?

"Breakfast?" She reached over and patted his stomach. He recoiled at the intimacy of the gesture, but not enough for her to notice.

"Not right now. I need to head out soon."

"Ah – to look for that artist."

"I told you about him?"

"A bit. You were very…coy. He's someone you met recently here in Paris, I think? I know he painted those paintings you're so precious about."

"I'm hoping to bag a deal. To pick up a few more. Paintings, that is."

"Do you want me to come with you?"

"Better not." He feigned regret. "Negotiations will be tough. I don't want him to be distracted by you."

She leaned over and kissed him on the cheek. "*Bonne chance*, my love. Very, very good luck!" She got up and picked up the empty coffee cups. As she left the room she glanced over her shoulder. "I forgot to tell you, Borivoj is coming to dinner this evening. Can I trouble you to pick up a bottle of wine?"

Oh great, he thought. The Czech had been hostile when he hadn't slept with Alouette, what would he be like now the deed had been done? Even if she didn't confide in Borivoj, he was sure to note she was acting like a frisky goat on a spring day. But the evening would look after itself; right now his priority was finding Gerome.

The thought of a potential deal cheered him. As he left the apartment he shouted goodbye and was halfway down the stairs when he heard Alouette's faint response. He smiled to himself - this felt like going out to work.

Contrary to the fear that Gerome would prove difficult to track down, Liam found him in his usual place in the Place de la Concorde. His heart beat faster at the sight of canvasses, stacked high on the stall; a potential fortune, there for the taking. Gerome raised a hand in greeting but remained seated on his deckchair.

"Back again, friend. Long time."

"Just a quick look," he said casually, taking care not to appear too eager. He did a mental calculation: from the sales of painting to Elaine, and the brooch, he would have enough for six month's rent and food. Or the money could be put to better use - to invest in the future. In Liam's mind, there was no contest. He was prepared to spend every cent he possessed if Gerome had something to offer. From the corner of his eye he could see Gerome, eyes narrowed, watching him. As a dealer, Liam was astute. He knew that if his hand or eyes rested for more than a moment on an object then the price would increase. He was soon disappointed as none of the efforts on the stall had been painted by Gerome's magical hand. Paris was the spiritual home to trainee artists. He'd seen scores of them, in squares and gardens, working on portraits, landscapes, cityscapes. Some of the paintings were reasonably good, others, like these, would have made his grandfather, who hadn't a clue about art, weep in despair.

Gerome stood up. "Good stuff, eh?"

"Not my style. Nothing here appeals to me."

Gerome frowned. "I haven't forgotten our deal if that's why you don't want to buy. Claudine returns tomorrow. I could set up your date very soon."

"That would be great," Liam said enthusiastically, obliterating all too easily the fling with Alouette from his mind. Then he recalled why he was here: Elaine, with her cute button nose and potentially limitless bank account. "Any more of your stuff? I'd like to see some more...assuming you've done more than three paintings in your life."

Gerome grinned. "Ah, *my* work. You have good taste, my friend. I can bring more on Saturday."

"I need them sooner. And I was thinking of, say, around twenty paintings. I've a big house to fill."

"And you want to fill your big house with *my* paintings. *Je suis tres flatte.* So very flattered. Such an honour."

"Look," Liam said impatiently, "give me a price for twenty paintings and we'll see if we can deal. But first of all, can you supply what I need?"

Gerome nodded. "I haven't exactly counted but I have at least twenty."

"Same style as the others?"

"Exact same style. It's the only one I do."

"Providing I like them, how much for the lot?"

Gerome flicked his cigarette stub, it landed on the ground. "Let's see….twenty paintings. They've gone up in price because of demand, so I think forty thousand."

"Two thousand each." Liam shook his head. "You're surely joking."

"No. I am first of all an artist, but I am also a market trader too. Part of my job is to barter."

Liam turned and started to walk away.

"Wait, friend. Thirty thousand. You can have all. All twenty of them."

"Twenty thousand," Liam countered.

"Twenty-five."

"Twenty and not a cent more."

Gerome shrugged. He spat on his hands and rubbed them together. He held out a hand, Liam shook it lightly.

"Deal."

"I need the paintings in a few days."

"OK. Meet with Claudine day after tomorrow and then afterwards she will bring you to my place. You can view the paintings and take them immediately, if they take your fancy."

"Odd way to do business."

"Two for one: the woman and the paintings."

Liam debated with himself for a moment. Gerome was a strange one and this was a curious method of conducting business. But, he reasoned, Claudine must have posed at Gerome's apartment, so she knew the way there. No reason why they couldn't go there together after dinner. Why not combine business with pleasure?

On his way back to the apartment he stopped at a supermarket and picked out a bottle of *vin ordinaire*. Liam's hangover had lingered and he had no intention of drinking this wine. Alouette too, he imagined, would also shun alcohol. He hesitated when he reached the till as it crossed his mind that he might be marked as a cheapskate, but his prior upbeat mood had decreased as the pounding of his head increased. He handed over the five euro note and made his way back to the apartment.

He was greeted by a rich, meaty aroma when he opened the front door. Alouette stepped from the kitchen into the hallway. In one hand was a wooden spoon, saturated in a brown liquid which dripped to the floor. He followed her into the kitchen. She tore off a piece of kitchen roll, bent down and wiped up the small pool of gravy. From his bird's eye view he noticed how doll-like her figure was, and envisaged picking her up and setting her on the living room mantelpiece. She stood up and smiled.

"Did you bring the wine?"

Liam held out the supermarket bag. He blushed, suddenly regretting the poor choice he'd made. She opened it and looked inside.

"*Merci*," she said with a frown. "I noticed you like meat so I'm making *boeuf bourguignone*."

"Terrific."

"I need to put some of this wine in the casserole. Did you bring another?"

"Just the one. I'm a bit hungover so I'm teetotal tonight. Not drinking."

Alouette nodded slowly. "I'm sure Borivoj will bring a bottle or two. This is fine."

"Need any help?"

"You go rest. I'm fine…absolutely fine." She waved a hand and turned her attention to the stove.

He lay back on the sofa and stared at the ceiling as he drew up plans for the following day. A final deal had been agreed on the brooch so in the morning, he would go to the jewellers to pick up his money. He'd negotiated payment in cash so if all went to plan he would bring the money back to the apartment and secrete it in a place where Alouette was unlikely to look. It wasn't that he was trying to cheat or deceive her, he reassured himself, he just needed to take control of his own life and there was no need to reveal every nuance, every twist and turn of fate. He pictured the blue linen shirt he'd bought in *Galeries Lafayette* when he'd first arrived. It was clean but creased so he would iron it when

Alouette was out. He flushed when he thought of the painting of Claudine; he had seen the paler colour of her skin under her clothes, had admired the V of her pubic hair, the curve of her thighs, the slight droop of her heavy breasts, the dark nipples. He began to perspire so he willed himself to forget the painting and concentrate on things as they were - a simple meeting with an attractive woman, which might or might not lead to something. He was single so he was doing nothing wrong.

Liam made further plans. On Saturday he'd bring three or four paintings to Elaine. If they were as good as the others, he was certain she would buy the paintings on the spot. If the price she was prepared to pay was right, he would ship the rest to the United States at a later date.

He congratulated himself on his business plan which he described as almost airtight. He wasn't aware of holes in the plan, but liked to prepare himself for the unexpected. If all went well there was a profit to be had, which he would reinvest in Gerome's work. Perhaps he could even arrange for a girl or boy to work the market stall giving Gerome more time to paint. He hoped the big man was up to the task ahead as once his work began to make a name, its value would rocket.

"Mental note to self," he whispered. "Get Gerome to sign a contract."

Chapter 17

Ezekiel:

Gerome got into his van and made his way across Paris. He stopped at a high-rise apartment building ringed by a forest of similar buildings, in northeast Paris. The area had a reputation of being edgy and populated with gangs. Riots would sometimes break out when police intervened in internal gang disputes and then shots might ring out and parked cars would be turned over and set alight. The trouble was often over almost as quickly as it started, and children playing in the burnt out shell of a torched vehicle might be the only evidence of conflict. The top floor, one bedroom apartment, belonged to his wife Marie, who had inherited it from an aunt. She and Gerome let it to subsidize their income and provide a pension nest egg. The rental for the run-down apartment wasn't much, so he was delighted when an illegal immigrant, a talented artist from an island in the Indian Ocean, who needed somewhere to stay, had agreed to his proposal of paintings plus cash in exchange for rent. Now it looked like his gamble was about to pay off. In a couple of days he would be twenty thousand richer, maybe more - if he could squeeze the Englishman until he squeaked and coughed up more cash. He made his way up the stairs. There was a small lift in the building but more often than not it was out of service. And even if it did work, an unfortunate passenger might find themselves trapped for hours, between floors, a few stories up.

Gerome stopped halfway up and sucked in air tainted by cat urine and heavily spiced cooking. He retched noisily both from the effort of climbing the stairs and from inhaling the pungent odour. He spat just outside an apartment doorway. Seconds later, a woman opened the door and began to scold in a loud voice. Gerome turned towards her. He opened his mouth wide and roared like a lion. She ducked back inside, closed the door and bolted the chain across. Gerome chuckled and made his way up to the top floor.

Gerome banged on the door of the flat. When no one responded he sighed and fished through his coat pockets for a bunch of keys. He selected a slim silver key and inserted it in the lock. He turned it and the door swung lazily open. Gerome sniffed the air. Where the hell had Ezekiel conjured up enough money for weed? Was the rent he was charging too low?

There was enough room in the hall to hang a coat on the one peg affixed to the wall, a bag of shopping could be placed in the corner and then, not even considering the impact of a human's presence, the hallway would be considered crowded. He glanced around the living room, which he could see from the hallway.

"Bastard, where are you?" Gerome whistled through clenched teeth. Ezekiel could be difficult and given to histrionics if a painting didn't work out as planned, or if he imagined his landlord had weaselled to the immigration authorities about his whereabouts. Gerome hoped he hadn't bottled out and returned to one of the foyers where many immigrants were housed. A year ago, on a trip through a foyer, looking for odds and ends to sell at the market, Gerome had discovered Ezekiel sitting on the ground, with all his belongings at his feet. A fellow countryman, who was legal and in possession of papers, had taken pity on Ezekiel, who had slipped into the country on a cargo boat and had no such papers. When Ezekiel had misunderstood his gesture of kindness for something else and had made a move on him, he'd been ejected onto the street.

Gerome, like most French, had been trained from a young age to appreciate art. The first thing he noticed when he drove down the street was the array of wonderful paintings surrounding the young man. Gerome had done a deal with him and offered the apartment, which had just been vacated, at a cash rent with several paintings a month thrown in. The deal had worked well for both, barring Ezekiel's occasional bouts of nerves regarding his illegal status. Gerome had ticked along nicely, selling the paintings almost as soon as he'd displayed them on the stall.

Gerome heard a cough coming from the bedroom. "*Merde*, still in bed. Lazy dog," he shouted. He opened the bedroom door and found the room shrouded in smoke. Ezekiel lay in bed wheezing and coughing. Gerome rushed over and threw open the window. Smoke billowed out, allowing Gerome to locate Ezekiel's prone figure.

"Don't do that! Leave it shut," Ezekiel squeaked.

"Are you trying to commit suicide? Crazy pig."

"Pig, dog. Make up your mind," Ezekiel croaked.

"I need paintings. You know, works of art of the painted variety," Gerome said fiercely. "And you're lying on your lazy arse, trying to kill yourself."

"I'm sick," Ezekiel whispered. "Get me water."

Gerome grumbled under his breath and then went to the kitchen. He returned with two glasses of water. Ezekiel gulped one down.

"Thank you. I needed that."

"*Mais certainment*. Your lungs are full of smoke – or grass, more likely, you fool. Of course you can't breathe."

Ezekiel shook his head. "I have a cold. I'm burning incense."

The smoke had cleared and Gerome could see, dotted around the room, more than a dozen incense burners.

"You crazy guy. Why so many?"

"Got a deal on these. Job lot at the market. My cold's been lingering. Thought I'd kill it off once and for all."

"Kill yourself off, more likely," Gerome grumbled. "But what about your paintings, how many do you have? Ten or fifteen, maybe?"

"Three or four. I've been sick."

Gerome threw his hands up in exasperation. If he didn't need Ezekiel to paint at double speed then he might just wrap his hands around his skinny throat and finish him off.

"Have a look in the living room," Ezekiel croaked. "Take what you want."

140

Gerome went into the living room. Leaning against the wall were three paintings in Ezekiel's usual style, with a touch of added genius. Fuck, Gerome muttered to himself, he was good!

He went back to the bedroom. Ezekiel gave him a wan smile. "If you'd do me the favour of closing the window, I might have a nap."

Gerome reached over and grabbed him by the collar of his shirt. "I need more paintings by tomorrow," he hissed. "No time for sleep."

Ezekiel, who had never seen such a volcanic rage welling up in anyone before, nodded.

Gerome was thoughtful as he left the apartment. For twenty thousand, he sighed, such a lot of work.

Chapter 18

They had just started on the main course. Despite Liam's resolution not to permit a drop of alcohol to cross his lips, he was already halfway through the third glass of a good Merlot, courtesy of Borivoj. The Czech had arrived glowing and triumphant, carrying a bag from the delicatessen, *Fauchon*. One by one, like a master magician, he revealed the bag's treats: two bottles of red wine, a Spanish goat's cheese, several slices of *jamon iberico* and a box of *marrons glaces*. Liam experienced a pang of jealousy when Alouette's face lit up as the contents were unveiled. Borivoj knew how to please a woman, he, for some reason unknown to himself, didn't.

Liam speared a piece of beef with his fork. He groaned and rolled his eyes.

"This is so delicious. Can't remember when I last ate so well."

"You've forgotten yesterday evening already then?" She shot a glance at him, then lowered her eyes and blushed.

Borivoj glared at Liam. He leaned towards him and narrowed his eyes. "Yesterday evening?"

Liam ran a hand through his hair, playing for time. From the moon eyes Borivoj was making at Alouette, Liam was sure he had a crush on her. He wiped his mouth with the stiff white linen napkin by his plate, which matched the starched tablecloth. He set the napkin down on the table, noticing that Alouette was staring at the brown blemish he'd made on the pristine material. He picked it up and put it on his knee, out of Alouette's line of vision. Christ, Liam said to himself, the napkin's for show, not for use.

He asked himself why Alouette had arranged such a formal dinner party between friends, particularly since she wasn't a serious cook. As far as he could tell her kitchen was rarely used for real cooking. She was adept at throwing together quick meals: pasta with aromatic sauces, breads, cheeses, pates and salads. She ate a bite or two of croissant in the morning, no apparent lunch, and an evening meal that wouldn't satisfy a gnat. He hoped all of this table paraphernalia, candles and the elaborate casserole wasn't in his honour. And he was equally suspicious of the mood music playing in the background. The Django Reinhardt Hot Club de France recording created a much too intimate atmosphere. He liked the music: violin and guitar with a soft background of horn and base. It was music that made him feel he'd been transported to the romantic Paris of the nineteen thirties. However, the particular album Alouette had chosen was slow and dreamy, perhaps too romantic for a dinner among friends. It was the type of music slyly played by a seducer to create a bewitching atmosphere, and best accompanied by a fine brandy or liqueur, warming the listener and lightening inhibitions.

"I'm confessin' that I love you." Alouette's face was flushed as she spoke. Liam dropped his fork on the edge of his plate. It clattered and his face reddened too. He glanced at Borivoj who had set both knife and fork on his plate and was slumped back in his chair. Alouette laughed. "The tune playing now: I'm confessin' that I love you. Django Reinhardt and Stephane Grapelli. Such fine guitar and violin, don't you think?"

Liam and Borivoj nodded in unison. Borivoj gave a small cough. "Yesterday evening... Liam?"

"We went out for a meal. A celebration, you could say."

"Good news?"

"A good deal, I hope. A business deal. It might lead to a new career."

"In England?"

Liam detected a hopeful note in the question. "No. I'm staying put. Here in Paris. I'm hoping to sell paintings. Deal in art, if you like. It's bad luck to say too much at this early stage – the deal is still in its infancy – but I might be onto a winner. Alouette shared my good fortune yesterday. We had a meal at that little bistro round the corner."

"I have walked past but never entered."

"It's expensive, but as I said, it was a celebration."

Borivoj turned to Alouette. "Ravishing. You look lovely. And such a nice meal you prepare. You are too kind to friends." He gave Liam a pointed look. For the first time that evening, Liam noticed the extra effort Alouette had made. Her bob was sharper, edgier. Her eyes were lined with sea-blue rather than black and her coral lipstick matched the silk scarf casually draped round her neck. The charcoal trouser suit she wore looked new. It suited her. The jacket, nipped at the waist, lent contours his hands hadn't detected the night before. He felt a wave of guilt. Alouette gave Borivoj a nod, acknowledging the compliment. Borivoj turned to Liam, a glint in his eye.

"I'm curious about you. Tell us about life in England – and Ireland. You don't say much about yourself." Borivoj's face lengthened with each swig of wine. He was trying to trip him up, Liam realised, so he decided to be as truthful as possible.

"I started out in Belfast. We – my mother and I – lived with my grandparents. They argued a lot, mainly about religion, about going to church and all that. I don't remember much else about my early years there as we left when I was two or three. But I have vivid memories of London. The size of it! A city with no start and no end, that's what it felt like. There were bright red double-decker buses everywhere. Streets and houses packed as sardine cans with people. For a treat we ate fish and chips seasoned with salt and vinegar or on a really good day we had chicken curry. We didn't eat fancy food like this...although I suppose the stew my mother used to make from scrag-end neck of lamb is a poor cousin."

"Scrag-end?" Alouette asked.

"Cheap meat," Liam said wryly.

"So you were not always rich?" Borivoj asked.

"I was never rich, in fact, we were the opposite of rich."

Liam took a deep breath. He was transported back to the winter he'd spent on a boat as a boy. His mother's boyfriend at the time had agreed to put them up when they were evicted from their flat. It was a bleak winter, the ground, sea and sky had taken on a grey colour. The lock on the tiny wooden door was broken so the door constantly swung open. Wind howled through the saloon, which was in reality not much bigger than a standard bathroom. The heating on the boat didn't work so they warmed their hands in front of a small electric heater. Liam recalled the pleasure that seeped through his body when it was his turn to stand in front of the heater.

There were two cabins. His tiny berth was located in the front V of the boat. At night time, when he curled up in his bunk, he listened to the wind whipping up until it gave a piercing whistle. Waves slapped against the side of the boat as he lay in the womb-like space. He had been comforted rather than frightened by the noise.

Liam took a few sips of wine. Feeling more relaxed, he leaned back in his chair and gave Alouette and Borivoj a rough outline of his childhood. He told of growing up without a father. He recounted how he and his mother had moved from home to home. Liam described how the fear in his belly grew, like a fast spreading cancer, as he saw paperwork mount up. Bills neatly stacked up in chronological order on a hall table. His mother was a good housekeeper so order was her priority – but the bills were never paid.

Liam fixed his eyes on a loose stitch in the fabric of the tablecloth as he spoke. He knew every twist of thread in that stitch yet he didn't know who his father was. He looked up at his dinner companions. Alouette was staring at him, an unmistakable look of love in her eyes. Borivoj, clearly embarrassed by Liam's frank reply to his question, turned his head away. Liam wondered why he had given so much detail. It suddenly dawned on him that Borivoj, with his dark beard and sober clothes, had the look of a priest. He had rarely been to confession, but his revelations about his childhood had lifted a weight from his chest. Liam began to laugh.

"What?" Borivoj said, annoyed.

"We all have our tales of woe. I didn't mean to depress you with mine. Anyway, the story gets better. I learnt a hard lesson which I never forgot. I was determined never to be poor again so I made my own small fortune, which I lost again. But those are the breaks."

"You will recover," Alouette said gently. "Remember your business meeting."

"I'm looking forward to that. Should be a productive night."

"I could come with you. Help with the language."

"He speaks English. Best if I go alone," Liam said, concluding that honesty was not always the best policy.

Later, Liam helped Alouette with the washing up. From time to time he stole glances at her. What was she thinking, he wondered? He knew exactly what was on his mind: sealing airtight deals with Gerome and the American woman. The first of many, he hoped. If there was a god, and he wasn't sure there was, no one would take him for a mug again. Still, his heart rate increased and his penis stirred as he pictured the flesh and blood Claudine. She was the icing on the cake.

He put the dishcloth down and yawned.

"Fantastic dinner, thank you. I think I'll turn in now."

"The bedroom is more comfortable."

"I'm exhausted. Is it okay if I bunk on the sofa?"

There was a flicker in Alouette's eyes. Hurt, disappointment, certainly not relief.

"What about a brandy and some jazz first?"

"I'm still a bit tired – the flu took it's toll – and there's the business meeting. I need to rest up."

"Of course," she said, biting her lip. He concluded that there had been more than one knockback in Alouette's life. He vaguely remembered her talking about an Englishman she had been in love with, but then he had dropped off to sleep. Right now he was worried she was becoming too attached to him. He would have to walk a delicate tightrope as, for the immediate present, he didn't want to hurt her and he needed to keep her onside. He had reached rock bottom when Will's telegram had arrived. Now he was on the cusp of something good, the first rung of the ladder back up again. Alouette's emotions he hoped he could manage.

Borivoj's resolution:

It was a fine evening and Borivoj's pace was slow as he strolled home. He had drunk wine and brandy and he was in a mellow, yet at the same time melancholy mood. Despite the soft light of the street lamps, the stars were easily visible as they twinkled against the blackness of space. The dinner had been superb: good company, mainly Alouette's, and equally good food, so why did he have this dull ache in his belly? He was, he finally admitted to himself as he passed a couple smooching in the street, falling for Alouette. Until this moment he had suppressed his feelings, even from himself. After all, Alouette was old enough to be his mother. But she had been kind and generous towards him in a way no one else in this city which seemed to be reserved for lovers had been. She had stopped and chatted and had bought him coffee when he was working on the street. He found her very attractive but was that enough? Perhaps he felt this way toward her because he was lonely and missed home? He badly missed his mother's roast pork with dumplings and her cabbage soup which warmed him on the coldest of winter days.

    He would have loved to hop onto a train bound for Prague, with Alouette in tow, but the thought of losing face haunted him. This was a fate he knew had befallen emigrants before him. They arrived in their city of choice, found themselves outsiders, excluded from good jobs, living in poor accommodation. Many had left home basking in a sea of celebration and good wishes. They were going to make their fortune, the world was their oyster. Reality was different, yet the shame of failure prevented them from returning and seeking comfort in the bosom of their family and friends. The hope of money versus the reality of community, in his eyes there was no competition, yet he still couldn't pluck up the courage to go home.

    He suspected that Alouette and Liam were having an affair. She was fragile and he hoped that Liam would be gentle with her. Despite calling Liam a friend, he didn't trust him. Borivoj had noticed how detached the Englishman was with her, yet she had thrown loving glances at him. And a glint had appeared in Liam's eye when he'd mentioned his business dinner. If it was truly a business dinner, Borivoj reasoned, why wouldn't he have wanted to bring Alouette, who was classy and personable and who would have been an asset. Why the secrecy?

"Well Liam, if you're being secretive, two can play this game," he said aloud, to no one and everyone.

He resolved to follow Liam to his business meeting to see if he was up to no good. He hoped not. Alouette was special and she deserved, at the very least, loyalty.

Borivoj stuck his hands in his pockets and made his way down a dimly lit, seedy side street, to the tenement where he lived.

Chapter 19

Liam tucked away his guilt. A bird in the hand's worth two in the bush, he told himself. But then he realised that this saying didn't apply to him as very soon he would have two birds - and wasn't sure how to juggle them without causing upset and mayhem. He was looking forward to his date with Claudine so much he couldn't help humming 'It must be love' under his breath while he dressed. Earlier, he'd gone to a nearby barber's. Patches of scalp, the size of a twopence piece, glinting in the mirror had startled him. His hair was his crowning glory, his best feature. While he had his hair, there was hope. He cursed Will once again for his duplicity and for causing him stress.

He put on his blue shirt and his only pair of jeans. He had observed Parisian street fashion and noted that men of all ages seemed to wear these on semi-formal occasions, giving the wearer an air of not trying too hard. Somehow, he reflected, as he studied himself in the mirror, the men he'd seen had carried the look off better than he did.

Alouette narrowed her eyes and took a long look at him when he went into the living room to say goodbye. She was drinking coffee. She put her cup on the coffee table and cocked her head sideways.

"Hmm…I think the expression is 'you scrub up well'."

"Well done, Alouette. You're remembering much more English now. Practically fluent, at least I've been of some use." He pointed to his jeans. "I need to make a good impression. Does this work?"

"Not too bad," she said in a low voice. "When will you be back?"

"Late. Don't wait up." He gave a smile which he realised was too wide, too forced, and hoped she hadn't noticed. He wasn't good at juggling women's feelings. He shivered inside as he remembered his mother and his ex-wife and how needy both had been. Women, with their fluctuating hormones, innuendos and inability to be direct, were too complex, in his experience. Would Claudine be the exception to this rule?

He made his way to the metro with long, lazy steps, savouring the notion of a night out and the sweetness of the impending tryst. Gerome had phoned earlier. He had arranged for Claudine to meet Liam in a small bar in the Haut Marais district, an upmarket area in central Paris. After dinner, they were to take a taxi to La Villette, the suburb where Gerome lived. Then, Gerome's voice had turned conspiratorial, after their deal was concluded, the night belonged to Liam and Claudine.

It was early evening and the sky was shaded in warm purple. He shoved his guilt to one side again and allowed himself to daydream about Claudine. Would she be even more lovely in real life than she was in her painting? And he wondered what was behind the come-hither smile as she posed. Surely that smile hadn't been for Gerome? Perhaps she was thinking of a past, or even future, lover. He grinned as he realised that this might be him. After he'd completed the deal with the American woman he would be around eighty thousand euro richer. Enough to buy freedom, maybe rent a small but luxurious apartment in central Paris while he worked out his business plan. He'd remain friends with Alouette but wouldn't have to depend on handouts from her. From past experience, Liam knew that generosity came with a price.

Claudine was already there when he entered the bar. She was seated at a table for two, trailing her fingers up and down the stem of her wine glass. Her eyes were focussed on the glass so he lingered by the door for a moment and watched her. He wasn't the only man doing this. The eyes of several customers standing at the bar were fixed on her. One of the men: average and middle-aged, brown hair, five foot ten, medium build, no facial hair, probably a wife and kids at home, crouched like a tiger awaiting the opportunity to pounce on prey. Liam wasn't surprised. Women of Claudine's beauty and quality were rarely alone and available. All eyes shifted back to the bar as Liam went over to the table and sat down. The disappointment of Claudine's admirers was audi-

ble: low sighs, shuffling where there had been none before, a barked request for a drink to soothe the pain of rejection. Claudine looked up.
"You must be the Englishman."
Liam nodded. "Irish, actually."
He smiled, although in reality he wanted to gasp as her real life beauty had winded him, sucked the breath from his body. She was his ideal woman: Sophia Loren, Jane Birkin and Brigitte Bardot rolled into one fabulous female. He leaned over.
"May I?"
"It's custom."
He kissed her on each cheek and made a mental note to thank Alouette for explaining the kissing etiquette, but he doubted she'd be impressed he was testing it out on a woman like Claudine. With Parisian women, when you first meet, you begin with two kisses and then, once you become familiar with the woman, you work up to three and finally four, Alouette had explained. Claudine's skin was soft, with the texture and scent of a ripe peach, so he hoped he would work up to four quickly.
"Pleased to meet you...at last, Claudine."
She gave a small laugh, a trill that came from the back of her throat.
"Can I get you another drink?" Liam noticed that the glass, which her long fingers tipped by blood-red nails was caressing, was empty. She shook her head.
"I'll wait for dinner."
Liam was impressed. Perhaps he was jumping in head first, but he preferred his steady women to drink little. A glass of wine here and there, like Alouette and the other French women he'd briefly encountered. He'd walked down the Champs-Elysées late at night many times but had never once noticed a drunk or scantily dressed woman. He compared that to running the gauntlet on city centre streets back home on a Saturday night. Like comparing World War One to a minor spat between children.

"Are you hungry now? Would you like to eat?"

The restaurant Gerome had recommended was decorated in warm colours with soft seating, candles and pink cotton tablecloths. The dining area was large and square with no hidden nooks or crannies. Tables were neither too close to each other nor too far apart. A comfortable yet neutral space, unlike the bistro where he and Alouette had eaten. That had been too romantic and, on top of that, he had made the mistake of reserving the most secluded table. No wonder Alouette had picked up the wrong signals.

He ordered the starter: foie gras for himself and mussels for Claudine. They ate in virtual silence, commenting only on the food, although Claudine appeared more interested in playing with the shells of the mussels than consuming their contents.

"Is everything OK?" he asked. He was suddenly concerned at her meditative air. Was she thinking of someone else and had his dream date taken a wrong turn already? He wanted to reach out and brush his fingers across her arm, just to validate she was real. Would her skin be cool to the touch, as though she had just stepped off the canvas and hadn't had time to take on warm blooded human form? It crossed his mind that Claudine might have interpreted this as a move. The last thing he wanted to do was to alienate her, so he resisted the urge.

"It's superb," she replied. "Good choice of restaurant." Liam mentally thanked Gerome for suggesting it.

"I love the painting of you. Enchanting."

Claudine smiled. "Gerome told me you bought it. I'm flattered."

"No need to be. You're very beautiful. I hope you don't mind me saying so."

She shrugged and took a sip of wine. He was worried. He had a patter, a selection of phrases he used to seduce women. He had tried a couple on Claudine and none seemed to work. Lost in translation, he assumed. Claudine was self-possessed in a way that few women were and didn't seem to care for trivial conversation. He wasn't used to strong, silent women. Searching for a topic that might interest her, his mind flickered back to the dinner table conversation with Alouette and Borivoj. Then, he had felt much more at ease.

"Tell me about yourself," he said. "What do you do for a living?"

She raised her eyebrows. "This and that."

"I know you're a model. Do you model clothes as well...?" Liam's voice trailed away. A coldness in her eyes told him she didn't want to pursue that line of questioning.

"Yes, yes. I do that sometimes."

"How did you meet Gerome?"

"I posed for a friend of his."

"And you posed for Gerome too."

"Yes, of course, Gerome painted me."

"I'll commission another painting of you," he said grandly.

She smiled and her dimples showed. He instantly forgave her poor conversational ability. After all, when a woman looked like that, he remarked to himself, she would hardly need to fine tune her social skills.

He took over the dinner conversation, telling her about his antiques business and how he had built it up. He neglected to tell her about his failures: the potential bankruptcy and the disastrous deal he'd done with Will. He was thinking of dealing in art as a sideline, he explained. Perhaps he'd stay here in Paris, rent a luxury apartment and live the good life.

Claudine smiled and nodded at the right bits, but he couldn't tell if the fishing expedition was successful and he was managing to reel her in. They finished their main course and he called the waiter over.

"A bottle of Moet. Bring it with dessert," he said, keeping one eye on Claudine, who giggled girlishly. He smiled back. Her laugh reminded him of the melodic pealing of church bells. He was, he realised, already besotted.

"Champagne with dessert? You're extravagant."

"Nothing but the best for you." Normally he would have been proud of this patter, but he suspected Claudine was accustomed to big spenders. He would need to deal fast and hard to hold onto her.

They each drank two glasses of champagne and he asked for the bill. He looked regretfully at the half-full bottle. A week's wages, gone in a matter of minutes. Still, he needed to keep a level dealing head as Claudine was enough of a distraction.

He took a heavy brown envelope from his inside pocket and set it on the table. The jeweller had paid cash for the brooch so the envelope bulged with one, two and five hundred euro notes. A well padded envelope such as this was a familiar sight for Liam. Large amounts of cash were commonplace at auctions, where the thickness of the wallet or envelope defined the success of the dealers, at least in each other's minds.

When the bill arrived, he scanned it, consciously ignoring the large sum printed at the bottom. Claudine was watching and he didn't want her to think of him as a skinflint, or even worse, a flimflammer. He removed several notes from the envelope, inserting them inside the embossed folder the bill was presented in. Claudine's eyes widened. He smiled to himself, finally she seemed impressed.

"May I," she reached her hand out and lightly touched the envelope. "I have never seen so much money in one place."

He nodded. She took the notes out and flicked a finger across the edge of the notes. She laughed, curled them over and inserted the notes between her breasts. Liam's eyes bulged as he watched the tip of the notes disappear between the two globes.

"That's Gerome's money."

"Yes, yes, I know. Just a game. Besides, it's safer here than in an envelope. You can take it out later."

He flushed, uncomfortable with Claudine's game, yet he didn't want to appear less than cool. Claudine was out of his league, used to major players, he suspected, but then she smiled and reached out her hand, entwining it in his.

They left the restaurant hand in hand. Every inch of his

body tingled with desire. He wanted to rip his clothes off then and there, but there was the deal to think about first, that had to be his priority. They got into a taxi, Liam gripping Claudine's hand tightly as he didn't want to lose either his money or the possibility of hot sex.

Twenty minutes later, the taxi pulled up in front of a seventies style apartment building in the Nineteenth Arrondisement. He stared up at the block of flats: this could be any big city, anywhere in the world. Claudine reached over and opened the taxi door. She gave him a gentle shove.

"Go on. It's perfectly quiet here. I know the area well."

"Not many people around."

"If you think this is scary," she laughed, "wait till you meet Gerome's wife. A real fishwife if ever you saw one."

He got out of the taxi, still gripping Claudine's hand. She pressed the apartment buzzer with her free hand. There was a sound of footsteps hurrying down the stairs and the door opened. An unsmiling middle-aged woman, who appeared to be expecting them, ushered them upstairs to a large dowdy living room. Gerome was on a sofa in the centre of the room, watching TV. His wife pointed to the sofa and Liam and Claudine sat down. He was relieved when she turned off the television as the rapid French at high volume made his head spin. He took a sly glance round the room. It was decorated in a mishmash of styles with the predominant colour being a dirty olive shade.

"A drink?" Gerome asked.

"Coffee, if you don't mind."

"I have to go to the bathroom," Claudine said. She stood up and followed Gerome out of the room.

Liam balanced his coffee cup on his knee, trying not to yawn. He cursed himself for combining romance and business and hoped that would be the only mistake of the evening. In the past, he'd made a point of not bringing girlfriends to auctions. He'd once lost the plot and had bid too much for a Victorian glass bowl when his girlfriend at the time had nuzzled up and licked his neck.

The paintings were stacked up in three lots of seven against the living room wall. Gerome pointed to them. "Twenty-one. One extra for good luck."

Liam drained his coffee cup. Gerome's wife was an odd fish who darted cold glances at him with her pale blue eyes, but she made a good cup of coffee. As the caffeine hit took effect, he recalled exactly why he was here. Dealing, that was the real point of the evening. Claudine was a sideline, albeit a lovely one.

"I need to take a look." He got up from the sofa and went over to the paintings. At the front of each bundle was a landscape. One was a desert scene, so truly painted he sensed the burning heat of the sand under the soles of his feet. Simple colours: burnished yellow, ochre and blue, yet applied with such a subtle hand, the essence and soul of the desert had been captured. The canvas at the front of the second bundle depicted a garden filled with flowers, tightly planted, blooms jostling for space: tulips, pansies, irises, daffodils. A feeling of joy swept over Liam. If only he could step into the canvas, inhale the perfume of the flowers, bathe himself in colour. For a moment he imagined the air in the musty room was filled with a flowery scent, then he moved on. The third painting was a park scene, with children playing and women sitting on benches. One was reading, while the eyes of the others kept watch over their charges. He shook his head in disbelief. How could one man possess so much talent? All the paintings were stunning, but they were also very commercial. Liam had no doubt the American woman, would snap up every single one, and then beg for more.

He glanced over at Gerome.

"Can you untie the bundles, please?" Liam's voice became commanding, an actor addressing his audience. He was in deal mode and could taste the profit to be made. It was sweet on his tongue, a rich sponge cake crammed with clotted cream and topped with strawberries. He suppressed a smile for he would have his cake and eat it too.

"It's late. I don't have time for chitchat." Gerome gave a

dismissive wave towards the paintings. "Take them now and go."

"Not before I see them all."

Gerome got up and moved to where Liam stood. He pressed his face inches from Liam's. A wary Liam took a step back.

"What's the matter? Can you open the bundles, please – or you won't get your money."

Gerome narrowed his eyes. "Maybe I'm selling too cheap. Ten thousand more. Thirty thousand and you take my paintings. That's a fair price."

"No way. Stick to our agreement or no deal."

"Our agreement?" Gerome began to laugh. His wife entered the room and joined in with the merriment.

"Are you both crazy?" Liam fiddled with the complex knot of the rope tied round one of the bundles. Finally he loosened it and extracted a painting. He drew a sharp breath as he recognised it as one of the inferior paintings he'd seen days ago on Gerome's stall.

"I told you I wasn't interested in these."

"You shouldn't have bought them then," Gerome said.

"Fuck you." Liam moved closer to Gerome. "You'll not get a penny."

Gerome reached out a calloused hand and shoved Liam backwards. He toppled onto the dusty olive carpet. Gerome helped him up.

"I owe you at least this," Gerome said as Liam brushed flecks of dust and dirt from his clothing. Liam shook his head.

"I'm off. Leaving with my cash – you'll not get a penny..." He paused. Something was out of place; it was as though the earth had tilted on its axis or a parallel universe had suddenly revealed itself. He had been here a while, hadn't he? Claudine had gone to the bathroom minutes after they'd arrived, how could he not have missed her? Were Gerome's paintings such a distraction they'd dulled the sheen of her hair, made him forget her come-hither eyes, covered over her large breasts.

He pictured her breasts: soft as goose-down pillows. A feeling of dread wormed its way through his body. Her beautiful breasts. The last time he'd seen his money was when she'd tucked the notes between them. He glanced at Gerome. The smirk on his face told Liam that not only was Claudine not in the room, she was no longer in the apartment.

"Claudine?" he said weakly.

"Gone," Gerome replied, clicking his fingers.

The sweet taste of profit turned immediately sour on his tongue. Both the paintings *and* Claudine had bewitched him. Now the spell had lifted.

"All a scam?" Liam whispered. How could he have been so naïve, not spotted this outcome?

Gerome smiled and nodded his head vigorously. "No problem, my little Englishman. For a mere ten thousand more, you can take your paintings. All three of them. I'll throw in the others if you want them. I'm an honest man."

"Bastard. You've stolen my twenty thousand, now you want ten thousand more!"

"Good deal, no?"

Liam felt his anger rise, adrenaline coursed through his veins. He launched himself at Gerome. They scuffled and threw punches in the living room, then rolled into the hallway. Liam heard a crack. A pain shot across his head. When he looked up, Marie was standing over him clutching a baseball bat.

"*Connard*...get out and don't come back," she taunted.

Gerome opened the apartment door and shoved Liam into the hallway.

"You heard her. Don't come near us again."

"My paintings…"

"*Je m'en fou.* You forfeited the right to these paintings. I was willing to be reasonable but you had to be greedy." He hauled Liam down the stairs and ejected him onto the street.

Earlier that evening, Borivoj had followed Liam to the metro. He wore a long overcoat which he knew Liam had never seen, and a dark blue baseball cap. He felt important, like a detective trailing a suspect. Perhaps that would be his next job. Fishing was out of the question and he was tiring of street performance with its poor financial rewards. His basket of tricks was becoming exhausted and even though he sat at his pitch day after day, trying to drum up new moves, his mind was a blank canvas. He was an artist whose creativity was as dried up as a bunch of shrivelled flowers. Perhaps the gods, along with his mother, were sending him a wake up call, telling him it was time to return home. Maybe he would set himself up as a private eye and tell potential clients of his escapades in Paris and his rich and important clients. He would get Alouette to write a reference for him. His clients in Besiny and the surrounding districts would be none the wiser.

He got into the carriage next to Liam's and watched him through the window. He needn't have worried about the disguise as Liam was deep in thought. Liam had been in such a daze, he'd only just made it out of his carriage at the last minute, leaving Borivoj to briefly become trapped in the doors as he tried to follow him. He trailed Liam out of the metro and found himself in one of Paris' high-class districts. He remained around ten metres behind as Liam made his way down the street. Liam was easy to follow. He was wearing jeans that sagged at the knee and curved in a bell shape at the bottom, not like the slim designer jeans most Parisian men wore. He noted that Liam had been to the barbers, his hair seemed tidier than usual.

Liam went into a bar and Borivoj waited outside. After around fifteen minutes, he became impatient. He pulled his hat low, over his eyes, as he prepared to enter the bar. At the same time, Liam exited arm in arm with a very attractive young woman. The woman was so striking Borivoj forgot he was supposed to be undercover. He stood motionless as a statue, staring at the woman's ample bosom as she edged past. Liam, fortunately, was also similarly distracted and didn't notice him.

Borivoj followed the couple to an showy restaurant. He

cursed Liam when he recalled that only a couple of nights before, the Englishman had escorted Alouette to an equally pricey establishment. Borivoj settled in a bar opposite and ordered a coffee. From the looks of the woman, it was going to be a long meeting.

He finished his third coffee and boredom had set in. The bar gradually emptied and the one remaining barman began stacking chairs on tables. Borivoj debated gate crashing Liam's dubious meeting. If Liam was enraged to see him, he would smile sweetly and comment on the long odds of running into him. The woman was almost too beautiful to be true. Borivoj remembered seeing her portrait when he and Alouette had rescued the then ill Liam from his hotel room. He now wished they hadn't bothered. If Alouette was wounded then it was his fault for introducing such a callous bastard into her life. Borivoj paid for his coffees and positioned himself in a doorway opposite the restaurant.

Half an hour later, Liam and the woman left the restaurant. As they lingered on the pavement, Liam, who was clearly tipsy, made snapping gestures, like a crocodile, with his hand. They both laughed heartily at the game and when a taxi pulled up in front of the restaurant, they climbed into the back seat.

There was no point in following them, Borivoj decided. He now knew that Liam was up to no good and, as he had suspected, the meeting was a sham. Poor Alouette.

Chapter 20

When Liam awoke he was in Alouette's bed. Despite the soft pillow, the rose perfumed sheets, the spongy mattress, all wasn't right with the world. A sensation of dread sat like a tumour, in his chest. He hoped he was in the throes of a bad dream, but memories of a fight, a blow to the head, and being shoved onto the pavement, were too vivid. He reached down, touched his right knee and winced. Was that where he'd cushioned his body when he'd fallen?

He tried to edge into a sitting position but pain drove his head back onto the pillow. He heard voices, raised and sharp: Alouette and Borivoj. He shut his eyes and kept them closed when they entered the room. Their voices dropped to a whisper and he strained to unravel their words. Alouette, he thought, was arguing that he should stay where he was. Borivoj, whose French accent at times was difficult to understand, appeared to argue in favour of his ejection. They left the room and he drifted back to sleep.

Alouette was sitting in the bedside chair when he opened his eyes again. "What...what happened?" he said.

"Mugged. You were mugged."

"A big man," he said after a moment's pause.

"A beautiful woman," she said dryly.

He reached up to his forehead and felt the wadding of a bandage.

"A man. I can only remember a man."

She gave him a severe look. "I can assure you it was a woman - the beautiful woman in that painting you're so fond of. Borivoj saw her with his own eyes."

Claudine. She'd been there too, of course she had. How could he have forgotten her dark, deceptive beauty? Then he remembered the vanishing act she'd pulled.

"My wallet. Was it on me?"

Alouette nodded. "It was. And it contained seventy euro, if that's what you're going to ask next."

He'd left Alouette's apartment with more money than that, much, much more. "Was there an envelope in my pocket. A big brown one."

Alouette shrugged. "I don't know anything about an envelope."

As he eased himself up, the evening before was playing back in his mind. A movie with a nightmarish focus, menacing yet fuzzy round the edges. The fuzziness cleared. Marnie. Was Claudine like Hitchcock's Marnie: a thief, frightened of men? He'd taken her lack of conversation for poor social skills but could she have been afraid? Afraid of him, afraid of Gerome, afraid of all men.

"Wait a minute," he said. "You said Borivoj was there. I don't remember being with him."

"He followed you. He didn't trust you. He was right not to do so, wasn't he?"

Liam nodded slowly. "That woman - I remember her now - we only had dinner, I swear to god. It was part of the business deal. I didn't want to tell you my meeting was with a woman. Didn't want you to feel insecure."

"Business deal. You and your fucking deals. Life is one long deal to you, isn't it? I suppose sleeping with me was part of some arrangement, some game you were playing."

"No, that's not true. You've been so kind."

"You're lucky you are still here. Borivoj was consoling me when a taxi dropped you off in a bloody state. Borivoj wanted to eject you and your luggage onto the streets immediately. I wouldn't do that to my worst enemy. Despite how much you have hurt me, Liam, you are not my worst enemy."

He lay back on the pillow.

"Thank you for rescuing me - again. I won't let you down this time."

"Don't think I've forgiven you. Borivoj is coming back in a day or two. We'll decide then what to do with you. In the meantime, sleep. I don't want to look into your untruthful eyes."

"I don't blame you." He shook his head, suddenly aware

of the human cost of his entanglements. Women weren't commodities to be bartered for, as he'd done with Claudine, or exchanged for a fancier model, as he had done with Alouette. Claudine ripping him off, he had probably deserved, but Alouette hadn't merited any of the fallout of his disastrous wheeling and dealing. He had no business hurting her. Another woman's face drifted into his consciousness. Elaine. Blonde hair and snub nose. He had to find her before she returned home. He drifted into oblivion.

Liam got out of bed. Borivoj was due at any moment so he dressed quickly. Elaine was on his mind. According to Alouette, he'd slept on and off for almost two days. Would the American still be in Paris or would she already have returned home? He searched for the card she'd pressed into his hand. He recalled inserting it into the back pocket of his trousers, but when he checked it wasn't there. *Hotel Aceline*, he was sure that was the name of her hotel and if he remembered correctly, it was in the fifth arrondissement. He resolved to make his way there, once the ordeal with Alouette and Borivoj was over.

   He frowned as he studied his face in the bathroom mirror. Bruising ebbed from the edges of the bandage Alouette had wrapped around his head, and his nose and cheeks were blotchy. Despite his injuries he had been lucky. Marie's swing with the baseball bat had missed its target: the top of his head. The cut on his forehead was small but bloody, Alouette had coldly informed him when she'd changed the bandage the night before. Despite the frosty tone, her touch was deft and gentle. When he'd tried to compliment her on her nursing skills and make light of his injury, her eyes had flashed and she'd sworn at him. Filthy words, he'd never have imagined she knew.

Liam lay on top of the bed, gathering his strength for the coming ordeal. He left the bedroom twice, once to go to the bathroom, the other to fetch a baguette and cheese from the kitchen. He did this hurriedly, as though the flat was no longer his sanctuary and he had no business being there. Not wanting to further anger Alouette, he took care to pick crumbs off the bedspread. He was a little frightened of her, he realised. Her features had distorted when she'd sworn at him. But it was her eyes, the mirror of the soul, which had shocked him most - they'd taken on a crazed look. What would happen if the cling-film of respectability encasing her, suddenly ripped. He doubted she was capable of lashing out physically as she was too refined and controlled. But Lily had also been quiet and demure when they'd first started dating. Only after their wedding did she permit her true colours to shine through. Was Alouette like Lily - one of the quiet ones you had to watch?

He became more and more unsettled as he waited. The unknown was worse that even a dreadful known. If you knew where you stood, you could always act to remedy a situation. Lolling around here was like being in limbo; there was nothing he could do, no plots to hatch or apology script to write. Finally footsteps clattered on the stairs and the front door lock of the flat clicked. Two sets of footsteps entered. He picked up a low hum of conversation, probably from the lounge. One set of footsteps proceeded along the hall to the kitchen. The fridge door opened, a saucepan lid clanged and the sticky oven door, sprang open and slammed shut. He surmised that Alouette was preparing lunch. His stomach growled and he hoped he would be invited to eat. Above all, he hoped he had been forgiven.

Over the next half hour, various delicious smells worked their way through the gap under the door: basil, cheese, pastry browning. He waited in anticipation but the bedroom door remained shut.

 He soothed his nerves by guessing what they might be eating: quiche Lorraine, broccoli, asparagus? The possibilities were endless. Finally, one set of spongy footsteps, neared the bedroom. He hurried to the window and casually leaned against the sill. The door handle turned and Borivoj entered. Today, Borivoj did not resemble a priest. With his black hair, dark sweater and sombre expression, Liam likened him to an executioner.

"Come to Alouette's salon," Borivoj beckoned. He straightened up and followed him.

"Sit there," Borivoj pointed to one of the dining table chairs. Alouette rose from the sofa and sat opposite Liam. Borivoj edged his chair close to her's.

"Judge and jury - it appears I'm on trial," Liam said playfully. His smile hid the dread creeping like a fungus through his body.

Alouette's eyes flickered from the table to the window. She rocked her elegant clasped hands back and forth, in small, barely noticeable movements. Borivoj's body seemed to expand and fill the room. Liam was quietly incensed. He'd suspected that Borivoj was in love with Alouette, so was he using the whole sorry incident to oust a love rival? Borivoj was the one in possession of a full set of cards and it looked like he was playing to win the game. He had Alouette's ear; he hadn't betrayed or let her down. Although he was aware that he had treated her badly, there was still a glimmer of hope that he might charm his way out of this mess.

More time - that was what was needed. Time to figure out how he would force Gerome to hand over the paintings he'd bought and paid for, fair and square. A deal was a deal and Gerome was a trader, surely he could win him round? He would tell him what a great artist he was; offer to help with marketing, exhibitions, publicity. Assure Gerome that with his help, he could become famous. With just a little more time he could contact the American woman and make that vital next sale. Time was the key to his future, his survival. If necessary, he would get down on his knees and beg Alouette's forgiveness. Borivoj spoke first.

"Alouette would like you to leave."

"What?"

"Go. Now. Today."

Liam had expected arguments, recrimination, even aggression on their part, and cajoling on his. He had not, in his wildest dreams, anticipated anything so direct.

"Maybe we can come to an arrangement?" he turned to Alouette, softening his eyes. Had she spotted the tear forming in the corner of one eye? "I'm willing to pay for my board. That would help towards your bills, wouldn't it? Make life a bit easier for you."

Borivoj shook his head. "Unless you have secret stash of money, you have grand total of fifty euro. The taxi fare was twelve and we gave driver the change from twenty for his troubles."

The air in the room was suddenly hot and suffocating. It seeped through his gaping mouth into his ears. There was no secret hoard of money. Almost everything he possessed had been stolen by Gerome: the proceeds from the sale of his mother's brooch, his paintings, his relationship with Alouette. All he had to show for his forty-something years was fifty measly euro. He gripped the table as the room began to spin. There was no question in Liam's mind, he had to stay here and he would say anything to make it possible.

"This is all so sudden," he said. "I'm sorry. I don't feel so well."

"Well enough to walk around. To plead. To lie. To cheat on Alouette."

"I'll do all the cleaning and washing up. I won't go out unless you come with me, Alouette. I'll be your willing prisoner. I swear I'll find a way to make money again."

"And then what would you do? Drop me for the first pair of young breasts and long legs that comes your way? Throw me on the scrap heap?"

"No, no," Liam protested. "I made a mistake and I'm sorry. Can't you forgive me?"

Borivoj looked at Liam gravely. "You must pack suitcase and go." He pointed to the door.

Liam shook his head. "Where…?"

"To England. To hotel room. To other country. We don't care."

"You care, don't you?" Liam attempted to place his hand

on top of Alouette's. She snatched it away and hurried from the room.

"Pack now," Borivoj's face was pale with fury. "I will sit here until you have departed."

"I'm still not well."

"Well enough to walk. Well enough to eat."

"Give me a second chance."

Borivoj's shook his head. He folded his arms and glared until Liam got up and left the room. He knocked on the bathroom door which Alouette had bolted behind her.

"You'll change your mind, give me another chance, won't you?" There was no reply, only the sound of snuffling, nose-blowing, then sobbing.

His energy depleted as a flat battery, Liam packed his suitcase. Almost all he had in the world was in this nylon and leather container. He glanced around the room which had been his sanctuary for the past few months. What he would give for another month in that soft bed, with its starched sheets and feather pillows! Thirty days of Alouette's breathing next to him, feeling her warmth. He willed himself not to be paralysed by fear. 'Look on the bright side, Liam' he muttered. He had two of Gerome's paintings. The deal he was about to conclude with Elaine was his sliver of sunshine, the route out of this mess.

He went over to the wardrobe, reached up and patted his hand along the top.

"Fuck. Where are they?" He dragged a chair over and stood on it. There was nothing on top of the wardrobe, not even a layer of dust. He climbed down and willed himself to breathe slowly, although his heart was beating so fast he thought it would spring from his chest.

"Where did I put them?" he said aloud as he checked behind the wardrobe and the chest of drawers. He bent down and peered into the empty dark space under the bed. It suddenly dawned on him that someone else had removed them. He hurried to the living room.

"My paintings. They're not where I left them."

Borivoj glared at him. "Alouette showed me secret. Hiding place."

"I need them. Now."

"I will keep for now. Safe and sound. But if you come back and bother Alouette, they will be destroyed. I know they mean a lot to you. More than Alouette and I."

"You've got the wrong end of the stick." He shook his head. If he could catch Elaine before she returned home, and make the sale, then he wouldn't be homeless.

Homeless: a word that sent a shiver down his spine. The image of the poor sods that lined the streets both in Paris and at home sprang to mind. He saw the soiled blankets round their shoulders, the only means of keeping the elements at bay, the expressions of despair plastered on their faces. How could this be happening? The thing he feared most in all the world was about to happen to him.

"No. Please," he began. Borivoj clenched his fists and stood up. He was head and shoulders taller than Liam and, given the beating Liam had received from Gerome and his wife, in far better shape.

"You must go."

Chapter 21

Alouette remained in the bathroom, seemingly unmoved by his pleas and whispered goodbyes through the door.

He pleaded again with Borivoj to return his paintings, but Borivoj was in bullish form, adamant he would return them only when he was certain Liam would not bother Alouette again.

"Send us postcard. We will mail to new address." He gripped Liam's arm with fingers stronger than a sturdy pair of pliers. "If you are planning on returning later, do not. I am staying here to care for Alouette." Borivoj's words were measured and calm, but the expression on his face was not. It dawned on Liam that an angry Borivoj was just as dangerous as Gerome.

He scribbled a note for Alouette and left it on the kitchen counter. He still cared for her, he wrote, and was sorrier than she could ever imagine for his appalling behaviour. There were no excuses, other than that of him being a weak man who had endured too many traumas in life. He added that he hoped she could find it in her heart to forgive him and asked her to intervene, to plead with Borivoj to return his paintings. They were all he had, a reminder of the good times the three of them had enjoyed.

He made his way down the street. He was still aching from the beating Gerome and his wife had inflicted, but for the first time in his life, he realised, he was free. Free from wheeling and dealing. He had no roof over his head so no one could take it away from him, as bailiffs and their masters had done in the past. And if there were only cents in his pocket, then no one could defraud him, nor could they pull a fast one in a business deal. Aside from the clothes in his suitcase, he was as he was brought into the world: without goods or possessions.

His new philosophical mood lasted only a few hours. A night on the nearby cold park bench, chasing away the occasional human vulture that came to prey on him, erased his newfound humility. He had time to reflect on the wrongs perpetrated by Gerome, Will, the women in the hotel, Claudine and now Borivoj. By dawn he was seething with rage. When it began to pour he hunkered down under a tree, wet and chilled to the bone. The rain stopped and he went to a bar - not the one with the red and white canvas canopy as he didn't want to bump into Alouette - and washed his face in a basin in the toilet. He changed into a wrinkled dry shirt and when he looked in the mirror, aside from a purple bruise across his forehead, he looked almost human.

Today was a day for rest and reflection, but tomorrow would be a new day, one that held a crumb of promise. A day to draw on courage reserves and break away from the circle of despair he'd once again been sucked into. He wondered if there was something wrong with his mind. Was a crucial decision-making part of his brain switched off? How many times of being duped and duped again would it take for him to learn his lesson? He was like a habitual criminal who hated prison cell walls - once freed, committing the same mistake again.

Liam stood at the reception desk of the Hotel Aceline. The lobby's polished marble floor reflected the sparkle of a large chandelier suspended from the ceiling. The chandelier would probably have cost more money than he'd made in a lifetime, where was the justice in that? The overall blondness of the space was broken up by plush red rugs embellished with golden dragons. Forgetting for an instant how out of place he looked, he drank in the opulence. This was like the reception area of many luxury hotels around the world: impersonal yet luxurious, a space where only the wealthy, accustomed to marble hallways, vast swimming pools and contrived luxuries, could relax, kick back, and feel at home. When he'd walked up to the front doors minutes earlier, the doorman had blocked his passage with a raised hand. Despite his scruffy appearance and the bandage round his head, largely hidden by a baseball cap, Liam had begun to protest. The doorman's eyes flickered suspicion and doubt. For all he knew, the man he had stopped was an eccentric tech billionaire, or a scruffy star maker in the manufactured music industry. He had lowered his hand long enough to allow him to slip by. When he arrived at the reception desk, he turned and saw the man's eyes were fixed on him.

"May I please help you, sir?" the receptionist asked in a surprisingly non-judgmental voice.

She was sleek, with dark hair pulled back into a bun, a shiny prison from which no tendril could escape. Her face was bare of make up aside from a slash of scarlet lipstick across her thinnish lips. The professional smile fixed on the young woman's face was not reflected in her eyes and Liam pictured her painting it on just before starting her shift. If he had been in the market for a PA she would have been a perfect candidate: detached, glossy, hard to read. He imagined she often came across customers who dressed in designer labels, wore flash jewellery and carried expensive luggage, who weren't what they seemed. Perhaps they were poor tippers or had slipped out, leaving behind an unpaid bill. On the other hand, apparently down and out clients, wearing ripped jeans and tee shirts, might have turned out to be rock stars or web billionaires. In a hotel such as this, appearances were deceptive and nothing could be taken for granted.

"I'm looking for a friend. Elaine..." he searched his mind for her surname. "American. Tall, blonde. Elaine."

"You don't know her full name?"

"Of course I do." He fiddled with his hair, willing the writing on Elaine's card to appear in his mind. "Richards. Elaine Richards. American."

She clicked on the keyboard of her computer several times and looked up at him. "I'm afraid Mrs Richards has checked out."

"When did she go?"

"Yesterday. She left a few days early."

"Do you know if she's still in Paris?"

The receptionist shook her head. "She ordered a taxi to take her to the airport. I believe she encountered an emergency and had to return to the United States. I can't tell you any more than that."

"Did she leave a phone number - or home address?"

The woman looked at him severely. "Now sir, I can't give out that information. Data protection."

He didn't argue, there was no point, besides the doorman had taken several paces closer to the desk. He gave a small nod of thanks and left the hotel. Things were bad, very bad, even if he recovered the paintings, he had no one to sell them to. He walked down the street deep in thought. With each step the wind cut through him and people averted their eyes. He imagined he had shrunk in size and that he was, in fact, becoming invisible.

He bought a tuna and olive baguette from a stall by the roadside. He counted the jingling loose change in his pocket and bought a coffee at an adjacent stall. He returned to the park. In the daylight it was a serene, green and non-threatening space, but he had become a night dweller and the world appeared to do a one hundred and eighty degree turn when the moon and stars came out. The peaceful space he now sat in would later become a place of shadows with malevolent creatures prowling, searching for victims. The sun which gave out intermittent bursts of heat, warming his bones, at night withdrew its favours, allowing its cold daughter moon to shed a frosty light. Morning or night, the fabric of the park was still the same. It had trees, benches, grass and flowerbeds. External forces, it seemed, changed the nature of a thing. He compared the park to himself: externally he had changed beyond recognition. If a former friend or auction adversary passed by at this very moment, they would walk on, turning their heads in the opposite direction, not realising it was him. But inside he was still the same man, determined never to be poor. He had always been, and still was, willing to walk over others to gain the upper hand in a deal. Now he would do anything, without exception, to claw his way back up again.

Elaine, he concluded, would not be the answer to his prayers. But in a city like Paris surely there would be a hundred, or even a thousand Elaines, who appreciated good art as much as he did?

Over the next few days, he alternated between sleeping and dodging rain showers. He slipped into survival mode, conserving energy for the next run in with Gerome. He lay on a bench and pictured their next meeting. The artist would hang in head in shame when confronted by him. Gerome would reach into his pocket or bag and take out a roll of notes, adding a few extra, before handing them over. Perhaps, to complete his act of contrition, he'd even throw in the three genuine paintings. Liam did not allow himself to consider another, more negative outcome.

His unwashed fair hair had darkened to the colour of a wet tea-bag, and when he looked in the mirror of the café he visited in the mornings, he noticed strands of white threading through. Once he spotted Alouette walking by the park. He longed to speak to her but was ashamed by his down-and-out appearance. She had seen him ill and ravaged by flu, but homelessness was another thing. Who but an idiot would give up a good woman's love for a foolish fling with a painting? There was also the possibility that where Alouette was, Borivoj would soon follow. He dipped into a doorway, but as she approached he saw that this subterfuge wasn't necessary. Her eyes were fixed on the grey paving stones, the expression on her face sombre. She had neglected to wear one of her array of jazzy scarves and that made him particularly sad.

When he had sufficiently recovered from his injuries, he made his way to the Place de la Concorde. He had no intention of visiting galleries and viewing paintings: his only purpose was to collar Gerome.

Gerome sat behind his stall smoking a fat cigar. He tipped his chair back and swung his feet onto the edge of the table. His body stiffened when he noticed Liam, who stood motionless as a beaten statue, on the other side of the stall.

"I want what's mine," Liam said hoarsely, forgetting his earlier intentions of disarming Gerome with flattery. His eyes flashed across the stall - he was relieved to see the three Gerome paintings weren't on sale.

"Fly, insect, bad smell, go away."

Gerome made shooing motions with his hand. He then pinched his nose with his thumb and index finger.

"Give me my money or give me my paintings," Liam said. He did not possess the strength for a physical fight so he hoped the direct approach would work.

"I have nothing of yours," Gerome got up and leaned across the stall "Do – you – hear – me. Nothing!"

Liam stepped back. As reason was not going to work, he decided to try threats.

"I'll go to the police."

"And they would believe you? A foul smelling tramp, a cheat who preys on women. Claudine told me how you tried to grab her breasts. You can get prison for less than that."

"I want my things, or my money back," he hissed. He balled up his fists and pointed his head forward as though he was about to launch himself across the stall.

Gerome laughed. "Remember the last time you did that. Look at you and then look at me. Who came off best in that round?"

His body sagged. What was he thinking of? Gerome could fell him with one blow. But he wasn't about to leave with his tail between his legs.

"I'll get what's mine. I'll be back," he said.

Liam made his way back to the park, which he was now thinking of as home. The encounter with Gerome hadn't defeated or sent him scuttling off to a hiding place. It had strengthened his resolve, made him even more determined to retrieve his property. Revenge, he reassured himself, was a dish best served cold. Right now he was not cold, he was chilled to the bone. Gerome would feel the same pain he felt, experience loss, even if it was only cash. How could a man as evil as this paint wonderful paintings? Life had given Gerome more than his fair share of gifts so was it time they were taken away from him? He pictured creeping into Gerome's flat when the artist was asleep, taking a knife and cutting off the index and middle fingers on the artist's hands. Let him try to paint then. Money and talent removed in one blow. Liam, who didn't have a violent bone in his body, had no intention of doing this but the mere thought of depriving Gerome of his gift was a small comfort.

He'd hidden his case in a secluded corner of the park, a dark and damp area shaded by the branches of a large elm. After verifying it was still there, he went to the tourist information booth at a nearby metro station and picked up a street map of Paris.

He unfolded the map and located La Villette, the area where Gerome lived. The map illustrated features he didn't recall: parks, a canal flowing through, and wide-open squares.

Closing his eyes, he played back the last minutes of the taxi ride. Claudine had been a distraction, but even so he'd been aware of driving along a very wide boulevard, then turning into a long, narrow street. He pinpointed the main boulevard on the map. Around ten streets branched off this on either side. Gerome's apartment, he thought, was in one of these. He put the map in his pocket. He would find the street and pay Gerome and his wife a visit - when they weren't in, of course.

A good night's sleep was crucial to his plans. He needed to be alert, able to detect problems or danger, and react accordingly. 'Expect the unexpected', he muttered to himself. Liam gathered up some leaves and made a fresh bed under the elm. He couldn't guarantee that he would not be mugged or molested but the tree was in a remote corner, away from public view. He snuggled down and willed himself to imagine he was curled up in a bed in the Hotel Aceline. The leaves transformed into a medium-soft mattress, just hard enough to support his back, but soft enough for his body to sink into. His jacket was a goose down duvet and his suitcase a plumped-up pillow. He drifted off into a deep and dreamless sleep, not thinking about poverty, or lost riches, neither did he give much thought to what he was about to do.

Chapter 22

Liam rode the metro to Porte de la Villette. It was a matter of months since his arrival in Paris, yet in that short time his life had turned upside down. When he exited the station, he noticed for the first time that the sun was positioned higher in the sky. In a few weeks the cooler nights would completely disappear as summer's heat overpowered spring. Like the seasons, his own life had altered, and in a way he could never have predicted. He had been plunged into his worst nightmare: broke, friendless and without a roof over his head.

He stopped and shut his eyes. When he opened them he wished with all his heart to see a friendly face walking towards him: Victor, before he'd crossed him, Lesley on a good day, the version of his mother he remembered from his childhood. 'I'll sort it, my wee man,' she'd said more than once when troubles bubbled up, although, with her Belfast accent, it sounded more like 'Mah wee mawn.'

La Villette was an area of contrasts, rich with an immigrant population and dotted with kebab shops, yet the overall ambience was French. It was a place where old Paris rubbed shoulders with new. Street signs told him the city's biggest park, which was once the home of Paris slaughterhouses was nearby. The old bars, run-down cafes and music halls, haunts of the working class, had given way to more highbrow entertainment: museums, concert venues and modern art structures. Housing, on the other hand, consisted mainly of streets of flat fronted apartment blocks. It was in one of these, he recalled, that Gerome lived.

If he'd had the time and money, he might have spent half a day in the park, strolling, eyeing up pretty women, enjoying the funfair and maybe afterwards taking a trip on a boat down the canal. He would have watched the ripples as the boat cut through the water. Simple pleasures, but these were the thing that mattered. The scent of a rose, sunshine warming the skin and bones, a soft bed at night, the patter of rain on a window, orange flames from a mid-winter fire. Why had it taken all his life to understand these truths?

Before long, he found himself on the wide boulevard the taxi had driven down. He made his way along, stopping at each intersection to examine the streets which branched off the main artery. There was much more of the sky to see out here in the suburbs, he noted. The centre of Paris, though rich with the ambience of old France, felt hemmed in, as though newer buildings had been squeezed in gaps between old ones rather than spreading outwards. He pictured the Louvre's glass pyramid. In his mind it would be better off located in the suburbs, the far suburbs, away from the ornate and historic main building. As far away as possible.

He stopped and bought a coffee and a baguette from a street-corner vendor. He counted out his money carefully, waiting to collect the ten cents change from the seller, who muttered under his breath as he slapped the small coin on the counter. He moved on. No point in arguing with this man when he had bigger fish to fry.

After lunch, eaten on a bench, he continued on his way. Near the end of the boulevard was a street that appeared familiar. Narrow and lined with apartment buildings, it was similar to many other streets in the district, but a hint of menace was embedded in the bricks and mortar of the buildings. Could this be where he'd stumbled, bloodied and in a daze, before a passing taxi had picked him up?

Liam wore a hooded jacket and instinctively, sensing danger, he pulled the hood up. He was glad he'd had the foresight to do this as seconds later a thick-set woman with curly, dark hair strode towards him. A wicker basket was hooked over one arm and her steps were quick and purposeful. So formidable did she appear that if a pedestrian was walking on the same stretch of pavement, and approaching her, they would probably step out into the traffic. He pressed his body so tightly against the wall, nubs of concrete scraped the skin on his back. His new invisible status was paying off and Marie didn't as much as glance in his direction. She was a woman on a mission who had no time for the sorry likes of him.

He followed her to the *boulangerie*. It was late in the day as far as bread buying was concerned and the shop was almost emptied of goods, aside from a scrappy assortment of gateaux. Through the window he watched as Marie scowled, then raised a finger and scolded the shop assistant. She strode from the *boulangerie* and went to a small supermarket which sold a variety of household essentials. He trailed her round the aisles, watching as she selected flour, sugar and jam and tossed them in the basket. The contents of the basket told him she was planning on baking.

He followed her back down the side street. She stopped a few metres before the end of the street and turned into a short cul-de-sac, which led to the rear of several apartment buildings.

She stopped by a door and opened it, without either using a key or pushing numbers on a security pad fixed on the wall. He surmised the security pad was broken and nodded approval. He'd engaged in a brief spot of breaking and entering in his youth so didn't mind picking a lock, but not here in public view. His eyes scanned each floor of the building. Not long after Marie entered, a light was turned on and a window opened on the fourth floor. As he watched, he thought he saw the tip of Marie's dark curls pass the window. He hurried over, pressed the building door handle and when it opened he darted back to the doorway and gathered up his belongings.

He took the metro back to the centre of Paris and returned to the park and his bed of leaves. He counted out his remaining money: twenty five euro and sixty cents. With a cupped hand, Liam scooped dirt from the ground next to him. He wrapped a note and some coins in an empty crisp packet, set it in the shallow hole and covered it with soil again.

"You're all I have left," he said, kissing a finger, then lightly touching the soil. All he had in the world was hidden in a hole in the ground. A sum so meagre it would barely buy a cheap meal in a restaurant, yet this money represented the dividing line between life and death. Was that fair, he asked himself? He was so incredulous at the thought he forgot to be bitter. Was this how people in poor countries felt when they looked at the bloated West? He shook his head, forgot about philosophising, and went back to planning.

Organisation, he acknowledged, was the key to success. In the past, when he'd checked auction catalogues and researched the sale items, he'd been confident, even cocky, striding through the auction house door. He knew exactly what the item he was bidding for was worth and how much he could sell it on for. Profit margins would be carefully calculated before crossing the threshold. Knowing your enemy or adversary was important, but researching your subject was the route to a successful deal.

Liam decided to stake out Gerome's apartment and take note of the activities of the occupants. Did Gerome leave for work every day? If so, at what time? And did Marie always shop in the afternoon? How long was she typically out for? When he'd verified they were dull enough to need a routine to function, he would pounce. Half an hour, he calculated. A measly thirty minutes was the maximum time needed to get his life back on track. He crossed his fingers, hoping the paintings would still be there. If there were any other valuables in the apartment, well, they'd be fair game too. He would imitate Victor's brand of revenge: 'an eye for an eye'.

A soft yet piercing rain began to fall. He was instantly sad and thought of Alouette. Was she thinking of him and did she regret the harsh treatment she and Borivoj had doled out? How he would love go to her apartment, knock on the door, go down on his knees and beg for forgiveness, just as he would pay a million, if he had it, for a warm bed. How far had he travelled from that night when he'd blustered to himself that he'd pay a million for a Peploe painting? Not inches, nor miles, nor across continents - the distance could only be measured in light years. For the moment there would be no Peploe, no Alouette and certainly no bed in a hotel. Liam shook his head, fearing that Alouette would never speak to him again.

The following morning he made his way to the café. The barman, a youth with oiled black hair, wearing tight jeans and white tee shirt, glared at him. The barman leaned over the counter as Liam made his way to the toilet. Liam stopped and shrank back. The young man's severe look changed to one of compassion and he glanced at the toilet door, shrugged and gave a small nod. Liam hurried on, fearful he might change his mind. He splashed water on his face and ran his fingers through his hair, barely glancing in the mirror. He didn't dare reflect on how he'd arrived at this state, knowing that if he did this, the will to live might vanish. He left the toilet and closed the door quietly. As he slid past the bar, the barman raised a hand. Liam flinched. What was he in for: a telling off or a barked order never to set foot there again? The young man pointed to the far end of the bar, a quiet area that customers usually avoided. A coffee and two croissants sat on top of the counter.

"*Mange!*" the barman said severely.

He nodded.

"*Oui. Merci, merci monsieur.*"

He felt tears of gratitude welling up. At this moment, the hot, sweet liquid put to shame the best wines, champagnes and brandies he'd consumed in the past. He ate and drank greedily and nodded his thanks on the way out. Something deep in his soul was touched by this act of kindness. Strangely, he felt even more vulnerable.

Later, he walked down the street where he'd first stayed. Passing by the front door of his old hotel, he glanced in. Everything appeared the same: the impersonal marble lobby, the subdued lighting, the staff with bored expressions on their faces. In reality, nothing was the same: behind individual room doors, a myriad of life dramas were being played out, some perhaps even worse than his. He played a game of 'what if' with himself. What if he hadn't been greedy? Then none of this would have happened. What if he'd seen through

Will's slick patter and turned him down? Bankruptcy would have been the worst-case scenario. What if he'd tried to make a go of his relationship with Alouette? He might have remained warm, comfortable and cosseted. At each defining moment in his adult life he'd made poor decisions. Seduced by greed. If greed was a woman, he reflected, she would be as beautiful as Claudine, with almond eyes and flowing dark hair. She would have skin soft as cream and a smile that sucked you in. Her caresses would be like the warm Mediterranean wind. But greed would be all appearance and no substance. She would be fickle and, when a lover showed vulnerability, she would consume and destroy.

When he reached the end of the street he realised too late that Borivoj was perched on his stool. He turned his head and quickened his steps. Borivoj leapt up and stretched out an arm, blocking his path.

"Jesus Christ. What happened?" Borivoj drew his arm back and crossed himself.

He smiled weakly. "Hard times. I was thrown out of the apartment where I was staying... Oh, you already know that," he added with more than a hint of sarcasm.

"Why did you not go back home - to England?"

"Things a bit hot back there."

"Surely it is better than this. You are sleeping in garden, I think?" He pointed at Liam's dirt-splattered trousers.

"Your fault," Liam said.

Borivoj put his face up close to Liam's. He scowled and stepped back. "You stink. I am not sorry for you, Liam. You leave Paris, now. You don't go near Alouette." He dipped his hand in his pocket and took out a twenty euro note. "That will buy you cheap bus ticket to London. No return. Make sure you go...soon."

Liam was about to add that Alouette might want to see him again, but a dangerous glint in Borivoj's eye silenced him. He was too weak to fight. When he'd taken what he was owed from Gerome's apartment, perhaps he might think of quitting Paris. Until then, he was a prisoner in this city of lovers.

"My paintings?"

"Write and give Alouette address abroad. We will send."

Liam opened his mouth, intending to plead, but Borivoj raised a hand. "Get lost," he growled.

Despondent, he gave up and went back to the park. Just outside the wrought-iron entrance gates was a charity collection box where, according to the sticker on the lid, old clothes, shoes and other personal items could be dropped off. He waited nearby until an elderly woman stuffing a plastic bag into the box had completed her task and made her way down the street. Sure there was no one in the vicinity, he put his hand into the opening and rummaged around. His hand touched the plastic bag resting on top. Probably filled with women's things, blouses and skirts, he thought, discounting it. Underneath was a woolen object, thick and bulky. He pictured a blanket, warm and heavy enough to keep wind, rain and any other weather anomalies the gods decided to throw in his direction, at bay. A cover much like the ones heaped on his grandparent's bed. He pulled out the object and held it up. A duffel coat: big, brown and warm. He slipped it on over his clothes, even then it was too big.

"Perfect," he muttered. The coat would serve two functions. It would keep him cosy at night and, as it was several sizes too large, it would aid disguise by adding bulk to his slender frame. He bedded down under the coat and slept until sunlight filtered through the leaves of the elm. With this wake-up call, he rose, dressed, put the coat on and headed straight for the metro.

The day was warm, the sky blue with only a few scattered clouds, so he took off the coat and carried it over his arm. He rode the metro to Porte de La Villette and went directly to the street where Gerome and Marie lived. There was an empty shop opposite, with newspaper stuck to the inside of the windows and several bags of rubbish tossed outside. He arranged the rubbish bags at the front of the shop porch, a partial barrier from passing traffic, and laid the coat on the tiles.

The coat, this piece of brown wool fabric, shabby and shapeless, had many uses, he realised: carpet, blanket, disguise, shelter, and at the moment, it was of more value to him than a precious stone. How many other simple, yet valuable, things had passed unawares through his fingers? He briefly reflected on who the owner might have been as he couldn't recall seeing an overweight person in central Paris. In his mind they were all skinny and well turned out. He knew this wasn't true but was just an overall impression.

Out here in the suburbs, fat, skinny and medium people walked past the doorway. He perspired in the small space. There was an abundance of miniature dogs. Tiny pooches the size of rats stopped to sniff the rotting rubbish in the bin bags. The old Liam would have been disgusted, both by the dogs – he was more of a cat man – and by the fishy stench. The Liam in the doorway had more on his mind. First and foremost was the desire for revenge, which burned brighter as the days passed. The second thing he coveted was a night in a room with four walls, barriers to separate him from the rest of the human race, and a comfortable bed. No, he said to himself, strike the comfortable, simply a bed would suffice. As the dogs sniffed, lifted their legs, and used his doorway as a toilet, rage at his current situation grew.

He made a mental note of the street's comings and goings. A flush overcame him when Gerome left the apartment building around nine thirty am. The urge to leap up, block his pathway and confront him almost overwhelmed Liam, but he suppressed it. Gerome climbed into the driver's seat of a Peugeot van, yawned and scratched his head. His features were visible as the car pulled out and slowly passed the doorway. Liam could have sworn the artist's lips were curved into a self-satisfied smirk. Was he thinking of the fast one he'd pulled, how he'd got one over on him? Was he relishing the image of him, quivering like a fool on the other side of the stall? There was no question, so far the victor in this deal was Gerome. But what Gerome didn't realise was that this was only round one: round two would decide the winner.

"Brains over brawn," Liam muttered.

Marie exited the building at one pm. He followed her as she made her way towards the shops. She stopped at the *boulangerie* once again, where an older woman, evidently a friend, smiled and greeted her with two kisses on each cheek. The woman went into a back room and brought out a plastic bag with the tops of two baguettes jutting out. Marie gave a satisfied nod, paid for the goods and left the shop. She went into the supermarket and then the butchers. Afterwards she returned to the back entrance of the apartment building. Once again she didn't use a key to enter the building nor did she enter numbers into the security lock. He timed the entire outing: forty-five minutes. This was more than enough time to seize his belongings. To allow for a slight variation in her routine, he'd make sure he was in and out of the apartment in under half an hour.

The following day he settled in the doorway. At around nine thirty Gerome got into his van and started up the engine. Liam's view was suddenly blocked by a figure in black.

"*Mon enfant…que fais-tu ici?*"

He looked up into the face of a nun wearing a traditional habit and veil. Her shoes were laced and sturdy, good enough to play football in, he imagined, and a large brown wooden rosary swung around her neck. She folded her arms and fixed her eyes on him.

"*Pas ici.*" She pointed at Liam, then at the ground. She cupped her hand, indicating he should follow her. Just around the edge of her full skirted habit he could see Gerome's van shudder as the engine idled. Was Gerome watching the drama in the doorway unfold? Liam was relieved when he pulled away. He gave a dismissive wave.

"*Non, non. Bien ici,*" he growled in a low voice. He backed further into the shadows; he needed to stay here, to verify Marie would leave apartment at the same time as usual. Timing was crucial to his plan as he was still weak and had no appetite for confrontation. The apartment had to be empty.

The nun shrugged and strode down the street. With luck,

she wouldn't return with reinforcements. She was likely a do-gooder, sent out to look for unfortunates, in need of a bed and a meal. But food was superfluous to his needs; right now he had enough desire for revenge to fill his belly ten times over.

At around one pm the rear door of the apartment building opened. Marie headed down the street, the straw basket hooked over her arm. She went into the *boulangerie*. The woman she had been friendly with wasn't working and the girl behind the counter clearly hadn't set aside any bread. Marie jabbed her finger at the assistant accusingly. A narrow-eyed Marie left and went to the supermarket. Afterwards she stopped off at a general household goods store. Just after two pm she returned to the apartment. She entered the door at the back of the building, again without using either a key or the security pad. He punched the air. Victory. There was definitely no security.

"Game, set, match," he said in a low voice. This was going to be easier than he'd imagined. He followed her up to the fourth floor and examined the apartment door. It had a bog-standard laminated steel lock. A quick wiggle, a pulse and it would fall open.

Over the next few days, he continued his stakeout, taking an early metro to Porte de La Villette and settling in the doorway before Gerome left. He wrote down their actions and the timings of these on a piece of paper. When he had monitored them for just over a week and established there was no change of routine, even at the weekend, he considered the surveillance complete.

"Tomorrow then," he muttered as he left the doorway and made his way back to the metro. Liam's heart pounded with fear and anticipation. By this time tomorrow, if all went well, he would have his paintings, and would help himself to any money or valuables left lying around as an added bonus for his troubles. His revenge would indeed be cold, but it would also be sweet as a chocolate sundae with whipped cream and cherries on top.

He bought a bottle of Vin Ordinaire from a supermarket and a hamburger from a roadside stall. Returning to the park, he realised he had no corkscrew and searched for an implement to edge the cork out. He found a sturdy stick and scraped the end on the ground until it was sharpened to a point. The effort of opening the wine made the joy of drinking it even sweeter.

After dinner, he drew up a plan which was as clear to him as an architect's drawing. First thing in the morning, he'd take the metro to La Villette. Once there he would install himself in the usual doorway, disguised according to what he could find in the charity box by the park. He would watch Gerome drive off. If Marie didn't change her daily pattern, and she didn't appear the imaginative sort who would vary things, she would leave at around one. Using a screwdriver and bits of wire he'd gathered up, he would slip into the apartment. In and out in half an hour or less.

His head buzzed as he tossed and turned and struggled to sleep. Tomorrow night, if there was cash in Gerome's apartment, he might exchange his bed of leaves for one in a hotel. Bliss.

Chapter 23

Raindrops scattered from the sky, onto the leaves of the elm which sheltered Liam. When the leaves had collected as much water as they could support, the liquid dripped onto his makeshift bed. He pulled the duffel up round his face. Was the rain a good or bad sign? He wasn't sure. The past week the days had been warm and bright, so what would happen if Marie hated wet weather, changed her shopping pattern, and stayed at home? He answered his own question: then he would go the following day and the next if necessary. Borivoj's donation to his meagre funds would buy a week of metro tickets. There was nothing to worry about, he reassured himself. It would all fall into place.

He reflected on how easily he'd slipped into this nether world where right and wrong had blurred boundaries, like brush strokes in a watercolour. When there's no further to fall, is a human capable of anything? It dawned on him that he was more interested in the mechanics of robbing Gerome than the morality. Not that morality had been a strong point in the antiques business. He wasn't above using all his wiles to get one up on other dealers. How he'd laughed in the past when he had bagged a book or a painting for much less than it was worth. And the brief spot of breaking and entering, done in his youth, would finally be put to good use. On the other hand, he donated occasionally to charities, particularly ones which helped the homeless, as he could not erase from his mind the short periods he and his mother had survived by begging a night or two's shelter from friends. If an acquaintance was in need, he'd be first to dip his hand into his pocket. His life was lived in two extremes, yin and yang: the good cancelling out the bad.

Finally he got up and put on his driest shirt. On his head he wore a grey and black striped beanie retrieved from the charity box. It was pulled down low on his forehead, the first stage of the disguise. He scratched his chin. The beard had thickened and taken on a wiry texture, giving the odd sensation that a brillo pad was glued to his skin. He put on a long brown trench coat he'd fished from the box the evening before, which was to provide the final touch in his disguise. The morning was humid and under the bulky clothes he perspired. He studied his reflection in the park pond. A man, at least ten years older than the one who'd arrived in Paris a few months previously, was reflected amid rain splodges on the surface. Even his own mother, if she'd still been alive, might have passed him by without a second glance.

An hour later than usual, he made his way to the metro, cursing himself for his tardiness. Plans, he knew, needed careful and timely execution. A delay of even minutes could scupper a well thought out agenda. If he hadn't lingered by the pond, reflecting on both his mother and Alouette and how he'd disappointed them, his mood might have been more relaxed and upbeat.

There were plusses in looking and smelling as he did. The metro was crowded but Liam had two seats to himself. He looked up and examined the faces of his fellow passengers, many of whom appeared to be of African origins. Not one person made eye contact with him. Not even a fearsome looking, tattooed white guy, who wore his hair in a buzz-cut and listened to aggressive metal music. Liam noticed that he, too, had plenty of room in the carriage.

He disembarked at Porte de la Villette at ten o'clock and made his way to the doorway. He was pleased to see that Gerome's car was absent. His stomach growled. It would be several hours before Marie ventured out so he headed to her local *boulangerie*. His heart raced as he pointed to an onion tart and then a large cream horn. He turned his head to one side while he counted out euros and cents so the assistant wouldn't remember him. She might vaguely remember a down and out individual, but she would not be able to describe his features. Selective blindness - the homeless and the down at heel had that effect on people. Feeling more pumped up than usual, he made his way back to the doorway.

"Touchdown," he said aloud. "Well, almost."

After eating, he dozed, a few minutes at a time, on and off. At one point, he awoke with a start, but when he checked his watch an hour remained before Marie was due to leave. He gazed up at the fourth floor; the flickering light of what Liam imagined was a television could be seen.

Just after one, Marie left the apartment. She made her way down the street, clutching her basket in one hand and an umbrella in the other. He smiled. A baseball bat she could do damage with, but an umbrella was child's play. It dawned on him that the moment of revenge had arrived. What he was about to do would serve as payback to Will, the women in the hotel, Lily, Borivoj, everyone who had wronged him in the past. This one act would cleanse his body and soul and allow him a new start. He breathed deeply, not allowing even an ounce of fear to trick its way into his mind. Pumped up with adrenaline, his scalp tingled and he had the impression that his hair underneath the hat was standing on end.

When Marie turned the corner, he took off his coat and left it at the rear of the doorway. He made his way across the street, his steps as light and stealthy as those of a cat on the prowl. He imagined his body was suspended a few inches above the pavement, his feet barely making contact with it. He could not hear or sense his own breath or heartbeat. He was like a hunter in olden-time America.

He made his way up the stairs to the fourth floor, each footstep so light there was no click or echo on the staircase. He was aware of how many minutes he had to complete his task, but time had taken on a different consistency. It appeared fluid, a melting Dali clock, rather than fixed. He paused and took a deep breath as he stood at the front door of the apartment. 'Abandon hope all ye who enter', he told himself as he gave a nervous giggle and drew a deep breath. The stale air in the hallway became sweet in his lungs. His body tingled, more alive and vibrant than it had been in a long time. He jiggled the lock with the screwdriver and suppressed a laugh when the door swung open - easy as cutting soft butter with a sharp knife. As he stepped across the threshold, the feeling of invincibility disappeared and his heart began to pound. On a ledge just inside the front door was the baseball bat Marie had battered him with. Blood on the implement had dried to a rust shade. He shuddered as he pictured her fleshy arms swinging it in his direction. He picked up the baseball bat just in case Marie came home early. He had no intention of using it, but it was a useful deterrent.

For some reason, perhaps it was instinct, he walked along the hallway and entered the living room on tiptoes. Hairs prickled on his arms, tiny radio antennae picking up signals his brain was unable to process. There was nothing to worry about, he told himself, he'd done his homework and was certain the flat would be empty for at least half an hour. He looked down at his hands and gave a satisfied nod. At the last minute he'd found a pair of leather gloves in the charity bin. He saw these as a sign, a gift from benevolent gods who had finally decided to smile down on him.

In daylight, the living room walls were an even dingier shade of olive than he remembered, and the curtains, sofa, carpet, cushions were all tinged with various dull shades. The furniture was cheap and mismatched, likely from second hand shops, markets or skips. He had a strange thought which puzzled him: surely this wasn't the home of someone who was as gifted with colour and form as Gerome. The exception in the room was the television, a sleek flat-screen model edged with chrome, which took pride of place on one wall. It was switched on although the sound was turned down low.

He was relieved to see the three lots of paintings still stacked up against the wall. At the very least he would have his paintings back. But would that be enough, or should he make Gerome pay for the hell he'd put him through? One thing he was certain of: he would try to have his cake and eat it too. Although Gerome and Marie did not live in a splendid house and their furniture was shabby, they had the air of tight-wads so there was bound to be money hidden in the apartment.

The next moments passed in a dream-like state. He entered a vacuum, where he existed without feelings. He became a spectator, watching a drama unfold:

A creak of bedsprings, feet slapping on the floor, footsteps thumping down the hallway. A voice calling 'Marie', followed by a fit of coughing, then swearing. The living room door opening. Gerome's bulk filling the door frame. The incredulous look on his face slowly transforming into a sadistic smile.
Gerome roaring, then flying across the room, launching himself at Liam like a human cannonball.
Liam grips the bat and swings it hard: a batsman versus a cricket ball. It connects with Gerome's head. Taken by surprise, Gerome stumbles and falls to his knees. His eyes roll from side to side. He tries to get up. Liam swings again and again, his arms move back and forth, taking on a life of their own. On the fifth swing, Gerome's skull shatters like an oversized boiled egg, hit by a giant spoon. Blood and other matter shoot everywhere; in Liam's eyes, on his clothes, up the wall, on the TV screen. He stands over Gerome listening for breathing, a sign of life. Satisfied that Gerome is dead, he walks over to the bundles of paintings and pulls out the ones on top. Three paintings. The rest, he knows, are rubbish. On autopilot, his feelings are suspended: no fear, no remorse. His brain protects him. He takes the paintings and puts them by the living room door.
Liam's primal brain urges him to complete the task he has rehearsed so well. He goes to the kitchen and rummages through the drawers. He is still wearing the leather gloves.
A click, footsteps, a sharp intake of breath, gurgling, and then a strangled scream. Liam's unconscious tells him he must have silence. He grabs a sharp knife from a stand, rushes into the living room and plunges the knife into Marie's back. It goes in easily. She falls on top of Gerome. Her mouth flaps open and shut until the breath oozes out, just like the blood, from her body. He picks up a throw and flings it over the bodies as he can't bear to look at them.
He goes through the drawers in the untidy bedroom. The smell of Gerome's body fills the air: his sweat, his dirty socks, his aura of menace. He finds several hundred euro, in varying notes, in a drawer.

As he closes the drawer, he spies his suede coat, hanging on the back of a chair. He puts on the suede coat, which is spotted with dirt. He takes off his bloodstained trousers and puts on a pair of Gerome's. He tightens the brown leather belt looped around them so they don't fall down.

Liam goes into the bathroom and splashes water on his face. He cleans the sink with bleach, not fully understanding why he does this. Probably something he saw on a TV cop show. Returning to the kitchen, he peels off two bin bags from a roll on the kitchen counter. He goes back into the bedroom and stuffs his trousers in one bin bag. He goes into the living room and pulls the knife out of Marie – more blood. He throws the knife and baseball bat in the bin bag. He takes the other bag and puts the canvasses inside.

He has a quick look around the apartment and then leaves, clicking the door shut behind him. He waits on the stairs until he is sure the coast is clear, then lingers at the door of the apartment building to ensure no one is passing in the street. Liam takes off the suede coat and puts on the brown raincoat he left in the doorway. He stuffs the suede coat in the bin bag with the paintings, then heads down the street and goes into the metro. On the train, he looks down at his shoes. They are splattered with blood. He slips them off and checks the soles. Strangely, there is no blood on the soles. He spits on his hand and wipes the top of the shoes. Some of the splatters disappear.

There is a fight on the train. Two youths spill from the carriage onto the platform. Passengers stand up and watch as security guards pin the youths down. The train takes off and Liam breathes again: people are chattering about the fight, no one is looking at him.

Liam lay down on his bed of leaves and placed the two plastic bags he had taken from Gerome's apartment next to him. His eyes closed as sleep forced itself upon him. The thing he, or someone like himself, had done earlier, had taken effort. So much effort that any action other than sleeping was unthinkable at the moment. His brain began to chatter, ordering him to dispose of the plastic bag containing the bloody clothing and weapons, but he ordered it to shut the fuck up.

Evening light was just transforming from mauve to grey

when he woke up. He was instantly relieved to find himself in the park. He'd had a strange dream, about Gerome and Marie and pools of blood, but then he saw the plastic bags and feared the dream might be real. He took a deep breath, closed his eyes and concentrated. He recalled going to Gerome's flat, with the intention of stealing back his paintings, then this other person had taken over. The other person had looked like him, sounded like him, but he was a stranger. A fight had taken place and he experienced a hazy memory of someone being killed. The memory pulsed in and out of his mind, like a cheap neon sign outside a sleazy motel.

The following morning he quickly became aware that a harrowing event had taken place, and that he was somehow involved. Perhaps as an onlooker, perhaps more. He picked up the bag containing the soiled clothes and left the park. He walked for miles through districts he'd never been to before, past old and new buildings and churches and parks, until he happened upon the Canal Saint Martin. He walked along the edge of the canal until dog walkers and strollers filtered away and there was only the occasional putt-putt of a boat engine. Blood seeped through the heels of his socks. He sat down on the canal bank and removed his shoes. The skin on his heels had chafed and formed blisters, which had burst and then bled. How could this have happened with no accompanying pain? Stuffing dock leaves down his socks, he slipped his feet back into his shoes. He looked around, suddenly aware that complete silence had fallen over the area. There was no birdsong, no rustling of leaves on trees and the throbbing of boat engines had faded away. He gathered some large stones and placed them in the plastic bag containing the bloodied clothing. He pierced the bag several times with a twig, allowing trapped air to escape. Checking the coast was still clear, he hurled the bag far into the water. It landed near the middle and after a few seconds on the surface it disappeared from view.

He trained his eyes on the spot where the bag had vanished. A few bubbles appeared then the grey water grew still.

Relieved that it didn't immediately resurface, he returned to the park and fell into a deep sleep.

Several hours later, he awoke and saw a plastic bag hidden amongst the leaves. Had he dreamt the canal incident and was the evidence still by his side, awaiting disposal? He felt inside the bag and was relieved when his fingers rubbed across the corner of a canvas.

He took the bag to a storage shed he'd spotted days before in a remote corner of the park. He'd peered through a small gap in the wooden slats and as far as he could tell the shed was disused and full of broken gardening equipment, empty boxes and bits of wood. Spiders had woven webs across the bolt confirming the structure's status as 'currently abandoned'. He swiped a hand, dusting the cobwebs away and wiggled the bolt until it worked loose. Inside was a jumble of poles, broken rakes, planks of wood, bits of twisted metal, a random selection of once-useful objects, strewn like bones in an elephant graveyard. He stuffed the bag containing the canvases in an empty crate at the rear of the shed and buried it under a pile of similar crates. This was to be a temporary solution and not the best one, his rational mind observed, as at any point the disused shed could become functional again. He shrugged: nothing in life was guaranteed so he'd take his chances. Before he shut the door, he looked back. The jumble and chaos that would indicate no recent activity in the dimly lit space still existed and spiders would weave their webs again in no time. Relief washed over him when he worked the rusty bolt across. Perhaps he could begin to put yesterday behind him.

He slid a hand into his trouser pocket, fingering the notes he'd taken from Gerome's. Enough to buy temporary freedom while reflecting next moves. He stuffed some clothing into his bag and stopped at a waste bin outside the park gates to dispose of the rubbish he'd gathered. With regret, he pressed the cosy brown duffel on top. Although it was an inanimate object, a mere piece of clothing, he now looked on it as a friend. He patted the coat one more time before heading down the street.

Liam walked until he found himself on the Champs Elysées. In a daze, he made his way down the grand boulevard, only stopping twice: once to look at postcards by a newsstand, then to rest on a bench. Passers by avoided his gaze. He glanced down at his shoes and saw rust coloured spots sprinkled across the leather, then, and for just a brief moment, he allowed himself to acknowledge what had really taken place.

When he had gathered up sufficient strength, he took the metro to Montmartre, making his way to the residential part of the district, away from the street artists and tourist bars. In another life he might have lingered and watched the artists at work, then enjoyed a pastis or two outside a bar. Street theatre would have unfolded - dramatic, colourful, sometimes dangerous. The ghosts of his heroes: Picasso, Matisse, Leger, might have, in his imagination, dawdled alongside. Today he ignored all the trappings of tourist Paris and went into a shop and bought bread, meat, cheese and wine. He was tempted by a packet of Gitanes. The blue and white wrapper with its silhouetted image of a woman dancing took on a comforting guise. He shook his head. Alouette wholeheartedly approved of his efforts to give up smoking and hadn't he already done enough damage, both to himself and to her? Maybe when he was on his last legs, that's when he'd give in to life's torments and light up.

Liam sat down on a bench and checked the map he had picked up from the Tourist Information Office. His finger traced across a small area in Montmartre, finally pinpointing the whereabouts of a budget hostel. He made his way there. An elderly man with thick lensed glasses, resting on the end of his nose, was behind the reception desk. He barely gave his new client a glance as Liam signed the register, nor did he ask for identification. The pen felt strange in Liam's hand as he wrote his name: Patrick Doyle. A wave of relief swept over him as the old man scanned the register and nodded – with a stroke of a pen he'd become a new man. A private room cost thirty euro a night, which was a good deal. He paid in advance for five nights.

The room, at the back of the hostel, had views of an alleyway and some warehouse buildings opposite: brown wooden structures with few windows, anonymous in appearance. If he looked to the side, in the distance, he could see a grassy mound. He drew the curtains shut although there were no people visible in the buildings opposite.

The odd bits of furniture, made little pretence in furnishing the room. A single bed with a thin foam mattress and no headboard was pressed against a wall, a chest of drawers and a wardrobe, both made from oak veneer stood side by side. The brown lino on the floor was old but spongy. He rapped the wall behind the bed and felt it move. It was made of plasterboard, thin enough so the wheeze of a neighbour's snoring could be heard. The bathroom was a few paces along the hallway, but this was a minimal inconvenience as there was a sink in the room where he could pee without putting a foot outside his temporary sanctuary. To Liam, this was a palace. A private place where he would be safe. He ate the bread and cheese and drank some wine. He put the rest of the food he'd bought in a drawer. On top of the chest of drawers was a 'do not disturb' sign. He opened the door and hung in on the outside door handle.

Chapter 24

The following day he emerged from his room. He went down the corridor to the bathroom, took a pair of scissors from his wash bag and studied his face in the mirror. His hair was oily and matted and his beard had grown longer. He listened to the rhythmic clip of the scissors as he chopped his locks until only half an inch remained. The bare patches on his scalp had increased in size but even more astonishing was the colour of his hair; it has turned the same shade of grey as his beard. In a matter of weeks he had transformed into an old man. How was this possible, he asked himself as he trailed a finger across one cheek? The pale skin that Alouette had greatly admired had turned red and rough from exposure to the sun, wind and rain. Fair hair turned grey, pale skin turned red, pacifist turned killer - his entire physical and mental states now reversed, turned inside out. Was the theory of alternate universes with infinite outcomes true, and had he landed in the worst outcome of all? Moving closer to the mirror, he looked into his eyes. They were the things that had changed most. Wide and staring. He had the look of a haunted man.

Jets of tepid water from the shower pressed on his skin. A sliver of soap was wedged between the tap and the wall; he prised it out and rubbed it over his body until it softened and dissolved. He watched, transfixed, as the grey slime slid down the plug hole. Was that what life was all about: hopes and desires melting and dissolving into nothing as time passes? Were humans programmed to lie to themselves, to pretend their lives of quiet desperation were fulfilling? Were people, in reality, nothing more than bags of hot air?

He got out and dried off with a tee shirt. There was a thumping on the door as he dressed.

"Hurry up mate. Some of us here need a shit," a male voice said in an Antipodean accent.

He gathered up his belongings and checked the bathroom. Nothing. It was almost as clean as when he'd first entered.

Nothing remained that could identify or incriminate. He'd even taken care to scoop up stubby hairs with a piece of damp paper and had flushed the paper down the toilet. He opened the door and turned to check the room again.

"Come on, Pops." The young man who waited outside jiggled from foot to foot. He had the look of a backpacker: early twenties, dark hair curling round the nape of his neck, stubble on his chin, wearing a vest he'd probably slept in. His body gave off whiffs of beer and garlic. Liam moved to one side as the young man pushed past, slammed the door shut and bolted it. He went back to his room and closed the door behind him, although *he* did this quietly. 'Look like a ghost, act like a ghost, and become a ghost', he told himself. If the man on the desk was asked who was in room four, his room, by police, he wanted to make sure the old man would answer that he didn't know.

He opened the drawer and took out his remaining food. The bread was hard but he still ate it, telling himself that it would give him sustenance and after dark he could go out and buy more. He finished off the last of the wine and added that to his shopping list. The room was his for a few more days so what better way to pass the time than eating, drinking, sleeping, gathering strength in body and mind. Memories of recent events had begun to merge with the lies he told himself. He could only vaguely picture Gerome's body, face down on the floor. Marie, he couldn't remember at all, but he was on some level aware that she'd been there. He blinked and the image of the blanket and the outlines of his two enemies disappeared.

"Not possible. I was just a witness. Someone else must have done it," he muttered to himself.

There was no television set in the room, and Liam had no burning desire to read a newspaper. The comings and goings of those in the outside world was now an enigma which could remain hidden, as far as he was concerned. He lay back on the bed, one arm behind his head, reflecting on what he would like to happen next. There was only one possible outcome: Alouette. She had a kind and generous heart. She'd come to his rescue once and by now she would surely have forgiven him. Would she come to his aid again?

He had a dream. He was in a coffee shop, with a pencil in his hand, writing a list of significant names in his life:

His mother. A funny but vulnerable woman who found all aspects of life difficult. He'd loved her with all his heart, but he supposed he'd inherited her poor decision-making skills.

His absent father, whom he never knew.

His teacher, Miss Bullock, who used to bring extra sandwiches to school for him.

Victor.

His ex-wife, Lily, who took him for every penny he had when they divorced.

Will, or 'the bastard' as he now referred to him.

Alouette.

Borivoj.

Gerome the swindler.

Clau... His eyes flew open when he had written the first four letters of the last name. Claudine. His heart raced. Adrenalin pumped through his veins when he had no need of it, so he began to hyperventilate. He jumped out of bed, raced over to the sink and threw up. When he'd ceased retching he went to the window, drew across the curtains and opened the window. He poked his head through the gap and inhaled. After a few seconds, the evening air, sweet, cool and smoky, swirled around, enabling him to breathe.

Liam's legs wavered as he made his way to the bed and lay down. Claudine was a loose end. She could identify him. She could tell the police how she and Gerome had masterminded their swindle. He imagined her low, hesitant voice telling the police that Liam must have returned and killed Gerome and his wife. She was the chink in his suit of armour and he had no idea what to do about her.

"Sleep on it, Liam," he said, as though he was talking to another person. "That's what I'd do if it were me."

The following day, he went for a walk. He stopped at a supermarket and bought two large packets of Lays potato chips, a packet of chocolate croissants, a small bottle of fizzy orange and a bottle of wine. When he passed by a newsstand, he averted his eyes. An overwhelming urge to find out the latest news overcame him. He went back and lifted a newspaper from the stand and paid for it. He didn't scan it to see if Gerome's picture was on the front; that could wait until later, when he had fortified himself.

He sat on a bench in Montmartre. Paving stones shimmered in the sunshine and warm air rose in waves, giving the impression the ground was liquid. He opened a bag of crisps, took a handful, and stuffed it in his mouth. The saltiness whetted his taste buds and he took another handful. Soon the packet was empty. He scrunched it up. This reminded him of the last time he'd crumpled a piece of paper: Will's telegram. Not so long ago, yet it felt like a lifetime. Then, he had plunged into the depths of despair. Now, he had crossed some sort of line and, although intellectually he knew he'd done something terrible, the part of his mind responsible for guilt and compassion had become as frozen as a pond in a winter storm. He hoped it would never defrost.

He lingered on the bench, watching a group of artists across the square. They laughed and joked as they applied paint to their canvases, joyful and carefree in the nice weather. Even so, Liam noted evidence of friendly rivalry between them as they tried to catch the attention of passing tourists, competing with polished patter. Did a portrait mean the difference between eating a baguette and cheese for dinner or tucking into a three course meal?

Most of the paintings displayed were charming. Great souvenirs to bring home after a weekend away, not so great hanging in your living room. These were the type of paintings bought on a whim, a reminder of a fun day out. He surmised that most would end up in a cupboard under the stairs or in a spare bedroom. He visualised Gerome's paintings. They were much, much superior to the efforts in the square. He counted on his fingers: five. Once Borivoj had returned his property, he'd have five paintings to sell. Elaine had been willing to pay five thousand each. Suddenly a thought crossed his mind. Now the artist was deceased, the price might go up. Eventually, if they didn't catch him first, he was in line to make a tidy profit.

His heart rate quickened when he pictured the shed where the three paintings lay hidden. It had appeared disused, but this status, he knew, could alter at any moment. At the time it had been the best hiding place available, and as far as hiding the paintings was concerned he'd done what he could. He recalled an engraving on a gravestone in Menton: *He did what he could*. At the time he'd laughed at the backhanded tribute, wondering what crime had the unfortunate individual had committed? Now he understood the full meaning of the words: not all people can be successful movie stars or scientists or surgeons. Some lead desperate lives, only basically surviving. 'We all do what we can, some better, some worse', he muttered. If the authorities decided to clean out the shed then he hoped another homeless person would happen on the canvases. Right now he could not bear to set foot in that patch of green he'd briefly called 'home'; he knew he could not put a hand on the park gate, open it and step inside, until he'd recovered. If it was too late and the paintings had been turfed out or disposed of by another means, then that would be his punishment.

When Liam was a teenager, after a spate of breaking and entering, he'd found himself in a church during the confessional hour. An unseen hand had guided him into the curtained confessional box. Kneeling inside, waiting for the priest to slide across the hatch, he had been overcome by a sense of peace. A wrong could be turned to a right with a few prayers. One 'Our Father' and a few 'Hail Mary's' and the slate would be wiped clean and life could be started afresh. Perhaps he would pay a visit to a church here, find a priest with a sympathetic face, or one who didn't understand a word of English, and offload his sins. But perhaps telling the whole story wouldn't be necessary; his mother had once assured him that simply attending confession was enough. 'After all, love,' she'd said 'God isn't flesh and blood, with eyes and ears. He knows everything - no need to go into fine detail'.

He thought of Claudine with a degree of regret. She would only ever be accessible to him in her portrait. She was a loose end in the saga with Gerome so he decided to leave it at that. There was no appetite to confront Gerome's beautiful muse in person, no will to discuss the events of the past few days with anyone and he certainly didn't intend to do her harm. She was merely his dream woman. Dreams didn't really exist - they were fantasy, weren't they? Although he did not relish the thought of prison, and didn't think he would survive it, Claudine could remain a loose end.

He turned his thoughts back to Gerome's artworks. Imagining how the paintings might be disposed of in the future when things had settled down. Rich tourists like Elaine who appreciated good art must be two-a-penny in the right location. There were plenty of upmarket tourist hangouts in Paris. Or perhaps it would be easier to sell the paintings to a gallery. Not a showy, pretentious one, like the gallery near the Boulevard Montparnasse, but one that appreciated good art. There were serious collectors from all over the world gathered in this city. With his deal making experience and his keen eye, tracking them down wouldn't be an impossible task.

He got up and strolled across the square. The past few days he'd been grateful for a room with four solid walls where he could shut himself away from the world, but this morning cabin fever had set in. He liked his own company but he wasn't a recluse. The buzz of a busy auction or boot fair could lift his mood. Equally here, in the midst of the hubbub of Montmartre, he hoped to distract himself from the events at La Villette. He walked past the artists, not stopping but at the same time taking a closer look at the paintings on easels and stands. One artist, who wore a black beret and a white smock, had a blank canvas in front of him. He waved a paintbrush in mid-air as though he was wondering what to paint. As he passed by, the artist reached out and touched his arm. Liam flinched.

"Voulez-vous posez?" the artist tipped his beret and smiled.

Startled at being the focus of attention, Liam shook his head firmly and hurried on. The last thing he needed was his portrait on display.

He turned several corners with no destination in mind and arrived at the Sacre Coeur Basilica. This was the highest point in the city and from here he could look out over the Paris skyline. He'd never climbed the Eiffel tower and had only ever viewed the city at ground level, broken up into chunks which he likened to squares of delicious chocolate, where you enjoyed the part but not the whole. Now the cityscape unfolded in front of him like a giant map. The roofs and domes of the old buildings stretched out until they were replaced by the high rises of the suburbs. Even more impressive was the big sky. Up here on the hill, he felt closer to the clouds that skipped across the sky, than the earth. For the first time since his arrival in Paris, he experienced the lightness of being a tourist, with cares and troubles tucked away in a suitcase, not to be unlocked until the trip was over. Right now, the white stone of the Basilica dazzled and the rays of the sun deflected off the building onto his face. He went into the church's meditation garden. People were sitting on benches, on the grass, contemplating and taking the sun. Nobody paid him attention. He was free to enjoy the moment.

Liam's reverie did not last long. An opportunity, which seemed like a miracle, presented itself. A couple were sitting on a blanket nearby, enjoying the view, chatting in low, intimate voices. The man rose to his feet, held out his hand and helped the woman up. He was grey haired, middle aged and well groomed. She had dyed blonde hair, cut into a helmet shaped bob. They had the air of well-heeled but not rich tourists. The man put his arm around the woman's shoulder and they walked to a nearby bush, leaned over and sniffed the large pink blossoms. On the blanket were the remnants of a picnic: half a bottle of a peach coloured drink, paper bags, still fat and stained with grease. Next to the bags, lay the woman's handbag.

Liam did a three hundred and sixty degree turn, his eyes alert, taking in every living thing in the vicinity. A handful of people looked over the Paris vista, others were quiet and meditative, no prying eyes focussed on him. He cut across the grass as though he was taking a short cut back to the basilica. As he strolled past the blanket, he dipped down and his arm shot out, fast as the swish of a lion tamer's whip. He picked up the pace of his footsteps as he moved back onto the pathway. The bag was his. He passed the couple, who appeared to be enjoying a romantic moment. The man whispered in the woman's ear. She giggled back. They were happy and, for the moment, in love, he observed, surely they could spare a bit of cash, a morsel of happiness for those less fortunate? 'Give a little, take a little', he muttered to himself as he left the peace of the gardens behind. The bag was butter-soft beige suede, malleable and, unlike most women's handbags he'd observed, not stuffed to the brim. He shoved it under his tee shirt and melted into the crush of the Place du Tertre.

Back in his room, he opened the bag and tipped the contents onto the bed. A cosmetic bag contained lipstick, a bronzer and a small brush. A wad of receipts were held together by a paper clip. Impressed by the woman's organisational skills, he gave a low whistle of approval. A packet of pills spilled out from the bottom of the handbag. He tossed them in the waste basket. He was pleased to see there was no passport as losing a passport was a major hassle and he didn't want to cause the couple, who had been unwittingly generous to a fault, any grief.

He opened the woman's dark blue leather purse and counted the notes. Two hundred and seventy euro. He laughed aloud. There was a further nineteen euro in coins. He put the money in a side pocket of his bag and gave a satisfied nod as he noted the bulging compartment. Must be almost four hundred euro in there, he congratulated himself. Enough for another week's respite plus meals.

He slipped his arms into the sleeves of the suede coat. The sensation of luxury he'd felt when he'd first put it on was gone and the coat had been tainted by Gerome's short period of ownership. In addition, the artist's bulk had stretched the fabric so it hung loose on Liam's shoulders. He took it off; it was too easily identifiable and, just like his life up to now, he had outgrown it.

The newspaper lay rolled up on the bedside table. He imagined details of the La Villette murders would sit in a prominent position, probably front page news, so he hadn't yet looked at it. He put the paper in a plastic bag which contained leftover scraps from his last meal. In a day or two the paper would be grease stained and stinking of old cheese and bits of pate. Then he would throw it away - he might or might not read it first. He recalled a saying: 'today's news is tomorrow's fish and chip wrapper.' He hoped the saying had at least a degree of accuracy.

On his next outing, he stuffed the suede coat into a communal rubbish bin. An Armani, chucked away as though it was a piece of paper, he thought regretfully. At the very least he would have liked to donate it to a worthwhile cause.

"Charity begins at home," he said aloud, as he weaved his way through the cobbled streets of old Montmartre. Just around the corner from the Abbesses metro stop, in a street lined with butcher's shops, artisans, bakeries and cafes, he stopped at a small bar which was little more than a hole in a wall. Yellow lino which had hardened and cracked like a badly aged cheese covered the floor, and mismatched posters were hung on walls. Liam imagined the bar owner driving round Paris, removing posters from stands and walls, with no concern for content, only worrying about covering jaded wall paint. This was a place unlikely to be the hangout of tourists looking for glamorous Paris: the revues with showgirls who kicked high and sang French songs, or restaurants with domed ceilings, tiled walls, and stiff waiters dressed in black tuxedos and bow ties. Here, there were just a few tables and chairs. Opposite the bar was a shelf facing a mirrored wall. Drinkers lined up facing the mirror, shoulder to shoulder, yet aside from the occasional cough, shuffle and ringing of coins in silver saucers, the space was as quiet as a church congregation during Sunday Service. Punters were here to imbibe and reflect, drink and think, he concluded. There was no chitchat between bar staff and customers, no passing of day between clients, no drunken laughter, shrieking or arguments. He also noted there were no women in the bar. Liam was relieved. A woman would change the ambience, the dynamics in the room. Male customers might be reminded of what was missing in their lives, then the mating dance would begin. It was better like this, he concluded. This would be an evening of reflection first and later a modest savouring of food and drink. Tonight, he hoped to draw a firm line between recent events and the future.

Liam ordered a pastis. The barman poured transparent yellow liquid into a tumbler and pointed to a jug of water which a customer standing at the shelf was using. Liam dropped a two euro coin into the saucer on the counter and made his way over to the wall. He stood in a narrow gap between a small man wearing a flat cap and a tall, muscular one with dirt-splattered overalls. The small man slid the water jug in front of Liam.

"Merci," Liam nodded at his neighbour's image in the mirror. The man's reflection glared at him. Liam shrugged, turned to his drink and tipped in around an inch of water. The liquid turned cloudy, much like his life, he thought: clear at first then pissing down with rain. He raised his glass and toasted himself.

"To the future." He said this with such force, his neighbour turned and gave a look of disapproval. Liam understood the silent admonition; this was a place of reflection, and most of the customers, he imagined, were trying to figure out the enigma of life. He'd never been a man of many words, unless he was in the process of dealing, then words flowed as quickly as a mountain stream in flood. And the gift of small talk usually eluded him, unless it involved seducing a woman. It dawned on him that he mostly preferred the company of a good bottle of claret and a rare steak. Alouette was different though, he liked her, liked being with her.

Normally his childhood was a no-go area; a private, boarded-up compartment in his mind, yet hadn't he opened up to Alouette and Borivoj over dinner, spilling the beans about his past? Perhaps wine had loosened his tongue, made him chattier than usual, but Alouette had a gift, he acknowledged. She cared about her friends. Like groves of oranges and lemons in a Mediterranean valley, which gave their owners an abundance of fruit when tended with love, he could have been similarly nurtured by Alouette's love. He'd have been cosseted like those trees, if only he hadn't allowed greed to corrupt and rot away his soul. He glanced up from his drink into the mirror, and found himself looking, not at Liam, but at Patrick Doyle. What kind of clothes would Patrick wear, how would he style his hair, would he be able to brush the past away just as a barber swept up stubby bits of hair? Would anyone connect a man like Patrick Doyle with the vagrant the police were on the lookout for? Surely Patrick was worlds apart from that man.

Liam set his empty glass on the counter and tapped the arm of the small man on his left. *"Merci et au-revoir."*

The man's mouth opened as though he was about to reply but then he turned and faced the mirror again. At the door, Liam looked back at the row of men, shoulder to shoulder, faces sombre, even sad. Was drink their only friend, and had they done something they weren't proud of that had landed them in this state? Was being forced to gape at their own features, their individual map of guilt, part of their penance?

Near the far end of the street, he came upon a bistro with a three-course menu handwritten on a board outside. The main course was boeuf bourguignon, with a starter of wild mushrooms. The scent of garlic drifted into the street and Liam was hooked. Twelve euro for two courses was a steal, so feeling nostalgic for Alouette and her marvellous boeuf bourguignon, he went in.

When he returned to his room, he dared himself to look at the newspaper. He removed it from the plastic bag and dropped it on the bed. After a few moments of indecision, he took a deep breath and picked up the paper. He scanned the front page, at the same time as listening to the quickened beating of his heart. With dismay, in the right-hand corner he saw a photo of a younger Gerome next to a woman who was probably Marie. She wore a long white puffy dress and carried a bouquet of flowers. The much thinner Gerome was barely recognisable in a light coloured suit with a strangely large flower inserted in the buttonhole. Neither party was smiling, nor did their hands touch or bodies connect in any way. The words *'meurtre'*, *'cambriolage'* and *'clochard'* jumped out at him.

"Murder, burglary and vagrant," He translated aloud. These three words told him everything he needed to know. He read on: the police were treating it as a burglary gone awry, and they were looking for a vagrant, who was either the perpetrator or a witness. Liam knew from watching crime shows on television that advanced new methods of detection existed which could identify the guilty party via a number of things – shoes, fingerprints, clothes, CCTV. He couldn't comment on the CCTV, but the other things didn't cause him undue worry. Hadn't he worn gloves on that fateful day and then disposed of them, along with his clothes, in the river? Even if they found a fingerprint or two from his first visit to the apartment, he doubted they would be able to identify him. Despite his borderline shady background at home, he'd never once been picked up by the law, so to his knowledge there wasn't a jot of information concerning him on any police file. Claudine and perhaps the man on the next stall to Gerome might mention the scam concocted by Gerome. But a scam was hardly a motive for a double murder, and Gerome with his belligerence and aura of menace surely had a long queue of enemies.

He reread the article. Afterwards, he set the paper down

and gave a satisfied nod. No one knew where he was. His appearance had changed so much, he could probably step in front of Claudine and she wouldn't have a clue who the man facing her was. He got undressed and slid under the covers, a happier man than the one who had checked into the hostel. He had fallen into the abyss and had clambered out, not exactly smelling of roses, but smelling okay.

"Patrick Doyle," he muttered. "Has a nice ring to it."

Chapter 25

The following day, a more peaceful Liam ventured out. It was weekend and the streets of Montmartre village were alive with performance artists. Acrobats, musicians and singers jostled with artist's easels for a few feet of space. A scent of baking bread lured him into a *boulangerie* on the Rue des Martyrs. If he was asked what reminded him most of Paris, he reflected, he would not enthuse about the beautiful women or the elegant fashions. What he found most evocative of the city was the variety of scents that shaded the air, subtly, like a watercolour wash: lavender from Provence, black tobacco mixed with strong coffee, wild garlic and seafood, grilled steak with bright yellow mustard sauce. Spices: cumin, coriander, cinnamon, floated from doorways of North African restaurants. The scent of wealth had been heavy in the air in the vicinity of his first hotel. Strangely enough petrol fumes from a Rolls or Bentley weren't all that offensive.

He opted for two beignets, one with raspberry jam and the other with cream. Melting dark chocolate oozed from the ends of pain au chocolat so he bought one. He ordered an espresso, drank it as he waited for the pastries to be set on a plate, and asked for another. The experience was hedonistic and he felt pleasure pumping through his veins. He recalled his grandfather telling him that a glass of amber liquid the old man had held in his hand was water. 'Water of life, king of liquids, that's what I mean…not the stuff from the kitchen taps', his grandfather had added, with a wink and a gummy grin. The Irish were wrong, he mused. Whiskey was the pretender - the espresso on the counter could truly claim the crown. He took his tray and sat down at a table.

An unwelcome thought pushed its way into his mind. Neither espresso nor whiskey or any other stimulant could now be appreciated by Gerome. He no longer existed, yet the talented artist's death mask was still etched in Liam's mind. He reflected for a moment on the meaning of death, the cessation of existence. Then he packed Gerome's memory away.

Liam's body melted back into his seat and he gave a sigh of pleasure as he consumed the cream beignet. Two women entered the bakery and waited by his table, patiently, with no sighs or stares. Even so, he noted all other tables were occupied so he finished his breakfast quickly, got up and left. There would be no opportunity for argument, no drawing attention to himself.

He made his way down the steps in front of Sacre Coeur to Barbès-Rochechouart. This was an area packed with discount and second-hand stores, and shops selling rolls of material. He joined the throng of shoppers, spilling onto the roads, weaving through queues of cars and buses caught in traffic jams. Horns honked, street traders shouted, a frisson of excitement ran through the collective crowd. There was a bargain to be had and they were determined to find it.

He came across an outdoor market. Spices, soaps, leather handbags and colourful clothes sat in a jumble on tables. Although he appreciated the foreignness and anonymity of the space, the crush sucked the breath from him, so he left.

Back on the main shopping street, a charcoal grey suit in the window of a second-hand shop caught his eye. It was sober, restrained and decent, exactly how he longed to be, exactly how he imagined Patrick was. The loud trill of a bell announced his entrance. The assistant, a young Arabic-looking man, rushed forward and shook his hand, a glint of excitement in his eye. Liam surmised that he was either new, therefore eager, or he hadn't had many customers that morning. 'A bargain to be had for sure,' he told himself as he prepared to deal.

"*Bonjour,*" the shopkeeper said.

Liam nodded and smiled: *let the dance of dealing begin.*

"*Bonjour.*"

"English?"

"American."

"New York?"

"California."

"I have never visited…it must be beautiful."

The shopkeeper's hesitation told Liam the man had momentarily lost his guard. One-nil to me, he congratulated himself. "It must be." He pointed to the suit in the window. "How much?"

The assistant went over to the window, he took a fold of the suit material between his fingers and caressed it .

"Nice quality. Two hundred."

"Two hundred! I could go to Chanel for that much."

The assistant gave an unsure smile. "I think monsieur is making a joke. Try on the suit. See if it fits."

Liam shook his head. "Too expensive. Do you have anything else? Like that one but cheaper." He cursed himself for losing focus and not making any attempt to deal. Had the terrible encounter with Gerome altered the sharpness of his mind, turned him into a dullard who was finished as far as the antiques business was concerned? The assistant went into a back room and emerged minutes later with several suits hanging over one arm.

"One of these will be suitable, I think." He laid the suits on top of the counter. Not too long ago Liam would have pointed out a mid-brown suit, a shade darker than an oak leaf in autumn. Now, that colour reminded him of the park and his bed of leaves. He pointed at a silver-grey suit. "Maybe this one."

He tried on the suit; the single breasted jacket was a few centimetres too tight but the trousers fitted perfectly. He opened the jacket buttons. It would do. The assistant asked for one hundred and twenty euro. Liam recovered his deal-making skills and paid sixty.

On the way back to the metro, he stopped at a barber's shop. He sat down in a chair in front of a large mirror. A full length painting of a nude female reflected in the mirror caught his eye. He turned and took a closer look. No, it couldn't be, he told himself. He turned to face the mirror, his face as ashen as his beard, his thoughts jumbled up. The reflection of the painting looked back at him. "Claudine," he

213

whispered.

A squat man in a white barber's coat moved behind Liam's chair, blocking the view of the painting. "You like the beautiful woman?" the man said, twirling Liam's chair round again to face the painting.

"Nice enough," Liam replied. "I was admiring the quality of the painting."

"Ah, quality... of course! One should admire the curve of the brush strokes rather than the curve of her arse."

"No, really. I'm not interested," he protested.

"Then you must be gay."

"Not that either, but it wouldn't matter if I was. Gay or straight, I can enjoy a good painting just as easily as the next man." He blushed, but his eyes were drawn to Claudine's breasts. He had hoped to see her undressed once again, but preferably in the flesh.

"No need to get hot and bothered. You're not the first customer she's had this effect on."

"Do you know who she is?"

"Just a painter's model. Beautiful, but women like that are two a penny here in Paris."

"So, you don't know where she lives?"

The barber shook his head. "You from England?"

"American."

The man tutted while he examined Liam's head. "American barbers not so good."

"Do what you like," Liam replied. The chair was padded and comfortable and he needed time to recover from the encounter with Claudine via her portrait. A young man with a subservient air, wearing a black coat, which Liam surmised was for novices, set a coffee in front of him. He sighed and relaxed. In spite of Claudine's enigmatic gaze and the smile painted on her lips, the experience in the barber's would be relaxing and enjoyable. Well worth the twenty euro advertised on the door.

The barber pointed to a man seated in the next chair, who was in the process of acquiring a cut Liam would have described as a number three. Liam gave a thumbs-up and ten minutes later he left the barbers lighter in both pocket and hairstyle. He caught a glimpse of himself in a shop window. A stranger. An elegant man, at least ten years older than the previous version of himself. He caught passers by glancing at him approvingly.

Soon he would pay Alouette a visit. He wasn't sure why, but all his hopes were pinned on her.

That evening he went for a pre-dinner stroll. He stopped at the bar he now labelled 'the quiet bar'. Only the occasional shuffle and ring of coins in a saucer broke the silence. There was an oddness about the place, he thought. Unlike English bars where you chatted with your neighbour, communication appeared to be frowned on here. That suited him, but today there were too many punters inside and, not in the mood to join the crush, he continued on his way. He'd only progressed around twenty paces when a vaguely familiar voice called out.

"Hey mate. You from the hostel."

The youth who'd been in a hurry to get into the hostel bathroom was seated at a table outside a bar across the street. In one hand was a glass of gold liquid, in the other a cigarette. Liam was tempted to ignore him when the voice rang out again.

"Over here, Pops." The young man set his glass down and pointed to the chair opposite.

Liam hesitated. If he continued on his way, the lad might confront him later and demand to know why he'd blanked him. He was loud and cocky so there might be a scene, unwanted attention could be drawn to him. He shuddered at the thought, then crossed the road and stood next to the empty chair. The young man spoke first.

"Wanted to apologise for the other day," he gave a wide grin. "Dodgy shellfish the night before. I was in a hurry."

"Better now?" Relief washed over Liam. Perhaps the conversation would be brief, they would shake hands and then he would continue on his solitary way.

"Stomach of an ox. Sit down," he said. "Good to have a

chat with someone who speaks the lingo." Another time, Liam would have refused, but right now he did not want to draw attention to himself, so he sat down. "Beer…on me, Pops?"

"A small one, I haven't much time."

"You're the right goer, Pops. Places to be, people to see." He reached out his hand. "Mikey, from the lovely city of Townsville."

"Australia," Liam said. "I'm Patrick – from Dublin."

"Aw, geez. Coincidence or what mate. I'm heading there next. Might do a world tour."

"Me too," Liam said, masking the disappointment he felt inside from his voice. He should be on a world tour. The luxury variety. Staying in top hotels. Instead, here he was, sleeping in a hostel, drinking beer in the glorious city of Paris with an Australian young enough to be his son. All thanks to that bastard, Will.

"You look smart, Patrick," Mikey commented. Liam was wearing a pale pink shirt he'd picked up in a charity shop. "Maybe you could give me some tips on Dublin. Where's the best Guinness, cheap place to stay? Any info gratefully received," Mikey beamed.

Liam stared into the glass the waiter set in front of him, wishing that it was indeed Guinness.

"You're in luck. All the Guinness is fantastic." Liam could count on the fingers of one hand the times he'd been to Dublin – even then he'd have a finger or two to spare. He pictured the streets he'd walked down, racking his brains for the name of at least one pub. He could remember the taste of the beer: malty and bitter, infinitely pleasurable, but the names of the bars eluded him. Liam shrugged.

"Must be one better than the rest?"

"Check the internet."

"I find word of mouth is better."

Liam had a flash of inspiration. "The Crown. That's a particular favourite of mine. Can't remember the street but it's right in the middle of the action. Good music too." Liam was thinking of the Belfast pub where he'd passed the afternoon after his grandfather's funeral. He hadn't wanted to crowd with strangers in the small terrace house, trading stories of the old man. Instead, he'd leaned against the pub's marble counter, gripping the glass of Guinness as tightly as, only a few hours earlier, he'd gripped the brass handle of the coffin.

Mikey was distracted by a group of teenage girls, giggling as they passed by him and entered the café.

"Good looking chicks over here. Not sure how to chat them up. I could offer to teach them how to surf, but there's not much of a wave on the Seine." He flashed a grin as Liam seized on the opportunity to escape.

"The direct approach is best. Why don't you go inside, stand at the bar, close enough so they can ogle you. Drop something or pretend to trip. You'll have their attention. After that, use your charm."

"That would work?"

"I think so. I'd give it a try if I were thirty years younger. You'd better go now. A bird in the hand and all that."

"A bird in the hand makes a happy Mikey." Mikey grinned and stood up. "Wish me luck."

"Break a leg," Liam said to his disappearing back. He crossed his fingers. If Mikey pulled, then he wouldn't see much of him over the next few days. He valued his silence, his solitude. Let Mikey have his fun, what *he* needed was peace and quiet.

He crossed the road to a symphony of hooting horns. He wasn't upset at the drivers' impatience; when a person did a decent day's work, they were entitled to rush home to whatever joys or disappointments awaited them there. Today, however, impatience was futile. The line of cars snaked around the corner, moving a foot or so every few seconds. He was glad he didn't need to be anywhere soon.

As he walked he dwelt on the crises that had inflicted themselves upon him during his life. When he and his mother, Mary, had been first evicted from their London lodgings the only thing he craved was somewhere to lay his head at night and a TV to watch. It didn't matter if the TV was black and white, he simply needed a distraction. Later, when his marriage had broken down and he needed somewhere to stay, he'd turned to his friend Michael, who had both put him up and put up with his misery until he'd pulled himself together and rented a flat. When Mary died, his support network had broken down and the only ears he could find to bend were those of the priest who had buried her, and of course, Victor. Then 'the bastard', Will, had double-crossed him. He'd fallen ill here in Paris but Alouette had come to his rescue, even though she'd probably guessed there was no prospect of reward. There were many, many more crisis points in his life, he realised, but he forgot about them as the scent of frying steak floated out from a familiar doorway.

He ate in the small restaurant he'd dined in the night before and ordered a bottle of house red to accompany his medium-rare steak, although he already knew the meat would be served bloody in the middle and only lightly seared on top. The accompanying fries were the skinniest he'd ever set eyes on. He wondered if they used a machine to slice the potatoes or if some unfortunate individual was employed to peel and slice spuds into matchsticks all day long. Or perhaps they weren't so unfortunate. Would he trade his current position for that of a dogsbody job in a kitchen, earning minimum wage, or less, he asked himself? Damn right. There was no hesitation in the response. If he could switch places with the lowly peeler and slicer of spuds, he'd consider himself the luckiest man in the world.

Liam ate slowly, slicing the steak into thin wedges which he cut again in half. He savoured each mouthful, occasionally lifting his glass and toasting the empty chair opposite. He finished his main course and the old woman who was serving, gruffly set a plate of blue cheese from the Auvergne on the table. She returned a minute later, took the cheese away and set it on one of the neighbouring tables. Liam ate his dessert - peach melba - slowly. Afterwards, reluctant to face his own company on the walk home, he lingered over two coffees.

While he ate, he set his troubles to one side. But as he got up to leave, the image of Gerome's living room sprang into his mind, like a puckish sprite, unwanted, causing mischief. He saw the brown blanket, the lumps and bumps where the bodies beneath shaped the fabric. There was no way of controlling these images, he realised. They could pop into his mind at any time. A searing pain shot across his forehead.

"Christ, no," he muttered. "Don't let me remember." He left the restaurant without waiting for his change, fearful that the pain of remembering would be too much. Scared that he would declare his guilt in full earshot of the staff and diners.

On the way back to the hostel, he distracted himself by thinking about his first few days in Paris. Before Will's telegram, he'd been hopeful. Zarek would turn itself around and in the end win the contracts, Victor would have his money back with interest, he had told himself. Maybe they'd even laugh off the whole affair over a glass or two of Glenfiddich. Overcome by the glamour of his surroundings when he'd first arrived in Paris, he had decided to treat himself. The first indulgence was the suede coat, which now languished in a rubbish bin. The second was dinner in a top class restaurant. The concierge at the hotel had recommended La Rose, designed by an architect and located in a seventeenth century townhouse in La Cite. It was seriously stuffy: the walls were lined in ox-blood linen, the tables, polished glass and steel, reflected the russet walls, creating the impression of a room ablaze. His waiter, dressed in black tuxedo and gold bow tie, hovered by the table, fussing over Liam's menu choices and the wines he'd chosen to accompany the very pretty but mean portioned courses. Although he couldn't describe the experience as the ultimate in pleasure, he remembered how important he had felt when he'd left the restaurant. He had dined amongst the rich, the important, the elite. With a smidgen of luck he could be one of them. He pictured the thirty euro tip left casually on the table and the look of disappointment etched on the waiter's face.

"Thirty euro, fucking fortune!" he said aloud. The meal he

had just tucked into had cost less than the tip and had given him much more pleasure.

He wished he could turn the clock back. First of all, he wouldn't have eaten at La Rose when he clearly couldn't afford it. But even more than that, he wished he'd never gone to the Colourists exhibition, or had become involved in Will's mad scheme. Above all he wished he'd never met Gerome.

Life, like a painting, was shaped by choice: choice of the brushstroke, freedom to shape the picture and make good or bad decisions. Free will was overrated. How many other people, he wondered, were pacing the streets of Paris at this very moment, wishing they could turn back time or change the choices they'd made? Not one as much as he, he concluded.

Chapter 26

Unable to face the rest of the evening with only dark thoughts as company, he wandered the cobbled streets. He was drawn once again towards the Place du Tertre. During daylight hours tour buses eased through the crowded streets, finally stopping to eject camera-clicking tourists for an hour or two. Drivers chatted and smoked by their vehicles, oblivious to the traffic jams they were causing. In the evening, when the buses and sightseers had left, the square took on a magical air. Light spilled from restaurant and bar windows, spraying a gold wash across cobblestones. Fairy lights winked on tree branches. The illuminated spire of the Sacre Coeur Basilica was visible through a gap between buildings and the air was smoky and fragrant.

How much had changed from the days when Utrillo and Picasso had wandered round the streets, Liam wondered? If he'd been an artist then he'd have aspired to emulate the rise and rise of Picasso's star. The short and balding Spaniard had started out penniless, swapping paintings for food - yet he'd ended his days rich, well fed and in the company of beautiful women. Liam stopped by a wall to reread a quote from Picasso, which he'd seen on an earlier visit: *'art washes away from the soul the dust of everyday life.'* He nodded in agreement. Not an artistic bone in his body, but that didn't stop him from appreciating a good painting. Art had the ability to inspire, to lift his spirits. When he looked at Gerome's paintings he was transported to another world; one the unfortunate Gerome had donated a pass to enter. The only certainty in Liam's mind now was that Gerome was a sure thing, an undiscovered genius who would one day be as admired as Picasso.

He pictured an auction room, ten or twenty years from now. He saw an assistant holding up a painting by Gerome. There would perhaps be global interest. Press and TV present, jostling for space near the auctioneer's podium. In that particular future a *Gerome* might generate more interest than a Picasso, not simply due to the brilliance of the painting, but also due to the circumstances of the artist's death. Scandal, that's what the art world loves, he mused. An outrageous newspaper headline could add millions to a piece of art.

As he walked, deep in thought, someone bumped against him. He turned and saw a couple, arms entwined. Each wore a beige mac so it was difficult to see where one person ended and the other began. The woman suddenly turned and caught his eye. He stared back: Lily. She reminded him of Lily when they'd first started going out. She too had been tactile, wrapping her arms around him at every opportunity. 'My rock,' she'd called him, to his delight. 'Well, perhaps not so much a rock as a bendy tree-trunk.' At first he'd been flattered: she needed him, depended on him. He was in his twenties, still a novice in the auction game with not much to offer a prospective girlfriend, so her neediness was an addictive drug. As a bonus, she was attractive with long dark hair. It wasn't thick and luxuriant, nor did it gleam and bounce when she walked, but he was partial to brunettes and Lily fitted that bill. Her eyes were a shade of blue that was difficult to describe -somewhere between the blue of the sky on a fine winter's day and the murky grey of the sea after a storm. She was petite and delicate in appearance, but was also capable of doling out barbs and put-downs: his clothes were bland, his haircut old fashioned, he was too quiet at dinner parties with her friends, who he hated anyway. He wished he had paid attention to the saying 'Love is blind, marriage is the eye opener'.

"Good luck, mate," he muttered.

Weariness overcame him so he returned to the hostel. As he turned into its street, he saw Mikey, each arm linked with the arm of a young woman.

"One - or two - nil to Mikey," he said. He watched as Mikey entered the hostel, envying him not for his youth but for his exuberance. Mikey was energy personified, he bounced when he walked. Had *he* in his entire life ever moved like that? It was as though the young Aussie's joints were made of rubber. Perhaps the Australian climate was responsible, he mused, after all, weren't kangaroos known for their bounce? Heat did something to the human body, made it more languid, less uptight. Mikey was surely one of the lucky ones; the type who'd fall into a septic tank and climb out smelling just fine.

Mikey was nowhere to be seen when Liam entered the reception hall. He surmised he had gone to his room with his conquests. But maybe he was reading more into the situation than he should. Weren't women equal these days? Perhaps they were listening to music or drinking tea. Liam knew that as far as women were concerned, he was a dinosaur. Hadn't Lily worked, yet he'd always considered himself the breadwinner?

He had a sudden epiphany, imagining all his flaws were visible, out there for the world to see. The events of the recent past and his responses had been caused by stress piled on top of stress – the domino effect. His whole life had been a torrent of stress, like a mountain stream in flood. The mind could only take so much, he acknowledged. Had he had a psychotic episode? He wasn't sure. He hadn't ripped his clothes off and run naked through the streets, like others he'd read about, but at some level he acknowledged that what he'd done was much worse.

The events at La Villette influenced his perception of himself in ways he did not understand. When he looked in the mirror he saw his features twisted and misshapen. His chin appeared to jut out further than before and his nose was longer, Napoleonic. He tried and failed to avoid looking down at his hands. They appeared detached from his arms, large and rough. Not the hands of a man who had once handled delicate antiques. Could these be the hands of a murderer, he asked himself? He thought of himself as a living Dorian Grey portrait: the bad things he'd done were affecting his living canvas rather than one stuffed away in an attic. He wondered if others could see him as he really was. Could they look at him, read his features and tell what he had done? Was he, or the person who had committed the murders, a bad person, or had they simply done something bad?

When he played a mental film of his past life, he saw himself as a man with a multitude of faults. He ticked off his personal deadly sins: greed, misogyny, lust, arrogance. There were probably reams of others, but that would do for the moment. At the very top of the list he put greed. Greed was the catalyst for all his current problems. He could bluff and bluster and try to pin the blame on Will and Gerome, who were also filled with greed - but they hadn't committed the ultimate crime. If he hadn't been looking for a quick financial hit, he would not be sliding down life's mud-caked slope. He wondered if greed had been sent to test him: first in the guise of Victor arriving with a suitcase full of cash, secondly in the shape of Will's 'sure-thing' deal, and thirdly in the lure of Gerome's paintings and the beautiful Claudine. Perhaps there was structure in the universe and everyone was faced with a test at some point in their life. Some would pass the test and some would fail. He had royally screwed up.

He had been touched when he'd read a newspaper article about a homeless man who'd found a diamond engagement ring in tin cup he used for donations. The man had returned the ring to its owner. He was well aware what *he* would have done. But could he change? Was the encounter with Gerome, with his oafish manners and taste for violence, a pathway for change sent by the universe?

He sat on the bed and pondered on the curiosities of life. Some people were born to sail on a flat-calm sea. Others encountered choppy waters. The unfortunate few were subjected to a perfect storm. Where was the justice in that?

He longed to be in the centre of a still ocean. He imagined himself on a lilo, floating on a sea so flat it resembled molten metal. Warm, but not hot, sun caressed his bones, his internal organs, his core. He was at one with the sea and sky. Not a sound, aside from the occasional cry of a gull. This was the peace he needed to achieve on dry land. Alouette's apartment had this aura of calm. She had a heart bursting with love and no one to give it to. Liam was suddenly ashamed. He had been planning to go to Alouette; to try to persuade her to forgive him and to take him back. He'd been thinking only of his own needs and not of hers.

It dawned on him that he had just completed one of the twelve steps: examining past errors. Soon, he would participate in another step and make amends for these errors. He wasn't about to seek out all of the people he had trodden on and upset in the past, partly because this would involve going back to England and incurring Victor's wrath, and Gerome and Marie were dead so there was nothing he could do there. He could patch things up with Alouette, though. Even though their relationship had only been in its infancy, he knew she cared for him. If she still wanted him, then he would try to fulfil her needs. Liam realised he was no longer in charge of his destiny - the ball was in Alouette's court. She was in control of the future and if she chose to reject him, which she might well do, then he would have to accept that.

There was a commotion in the hallway. Objects hitting walls, shouting, doors banging. Liam rushed over to the bed and put his head under the pillow. The sound of arguing distressed him so much, he'd likened it in the past to a gramophone needle scraping across an LP: Mary and her father, Mary and her boyfriends, he and Lily. To Liam's ears, a torrent of threats, accusations and recriminations was worse than the physical act of throwing a punch. Yet when he thought of La Villette and Gerome's apartment, he could not recall one sound. Not Gerome's cries, or Marie's scream, or the sound of the bodies falling to the floor. Liam shook his head, he was aware that his mind was playing the joker and he wasn't in the mood to argue with it. He recalled a saying: *arguing with a fool only proves that there are two.*

There was an urgent banging on the door. Liam got up from the bed, went to the door and put his ear against it. He heard the sound of footsteps, quick and urgent, pacing in front of his door. Liam pictured a squad of police outside, waiting to cuff him and take him into custody. Was this the moment of discovery? He edged the door open an inch and saw Mikey

"Doing a bloody dance outside my door? What the hell."

"Let me in, mate. Fuckin' women trouble."

Liam looked down the hallway, where pillows, a lamp and other objects were strewn about. Mikey hurried past him, into the room.

"What's going on…all that stuff outside your door?"

"Fuckin' awful, mate. I had to get away."

Liam's heart began to pound. Had Mikey done something terrible? Had La Villette repeated itself? He went down the corridor to the Australian's room. He gave the door a shove and entered. Barely an inch of free floor space existed amongst the pizza boxes, food leftovers of various descriptions and a tangle of sheets. His shoulders relaxed when he saw there was no other person, living or dead, in the room. He went down the hall and checked the bathroom; it too, was empty.

He went back to his room. Mikey, partly hidden by the open wardrobe door, was sweating.

"It's safe now." Liam shut the wardrobe door. "There's no one there."

Mikey wiped his forehead and sat on the bed. "Thanks, Patrick. Thought I was a goner."

"What happened? I saw you come in with a couple of girls earlier."

Mikey nodded. "Thought I'd lucked out, mate. They were up for partying. We bought wine, beers. I was ready for a right soiree." His voice trembled as he spoke.

"I heard the banging and shouting. Are the girls okay?"

"They're fine. I'm not. Look at me, mate, I'm in bits. It was mental. One minute we were drinking. I was thinking I was in with a chance with the small blonde, a real honey. Then they both started jabbering in their language…"

"French," Liam said dryly.

"Yeah, that. I hadn't a clue what they were saying but I knew they were mad at each other, and getting madder. PMT hell, Patrick. One picked up a cushion and threw it at the other, then the beer and wine was chucked around. The small one picked up a chair. It was getting heavy, I think she was about to smash it on her mate's head when I managed to shove them out the door. They were at it hammer and tongs as they went down the stairs. I'll be lucky if I'm not chucked out."

"So, none of this was your fault?"

"Didn't lay a finger on either of them. Didn't have the chance."

Liam felt a flash of fear. What if someone heard the noise and called the police. What if Mikey was lying and he'd tried it on with one of the girls?

"You'd better get back to your room and clean up," he said. "The management, or police, might check on you."

"Police? I'm outta here man."

"Best if you lie low. Hide out in a bar. Not the one where you met the girls…"

Mikey thanked Liam for his help and advice and left.

Liam shut his door and locked it. He sat on the edge of the bed and wondered if he should pack his belongings and leave. But where would he go? He'd paid in advance for a few more nights at the hostel. This was his safe haven. Had Mikey's stupidity ruined his hopes of rest and recovery, put paid to his aspirations of smoothing out his life before he faced Alouette? Stupidity, Liam mused, was *his* domain. Compared to his own knack of taking the wrong fork in the road, Mikey was a novice.

Half an hour later, he ventured downstairs. The old man sat behind the reception desk, eyes down, an open book in front of him. He appeared peaceful, oblivious to the commotion, although Liam wasn't sure he was actually reading. He breathed a sigh of relief. The hostel would remain a sanctuary for a few more days.

Routine, he knew, was an antidote to chaos, so he drew up a daily schedule. *Know where you stand, prepare for the worst, hope for the best,* that would be his motto from now on. The day would begin slowly, like that of a bargeman without a load slowly drifting down the Seine. Mornings would be filled with contemplative activities: a long shower, breakfast, as much coffee as he could drink and, afterwards, a gentle stroll. After lunch, he'd venture further. He was still a free man so why not expand boundaries and become familiar with the city. He'd feel the fear that had kept him prisoner in the vicinity of the hostel, and then let it go.

Chapter 27

The following morning, after breakfast, he explored the outskirts of Montmartre, a quiet area with few tourist trappings. In the afternoon he ventured further afield, to the Boulevard de Clichy, a street lined with bars, kebab shops and peep shows. He wasn't interested in the peep shows and found them a turn off. In his present mood, sex was the last thing on his mind.

The next day, he strolled through the cobbled streets near the hostel. He put his hand on an old, rough wall, felt its warmth and energy, and wondered if once Picasso, after one too many, had stumbled down this street and bumped against this very stone.

In the afternoon, he took the metro to the Musee D'Orsay. While he viewed the swirls and circles in Van Gogh's *The Starry Night*, he was reminded of the paintings in the park. How much for a square or rectangle of canvas with paint applied, he asked himself? Van Gogh's fame was accelerated by the lingering mystery surrounding the circumstances of his death - would Gerome's death bring him the same level of fame?

He wondered again if the paintings would still be where he'd left them. If they'd been discovered would the finder have contacted the police and would they have recognised these as works by Gerome? Perhaps police were already in the park, hiding amongst other shadowy individuals, waiting to pounce.

On the way back from the museum, he stopped and studied the boards outside a group of restaurants, advertising fixed-price menus. The words *coq au vin* on one board, written in bold purple chalk, caught his eye. The artistry of the letters reminded him of Van Gogh's sweeping brush strokes and the price was reasonable, so he decided to eat there. As he ate, he pondered the effects of advertising. The meal he ate was ordinary, yet he'd been drawn into this restaurant. Advertising was key to his decision making and perhaps lack of that was why Gerome's genius had lain undiscovered. Later, when the chaos and fuss surrounding Gerome's demise had died down, he would think of a suitable campaign to launch Gerome's art – in another location, of course.

The routine suited him and a few days in, when he looked in the mirror he caught a glimpse of the other Liam, the one who'd bought and sold antiques in London. His hair was still grey, the beard still grew on his chin, but his eyes had changed and only a glimmer of the haunted look remained. Liam ran his fingers through his hair. The steely shade and the beard, which gave the air of a learned professor, pleased him. If the real Patrick had existed, he would have found it difficult to pay him back for the loan of his persona. He tipped an imaginary hat to the alter ego who'd taken him by the arm and guided him through a thorny maze of his own construction. Each turning, each scratch, a reminder of the poor choices he had made. Without Patrick, he would have succumbed to the bites and scratches, would have become snarled in twisted branches. Yet, despite Patrick, Gerome's image and memories of his genius were never far away. Contentment was like a blushing apple on a high up tree branch. Lovely to look at but too far away to reach.

He bought several shirts from a second hand shop and laid them on top of his bed. He hung a blue denim one on a hanger, ready for the following day. It had the most possibility, it would please Alouette.

"Tomorrow," he muttered aloud. Tomorrow he would leave this room and his fate would be in the lap of the gods. Tomorrow he would say goodbye to Patrick. He'd known him only briefly but he was the best friend he'd ever had.

He went for a beer with a somewhat subdued Mikey. Mikey was leaving Paris, heading off to Dublin, the young man confided. His enjoyment of Paris had been spoilt by the bizarre behaviour of the two girls.

"Can't see why you invited both back to your room," Liam said, as they sat outside a café in the Place du Tertre. "Double trouble."

"Not my usual style, Patrick. I thought it might be different here. Different customs. They offered to come back. I could tell there was bad blood between them, but I thought it might be bad manners to refuse."

"Paris is certainly different, a cut above the rest," Liam said, "but as far as women are concerned, they're the same the world over. If they like a man, they want him to themselves. I've had a few hairy moments in my life when it comes to the fairer sex, but if I had it all to do again, I'd make sure I put respect at the top of my list. Show a woman respect and you're halfway there."

"Jeez, you're quite the gentleman and philosopher, aren't you? I suppose that's the Irish in you."

Liam eyes were drawn to the centre of the Place du Tertre, where the number of performers and artists had dwindled to a handful. Liam, who was about to take a sip of beer, set the glass back down as he spotted a familiar, and not so friendly, face amongst the few who had remained. Borivoj crouched on his stool, around thirty yards from the table.

Liam shifted his chair round so his back faced the performers.

"Missin' all the action, Pops."

"Bored with it. If you've seen one performer, you've seen 'em all." He raised his glass. "To peace and quiet." He shrugged and hoped that Mikey hadn't noticed the change in his demeanour: his movements becoming stiff, his eyes filled with fear. He pictured himself, tied to a chair with Victor standing in front of him, his fingers inserted in a knuckle duster. Would Victor's punishment be worse than that which Borivoj might dole out? Borivoj was certainly an enigma: caring and kind towards Alouette, yet he'd seen something in his eyes the day the Czech had thrown him out of the flat. A chill surpassing Victor's form on a bad day. On some deep, intuitive level, he knew that Borivoj might be capable of cold-blooded murder. Liam shook his head: the worst had already happened and no external torture could top the angst he felt inside.

"Alright, Patrick? Gone a bit pale."

"Fine and dandy, just fine."

"Why don't you kick loose, come to Dublin with me. We'll have a blast."

Liam was sorely tempted. If he could afford it, then where better to go than Dublin? He spoke the language, the beer was excellent, the scenery and nightlife fantastic. He might even get some work. He could take a new name, or hang onto the Patrick Doyle identity and start a new life. But then he remembered Alouette. For some crazy reason he had to see her and in reality he couldn't afford a new start.

The paintings, he knew, were the key to the future, so transporting them out of the country when Gerome's body was barely cold was risky. Perhaps border guards already knew his name and were in possession of a photo. It wouldn't be an up-to-date one but the bastards were clever. He massaged the wrist of his left hand, imagining the bite of cool steel on his wrists. Freedom, that was all he wanted. Freedom was worth much more than Victor's money. Paradoxically, before he'd frittered his freedom away, he'd had as much as any individual required. Right now, he told himself, it was best to lie low.

"Nice offer. I think I'll stay awhile. Galleries to see, restaurants to try."

Mikey nodded. "I can see you're into all that. More an outdoors man myself. I've heard the Irish are pretty laid back. That'll suit me down to the ground. Anyone you want to give your best to?"

He shook his head. "I left on bad terms with the missus and a few other people, so best if you don't mention my name."

He got up, shook Mikey's hand and made his way across the square. His heart beat faster as he neared Borivoj, who was distracted when his sunglasses fell to the ground. Liam bent down and picked them up. His heart was pounding so hard, he wondered if Borivoj could hear it too.

"*Merci, monsieur.*" Borivoj held out his cup. Liam shook his head and hurried on, thanking Patrick for this final act of cover.

The following morning, Liam packed his bag and settled the remainder of the bill. He resisted the temptation to slip past reception without paying. Was there any point in risking a brush with the law? he asked himself. He'd not kept up with current affairs so had no idea if the police were still looking for him either in his vagrant or in any other guise.

As he made his way to the metro, he planned what he would say when he knocked on Alouette's door: he had gone to England for a few weeks but had missed her so much he was compelled to return. The latter part of this wasn't untrue, he realised. But would she take him in like a stray cat, or would he once more be homeless, without a bed to sleep in or a roof over his head, counting the stars, wind, rain and sun as his only companions.

Chapter 28

Liam's footsteps echoed on the marble staircase. Marble, he thought as he made his way up the stairs, was a grand word, evoking images of Roman or Florentine interiors or statues in charming piazzas, but in reality these stairs were tiled in a cheaper variety: cream with an dull greyish shade running like a varicose vein across the surface. The tile colour matched the yellowed walls, which had likely sucked in years of cigarette smoke without the occasional freshen up. He wondered why Alouette chose to live here, but perhaps it wasn't a choice, maybe it was simply cheap.

He climbed the forty stairs to the fourth floor. Everything was perfectly symmetrical: ten stairs leading up to each floor. Each block of stairs was broken by a small square landing. There were no flowers, prints or paintings to soften the hallways but neither were there sickly smells of cooking or heavy cleaning materials, as the window on each landing was wedged open.

He stood in front of Alouette's door and smiled as his eyes traced round the golden yellow beading on the cream door. He pictured her standing in the cold, melancholy hallway, a paintbrush and tin of yellow paint in her hands. Making the best of things, that's what women like Alouette did.

Taking a risk, he gripped the brass knocker and rapped twice. These first knocks were timid, the knocker barely making contact with the brass plate on the door. He listened: there was no evidence of movement inside. He rapped again, this time with more force. He put his ear to the door and thought he could hear a voice singing. Strange what tricks the mind can play, he thought. His own mind had likely played the biggest joke on him when it had urged him to return to Alouette; to rely on her to save him when for all he knew she might have moved elsewhere, or maybe she'd taken a new lover and was singing to him.

Heels tapped on the hall floor, a lock was fiddled with and the door opened several inches. The gap was big enough to observe her eyes, at first wary, turn curious. Her puzzled gaze said that she knew this person on her doorstep, but couldn't remember from where.

His eyes took in every aspect of her appearance. She was unchanged, the calm in the midst of his stormy sea. He imagined if he returned in a year, or two, or more, he would find her preserved 'as is', like the contents of an unopened luxury tin. Truffles bought from Harrods one Christmas came to mind. The smell of damp earth was still strong, almost overpowering, when the tin was finally cut open two years later.

Whatever turmoil existed inside, Alouette hid expertly. She wore her standard uniform of black sweater and trousers, perfectly clean, perfectly pressed. A grey silk scarf dotted with tiny yellow roses was casually draped round her neck. Not a strand of hair escaped from its allotted place in her glossy bob. Such order in life astonished Liam and he wished he was more like her.

"Alouette," he said, not knowing what else to say.

"I..." her voice trailed off. She squinted, moved closer to him and put on her glasses, which were hanging on a cord looped round her neck. Her eyes widened behind the lenses. "Liam? Pas possible."

"It's me, Alouette, the bad penny. I've come back."

She allowed the door to swing open, then turned and walked towards the living room. She didn't wave her hand, or ask him to follow her but he knew that was what she wanted. She sat down at the table. He started to pull out a chair opposite, but she shook her head and pointed to the sofa.

"There, better over there for you."

He sat down; the sofa cushions were springy yet soft. He leaned back against the cloud of comfort – not far enough back to make her think he was already settling in. He wished he'd brought a bottle of wine, flowers, some sort of peace offering. Instead all he had to offer was himself. Not much, he thought, despite the new haircut and light blue shirt. There was so much he wanted to say but he decided to begin with sorry. "I came back to apologise. I treated you badly."

Alouette nodded. "It's not the first time in my life. Others have done it, I'm sure it will happen again."

"You didn't deserve it...what I did."

"You're right. I didn't, but perhaps I should accept some of the blame."

"Can't think why," he frowned.

"We had known each other a short time; just enough for a holiday romance - although I suppose holiday romances sometimes work out. I opened up to you too quickly, without verifying what *you* wanted."

"I was confused as hell. I'd just blown a fortune. Greed and stupidity, I'll own up to that. All I could think of was making money and the next deal. Poverty and I – well we don't make good partners – but *we* were good together, you and I, weren't we?"

"That woman? Borivoj said she was young and beautiful, just like the painting. Are you still seeing her?"

"Not since that night." Liam flushed. In this instance, he was telling the truth and liked how that felt. In reality, even if Claudine came begging, he wouldn't be interested. Dreams weren't reality, a big-hearted woman like Alouette was.

"So, where have you been?"

"England. I went back and tried to sort out my mess but there were too many problems. I left while I still could."

"So, your associate is still looking for you?"

"With a fine tooth comb, I'm sure." Already he was slipping back to a world of untruths, ducking and diving, but these small white lies, told with a silver tongue, were solely for Alouette's benefit.

"You don't choose your friends well, but neither, I suppose, did I."

Liam raised his eyebrows.

"You don't remember the tale I told you, about my stay in England? I think you fell asleep. Never mind, it was good to let it all out, even if I wasn't heard. But like you, I too can't go back there."

"Why?"

"Another time. Let's put the past to bed, tucked away under the duvet. Tell me what you are doing back in Paris and what your intentions are."

"No idea what I'll do, Alouette. I wanted to see you. To tell you I was sorry for lying. I'm a different person now. I want to make amends."

"Borivoj told me he saw you on the street. He said you were dressed in old, stained clothes."

"I had nowhere to go and no money. At first, I wasn't well enough to go back home. Borivoj gave me a little money so I went back to England. I stayed with a friend but it didn't take long to realise there was nothing there for me. I'd burnt my bridges. Paris is my home."

"And what now?"

"Still no money, I'm afraid. But I have my health back again, I'm sure I can find work."

"What work will you do?"

"No idea. I'm sure I'll think of something."

She tapped the nails of one hand on the table. "Perhaps your language is of some use. Your pronunciation is very clear, you speak nicely, have a wide vocabulary. You could give English conversation lessons? I might know some people who would be interested."

He nodded vigorously. Alouette was warming to him again. If he had to give English classes to win her back, then he would. Besides, what was wrong with adding another string to his bow?

"That would be fantastic. And I almost forgot. I have paintings to sell. They might be worth a bit. That'll help me out for a while."

"Ah, those paintings. The source of all your troubles, if you ask me. They're under the bed, along with the rest of the things you left. Borivoj returned them. I think he knew you would be back."

"He recognises a bad penny when he sees one." He stood up and reached out a hand, wondering if she'd take it.

"There's so much we need to talk about. Let's go for a walk in the fresh air."

Alouette flushed and ignored the outstretched hand. Liam felt his heart sink; he'd been too presumptuous, assumed that as she'd let him in, he would be forgiven. Then she waved a hand towards the door.

"It's a beautiful day and I suppose we need to top up your new suntan. Did I tell you I prefer the grey hair and beard, very distinguished." Alouette's eyes drifted to the window. "Let's go down by the water, Liam. Water makes me feel alive. The Canal St. Martin is so pretty, I want to show it to you."

Despite his relief at her gradual thaw, nerves gripped his stomach. He could not admit he'd been to the Canal St. Martin recently, as it was there he'd disposed of his bloody clothes and the murder weapons. He willed his mind to continue protecting him.

They arrived at the Canal and sat on a grassy bank near a bridge. He shivered as he looked at the grey stone blocks that made up the bridge's structure. Serving a harmless function now, but how different, even menacing, they'd appeared that day. Then, he'd stood on the bridge and hoisted the plastic bag onto the ledge, intending to tip it into the river, but a woman waving from a passing barge had thwarted this plan. He'd walked further. Miles, in his imagination, before disposing of the bloody baggage, but perhaps in reality it wasn't that all that far. Liam stood up and held out his hand.

"Let's take a stroll along the bank. Nothing like being next to water on a fine day."

He and Alouette walked a while then sat down on the canal bank. He unscrewed a bottle of wine bought from a wine merchant on the way, and filled two plastic goblets. He raised his goblet and tipped it against Alouette's.

"To old friends – and much more."

"Friends, yes. Good idea to take it slowly, to enjoy the scenery. Like taking a horse and cart through a lovely valley rather than racing along in a Ferrari," she toasted him back. "To old and not so old friends."

She set her glass on the grass and trailed a finger over his hair. "Mmmn, nice."

He flinched.

"Sorry, I didn't mean to startle you. I was simply admiring the colour of your hair. It suits you. And the texture of your beard, like fine wire - you know the thing you use for scrubbing dishes."

"Like a Brillo Pad, you mean. I'm not used to the new me yet. When I look in the mirror, I think someone else is looking back."

"Do you like this new man better?"

"Than what?"

"The old one. The old Liam."

He shook his head firmly. "That one is dead and gone. He's a shadow, a ghost."

"You didn't like yourself much. I could tell that right away when I met you. That first night at Le Chat Rouge."

"I was ghastly. Vile. I'm amazed you and Borivoj bothered to rescue me. I suppose it's possible to change, isn't it?"

"If you want something enough, then yes. I think we can change when we drop our facades and let our weaknesses shine through. I find vulnerable people much more attractive. We are, some say, the sum total of our weaknesses."

"I could never do that," he said cryptically. "I mean I could never let my guard down. That would be like opening that old cliché: Pandora's box. But moving forwards, I could promise to be truthful. That's a good start, isn't it?"

Alouette gazed into the water. Her eyes glittered, reflecting back ripples that skimmed the surface.

"I love these tiny waves on the top of the water. They're like the waves in Venice, the ones the artist Canaletto painted."

"I know Canaletto's waves," he laughed. "Nice from afar, like a child's cartoon up close. Some things, Alouette, are best seen from a distance."

He was distracted by two men walking past. They had an aura of importance about them, an air of officialdom he'd come across before. Council officials, social workers, bailiffs: he could identify them a mile away, and in his mind, their business involved making life difficult for some hapless individual. The men picking their way along the canal bank, slowly and curiously, wore dark raincoats and heavy work boots. Liam noted that their eyes flitted back and forth in synchrony. The moment the one nearest the river looked left, into the water, his companion's head head swivelled right. He felt the one set of eyes momentarily scrutinise them, then both men moved on.

"Police," he murmured.

"Looks like it. They must be looking for someone."

"It's so quiet round here and not many places to hide. Can't imagine criminals hanging out in this area."

She shrugged. "We have crimes. Plenty of crimes. While you were in England there was a murder. A market trader and his wife. Terrible thing. Both killed in their own home."

"Did they catch them? I mean the people who did it."

"I don't think so. They were looking for an old man who was hanging around the district, but it's all gone quiet now."

His eyes tracked the two men as they rounded a bend and disappeared from view. Fear clutched at his stomach, twisting until he could barely breathe. He imagined the worst: had the bin bag popped up to the surface after he'd left, revealing its deadly contents? Had a passerby found the bundle and turned it in? If so, the authorities might be looking for him. He reached over and gripped Alouette's hand. She gave him a curious look.

They made their way to the metro. As they boarded the train, she asked him to move back in with her and he agreed. He was being given a second chance, an opportunity to build another life. This was a wildly different life to the one he had imagined almost six months ago. There would be no expensive apartment on the left bank, no fancy holidays, no young and beautiful women in his bed. But Alouette was attractive and a good companion. Given what he had been through recently, wasn't this the best outcome life could offer? It dawned on him, that if he could put his greed and insecurities permanently aside, then he might achieve a degree of happiness. Wasn't that what life was all about?

She gave him an odd look as they sat down in the almost empty carriage.

"I made a call while you were buying the tickets."

His insides once again began to churn. Had Alouette sensed the fear oozing from his pores when the two men had walked by?

"I invited Borivoj round for a drink later. I think we all need to make peace."

"It's your call. He hates me, though."

"He doesn't trust you, that's not the same as hate. Borivoj is a good friend. If you're staying with me then I need things to be harmonious. I hope you boys can act like grown-ups; put your differences to one side."

"Not a problem for me," he said, feeling like a moody five year old forced to visit an aging relative they didn't like. He wasn't looking forward to seeing Borivoj again. The last time they had properly spoken, he'd been crazed and about to do something he'd regret for the rest of his life. Here with Alouette, all that seemed like a distant dream, and that's how he wanted to keep it.

"Would you prefer to go out? What about Le Chat Rouge? I haven't been there in ages. If I remember correctly, there's a Django Reinhardt tribute band playing this week."

Liam and Borivoj scowled at each other.

"No," they said in unison.

Alouette sighed. "Now, you two!" You are my favourite men in the world. Why can't you get on?"

Borivoj waved a hand towards Liam. "I must be frank. This man is not honest. He is not good for you, Alouette. I am sorry to say in such a public manner."

"I've changed." Liam's voice was soft yet stubborn. He

needed to turn Borivoj round, to get him onside. A voice whispered in his ear: *keep your friends close, your enemies even closer.*

"When I last saw you, you looked like crazy old man, wild person living in garden. Alouette is woman of refinement, too good for you."

"My fault. I shouldn't have thrown him out. I knew he was vulnerable." Alouette bit her lip and looked at Liam. He was suddenly jittery. She'd spoken earlier about the police looking for an old man in connection with the murders. Didn't that fit with Borivoj's description of him? Alouette could be naïve but she wasn't stupid. It wouldn't be long before she put two and two together.

"I gave money to go back home," Borivoj said.

"And I did. I was grateful, I went right away," Liam added quickly. "I missed Alouette; that's why I came back."

Borivoj got up from the sofa and sat on the floor crosslegged. His back was as straight as a steel rod.

"Dear, dear Alouette." He shook his head and tutted.

"What are you doing down there, Borivoj?" Alouette gave a faint smile and patted him on the head.

"I'm a poor man, a simple man, not fit to sit on your chair."

Liam got up and sat on the floor next to him.

"You are taking fun of me," Borivoj said huffily.

"Making. But not at all. I agree with you. Neither of us is fit to sit on Alouette's sofa."

Borivoj ignored Liam and looked up at Alouette. "I am returning to Besiny."

Alouette nodded slowly. "I thought that day was coming soon. I don't blame you. It's hard enough here for me and I'm French. I can imagine how difficult it must be for you, so far away from home, from your language and people. We all need to find a place we can call home."

"Come with me. At least for holiday. You can take time away. Far away from this… scoundrel. You can relax at house of my mother and plan future."

Alouette shook her head. "Too late. I've no appetite for

starting afresh. My future is right here."

"With him?"

"Yes, if things work out, that wouldn't be so bad."

Liam's heart swelled with gladness and Borivoj stood up.

"Then I have said enough. I bid you adieu, dear Alouette."

Alouette followed him out to the hallway. Their whispering was like notes on a scale - at first low then high. Then the front door clicked shut. He breathed a sigh of relief. Borivoj was one more hurdle he would not have to overcome in the future. At the moment all that was required was peace and quiet.

Chapter 29

Days later, while Alouette was out, Liam collected the paintings from the shed. He arranged them on the bedroom floor, first scanning the desert scene, taking in every variation in shade and colour on the canvas. Like a fine wine which had reached the perfect moment of maturity, the painting was better than he remembered. Gerome had captured the very essence of sand, its grainy texture and colour. In confident strokes, the light and shade it had taken nature millions of years to create had been captured, and for a few seconds he'd been transported to a hot southern land. Then he remembered Alouette. If she happened on the paintings, he would say he'd spotted them in a market and had snapped them up with the idea of flogging them later. That wasn't much of a lie, was it?

As days slipped by, his sense of wellbeing increased. Sometimes he managed to convince himself that the terrible events at Gerome's had been simply a bad dream. On other days, he told himself that someone else committed the murders and that he'd simply stumbled upon the crime scene.

Routine and good companionship were the keys to mental health, he'd realised, and for the first time in years he had a rough idea how his day was going to pan out: food, music, walks and the occasional sex. Their relationship slipped into a gentle rhythm, natural and unforced, and he likened it to the lapping of waves against the shore on a calm day.

There were no rows or bouts of bickering. It was an unspoken rule that whoever cooked didn't wash up. He had little interest in television so Alouette was in charge of the remote control. If she was up early, which she often was, she would pick up groceries. She liked shopping, she often declared, so he knew this wasn't much of a chore. If she was in a lazier frame of mind, they stayed in bed late.

He sometimes went with her to the local market. There was something about the hustle and bustle and the shouts of the traders that lifted his spirits – perhaps he was reminded of auction days. The scent of soaps from the South lingered over one particular stall: at one end, the air was heavy with lavender oil, in the centre, honey dominated, and at the other end a sharp lemony scent clung to small yellow balls. Then there was the piquancy of the tapenades on offer. The sharp smell brought to mind a long-distant holiday in Menton: five days in the old town with his mother, in a higgledy-piggledy tall house, airbrushed yellow, the same shade as the sun. Like most of the other houses in the old town it had no garden, but the view of the Mediterranean from the roof terrace more than made up for this. He'd paid for the holiday with a big auction win. A small price to pay to fulfil one of her dreams - holidaying in the South of France.

Alouette was the most undemanding woman he had ever crossed paths with, yet he was still occasionally compelled to wander the streets on his own. He treasured these moments of solitude as they reminded him of who he'd been in the past, before Paris. When an attractive woman passed by, his eyes would flicker downwards, fixing on the pavement. Alouette had taken him in, given him a lifeline so he owed her everything. He made an oath to himself that he would be faithful for as long as they were together. Their current arrangement suited him so he allowed himself to imagine that the relationship would last.

When his mood took a low, melancholy turn, he relied on art to lift his spirits. He learned to negotiate the glass and steel pyramid of the Louvre and studied the Old Masters. Other days, only the colourful delights of the Impressionists in the Musee D'Orsay would suffice. He dawdled in galleries and allowed himself to dream: in another life, given the right opportunities and circumstances, he might have studied Art History. He would have hung out with artists, basked in their reflected glory. Maybe discussed the meaning of their paintings, or imbibed a glass or two with them at La Coupole or Le Select in the Boulevard Montparnasse.

If he didn't allow the murders to worm their way into his thoughts, peace was like a ripe apple on a low branch – there for the picking. Alouette was a considerate and undemanding lover. This did not surprise him, nor did he want to alter her in any way. The most important aspect of the relationship was their closeness. He did not want to be alone with his demons.

Money was the only difficulty, the proverbial spanner in the works, so the option of stealing another handbag crossed Liam's mind. He didn't relish the thought of causing, yet again, distress to a fellow human being, but could see no other option. Alouette came to his rescue.

"You know those classes we were talking about. The daughter of an acquaintance needs some help with passing her university entrance English exam. Interested?"

"Definitely up for it. When do I start?"

After a few lessons, which to his surprise went better than expected, Alouette's friend recommended him to others. His client list expanded from one to four. Eight hours a week teaching at ten euro per hour. He calculated that taking into account metro fares to his students' homes, he was earning sixty euro a week. Enough to buy an occasional bottle of wine, not enough to eat in a good restaurant or go on a trip. He'd always claimed that slogging for a pittance was a hopeless way of making money yet he found a strange satisfaction when a student's English improved, when they used the right tense, and the right word. Job satisfaction without real financial gain: for him, that was a novel concept.

Some evenings, he and Alouette made their way to one of the city's boulevards, where they sat at small round tables in cafes, eyeing up the latest fashions, observing, judging, just as others had done for centuries. They lingered over a glass or two of wine or an espresso, then returned home. Liam had never experienced this form of gentle companionship before as he and his mother were usually one or two steps away from the next crisis, and with Lily, he never knew where he stood.

One evening, a few months into his stay with Alouette, there was a TV news update on the La Villette murders. To date there were no arrests, the reporter said, and the only witness appeared to be the old homeless man, who had subsequently vanished into thin air. There were rumours of an underworld hit; Gerome had a swarm of enemies which the authorities were in the process of tracking down. Alouette didn't comment on the news report. Instead, as the remote control wasn't at hand, she got up and manually switched the TV to another channel. She was subdued for the rest of the evening, but in bed she was more passionate than usual.

"Are you happy?" she asked after they'd made love.

"Yes, of course."

"I mean, really, really, happy."

He squeezed her hand. "You've no idea. I'm at peace. I've never felt like this." He briefly reflected on his childhood. "No. Never as peaceful as this."

"I hope nothing takes that away," Alouette said mysteriously.

He wondered if she had prophetic powers. Could she see into the future? Could she foretell his undoing?

Alouette was keeping a secret. It wasn't anything she'd said that made him suspicious; he simply had a gut feeling. He noted she was quieter than usual the following evening. In the kitchen as she prepared dinner there was no humming, singing or tapping of feet. At the dinner table she had a faraway look, as though the pasta they ate was tasteless, taken simply for nourishment. He wanted to ask what was wrong but fear at first prevented him. Then he took a long drink of red wine and drew a deep breath.

"You're quiet."

"I suppose."

"Is everything okay?"

"Mmmn, yes," she said dreamily.

"You seem a bit distracted."

"You could say that."

"Anything you want to share?"

"Maybe later."

Her words floated like a lilo on the sea. There was no dismissing or pushing them down and even when he tried, they popped up again. He took another sip of red wine and set the still half-full glass on the coffee table. Losing his guard, the barrier he'd set up between himself and the events at La Villette, was the last thing he wanted. With a glass too many, secrets that were best kept under lock and key might be blurted out. Alouette was planning something, that was clear. Had she become tired of him? Earlier, she'd mentioned how much she missed Borivoj, then she'd laughed and shook her head. What did all that mean?

Liam was worried. He was prone to talking in his sleep so perhaps his unconscious, freed from waking-world conventions, might have owned up to something his conscious mind might tuck away. He recalled a line from a George Orwell piece: *If you want to keep a secret, you must also hide it from yourself.*

Later, in bed, he reached out and rested his arm across her breasts. He was tired and not in the mood for sex but he wanted contact, to reassure himself that all was well.

"How long have you been living with me, Liam?" Alouette asked.

"A few months. Almost three, I think."

"And you've never asked when my birthday is."

He propped himself up on one elbow, trying to read the expression on her face, but it was too dark. Was she angry, sad or content? He had no idea. To Liam, most women were puzzling, enigmas too difficult to break. He had frequently described them in boozy all male sessions as being from a different universe, never mind a different planet. There was one thing he knew as gospel truth: you never forgot their birthday.

"Shit, I've missed it. I'm so sorry..."

Alouette covered his lips with a tiny hand.

"No, you haven't. I'm Aquarius. A typical one. Humane, intellectual, sympathetic. At least I like to think I am."

He felt like he should have scratched his head - he wasn't into astrology.

"January twenty sixth, Liam. You haven't missed it."

"Phew. Thought I was in trouble."

"I had a look at *your* passport."

His head was beginning to pound. Was Alouette toying with him: a cat with a mouse, a fox menacing a chicken? He pictured her nails become longer, claw like, pressing into his flesh.

"Enlighten me, Alouette," he sighed. This was the closest he'd come in the past few months to being cross with her.

"Your birthday, silly, is next week." She slapped his arm playfully. "Why didn't you tell me?"

"Nothing to celebrate," he said. "Better if I hadn't been born."

"You're letting the glass or two of red wine talk for you. You know it always makes you morose. Better to stick to a nice, light Chablis."

"I'd prefer if we ignored it. Not the Chablis, the birthday, I mean. After all, do *you* want to be reminded of passing years?"

"It's different for women. Society dictates that we should be forever young and we women comply by dyeing our hair and spending a fortune on creams that may or may not work. On the other hand, lines and grey hair are practically mandatory for the male species. They turn gauche boys into handsome men. But never mind. I have a surprise that will make you welcome your special day rather than dread it."

He narrowed his eyes. These days, he wasn't sure he liked surprises. He preferred to know things in advance: where they were going, what they would do, if not hour by hour, then day by day. As a child he'd detested clowns in circuses, with their sudden tricks, japes and jokes, and had never found a jack-in-the-box in the slightest funny. What kind of idiot would want to be startled out of their skin by a rubber head popping at them from a box?

"We're going away for a few days," she said.

"Away…away from Paris?"

"Yes, but not too far."

"Are you going to tell me where, or is that top secret too?"

"You'll find out when we get there."

Although the idea of another birthday didn't appeal, particularly this one which marked a year of failure, he was pleased at the thought of leaving Paris.

He had been living with Alouette for almost three months. Had it really been that long? He cast his mind back and realised he couldn't recall specific conversations between them. There were no grand topics, no discussions of war, politics, divorce or similar. It had all been small stuff, things of the moment: scents in the market, pretty flowers, a good wine, the weather, nothing that drilled into inner thoughts. There were no visits from her smattering of friends; it appeared she enjoyed relative solitude. Yet she wasn't one dimensional. Another side of her had been unveiled at Le Chat Rouge, where twice she had stepped onto the stage and sung. She'd done this solely for her own enjoyment, with no accompanying ego and no embarrassment. She had been clapped enthusiastically by the audience, who'd consisted mainly of tourists, apparently grateful for the typically Parisian songs she'd sung in her unique and charming way. You could see nostalgia for the Paris of the past etched on faces in the crowd. This was why they'd come here and they had clapped with such enthusiasm, she'd had to perform several encores.

"You could go on stage, sing again, if you wanted. I bet they'd give you a regular slot here," he'd said on the last occasion, when the applause had dwindled. Her eyes had taken on a fearful, haunted look, so he'd dropped the subject. Perhaps she was reminded of the past and he, above all people, understood the need to wipe the slate clean and begin again.

They had plenty in common: both were only children with no close relatives, money was in tight supply although Liam's situation was far more dire than Alouette's. She had what she called her *petit* trust fund so she would never be homeless. He knew much about her yet he knew nothing about her inner feelings. And she, in turn, could never know his deepest secret.

He rested his head on the pillow again and squeezed her arm. "Can't wait for my mystery trip," he whispered, surprised to discover he meant this

One week later, they made their way to Paris Saint Lazare station. The only clue she would give was that they were going on a fairly short journey. Liam carried a weekend bag in one hand, and Alouette's larger bag in the other. She took his arm as they walked to the metro. Her step was light and her eyes mischievous. He asked again where they were going and she smiled in an enigmatic way, he was reminded of the Mona Lisa - who knew what wicked thoughts lay behind that smile! He guessed there would be few moments in her life when worries about money, loneliness and her past could be tucked away. Today she'd taken on the role of 'tour leader', in charge of their destinies, so he accepted the role of 'willing tourist'.

It was a fine day in late September and the sun gave off a hazy heat. He removed his jacket and packed it in his bag.

"I didn't bring swimming trunks," he said. "Actually, come to think of it, I don't have any."

"You won't need them."

"But we are going to the coast, aren't we?" He was anticipating a trip to the coast, perhaps somewhere in Brittany. He could practically smell the seafood as the imaginary chef whipped up a fabulous dish: mussels in a wine sauce, Sole Veronique or even sea bass with burnt fennel. The pleasure of the food would be doubled by the views - cliffs reminiscent of Gerome's seascape, towering over a stormy sea. Afterwards they might stroll along the promenade, a warm wind blowing. He imagined if he stuck out his tongue, he'd taste the damp, salty air. There would be enough pleasures to shake away the cobwebs of deceit he'd weaved in Paris, far, far away.

"Can't say. It's a birthday surprise. Let the word 'surprise' be a clue."

"Well, I don't picture a birthday party with cake and candles and all my nearest and dearest present."

"That's correct, Liam. There's no crowd. Just you and me. And stop trying to guess." She elbowed his arm.

He took a long look at her. Earlier that morning, she had emerged from the bathroom with a rosy glow. The pink shirt she wore reflected on her cheeks, giving her skin a youthful blush. The scarf usually knotted round her neck had been discarded; in its place was a gold chain with a fish pendant. She wore slim jeans and flat shoes, making her even more petite. Her hair was loosely piled on top of her head. He was astonished: she appeared at least ten years younger. Looking at her was like admiring a painting with soft edges, maybe a Renoir, he thought. He took a deep breath.

"Wonderful. You look wonderful."

Fresh and pretty. He felt a stirring inside and realised he fancied her. Were the months he had spent with Alouette sprinkling water on his own emotional wasteland? He had imagined the ability to share his soul with another individual was lost. Surely that was good, though, as his emotions, like freshly ironed underwear, needed to be tidied away, out of public view? He was suddenly frightened. If he fell in love with Alouette, would that destroy the barrier that shielded him from that darkest moment?

When he had returned to the shed, he had been astonished to discover the paintings were still hidden under the stack of crates. The part of him which longed for a new start in Paris had hoped to find the structure demolished, a pile of rubble, its contents destroyed. Or even better, he'd thought, one of the homeless people living in the park might have discovered and sold them. He could have lived with any of these scenarios, which might have drawn a thick black line under the shambolic mess he'd created. But another part of him, the part of his mind where greed lurked, was relieved when his hand reached in and made contact with the corner of a canvas. Once Gerome's genius was posthumously discovered, he could be sitting on a goldmine. He hadn't reckoned on falling for Alouette, though, if that's what you'd call the butterflies in his stomach when he looked at her.

A little more than half an hour after the train left the apartment blocks and industrial estates of Paris' suburbs behind, she stood up. The train slowed as it pulled into a station. The sign above the platform announced they were in Vernon.

"We have arrived at our destination," Alouette said in a commanding voice as she led the way to the exit. Liam followed, carrying both bags.

He stood on the platform, gazing around. The station was small and the only amenity he could see was a newspaper stand. The doors at the front of the station were wedged open and a scruffy bar with motor bikes parked outside was across the road.

"Vernon. ... Never been here before. Seems nice, quiet, not too much here."

"Very droll, Liam. This is actually an attractive town, if you walk a few hundred metres over the bridge."

"Not the seaside?" his voice trailed off as Alouette erupted with laughter. When she had composed herself, they exited the station and waited across the road for a bus. Liam scanned the timetable.

"Giverny. We're going to Giverny. Is that right?"

She smiled and nodded.

"I'm afraid you have discovered your destination a little early. Although it would have been impossible to ask the bus company to keep my secret."

"Wonderful...bloody magic! Monet's house - I'll want to visit that. I've never been to Giverny. I've always meant to go."

"It's very beautiful. We have two days. We are staying in a nice hotel near the village. I have arranged tickets for Monet's house and gardens, but aside from that connection, Giverny is a perfect place to relax, eat and walk. Just what you need. What *we* need."

He leaned over and kissed her cheek.

"Perfect place, perfect companion, perfect birthday present. Right now, I'm as happy as I've ever been. Do you know the expression 'happy as Larry' "

She shook her head. "Who is this Larry?"

"No idea. But he must be a very happy person."

The bus journey from Vernon to Giverny was short and took them through pleasant countryside. If Alouette had presented him with a list of possible things to do on his birthday, this would come out tops. His obsession with art was almost as great as his need to craft the perfect deal. It was like cracking a combination lock on a safe - part luck, part skill. Art, like women, or antique books with foxed and yellowed pages, he'd never tire of. Alouette, it appeared, had tuned into his desires and he was touched by her generosity. 'The heart that keeps on giving', he said to himself as he glanced at her. He was suddenly deeply touched that she'd taken the trouble to check when his birthday was. On the other hand, he gave thanks that the habit of stamping passports at border crossings had virtually disappeared. He'd lied to her when he said he'd gone back to England, that was true. But was it really a lie, he reasoned, when Alouette believed what he'd said? Surely a lie took two parties to make it complete: the teller and the recipient. Without both understanding their complicity, did a lie really exist? In any case, he was grateful to Alouette for her generosity and hoped he had the strength of character not to disappoint.

When he examined his thoughts, as he frequently did, he found they were transforming on an almost daily basis. This change operated on a deeper level; he was becoming more like the man he wanted to be. He wished he could swat away the old Liam, who he now thought of as an annoying fly, buzzing, teasing, tainting his space with its germs. When the fly called a truce, he allowed himself to be grateful for small pleasures: a walk in the park in a rainstorm, a glass of chilled Chablis, rather than a bottle or two, breakfast in bed, watching a romantic film. He was becoming a better person yet a terrible deed was responsible for this metamorphosis.

Would the change only be complete when he had fully acknowledged what he'd done and had made amends? But how could you make amends for taking a life? That was the ultimate wrongdoing, a deed that couldn't be reversed. He shook his head. Remembering La Villette could wait and for the next few days, he and Alouette would eat, drink and view wonderful art.

"Happy birthday, Liam," he muttered to himself.

They arrived at their hotel, a converted watermill. The walls were thick yellow stone, interrupted by a functional watermill. Their room was decorated in a comfortable French country style: lemon walls giving off a summery glow, a bedspread dazzling with bright flowers, polished floorboards. Liam ran his fingers over the top of the oak dressing table. The grooves, marks and wear of the old furniture were comforting to the touch. Things happen, time passes, we move on, he told himself.

The floor to ceiling windows led to a small terrace overlooking a broad expanse of green. A thread of silver curled across the land.

"River Epte," Alouette said. "Like silver yarn in a green knitted jumper." Liam smiled at the jumper comparison: his mother, a prolific knitter, would approve of Alouette, he thought. A lump formed in his throat and he found it difficult to choke back the tears that threatened to overwhelm him. He wasn't worthy of Alouette's kindness. She surely deserved better than him: a thief, a liar, a murderer. He felt like picking up his bag and leaving.

"Don't you like my surprise, Liam?"

"I love it. All of it. You've done too much, though. I don't deserve you."

Her face suddenly fell. "I've gone too far, haven't I? I didn't mean you to feel trapped…claustrophobic, I think you call it. Someone once said they felt like that when they were with me. My intentions were innocent; you've had a hard year. I simply wanted your birthday to be perfect. Is that so wrong?"

He took her hand and gave her a watery smile. "It's not that. I love what you've done, but I don't deserve it. I'm not a good person. Borivoj was right, you deserve much more than I can give."

"Tsk, tsk. Accept the holiday with grace. It's for both of us and it's not like I'm asking you to marry me, is it?"

Chapter 30

Ezekiel's stroke of luck:

The studio was large and bright. Light flooded in through windows overlooking the river, illuminating the clotted-cream walls. The river outside was the Seine; he was where he belonged, right in the thick of things.

Ezekiel was working on a new painting and had barely tipped the canvas with his paintbrush when there was a knock at the door. A shiver ran down his spine as usually happened when someone called. This was an old habit. When he'd lived in the Foyer, the police had been constantly seeking out illegals. And after his move to Gerome's flat, the big man had threatened to inform on him - or worse - if he didn't produce enough paintings.

Now, things were different. It was amazing how life panned out if you let things take their own course. He compared himself to a stream, fresh and clear at its source. Just as the force of gravity took control and propelled the stream towards its larger destination, he was being led forward to fulfil his promise. He had little choice in the matter, his art had a mind of its own - it demanded an audience.

He had fled Gerome's flat as soon as he'd learned of the murders and had gone back to the last place he'd felt safe, his friend's flat in the Foyer. He hadn't been sure if the former friend would take him in, given the circumstances of his previous departure, but he had no intention of going back home. Paris was his home now. Just as this city, with its silvery light had provided a home for painters over the centuries, it was providing one for him now.

He had been waiting in the street for his friend to come home. He'd intended to beg, plead, to give him everything he had, which wasn't much, even offer to cut off his balls if his friend would just give him sanctuary for a while. None of this had been necessary. As he'd hunched on the pavement outside the building, his paintings stacked up against the wall, a car had stopped, mirroring what had happened when Gerome had first spotted his work. A woman, sleek as a cat, with short reddish hair, navy suit and crisp white shirt, had swivelled out of the driver's seat. She'd strode over to him, ignoring his curious look. Instead she'd focussed on one of the paintings: a view of Paris roofs, a jumble of colour from afar, yet close up the eye could trace perfect roof structures. Ochre, terracotta, green, a shade of grey that mimics the sky on a dull, rainy day. The rooftops and sky were painted in more or less equal proportions. Although it wasn't a copy, the theme of the painting had been inspired by a skyscape of Paris, painted by Van Gogh over a hundred years earlier.

Things had moved quickly, just as they had when Gerome had discovered him. He'd been whisked away to a gallery where his paintings had been examined. After much discussion and whispering, the red haired woman had brought him to this studio. The woman, a well known art dealer, had asked him to paint. But her request, unlike Gerome's, hadn't been accompanied by threats of police or hints at violence. He could still remember the thrill he'd felt that day when she'd handed him the front door keys and an envelope containing several fifty-euro bills.

He opened the door. Claire was waiting patiently in the hallway. She was here to inspect his latest work. He'd been painting like the devil, or angel, dependent on how cynical his worldview was at any given time. He had three new canvasses to show her and had already delivered five. His offerings for the exhibition were almost complete. He wished he could have retrieved the last three paintings taken by Gerome. The desertscape was particularly haunting and in his opinion was probably his best work. He had tried to reproduce it but the colours he'd mixed were wrong, the strokes of the brush unable to capture the mood of the original. Once the energy is spent on one painting then the artist has given all they can, he acknowledged.

Claire went over to the new canvas. She studied the three strokes of yellow paint Ezekiel had sketchily applied.

"Unusual shade of lemon. Could almost be described as green. What will this be?" she asked.

He pointed to a table near the window.

"Nature morte. Still life."

"Interesting. Your other paintings reflect life, this one death."

He smiled. He liked Claire's visits. She was one of the few people with whom he could discuss art.

"Death is a part of life, as far as I'm concerned. We live on a spectrum, a line, if you like. We're born, we go to school, we paint or do other things, some might marry. Death is the final point of this line, as far as we're aware. I suppose though, that's dependent on your beliefs."

"So you don't see nature morte as relating to death?"

"No, despite the name, it's part of life. You'll see how I paint the objects. The lemons have been picked from the tree so they don't have any more of nature's nourishment. But they still have energy." He went over to the table, picked up a lemon and gave it to Claire.

"Take this young lemon in your hand and close your eyes." She nodded and shut her eyes. "Wait a minute and tell me what you feel."

He watched as her puzzled expression dropped and a smile appeared.

"I can feel tingling, warmth. What's going on?" She opened her eyes.

"You're feeling energy. Pure energy. When I paint the lemon I will paint the energy. I try to capture that in all my paintings, animate or inanimate."

"Fascinating," she said, sitting down in an armchair.

"Would you like a coffee?"

She shook her head. "No. I'm here to tell you about the exhibition. It's not a solo exhibition, but the next one you appear in will be. We're aiming for ten of your paintings; they're certainly good enough. The gallery will bill you as the star. The name of the exhibition will be 'Rising Stars'."

Ezekiel's eyes glittered.

"After this canvas, I will paint the centrepiece for the exhibition. I will paint the stars."

"I've no doubt you will. Thank you, Ezekiel." She stood up and picked up her briefcase.

"Just before you go, what about those other things? My little problems...although they are, in reality, not so little."

"We've engaged an immigration lawyer. He's good. Because of our sponsorship and your talent, you will have a good case. He's confident of that and can't foresee any problems in getting your papers. He will present you as an asset to France; you certainly won't be seen as a burden."

"That's great! What about the other matter?"

"Your previous mentor? That will be more difficult. We need to tread carefully. My lawyer friend has a colleague in the police force. He has asked around, discretely. At the moment they're looking at two avenues: the underworld, which Gerome was a part of, and also there was an old man seen in the area who has subsequently disappeared. They're scouring Paris for him."

"I never knew where Gerome lived. He came from time to time to get money and paintings. That was my only contact."

"Then you've nothing to worry about." Claire patted his arm. "You are the next big thing, Ezekiel. Don't forget that."

He waited at the top of the stairs until he heard Claire's footsteps disappear and the front door slam. He went back into the flat, and prepared a thick, sweet, Turkish coffee. He sat in the armchair she had been sitting in. She was optimistic that he would get his papers - that was bloody fantastic and almost too good to be true. He wasn't completely aligned with her reassurances over the murders. It was true he had never been to Gerome's. This could be supported by an absence of his fingerprints on anything other than his canvasses. But any link with this investigation might ruin his chances of obtaining papers. He hoped the whole thing would go away quickly and they would discover it was an underworld hit, or maybe the old guy was intending to burgle the flat and it had all gone wrong.

He went back to the canvas. The coffee had revived him and given him strength to pick up his paintbrush again. Sometimes it was difficult to do that, just as it was for a writer to face a clean page. Anyway, he reasoned, as soon as the paintbrush made contact with the canvas the outer world would fizzle into insignificance.

Chapter 31

Liam couldn't pinpoint what had lifted his spirits: Monet's lush gardens, the paintings in the artist's villa, the old mill they stayed in, or the food they consumed. Gusto, that was a word he hadn't used in a long time. He wanted to live with gusto, inhale so deeply the clean air would chase the staleness from his blood. He wanted to lounge on dewy grass and feel its coolness on his feet, to walk past a restaurant and smell a beef stew cooking. He wanted to break into song or to jig around, act the fool, something he hadn't done in years. His good mood was shared by Alouette who could sometimes appear pensive and sad. Today, her whole being was puffed up with lightness, like a newly inflated party balloon. Despite her claimed shady past, she appeared as strong as a supporting beam in a building. Strength of character and good parenting could help form the adult, he mused, but lady luck determines where we end up in life. Alouette had failed to realise her potential but she wasn't bitter.

After dinner they went back to the hotel. The room was in virtual darkness when they entered, only rectangles of moonlight sifting through slats in the shutters interrupted the blackness. She went over to the table lamp.

"Don't do that," he said.

She turned to face him, a quizzical look on her face.

"Isn't this magical?" he said. "No idea what's going on, but I feel like I've been here before."

"Maybe in a past life, or perhaps you sense the presence of others who've stayed here? Maybe couples on honeymoon or solitary travellers, seeking out a place to disappear into, to hide from the world."

"I'm not a believer in ghosts or all that mumbo jumbo, but I reckon in the old days, when the mill was up and running, a clatter of children would have filled these rooms. Noisy. Boisterous. Just like children should be."

"Yes. I feel it now. It's like they left a tiny bit of their spirits here. I can sense different emotions: peace, happiness, maybe sometimes despair."

"Just like my life. Ups and downs. Bit too extreme at times."

"I hope it's full of only good things right now."

He nodded and pushed her gently onto the bed.

They made love enthusiastically, each consuming the best of the other, making up their own missing parts. It was as though neither imagined their love affair could last. As dawn light filtered through the shutter slats, they fell asleep.

Liam woke first. A wave of wellbeing swept over him when he realised he was not in Paris. This was quickly followed by a strong sense of vulnerability and a knot of fear tightening his gut. He glanced at Alouette, curled up on her side, fast asleep - not dreaming of ghosts he hoped. He remembered making love, allowing his guard to drop. He'd opened his heart just a crack, enough to let her in, but it must have also been wide enough to allow knowledge of his terrible deed to escape its hiding place. This morning there was no denial protecting him, he *knew* what he had done. He got out of bed, went into the bathroom, and threw up as quietly as he could into the toilet bowl. Afterwards, he pressed a fist onto his stomach, willing himself to vomit again. Perhaps the sickness would expel the horrors lurking inside. Why did happiness never last? In his case it was bloody fleeting, just like the kingfisher he'd spotted in Monet's garden the day before: a brilliant blue streak, gone before he'd had time to admire it.

His eyes were fixed on a flowery pattern on the inside of the toilet bowl when he became aware of another presence.

"Mon Dieu! Must have been the mussels in cider."

He raised his head and gave a weak smile. "Yes, probably. Think I've thrown up all the little buggers now."

Alouette soaked a facecloth in cold water. She pressed it against his forehead.

"Come back to bed and rest. You don't want to spoil the day, do you? For *you*, I mean. As you know, I've been here many times. I'm not eager to be out."

He allowed himself to be led back to bed. His head ached, his insides were on fire. Was another strange illness about to launch an attack? And were these illnesses he now frequently suffered of the mind or of the body? Weak and exhausted, he drifted back to sleep.

He got up at eleven. Breakfast at the hotel finished at nine so they went to a café in the village.

"Sure you're up for a walk?"

"Legs like steel goalposts. Not a wobble, unless you give them a good kicking."

She shrugged and pressed a finger against his cheek. "Your skin is white, like chalk. I'm not sure if I prefer the pale you. Perhaps the weather-worn Liam is more handsome."

"Better top up my tan then," he smiled. "Seriously though, I'm feeling much better."

"Well enough for another round in Monet's garden after lunch?"

"I fancy a go in the punt," he said, a mischievous glint in his eye, remembering the small green rowing boat that nestled amongst waterlilies.

"Go ahead, if you want to spend the rest of the day in the police station."

His good humour evaporated. The last thing in the world he wanted was to be interviewed by the police. Anonymity was key to freedom, like one of Alouette's ghosts in the mill: present but not seen or heard

The visit to Monet's house and garden the day before had been brief so today they planned to spend the entire afternoon there, lazing in the sun.

Flower beds, fruit trees and climbing roses dominated the area directly outside the house. Alouette stopped in front of a flower bed. She pointed to a large, blue flower. "Agapanthe, my favourite."

"If I had to choose a favourite it would be..." he looked around, "these fabulous pink rhododendrons. Remind me of a sparky girl. Someone who might have worked in the Folies bergère a century ago. She'd have kicked high and flashed her bloomers at the audience."

"Perhaps that's why Monet liked this plant?" she said mischievously.

They crossed over to the water garden, a feature Monet had created when he'd bought a piece of land adjacent to the house, Alouette explained. She was animated as she described how the artist had diverted a tributary of the River Epte, creating first a small brook, then the pond. Liam's eyes watered as he viewed the pink, blue and white flowers floating on the surface of the water.

"Never imagined nature could better Monet's paintings."

"Every time I see this I ask myself if his genius lay in gardening rather than art. Of course his paintings are wonderful, but to create many of them he first had to create this."

"How come you know so much?"

"I'm French. We like art. Going to galleries is a national pastime."

They sat down on the grass near a willow. The afternoon was hot. He took a bottle of water from his rucksack and held it out. "Thirsty?"

"Not right now. Would you mind if I went to the shop? Some posters for the apartment would be nice. A reminder of our trip."

"Suits me," he yawned and lay back on the grass. He could stay like this forever. He looked up at the sky as he listened to Alouette's footsteps on the path become fainter, then fade away. He was at one with the sky, the trees and all of nature. He drifted into a mindless state, which a friend who liked to meditate once described as transcending into nothingness. Now he understood what his mate had been talking about: there was nothing in his mind, only a vast emptiness. His body lost its muscle, skin, bone. Like Alouette's footsteps it had vanished.

"Free from suffering," he whispered.

Suddenly, he inhabited his body again. He sat up. Emptying his mind of all thoughts had stripped away the thin protective varnish, torn down the barrier between him and the terrible thing he'd done. Earlier when he was ill, he'd partially experienced this level of awareness. But now the knowledge of what he had done was complete, it consumed him so his body took on a life of its own. His arms trembled, then his legs. He imagined his movements were controlled by a novice puppet master, jerking wildly, yet when he looked down he only saw a slight tremor in his limbs.

The branches of the willow rippled in the warm breeze. They took on a sinister appearance, pointing at him, rebuking him. He might have been at one with nature, but nature, it appeared, didn't like who he was.

He stood up and stared at the pond. A patch of dark pink waterlilies brought an image of Gerome to his mind, the last time he'd seen him, blood and matter oozing from his head. Until now, any replay of that day had resembled an old movie, with no colours, only shades of grey. He curled his fingers tightly round the rail of the Japanese bridge as he experienced for the first time the terror of his encounter with Gerome. Delayed shock, he realised. But the fear that now consumed his entire being was so invasive, he considered leaping into the pond and immersing himself in the water to cleanse away the memories. A conversation with a friend who'd travelled to India flashed into his mind. His friend had been astonished as he'd watched people bathe in the muddy River Ganges, hoping to cleanse away pain and suffering. Perhaps they knew more than he did, he thought as he fixed his eyes on the dark and inviting surface of the water. He was leaning over the bridge when Alouette returned, waving a paper bag.

"Over here, Liam," she said. "See what I bought."

Alouette, distracted by her purchases, didn't see the flash of wildness in his eyes or the shaking of his hands. He followed her and sat on the grass. He hugged his knees against his chest. She reached into the bag and pulled out a silk scarf.

"Look. It's the waterlilies."

He could not bring himself to look at the scarf with its

abundance of pinkish-red flowers. When he steeled himself and took a glance, the flowers on the scarf looked like spots of blood.

"I feel sick again," he said.

She looked at him strangely. "You were fine when I left. Has something happened? Have I offended you, done something wrong?"

He shook his head vigorously. "No, never. You could never do anything wrong. It's me. There's something wrong with me."

She put the scarf back in the bag. "I shouldn't have left. You look feverish again. You were so ill earlier. Surely it can't still be the mussels."

"Can we go now?" he said in a weak voice. He would have to summon up the strength to walk back to the hotel, but more importantly, he needed to buck up and hide the true cause of his sickness from her. It was a fever all right, but of the soul rather than the body.

He spent the rest of the day in bed. He tossed and turned and Alouette sat on a chair at the bedside, alternating between reading a book and placing cool cloths on his forehead. She left once to fetch a carafe of wine and some bread and cheese from the kitchen downstairs. He had no appetite so did not eat. He muttered things in his sleep and once he woke up and grabbed her arm. 'Sick...in the head and soul,' he ranted, eyes bright with fever. He told her to go far away from him, lest it was catching.

The following afternoon they took the train from Vernon back to Paris. He was still weak so he slept for part of the journey. When he awoke, Alouette's eyes were fixed on him. She had an odd expression on her face as though she'd made a decision. It was the same determined look his wife had worn when she'd resolved to throw him out.

"What?" he said. "Did I say something while I was out for the count?"

"No. Sorry if it seemed I was staring. I'm worried about you."

"Just a weakness. I didn't properly recover from that first virus. I promise, I'll be better soon."

She held up her phone. "I made a call while you were sleeping."

His body stiffened. "Who...who did you call?"

"An old friend. We're not close, but she helped me out before."

"Why do you need help?"

"Not me, Liam. It's you who needs help. I know something's bothering you and you don't want to confide in me. My friend studied psychology at university. She's an excellent listener. I've invited her for dinner."

"I'm not into all that. I told you, I haven't recovered from my virus. I'm perfectly sane." His voice was slightly raised. The last thing he wanted was someone digging into his mind, trying to read his thoughts.

"She's coming for dinner anyway. I can't cancel. It would be rude. You can have a private chat with her, or not. It's up to you. Entirely your choice."

He squeezed her hand. "I must sound ungrateful. You've done so much, too much. I'm just not cut out for talking therapy. This is simply a weakness from the flu and the beating. I'll be right as rain before you know it."

"I hope so. In the meantime, I'll sure you'll be a polite host when Catherine comes."

When they arrived back at the apartment, he went straight to bed. Alouette left him alone and he was grateful to her for not fussing. If she had special powers and could have read his mind, he doubted that a decent woman like her would have allowed him to remain in her flat. It was all black and white: she was good, he was bad, if not evil. He had done terrible things and now he was living the pain. Like an abscess, in his brain rather than under a tooth, the pain radiated from his head, through his neck, to his arms and down his legs. There wasn't an inch of his body that didn't ache. He wondered if other murderers felt like this. Then he went to the bathroom and threw up when he recognised he had labelled himself a murderer. It had all been an accident. It was Gerome's fault. He wasn't supposed to be at home.

Chapter 32

The urge to confess his terrible deed grew. At night he tossed and turned, unable to sleep. Finally, after a particularly sharp dig in the ribs from Alouette, he shifted from sleeping in the bedroom to the sofa. Dark circles shaded the area under his eyes and food with its smells, textures and colours, failed in its seduction efforts.

"Now it's you who eats like a bird," she commented one day, eyeing his barely touched plate of food.

"It's the illness. Nothing more," he said. But the words were uttered without conviction. In whispered tones Alouette confessed she feared he was physically ill. Her face turned pale when she asked if he'd been diagnosed with cancer or some other terrible disease. 'Don't protect me, Liam. Tell me the truth,' she'd said. He knew too well the effect of guilt on the mind and body. He had no doubt some of the torment she felt was due to her banishing him in the aftermath of the Claudine episode.

As his depression worsened he cancelled the English conversation lessons and took to wandering around the flat, dressed in pyjamas. He didn't question where the paisley print pyjamas had come from. They had simply appeared in his drawer. They required no effort to wear, so why not?

The ease of wearing nothing but pyjamas suited him, as then he didn't need to waste effort thinking about what to wear. What was the point in bathing, getting dressed, brushing your hair? He had a sudden insight that none of these things mattered. So what if dirt was trapped under his fingernails or if even he found his own body odour offensive? Were these things really important in the grand scheme of life? Now *taking* a life, that was another thing. That was offensive.

He had nothing, he reasoned. No one, not even Alouette, would miss him if he died, so why bother making the effort to live.

"Catherine is coming to dinner in a few days. I was hoping

you might talk to her." Alouette said.

"Why?"

"To unburden yourself. She helped me when I came back from England."

"Oh. That story you told me when I was asleep."

"I'll tell it to you again, one day, but not now. It's you I'm worried about. You're nervous. Tight as the skin on a drum. I'm sure Catherine can help you loosen up."

He shook his head. If Alouette only knew his thoughts, his past actions. How could he unburden himself by confessing his terrible deeds to this friend of Alouette, and what words would he use: 'I'm a bit stressed because I killed two people' or 'I lost my money. I've been on a downward spiral, of which murder is just a part.' Alouette was right about one thing - the weight of the burden he carried was too great to bear alone. Yet if he confided in anyone the consequences would be dire. He toyed again with the notion of going to a church and confessing his sins. Wasn't the priest bound to keep his sins secret, but did that cover murder? He wasn't sure.

She fussed around him so much, he relinquished the pyjamas, washed his face, combed his hair and decided to go for a walk. She remained tight lipped and disapproving when he said he wanted some time alone.

"Not going to kill myself or have an affair," he snapped as he pulled his coat on.

As he stepped out of the building, the wind slapped his face with surprising vigour. It was tinged with an iciness which startled him. Wasn't it only days ago they'd returned from the heat of Giverny? Time had become fluid again. How long, he asked himself, had he been wandering around the apartment in pyjamas, and why had Alouette allowed this behaviour to continue?

He answered his own question. Fear. Fear he would stop caring for her. Fear he would leave. Fear, he realised, was responsible for many of life's ills. It corroded you from the inside out. It tossed and turned the mind at night, turning dark shadows into ferocious beasts. Fear hid behind curtains, wardrobes, in the bathroom, under your skin. When people were afraid they committed terrible deeds. Not that Alouette had done anything terrible, but she was too tolerant. She had lost someone she cared for in the past, someone he reminded her of. Perhaps nothing he did could make her hate him. But surely even patient Alouette had her limits. Could she forgive him if she knew he had taken another life - make that two - he corrected himself, and would she be afraid he would kill again?

His thoughts drifted as he walked aimlessly. After a while he found himself in the core of the city, walking down the Champs Elysee towards the Place de la Concorde. Halfway down he stopped and closed his eyes, imagining that when he opened them he would see Gerome's stall, still stacked with his beautiful paintings. Gerome would be lounging in a chair, puffing on a cigar, an indolent expression on his face. Gerome might perk up when he saw him, but this wouldn't last long when he discovered he was broke. He opened his eyes and began to cut his way through a group of tourists who had just disembarked from a bus.

He passed by stalls with coloured canopies and others, which, clearly not anticipating wind and rain, were open to the elements. There was an abundance of Paris street scenes, bags, tee shirts and souvenir key rings. His mood slumped when he saw no sign of Gerome. The burning hope that this had all been a bad dream sank like a rock tossed in the Seine.

He felt as though he held the earth on his shoulders. If it fell and broke, then he would break too. The heaviness lasted as he wandered aimlessly around the market, the weight of the world bowing his back. Gerome was gone, as was his neighbouring stallholder, who had probably scarpered to avoid trouble.

He walked on towards the Louvre. There were benches in the Cour Napoléon, the main courtyard. He sat down, intending to while away an hour or so before returning home. Perhaps his mind would transport him to another time, another century, and there he'd savour each and every second of freedom, rather than allowing fear to consume him. How much longer would he be able to do something as pleasurable as this, he asked himself? Alouette would surely tire of his ups-and-downs, his constant illnesses. She was probably sorry she'd bought the pyjamas and sick of looking at the jazzy maroon and navy pattern shuffling round the apartment. She would throw him out and he would be homeless again. One more night in a park, that thought was unbearable. Two choices would then face him: confessing to the authorities or committing suicide. He still found the idea of taking his life too awful to contemplate, but then so was living. Perhaps he should have jumped from the Japanese bridge in Monet's garden. But the pond wasn't very deep and some hero would surely have saved him. He remembered the woman in the painting in the Louvre, who had stood at her dead husband's bedside, pointing a dagger at her breast. Now he understood where she was coming from.

There was another option: taking an overnight bus to London, and turning himself in to Victor. But was he prepared for the inevitable consequence - a slow and painful death? Nothing more than he deserved. Victor had helped Mary, and he, in return, had double-crossed him. But that paled into insignificance when he thought about that day at La Villette. He had committed the ultimate crime: robbed two people of both their present and their future. Freedom was relative, he thought. There were no bars surrounding him but he was a prisoner of memory and conscience.

Two uniformed police officers strolled by. They smiled and chatted, appearing relaxed, as though they hadn't come across a villain for a while. He resisted the urge to chase them and beg them to take him away in handcuffs. He had killed and he could kill again, he might blurt out if he couldn't fight the impulse to get the murders off his chest. He got up from the bench and wearily began his walk away from the retreating backs of the policemen.

On the way back, no one seemed to notice him. It was as

though his skin was dissolving and he was becoming invisible again. A large billboard by the roadside drew his attention. He wasn't sure if it was the form or the colour of one of the posters that caught his eye, but there was a flash of recognition. He stopped a few feet away transfixed by the poster. An image of a painting. A work done by so sensitive a hand, the image appeared to float above the surface of the poster. He sat down on a nearby bench, eyes still fixed on the billboard. A night sky, pinpricks of colour forming stars, light pouring from café windows. This particular lightness of brush strokes he'd seen only once before, in the works painted by Gerome. A tear pricked his eye. Even in death, the dishonest, violent Gerome, with his perfect genius, was stalking him.

He went back to the billboard and took a leaflet from a side pocket. The front of the leaflet mirrored the poster. He noted the caption above the image: 'Rising Stars'. He opened the leaflet, which was advertising an exhibition of paintings by up-and-coming artists. Even though it was just a reproduction on the front of a flyer, he could sense the magic of the work - the sky, dark blue, brooding, majestic. The diamond-like stars more beautiful than the real things. He reread the leaflet. Even with his limited knowledge of French it suddenly dawned on him that there was something wrong. Very wrong. The name Ezekiel was mentioned. Ezekiel. Who was this artist from Baobab Island, which he'd never heard of, who claimed to have painted this? Ezekiel. Surely it was impossible that this man could possess the same magic as Gerome. Either this was a mistake or this Ezekiel was an imposter.

Liam sat down again. The word 'imposter' rang in his ears like an alarm bell. He put the leaflet in his pocket and stared ahead, not seeing the window display of the luxury handbag shop opposite. He took the leaflet out again and looked at the picture of the artist on the back. Ezekiel was standing next to a woman with reddish hair, his frame gaunt as though food wasn't high on his list of priorities. He looked closer, even in the picture, Ezekiel's eyes burned with passion. A passion that had always been missing from Gerome.

He slumped back in the bench. The web of deceit Gerome had weaved finally snapped as it dawned on him that Ezekiel was not the imposter. He, and not Gerome, was the true artist.

Liam seethed. The lying, cheating Gerome had probably never picked up a paintbrush in his life, nor stood in front of an empty canvas. Even before Gerome had attempted his double cross, he'd been mocking him, playing him for a fool, the jester in a deck of tarot cards. He clenched his fists. Even though Gerome was no longer a living resident of planet Earth, he would have given almost all he had to make him reappear. To give him a good kicking before he sent him off again. It all made sense now. Gerome had tricked him, but in return he'd paid the ultimate price: forfeiting his life.

Finally, he told himself, he had something to focus his mind on. Gerome had pulled the wool over his eyes. He had forced his hand, so, in a roundabout way, he was responsible for his own death. 'Got what was coming to him,' he mumbled to himself. Could he really convince himself that the market trader did not deserve to live? He hoped so.

He checked the date of the exhibition. It would take place the following week and tickets for the preview were on sale. He decided to swing by the gallery on the way home to pick up a ticket. He needed to confirm his suspicions and, if possible, to meet the artist. Viewing the beautiful painting of the stars would be the icing on the cake.

His anger had subsided completely once the ticket was in his pocket and each step he took felt lighter than the previous one. Alouette was in the salon, reading, when he returned home. He planted one kiss on her cheek.

"That's the way we English...and Irish... do it." He gave her a wide, beaming smile, then settled on the living room sofa with a copy of yesterday's paper. He secreted the 'Rising Stars' leaflet inside the newspaper. Occasionally, he glanced at the leaflet and smiled. The guilt at what he'd done was still there, but for the moment the thought that Gerome might have lied as well as cheated had diluted it.

A few days later, just before Alouette's friend arrived, he experienced a setback to his recovery. When he went into the kitchen to get a glass of water, his eyes were drawn to a silvery object in Alouette's hand. She wielded a large, sharp knife, and was cutting a steak into smaller pieces. Her movements were short, precise and rhythmic.

"Boeuf bourguignon again, I'm afraid. I think what I do is good... at least I've been told that... but I'm limited to a few dishes for entertaining. Liam?"

He turned on his heel and headed straight for the bathroom. He locked the door and breathed deeply. There was a small, high window in the bathroom. He climbed on the edge of the bath and opened the window. A slight breeze blew dust from the windowsill onto his face. He stepped down and sat on the toilet, head in his hands. A wave of remorse consumed him and he scolded himself for letting his guard down, allowing himself to think he'd pulled the wool over guilt's eyes. Had he really taken a knife, just like the one Alouette was waving around in the kitchen, and plunged it into Marie's back? Was he capable of such an act? He knew the answer. The buzzing in his head was as bad as physical pain. He wished he was a psychopath, as that sort of person would justify the murders, not give them a moment's thought. Still, Gerome was a terrible person. Strike terrible, he told himself, evil was a more fitting word. And Marie wasn't much better. Hadn't she battered him and helped Gerome in his dodgy dealings? In the past, although he wasn't averse to cheating a member of the public at a boot fair with a suspect antique, he'd never wanted to inflict physical harm on another. So, in a way, he reasoned, it was all Gerome's fault.

There was a knock on the bathroom door.

"I'm fine, Alouette. Needed the toilet."

"Thanks for the information, but I'm not Alouette. I'm Catherine, Alouette's friend. She invited me to dinner."

He flushed the toilet. "I'll be out in a minute."

His stomach churned. Catherine's voice was clipped and

sharp, she sounded like a busybody, someone who enjoyed meddling in the affairs of others. He couldn't comprehend why someone would bother studying psychology unless they planned to set up a practice and charge hundreds of pounds an hour. Who cared what made someone else's mind tick, he thought, wasn't it the actions that counted? He imagined standing up in court with Catherine at his side. 'Yes, your honour, I killed Gerome and Marie,' he would declare, wearing a contrite expression on his face. Catherine would then present his defence: 'he had been distraught at losing a fortune; his upbringing was hard; he found it hard to bond with other people.' Would the judge accept Catherine's defence and excuse him? Would he or she pat him on the head and say how sorry they were that Liam had suffered such a hard time? The answer was a resounding NO.

He sighed and opened the bathroom door. Alouette's friend was standing in the hall. He was momentarily distracted by her stature as she was even more petite than Alouette. Her hair was short, cut in a tight crop which emphasized her strong, square shoulders. Her large green enquiring eyes were her most attractive feature. He imagined they could hypnotise in a flash.

"Nice to meet you," he said firmly, trying to gain the upper hand. Act superior, be superior, he'd always told himself when thrusting forward to make a deal.

She shook his hand and smiled. All the while her eyes seemed to be studying his face, assessing every twitch, tic and movement. "Alouette has told me all about you."

They sat down at the table. He decided to disarm her with wit and told a couple of jokes, which neither Catherine nor Alouette appeared to find amusing.

"Lost in translation." He cracked a smile and looked from one confused woman to the other. They were not smiling, but still, he was pleased with his performance. He was chattering, filling space with nonsense and hot air, determined not to allow Catherine to get a word in edgeways.

"You're from Paris?"

"I'm actually from Nice."

"Fabulous city. Baie des Anges. So chic."

"I came here to do my Masters, and stayed on afterwards."

Catherine looked at him expectantly, as though she imagined he would ask what she studied. He didn't.

"Don't you miss the sea...and the colours in Nice? So amazing. I always associate blue and yellow with Nice. And silver with Paris." Alouette and Catherine looked at each other as he continued. "Of course, London is grey. With maybe red for the buses. Belfast – now that's another story. Shades of green and orange."

"We get the picture," Alouette said dryly.

He arranged his knife and fork on the plate and pushed the plate away.

"You know, ladies, it's been so nice to have dinner with you, but I think you need some time to catch up. Space to gossip." He stood up.

"Gossip?" Catherine repeated. She raised her eyebrows.

"Yes. Whatever you women chat about, when you're alone."

"Us women?"

He smiled. "I'll let you get on with it." He picked up his plate and took it to the kitchen, straining on the way to hear what the women were saying. There was only a low buzz. Whatever it was, it would be about him. He shrugged. At least he had escaped the inquisition. Who knows what he might have admitted to when Catherine fixed him with her hypnotic green-eyed stare.

He went into the bedroom and shut the door. He was just starting the second chapter of a John Grisham thriller Alouette had bought for him when there was a soft knock on the door. He ignored it. The knocking continued and he got up and opened the door.

"Come in," he said, not surprised that it was Catherine. Why would Alouette knock on the bedroom door in her own apartment? They had been sharing a room for several months, aside from his recent sojourns on the sofa. From a physical point of view there were few secrets between them. From a psychological angle things were very different: Alouette hid her feelings as expertly as a squirrel hiding its winter stash of nuts. The mask she wore gave nothing away. She gave the impression of being content with her lot in life, yet when he'd asked her if she missed her career, he saw a fleeting sadness in her eyes which was gone in an instant, so quickly he might have imagined it. These moments of vulnerability were like tiny black holes: visible for a millionth of a second, then gone. Most of the time he would describe her as a practical woman; one of those annoying people who 'got on with things'. The apartment was always tidy, dishes were never stacked up in the sink, dinner in some form or other was always planned. There were no extravagances as money was in short supply, but she budgeted carefully so what she had was sufficient. He was the anomaly, the chink in her armour - he knew she was dependent on him.

Catherine pointed to the bed. "May I sit down?"

"Sure. Where's Alouette? "

"Making coffee."

"Do you want me to join you? I thought you might want a girlie natter."

"First time I've heard discussions between grown-up women called that."

"Sorry if I offended. I guess that sounded condescending. I sometimes say the wrong thing. I'm sure you're both intelligent women." He smiled affably, wishing Catherine would go away. He wasn't in the mood for a cosy chat, nor did he want to pour his heart and soul out to her. He moved towards the door. "Best not leave her alone."

"Wait. I need a word with you."

He sighed, then sat down on the bedroom chair. "Look, I've been ill. I had a really bad virus. On top of that I have financial troubles. I'm trying to sort all that out. Alouette thinks I keep getting ill because I'm stressed. It's a chicken and egg conundrum. What came first: the illness or the stress?

I'm usually a pretty cool guy, so I like to think it was the illness."

"She told me all about you. I also had a call from Borivoj, who I know pretty well. Now *he's* a cool guy. He thinks you're taking advantage of Alouette, that you're with her until you can figure out another plan. Then, you will leave. I think the current English expression is 'dump her'."

"Borivoj said that?"

"He told me all about you, about the other woman. When Alouette asked me to dinner she told me her boyfriend was troubled. She asked if I'd talk to you; see if I could help in some way. I phoned Borivoj to get his opinion. He told me he was so concerned about Alouette he was considering returning to Paris."

"So, you're worried about my relationship with Alouette?" he said slowly. Catherine nodded. "And you don't want to analyse me?"

"I'm not properly trained. I think you would need an expert."

"Oh? Why would you say that?"

"You're a cold fish, Liam. I've been watching you. You're careful about everything you say. Nothing is natural. It's all contrived."

He stood up, strode to the bedroom door and opened it. "If you've finished assassinating my character, I think you should go. Have coffee with Alouette in peace. I won't upset her by telling her how rude you've been. She thought she was helping by inviting you to dinner, instead you try to break up her relationship. Not much of a friend, are you?"

Catherine swept past him. She stopped and pointed to her right eye.

"I'm watching you. If you hurt Alouette, you'll have me and Borivoj to answer to."

He closed the bedroom door. He needed to escape those all-seeing eyes. Catherine had made one mistake: she should have trained as a psychologist. One flash of those eyes and her clients would not only spill some of the beans, they would empty the whole tin.

When Catherine had left, he decided, he would have a quiet word with Alouette, to ask her not to involve him in her schemes. He knew well enough what was wrong with him, and none of her meddling would help. He hoped that now she would leave well enough alone.

Later, he made up his bed on the sofa. Alouette lingered for a while, drinking tea. She didn't talk about her friend's visit and he decided not to complain about Catherine's accusations. The following morning they chatted over breakfast and acted as though the evening before had never happened. Alouette, he realised, did not want to confront his strange behaviour. Was she afraid that their fragile relationship would end and how far would she go to keep him here?

Chapter 33

Alouette

For Alouette, living with Liam was heaven and hell all rolled into one. There were no soft edges, no greys in his thoughts. He was never a woolly, umming and ahhing, sort of man. He liked strawberry jam but not cherry. He liked plain croissants and pain au chocolat but detested fruit muffins, 'too sweet' he pronounced them. He liked his women dark rather than fair. Both she and Claudine were testament to that. He enjoyed Chablis but hated most other white wines. Everything was absolute: black and white. His moods were either up or down. He was a super confident deal maker, or so insecure he would have been more at home crouching under the bed or locking himself away in a cupboard.

She wasn't sure which Liam she preferred. The insecure version could be wearing, even frightening. More than once, when he was going through a low phase, she'd glimpsed madness in his eyes. Dreams might be accompanied by babbling and violent jerks of limbs. Sometimes he muttered a word or two in French: *clochard* and *parc*, seemed to be particular favourites.

On the other hand, the confident Liam, the dealer of antiques, reminded her of Trevor at his worst. That Liam had a ruthless streak. He coveted success and money and would do, she imagined, almost anything to get it.

More than once she'd considered ending the relationship and scraping up enough money to send him home. But, she admitted to herself, the suffocating loneliness of the past few decades had been hard to bear and she wasn't ready for another round of solitude. If only she could cut through his mental suit of armour, he might find that she was willing to forgive more than he imagined. She longed for a smooth relationship and companionship in her later years. Was that too much to ask?

Liam had come into the living room earlier. He was dressed in a suit and his demeanour was confident, even cocky. He was off to an exhibition, he'd said. There was some sort of potential deal involved so he didn't want her to come. She had reminded him that the last time he had done this, he'd been beaten up. But he had been insistent, once again he wanted to go alone.

She wondered if, now that he was going through a good phase, he was planning on meeting *her*. 'That bloody portrait woman', she'd labelled her in her mind. Liam was clever, he never mentioned her now, but the description Borivoj had given: 'more beautiful than Helen of Troy' still cut to the quick. Could any man resist a woman a lovely as that? Borivoj had been quick to add that she was probably a nasty piece of work. 'Good looking, but I think she has intellect of flea.'

She missed Borivoj. They had known each other just a year and a half but had become firm friends in that time. He was funny and protective. Right now she could use some kindness. She wasn't sure who the chameleon she was living with actually was. She wasn't even sure how she felt about Liam. The love she gave him was the same as the love she'd given to Trevor. It wasn't a copy, it was Trevor's love. Like a candle with the slowest burning wick, a string that could envelop the world twice over, her love for the pale English actor had never diminished. She had existed for all these years in a virtual museum dedicated to her passion for him. There was no day to day bickering, no committing errors and exposing personality faults that could grind her love for him down to a mere biscuit crumb. It had become too much to bear by the time Liam had come along. Transferring her burden of love to him had brought relief. She was an overfilled balloon waiting to be popped, he had provided the pin.

She picked up her mobile phone and dialled Liam's number. The phone went straight to 'messages'.

She switched on the television. The news headlines were dominated with the euro crisis. Greece, Spain, Italy, Cyprus, Portugal – which would bite the bullet and leave the euro first? Personally, she had no idea which way the wind would blow, but at least France wasn't in that list. The topic changed and a woman was pictured giving a press conference. She was the new detective assigned to the La Villette murders. She looked fresh, young and vigorous. She had a kick-ass air; a swagger that was a visual warning not to mess with her. There was no hesitation in her voice when she declared they would find the killer or killers. She said the people of La Villette deserved to sleep peacefully in their beds. They were interviewing associates of Gerome and were very keen to track down the old vagrant seen sleeping in doorways in the immediate vicinity of the flat just before the murders. It was a nun who had provided this last piece of information, she declared, as though this gave the information more credence. The nun had described a dishevelled *clochard* who spoke with a strange French accent and hid his face so she couldn't say how old he was, but she'd had the impression he was elderly.

She turned the TV off. That word again. Clochard. How many times had she heard that word uttered in the last few months. This wasn't a word she used frequently. In her view, people who slept on the street were homeless. What was the difference between a homeless person and a *clochard* or vagrant? The homeless, she supposed, had fallen from grace and might claw their way back into society. A tramp or vagrant was a free spirit, someone who chose the vagabond life. An individual who didn't mind sleeping under the stars or camping out in all kinds of weather. Liam wasn't a vagrant, yet Borivoj had once used the word 'clochard' to describe his appearance. She shook her head. Perhaps she'd been infected by Liam's strange behaviour and was now having equally bizarre thoughts?

She went into the bedroom and pulled his bag from under the bed. She unzipped it and rummaged though, looking for evidence of his prior return to England. There was nothing. No bus ticket stubs - and he'd said he'd travelled home by bus. No receipts from English shops. No books or toiletries that suggested he had recently crossed the Channel. She found one piece of paper folded into a tiny square and stuffed in an interior pocket. A receipt, but not an English one. This one was for a stay in a Paris hostel. Several hundred euro, paid in cash. She checked the date at the top of the receipt. It was just before he'd moved back in with her.

She shoved the bag back under the bed and paced up and down, agonising over what to do. Should she confront him, ask him if he was seeing that woman again, ask him to give her a minute by minute account of where he'd gone when she'd chucked him out? Should she tell him he had been talking in his sleep and ask what the significance of his ramblings were?

She could also do nothing. Despite his behaviour and her insecurities, it was good to have him here. For the first time in decades she didn't feel like crying herself to sleep. She didn't sense Trevor's touch when she closed her eyes, or hear him speak in his funny French accent. She didn't think of their lost child.

He had returned around eight o'clock and settled on the sofa. She had already eaten a light meal and when she offered to throw together a salad, he'd refused. He had eaten at the exhibition, he'd said. He'd leaned over and kissed her. His breath was heavy with red wine and garlic. Alouette doubted that any art exhibition would serve spicy food and red wine. Most, in her experience, dispensed flutes of golden champagne or bulbous glasses with a sliver of Chablis in the bottom. Trays of cheese, dips and olives, black or green, were usually the accompaniment to the champagne. This, she knew, what was an exhibition would serve the clients, rather than a garlicky accompaniment to a full bodied red.

His general demeanour had been quiet and pensive. He'd switched on the television, to avoid conversation, she'd imagined, glancing occasionally at him. She could tell he wasn't paying attention to the Jacques Cousteau documentary as his eyes had flickered to an empty space on the wall and remained there. Had he been mulling over a future decision he'd have to make? She likened his emotional state to 'the calm before the storm'. The period when the quiet thinking was done, the inward battle waged and resolved, and a decision, right or wrong, made.

"Are you intending to stay on the sofa permanently?" she'd asked.

"Of course not. I'll come back to the bedroom tonight, if you'll have me."

"Why not? We know each other so well. No secrets, Liam, right? You can tell me anything."

"Sure, no secrets."

He'd lingered in the living room; there were things he needed to work out regarding his latest deal, he'd told her. His voice had been soft, his eyes hooded. He was thinking of dealing in art, he'd confided. This time he was serious. There were so many talented artists here in Paris it would be a piece of cake to uncover a genius.

"Bad luck," he'd muttered when she asked him if he had an artist in mind. "You never talk about a deal until it's done."

Chapter 34

Liam's mind was spinning with thoughts of what he'd discovered earlier. Ezekiel. The true artist. The next big thing. His meal ticket. He breathed a sigh of relief as he climbed into bed and heard the faint trill of Alouette's snore: there was thinking to be done and he couldn't bear it if she was in a needy frame of mind, as she frequently was these days. Rather than comforting her, boosting her confidence, telling her that she was lovely for her age, he needed to mull over what he'd seen. Ezekiel. Bloody Ezekiel. Who'd have thought!

His future fortune depended on good planning. Planning was eighty percent of a deal, he knew. The rest was luck.

The exhibition guests had consisted of arty types and hangers on, with a few middle-of-the-road visitors thrown in. Liam had dressed in a low key, dark suit, light shirt and sober tie. Generic clothes, the anonymous businessman, nothing memorable about his person.

Visitors, sardines vying for space in a tin can, crowded into the gallery. Vivid colours were worn by many: red, yellow, azure. Like large birds of paradise, they moved from painting to painting. A jester in a red and yellow outfit brushed up against him. Liam deduced he'd been hired by the gallery when he handed him a fridge magnet with an image of the sky and stars painting. Ezekiel, himself, was dressed in simple flowing robes, like a character from the bible or the film, *Lawrence of Arabia*. Liam suspected these were not the typical clothes of Baobab Island, where the information claimed he was from, but were worn for effect.

The minimalist stood out again the fabulous, he'd thought as he eyed the artist. Ezekiel was even slighter than he'd appeared in the flyer and he noticed the tiny man spoke little, usually deferring to a tall red-haired woman clamped to his side. Liam assumed she was his agent.

He had shadowed Ezekiel as the red-haired woman singled out people in the crowd to chat to. He'd listened as he spoke about his work and the processes he had used to achieve the finished canvases. Ezekiel stood in front of one of his canvases, the painting of the sky and the stars. Raising a finger, he'd singled out one star: 'Resolution', alors c'est complete!'

"Resolution," Liam had whispered under his breath. He'd never heard Gerome say one word related to the creation of the paintings, nor had there been any mention of mixing colours, brushstrokes or resolution. This confirmed what he now suspected was true: Gerome was a fraud. Liam wondered what his relationship, if any, was with this artist. Had he stolen his paintings or paid a pittance for them?

He'd studied a still life. He could taste the bitter sweetness of the lemons on the plate. A card was fixed to the wall beside the painting:*Ezekiel manages to capture the very essence of his subject, with brush strokes that imitate energy and life.*

Liam smiled. Although he heartily agreed with this, it was a little pretentious. The paintings stood on their own; they didn't need this slick marketing. His stomach lurched when he looked at the price tag: twenty five thousand euro. There was a red sticker next to the painting. It had been sold. Bloody hell, he thought. Didn't he have five of these paintings? The ones he had were most certainly done by Ezekiel's hand. A small oriental man stood in front of the painting. He gave a satisfied, ear-to-ear grin, raised his glass and toasted the painting.

"Cheap," he said smugly.

"Did you buy this?"

"Fantastic, no? This guy is the new Picasso. In a few years I'll have a fortune on my hands."

He smiled and nodded. Fortune, indeed. Well bloody good for you, and for me, mate. In reality he wanted to drool. If he held onto one or two of the paintings for a few years then he would be well off. Not rich, but his wealth might be heading towards a million. If you added to the equation the fact that his needs had become more modest, then that would be enough to see him through old age in comfort. He could, of course, give some of it to Victor, but Victor was probably back in his prison cell and it was *he* who was in need of funds right now.

In the meantime, to test the market, he might sell one painting. If it sold for enough, then he, and maybe Alouette, might spend a year or so in Nice or Menton. If that didn't work out, they could bugger off to a tropical haven. For the moment he would content himself with the Riviera. Although he loved Paris, the city, packed with people and cars, so far away from the sea, made him feel as though his bones were being crushed and the breath sucked from his lungs. He longed to see big skies, to hear the wash of waves on the shoreline, dependable and non-judgmental. He needed to see the tip of the land, that last stretch of French coastline, and know that escape was only a boat ride away.

There had been enough trouble, strife and heartache in this city to last a lifetime and his welcome had long been exhausted. Life should be lived at a slow pace: a newspaper in the morning, preferably one not reporting Parisian news, lounging in a café by the sea, drinking coffee and smoking, if he took that up again. He longed to feel the warm Mediterranean breeze brush his face and wipe his soul clean. He would ditch Chablis and drink blush-pink local wines to his heart's content. He was filled with joy and hope but immediately he put a clamp on his emotions. There was no room for feeling, no room for optimism. The only important thing was planning and executing.

He had examined the paintings hanging in the exhibition gallery in detail. When he was satisfied the works he owned were painted by the same hand, that of Ezekiel, he'd set his empty glass down and started towards the door. Passing an animated group of well dressed people near the exit, his eyes had been drawn to a woman in the group. Not for the first time, her beauty stopped him in his tracks. Claudine wore a virginal white shift, not clingy or showy, but he could imagine the curvaceous body underneath. Her breasts were not visible, but he remembered the wad of notes disappearing between them, as though it was yesterday. Her hair hung in black rivulets, tipping her chest. If he'd been a few feet closer, his reflection might have been visible on the shiny surface. Her pale pink lipstick had emphasized the fullness of her lips: eternally kissable. Liam had stopped dead in his tracks, unable to put one foot in front of the other. He'd sensed the underarms of his crisp shirt dampen and a rivulet of perspiration slide down his nose.

Claudine's lips were curved upwards into a bow. She'd leaned towards and latched onto the arm of a handsome, older man. Liam had recognised him. He wasn't sure where he had seen him but he surmised he was a politician. He had that look: confident, smooth, full of charm and bullshit. Taking a deep breath, Liam had forced himself towards the door.

As he'd moved, Claudine had turned her head. Her forehead had creased as she unravelled her arm from her companion's. She'd whispered in his ear; he'd nodded and resumed his animated discussion with the others in the group. Claudine had glided over the door and inserted herself between Liam and the door handle.

"We know each other."

"Not sure I've had the pleasure." He'd willed her, and his feet, to move. Her beauty wasn't worth risking prison for.

"We've met. Come over here, we can talk." She'd pointed to a quiet corner. He'd glanced over at her companion who was still deep in discussion. Cocky bastard.

"I'll get to the point." Her voice was ice cool, as glacial as the colour of her dress. "We had dinner. I've forgotten your name?" He remained silent. "Anyway," she'd continued, "I don't want my fiancé to find out about that night."

"Fiancé?" This was a surprise. Why had she scammed him when she had a wealthy fiancé?

"Whirlwind romance. We're getting married soon."

"Politician? Has that look."

"He mustn't find out about us."

"Us? Nothing happened between us."

Claudine had frowned. "The other thing – in the apartment."

Liam had shrugged, he was becoming confident, pleased at his poker face "You have the wrong guy. But hypothetically speaking, does anyone else know about that night?"

"Neighbours recognised me. The police found and interviewed me. I told them the truth: I was a friend of Marie, nothing more."

"I've heard it was an underworld hit."

"Yes, yes. That's what it would have been. Gerome did not choose his business associates with care."

"Then it's all settled. You've never met me. There's no connection between us. I'll make sure your fiancé is kept in the dark." He'd looked into her eyes with a hint of regret. "I think we're done."

She'd nodded and returned to her fiancé, linking her arm though his. Her eyes had flickered towards him as he exited the gallery.

Needing time to recover from meeting Claudine and to process what he'd just seen, Liam had decided to walk home. On the way, he'd stopped at a restaurant and ordered steak frites accompanied a half bottle of house red. The steak was rare and garlicky, just perfect, and the frites were thin and crisp. Food helped him think and he had forgotten how much he liked to eat alone. He had eaten the meal with a new sense of appreciation. The loose end of Claudine had just been tied up in a beautiful black and white ribbon, like her hair and dress. Glimmers of hope for the future had sprouted as quickly as new shoots on a Russian vine. He'd bathed in the yellow glow of the street lamp filtering through gaps in the restaurant curtains. Now all that was needed was to zip up his guilt and store it in a compartment in his mind.

Later, unable to sleep, he mentally ran through images of the Ezekiel paintings he owned. The one he would sell first, he concluded, was the desert scene. It was both commercial and strangely beautiful. If it sold for as much as the current hype hinted it would, he would buy a pair of first class tickets on the overnight to Nice. From there, they'd rent a car and drive to Menton. A studio in the old town's warren of tiny, winding streets, would provide adequate anonymity. He sighed. How he longed to be away from Paris. The wide boulevards, clogged with people and traffic, now had an oppressive feel about them. He could no longer enjoy a stroll in the squares of Montmartre or along the Seine, as both these locations reminded him of Gerome.

Out of sight, out of mind. He hoped the saying would hold true in the coming months. The vivid colours of the South: blue, yellow, white, green, would brush away the charms of silver-grey Paris. And a visit to the Matisse chapel in Vence might blow away the cobwebs from his soul. He'd only ever seen the stained glass windows in books: blue, yellow, green glass, floor to ceiling, throwing coloured patterns on the white walls. Even then their stark beauty had taken his breath away. Beauty and simplicity, that what he needed. Surely not too much to ask?

A fresh thought crossed his mind. Perhaps Alouette would not fit easily into these plans. He was fond of her. She had provided companionship and shelter when he was at his lowest, a rudderless boat in a storm. But she was a Parisian through and through. Would she be able to leave this city and begin a new life? And as far as morality was concerned, she was as straight as the old iron poker that had sat on his granny's hearth. Do no harm either in thought or action. How would she react if she discovered what he'd done?

His brain was buzzing with contrasting thoughts. Would she fit in with this new life he was planning? Perfect clothes and perfectly ordered mind. Not the ideal companion for a man like him, more imperfections than an antique table riddled with woodworm. Perhaps he should do her a favour, maybe he should go alone.

Chapter 35

Over the next few weeks, Liam continued crafting his plan. Deceiving the person you lived with was tiring, he realised. Suddenly she was around all the time, clingy, watchful, suspicious, making it difficult to research the sale of the paintings.

"You won't leave, will you?" she said after dinner one night. Her face took on a sadness, her eyes moist, lips set thin.

"It's the red wine." He laughed without responding to her question. "It always gives you the blues. I'd stick to a nice dry white, if I were you." He echoed back words she'd spoken to him recently. Yet, despite batting her words away with humour, her new dependence on him grated, like nails scraping on a chalk board, and he discovered his plans now did not include Alouette.

He came up with two options for disposing of the desert painting: selling to the gallery that had exhibited Ezekiel's paintings, or putting it up for auction. The gallery option might bring the highest pay off, but there was risk involved. Provenance would have to be checked, and they might go as far as contacting Ezekiel. He had no idea if Gerome had acquired the painting legitimately, so quickly dismissed that option. An auction, he decided, was less risky.

He logged onto Alouette's computer when she was out. He was intrigued when he saw an online auction. He gave a low whistle. Online was easy and anonymous, no jostling, heckling, making yourself known.

He checked through previous auction results. Most paintings had sold for a few hundred euro but there was a handful of much higher hammer prices. This, he thought, would be the safest option. With the Web you could take on any identity, reinvent yourself, and neither your signature nor photo would be required. A thread of excitement ran through him as he clicked through the website: best of all, they took only ten percent commission and would transfer the money to

PayPal or a bank account. This was a method of selling with few questions asked. All he had to do was supply a photo of the painting and some details. Enter and click, that was it. It might sell for less than it would in a large Paris auction house, but that was a chance he was prepared to take.

He wondered how many other dodgy dealers followed this route and he elected to bear it in mind for the future. He retrieved the desertscape from behind the wardrobe and laid it on top of the bed. The starched white duvet was a perfect backdrop for a photo. He pointed and clicked his phone several times.

"Good," he muttered as he reviewed the images. He also gave thanks that Gerome had omitted to sign the three paintings he'd retrieved from the apartment. An art restorer would have to remove Gerome's signature from those he'd bought at the market, still, that was doable and a small price to pay for a big profit.

He logged onto the site again. after verifying he couldn't hear her returning footsteps. It wasn't that she minded him using her computer, for she was always generous. He just didn't want her to know what he was up to.

Following step by step instructions, he uploaded images of the painting onto the website, along with a brief description.

Painting by Ezekiel: new sensation in the art world. This desert scene will transport the owner to a hot and dusty land. As with Ezekiel's other paintings, the owner will be captivated by his use of colour and realism. This work is not signed, but the quality of the painting speaks for itself.

Acquired when the artist was unknown. His paintings are now selling for circa thirty thousand euro.

He set the minimum price at ten thousand, and pressed 'enter'. He sat back and gazed at his auction entry with pride. Done and dusted. He sniffed the air and the smell of success drifted into his nostrils. He imagined euro notes of large denomination, alongside mimosa and freedom. He crossed his fingers and allowed himself to hope.

A few minutes later his phone rang. The trill made him

jump. No one except Alouette called him. But then, this was a pay-as-you-go phone he'd bought in Paris, so who else would have his number?

"Bonjour," he said, slowly.

"Ah, this is the auction house. I would like to speak to Liam Donoghue."

"That's me," his voice was high pitched and defensive. There was no choice, he'd used his real name, as that was the name on his bank account. Could they have tracked him down already? Could a European Arrest Warrant be floating around with his name on it? The web had changed everything. You might be hiding out in a remote corner of the globe, but once the web for that area was up and running and your photo was on the internet, you were fucked.

"It's about the painting you are selling. You have just entered an item into our next auction."

"Yes?" his voice was by now barely audible. He'd been found out. Christ, the authorities were good! How was this possible in the space of ten minutes? His hand tightened around the receiver as he anticipated a knock on the door.

"Ten thousand is the minimum price you've set."

"Yes. It's a good piece. I followed the instructions on the site."

"You must have missed the small print, monsieur. Paintings which cost more than one thousand must be displayed in our showroom. The buyers must be able to view them physically and we have an expert authenticate – that's a service we offer to our buyers and sellers."

His immediate thought was to pull the painting out of the auction. Perhaps he would put it in a sale in the South of France. But the buzz around Ezekiel was here, in Paris, plus his pockets were virtually empty. He was a kept man. Alouette paid for everything, but he doubted even she would fork out for the Cote D'Azur adventure. He would need money for the train fare and to set himself up in a hotel. If he put the painting into the auction, what was the worst that could happen? It was genuine, he had no doubt of that, and could be authenticated. As far as he, and anyone else, was concerned, he'd picked it up from a market stall. Only the tenuous link between Gerome's death and the painting made him hesitate. But the saying 'he who hesitates is lost' came to mind.

"Monsieur?"

"Fine. I'll bring it down."

He wrote down the address and ended the call. This was a setback but not a huge one. The painting would be displayed in an auction showroom, but maybe that was a good thing. It would be authenticated and that might double the price, plus the buyer would have no recourse. The painting was magnificent. It was also non returnable, non refundable.

Alouette returned from her shopping trip. She popped her head round the the living room door.

"Everything OK?" she asked. Her lips were smiling but the supposed good humour didn't reach her eyes. Since he'd insisted on going to the exhibition alone, she'd been wary and watchful. Their relationship had shifted. She was not the same woman who'd whisked him away to Giverny. Once again, this confirmed his decision to make the journey South alone.

Chapter 36

His hands shook as he gave the painting over to the gallery assistant. A young woman approached him.

"Ah, the Ezekiel. I've been looking forward to seeing this."

He judged her to be an art history graduate. With her round glasses, hair pulled back in an efficient bun, and dark business suit, she looked authentic. The metier of working in a Paris auction house fitted her like a soft leather glove. Not for her the seedy barns he'd hung around in the past. And he doubted she frequented car boot fairs or low quality antique shows in remote English fields, wind howling, rain pissing down. She slid her owlish glasses down her nose as she studied the painting. First she stood, head to one side, a few feet away. Then she moved in for the kill, her eyes scouring every inch of the canvas, examining the brushstrokes. She took out a magnifying glass and passed it over the painting, then put it back in her bag. She stepped back again and shook her head. He felt his heart plunge. Had he been wrong? Was Ezekiel *not* the artist? He was on the point of snatching the painting from the wall when she spoke.

"Magnificent, isn't he?"

He nodded, unable to reply.

"This is definitely an Ezekiel. He signs his paintings now, but a couple like this have come up at auction in the past few weeks. He didn't sign the early ones."

"Yes, I bought this a while back."

"From a market stall?" He nodded in response. "Sounds right. You're so lucky. I'm guessing you paid a few hundred. I'd estimate the selling price at around thirty thousand, on a bad day. Fifty if the right person is online."

"Really?" His throat was parched. He desperately needed a drink. "Then I sure am a lucky man." He left the saleroom and headed for the nearest bar. He scanned the labels of the bottles behind the bar. "Jack...Jack Daniels, *s'il vous plait?*"

"*Avec?*"

"Nothing – *rien*"

"*Grand?*"

"Double," he said. Forty or fifty thousand! Enough to get him out of Paris, to the other side of the world if he wanted. He could go anywhere, do anything. Once he'd paid to have the signature removed from the canvasses Gerome had signed, he could flog the lot.

He stared into his glass and frowned. Alouette would have to stay here, he reconfirmed his earlier decision. He was grateful to her but she was too perfect, uptight even. Perhaps she wouldn't approve of his windfall, after all hadn't she said that these paintings were the source of his problems. He pictured the scarf drawer in the bedroom. Over fifty scarves she had said proudly when she'd first showed him the drawer interior. All folded into neat squares. 'Woman from Harrods been?' he'd laughed at the time. Now such perfection wasn't so funny. He doubted she'd ever done anything wrong in her life, not even dropped a chocolate wrapper on the pavement. And what would he do if she became bored and put pressure on him to return to Paris?

He ordered another whiskey, partly to celebrate, partly to seal the deal on his new life plan. He realised he was drinking to cover up his guilt, but he'd learn to live with a measure of that. And as the years passed it would grow smaller, until it became like a speck of sand on the beach. That much guilt would be bearable

Alouette was still out when he returned. She was at the hairdressers, he recalled, fancying herself up for dinner later. Liam took out his wallet and counted his remaining money. Just over forty euro – and even that he'd borrowed from Alouette. She'd given this with less grace than usual, folding and unfolding the notes before handing them over. This performance was accompanied by sighs and raised eyebrows. The change in her mood had taken him by surprise. Usually a small compliment, lavender soap from the market or a glass of good wine was enough to raise a smile. He was becoming aware that he might be outstaying his welcome but would he ever meet someone as pleasant and undemanding again? "Too bad. Attractive and good company. Quite a catch – for someone else," he said aloud.

He went to the bathroom, switched on the shower and adjusted the temperature to hot. As he scrubbed his back with a long wooden brush, he realised he was feeling good about his change of plan. Heading off alone to the South of France was the best outcome for this whole sorry mess. It had been madness to consider taking Alouette. A clean break, that was the kindest thing to do. After all, could he really ask her to go on the run with him? One last piece of decision making was required to complete the jigsaw puzzle of his escape. Should he take off one morning when she was out, or should he tell her what he planned to do?

He recalled Lily, her glittering eyes, the feline smile on her face when she'd announced the end of their marriage. He was nothing like Lily. He was a man of compassion – the thing with Gerome had been an accident. As far as Alouette was concerned, he'd break the news gently. The easiest and least painful option would be to tell her that he was going home. Genuine tears formed in his eyes as he pictured wringing his hands, declaring he couldn't live his life as a stand in for her past English lover. He sighed, as he was genuinely fond of her. There might be a small scene but she would eventually acknowledge that he was right to go, and Borivoj and Catherine would back up his decision: he was a ne'er do well, a black sheep, best far away from her. He dried himself off and dressed. Like tumbling dominoes, the future was falling into place, each decision influencing the next.

He received another call from the auction house. As a Chagall was featured in the auction, it would be held both online and in the saleroom. 'More exciting, don't you think?' the young woman he'd spoken to previously said. He agreed with her. Butterflies were already fluttering round his stomach. Two weeks until the sale, a fortnight before freedom, and he still had plenty of time to finalise his exit plan.

Chapter 37

Ezekiel's lost painting

Ezekiel wiped away a tear. He stood in front of his lost painting, the one he considered his best work. His agent had been surprised when she'd received the call from the auction house. They had asked if she would mind authenticating the painting. She had hurried over to the Rue des Martyrs, only too happy to oblige.

When she saw the painting she was more than a little peeved that this hadn't been included in the exhibition. Ezekiel's painting of the sky and stars was beautiful but this was a masterpiece. It was unique: hot, lonely, achingly beautiful. She had flipped open her mobile and phoned Ezekiel.

"You have to come and see this. One of your paintings has come up for sale. I suppose that Gerome guy sold it for a pittance."

Ezekiel had hurried to the auction house and now he couldn't tear his eyes away from the painting. It wasn't simply the fact that it was beautiful that drew his eyes – he felt something wasn't right. The resolution had been disturbed. Something had been added to the canvas. Something that shouldn't be there. He moved closer to the painting and focussed on a yellow sand dune. Rust coloured spots had appeared at its summit. He knew he hadn't painted them, so who had put them there? He looked even closer. Speckles of rust had drifted across the canvas, into the pinkish hue of the sky. This paint was strange; not something he used, but he remembered seeing this exact shade of rust once before:

Ezekiel's father was a bus driver. In his spare time he painted large landscapes and portraits. The walls of their modest home were completely covered in paintings of desert, oases, portraits of Ezekiel, his brother, his mother and his aunt, Fatima. The family was not well off but their interest in art elevated them to a higher status. They were considered artisans, painters rather than labourers. Disaster struck when

Ezekiel's father was laid off. The bus company was losing money and they decided to cut down their schedule. Last in was first out so his father, who had a mere eight years with the company, lost his job. There was no redundancy money, no unemployment. The family turned to relatives and their meagre savings to meet ends.

Painting was the one thing Ezekiel's father could not give up. Unemployed, he was under stress, so what better way to relieve this than painting. He was like a whirling dervish when he started a new canvas. The children stayed out of the way, and their mother remained in the kitchen, complaining about the waste. 'Our money gone on canvases and paint. What's to become of us?'

Ezekiel thought that his father was quite brilliant. After all, none of the other men in the village could pick up a paintbrush and produce something spectacular and spellbinding.

One day he found his father in his studio. Tears were running down the older man's face. Something caught Ezekiel's eyes. He looked down and saw a blood-soaked rag wrapped around his father's lower arm. "What has happened, father?" he'd cried. His father shook his head and put a finger to his lips, indicating Ezekiel should be quiet. He pointed to his canvas, a scene of rust coloured mountains tipping the edge of the desert. Ezekiel ran from the room crying. He realised that the colour reflected was blood. Later, his father explained that he had no money left for paint. He needed a particular dark rust shade, the colour of dried blood, so he had used what God had given him. Ezekiel never forgot this lesson. It was one of the things that had influenced his move to Paris. If he was to be a painter, he wanted to be in the thick of things. He wanted to be in a place where a man was appreciated for his art, rather than laughed at and left to paint in blood.

A chill ran down Ezekiel's spine. Blood on his painting…he hadn't put it there. That was the last thing he would do. He turned towards his agent.

"You're very pale. Something wrong?" she said.

There was indeed something wrong. Ezekiel's head was spinning. This painting hadn't come from a market. The rust stains had to be Gerome's blood!

The day before the auction, he sat in his agent's office. Ezekiel didn't know whether he should be down-in-the-dumps, scared or happy. If he spilled the beans about the blood on the painting, would his agent insist they go to the police? He'd no idea if he would be on the first boat or plane out of France, or if they would even listen to his suspicions. Gerome had taken the painting from his apartment, not long after, he was dead. If the painting was in the apartment when Gerome was killed, then the blood on the painting would be his.

It was all cut and dried - Ezekiel decided not to use this pun if and when he put his theory forward, as it reminded him of his father's bloodied arms and the rust spots on the canvas. Could the individual who'd put the painting into the auction have had something to do with Gerome and Marie's deaths? If that was the case then they'd done him a favour, so perhaps he'd keep quiet. On the other hand if he helped solve the murders, perhaps his immigration application would be fast tracked. After all, wouldn't it look bad if the person who solved the 'La Villette murders' was deported?

"So, Ezekiel, what's our next move, where do we go from here?" his agent said.

Chapter 38

The air crackled with both tension and hope. Ten thousand, twelve thousand, the bidding continued both in the room and online. Ezekiel's paintings were creating a stir in the art world. *At last a new school of painting*, articles which had appeared in papers had trumpeted. Privately Liam thought the style wasn't so much 'new school' as a combination of existing schools perfectly executed.

Finally, the auctioneer banged the gavel on the rostrum. Liam slipped out of the auction room, heavily perspiring. Fifty-two thousand. Fifty-two bloody thousand, he congratulated himself. No more scrimping, no more stealing handbags, no more hoping for a handout from Alouette. He had been down and out, but like Ezekiel, his own star was rising.

"Deal well done," he said aloud as he made his way to a bar. He sat down, oblivious to his surroundings.

"Champagne, *s'il vous plait*," he asked the waiter.

He paid for the drink with a twenty euro note Alouette had left on the hall table. He twirled the glass by the stem, admiring the straw colour of the liquid and the fine bubbles bouncing enthusiastically like can-can dancers at the Folies Bergere. This was a beverage fit for a winner.

In a few days, when the sale money was in his account, he would drink a bottle of champagne with Alouette. It would be their last dinner together. He would cook for her at the apartment rather than go to a restaurant as there might be a scene when he announced his intentions. If there was one, it would be small: Alouette was too refined to plead. He suspected that rather than being upset at losing him, she was afraid of the prospect of an empty space next to her in the bed.

Once the money was in his account, he'd be a free man. The past few weeks had been difficult. He'd found it almost impossible to hold his tongue, not to openly declare that he thought his and Alouette's romance had run its course.

And her mood had been stranger than usual. She was

pleasant but distant. At some level, she knew that he was about to leave, he realised. It wasn't that he had been cruel or deliberately hurtful, but a coolness had slipped into everyday life. They were, he knew, plunging headlong into the winter of their relationship, with no fires to keep them warm or hot chocolate to enjoy together. There was no blanket to join together under. Each was separate in their own chilled cocoon.

Alouette no longer enquired about his comings and goings. When they went to the market she did not discuss the herbs that might be appropriate for special dishes she wanted to cook in the future. One day she picked up a bar of lavender soap and said that it reminded her of Provence. She would like to visit Aix soon, she said wistfully, but she supposed she wouldn't have the opportunity.

Tired of guilt weighing him down, he put Alouette's feelings to one side. She had survived the break up with her old boyfriend, who was much more important to her, so she would survive the break up with him.

The money duly appeared in Liam's bank account. He withdrew forty thousand euro. His heart sang as the cashier flicked a finger through the notes, counting them. Money was bliss, money could heal everything. All his childhood fears, his adult worries, evaporated under money's spell. Perhaps money could even buy reprieve from guilt.

He left the bank feeling like a bird whose cage door had been accidentally left open. There would be no prison for him now, either physically or metaphorically. He made his way to the Gare de Lyon and bought a ticket for the Nice train departing early the following morning. With the ticket safely in his coat pocket, he checked the station lockers, noting there were several oversize ones which would easily hold the remaining canvasses. He paid for two lockers and picked up the keys. If the opportunity arose later, he would transport the paintings here. Safe and sound, just in case Alouette caused a scene.

He bought a new phone. Tomorrow, he would toss the

one he currently used out the train window. Better to break off all contact with Alouette. He justified his actions by telling himself he was doing her a favour: he'd too much personal baggage, she should find someone steady and uncomplicated, maybe get married and settle down.

He went to the supermarket near the apartment and bought a bacon and leek quiche, new potatoes, green beans and a bunch of parsley. Something quick and easy. There was no time for fiddling around and he certainly didn't want Alouette hovering in the kitchen while he cooked.

Over dinner he'd come clean. The bottle of champagne he'd bought would provide their farewell toast. He was going back to England, he'd say, to face the music with the authorities, his guilt weighed him down, was too much to bear. This was almost true, except the guilt he felt was for the murders he had committed rather than financial fraud - and he was heading South, as far away from London as possible.

He would wear a mournful expression on his face when he told Alouette that Borivoj was right, she was too good for him. There was no choice, he had to go home. His voice would be low and contrite. She would understand.

He left the groceries and champagne in the kitchen. Alouette was out, so he collected the paintings, called a taxi and returned to the Gare de Lyon. He stored the paintings in the lockers as planned. As he turned the key in the second one, a young woman caught his eye. Petite with dark, chin length hair. She had a look about her – creative – maybe an artist or dancer? Was this what Alouette had looked like thirty years ago: navy jacket, blue scarf round her neck, elegant, delicate and pretty as a picture? He was suddenly breathless when the young woman turned and looked at him. Her eyes were large, dark and vulnerable. Mascara ran in rivulets down her olive cheeks. The mournful look on her face pierced his heart so deeply, it might as well have been the dagger in the Rubens painting in the Louvre. He was pondering over asking if he could help when a tall man, much older than her, appeared. He carried a bunch of raspberry hued flowers. Alouette's colour. Was this a sign? He watched them hug, then walk off, arms wrapped around each other. He sat down on a nearby seat. What would have happened, he thought, if the older man hadn't appeared? Would the rest of her life have been blighted by such cruelty?

"Never mind," he muttered to himself. "All's well that ends well."

He took the metro back to the apartment. A slower method than taking a taxi but he needed to think, to process what he'd just seen. The woman's tears had tricked their way into his heart. For the first time he was truly aware how his actions could impact another. Could he really take off, destroying Alouette's life, when she'd come to his aid again – and again? She didn't have the luxury of youth, resilience and time to bounce back. But more than all that, she'd been the port in his perfect storm, had given him a refuge from the world. One day in the distant future, he would need to confide in someone, he suddenly realised. Alouette was the only person that could fulfil that role. When the time was right he would reveal his terrible deed to her. With luck, she would forgive him.

Liam's heart swelled with joy as he reached his final decision. He would change his ticket to leave a few days from now, pick up an additional one, and ask Alouette to accompany him. A surprise, he'd tell her, just like the Giverny trip. If all went well she could return to Paris to pick up her things. He would wait for her in Nice or Menton or wherever they set up home. He would never set foot in Paris again. Liam's mind bubbled with future plans. He couldn't wait to reveal these to Alouette.

She gave a start when he entered the living room. "Oh. I didn't hear you."

"I'm just about to cook , an early dinner would be nice."

"I suppose," she nodded slowly, as though she wasn't in the mood for food. He brought her a glass of chilled champagne. "Merci." She raised her eyebrows. "Are we celebrating?"

"I'll tell you over dinner," he said mysteriously. Alouette's face paled and he gave her a curious look. He went over to the window and looked out. The sky was pink, casting a rosy glow on the building opposite. He dismissed the sense of dread that was beginning to envelop him. Had Alouette picked up on his earlier plan to leave without her? She was astute enough to have done so. But if this was the case, then she was in for a nice surprise.

He set the table and carried in the quiche, potatoes and green beans. He poured another glass of champagne and sat down. Alouette sat down opposite. He raised his champagne flute.

"To you, Alouette. To a charming and lovely woman who has helped me through the worst of times."

She nodded slowly, but didn't take a sip of champagne. The living room window was open, Alouette got up and shut it. She remained by the window, her eyes focussed on the street below.

He sighed. He was impatient to break the news to her, wanted to see the sparkle in her eyes, the smile on her lips, yet she seemed skittish, unable to settle. "Sit down. I've something to tell you."

Alouette reached over and stroked Liam's hand. The gesture was regretful rather than gentle or loving. She shook her head.

A faint wail of sirens, becoming louder. A screeching of brakes. Blue light flashing on the ceiling. Footsteps on the marble stairs. He looked into her eyes, dark pools, devoid of emotion.

"No, Liam. It's me who has something to tell you."

The End

Carol McKee Jones is originally from Belfast, Northern Ireland. She was joint winner of the Rethink Press 2014 new novels award (Forget Me Not). She is also a writer of short stories and has been short/longlisted in the Fish and Ink Tears competitions. She was longlisted for the Mslexia women's novel competition (2014).

She has lived in Spain, France and Canada and for several years worked in passenger services for Air Canada in Toronto.

She studied International Relations at the University of Sussex and also took a year of Caribbean Literature. Afterwards she studied for an MSc at the University of Brighton.

After years of travelling, she has settled on the South Coast of England and lives on a 46 ft motor cruiser.

She enjoys reading, writing, painting, and seagulls.

Printed in Great Britain
by Amazon